Praise for Kimberly Belle and *The Last Breath*

"Painstakingly emotional…will surprise readers to the very end…it's so worth it!" —*RT Book Reviews*

"Belle's engaging debut brings the reader into [an] emotionally tangled world." —*Booklist*

"Belle's a smooth writer whose characters are vibrant and truly reflect the area where the novel is set."

—*Kirkus Reviews*

"*The Last Breath* will leave you breathless. This edgy and emotional thriller will keep you guessing until the very end."

—*New York Times* bestselling author Heather Gudenkauf

"Powerful and complex with an intensity drawn out through each page, *The Last Breath* is a story of forgiveness and betrayal and one I couldn't put down!"

—*New York Times* bestselling author Steena Holmes

Also by Kimberly Belle

The Ones We Trust
The Marriage Lie
Three Days Missing
Dear Wife
Stranger in the Lake

THE
LAST
BREATH

KIMBERLY BELLE

PARK
ROW
BOOKS

PARK ROW BOOKS™

Recycling programs
for this product may
not exist in your area.

ISBN-13: 978-0-7783-1163-8

The Last Breath

First published in 2014. This edition published in 2021.

This edition published by arrangement with Harlequin Books S.A.

Park Row Books
22 Adelaide St. West, 40th Floor
Toronto, Ontario M5H 4E3, Canada
ParkRowBooks.com
BookClubbish.com

Printed in Spain

For the Dutchman,
for allowing me roots while also giving me wings.

And for Evan and Isabella,
living proof we did the two most important things right.

THE
LAST
BREATH

Ella Mae Andrews, April 1994

PROLOGUE

Some guy on Oprah *last week said there is no such thing
as an accidental lapse of memory. That every phone call
you forget to return, every errand you forget to run on the
way home is a whisper of your subconscious.*

Listen really hard, *he said,* and you'll hear the reasons
behind your resistance. *Why do you keep putting off calling Marla Murphy back about the church bake sale? Why
should your husband have to wear last week's dirty slacks?
Why did you allow your misery about Dean to distract you
from the fact that the letter you wrote is still upstairs, lying
forgotten on the bed? Ella Mae Andrews would especially
like to know the answer to that last one.*

*Unfortunately, she couldn't hear a thing her subcon-
scious was trying to tell her over all Ray's sobbing.*

*You'd think that when confronted with concrete evidence
of your wife's infidelity with the next-door neighbor, there'd
at least be some screaming. Screaming and cussing and
angry accusations and blame.*

*You'd think Ray would have tossed her out and changed
the locks and shredded her clothes, that he would have*

marched next door to Dean's house, fists slinging, or maybe even shoved her onto the bed for a heated round of revenge sex.

But there was none of this. There was only sobbing, which was so, so much worse.

Ella Mae may have not been able to hear the whispers of her subconscious, but her conscience was roaring, and it was telling her this was wrong. Wrong to have spent her afternoons in bed with a married man who was not her husband. Wrong to have let Dean talk about a future together, after divorces have been settled and families have been broken to pieces. Wrong to stay in a marriage with a man she no longer loved.

By now it was dark out, and Ray and Ella Mae spooned on top of the very same sheets that still smelled of Dean. The full spring moon outside the window acted like a nightlight, bathing the room in a buttery glow. Ray's tears had finally petered out but he was awake, his mouth pressed against her ear. She closed her eyes, and tried to process what he was asking.

"Let's give it a month before either of us makes any decisions." Ray buried his face in the damp hair at the side of her neck. "Please?"

"A month won't change anything."

"We'll go to therapy. Cal will know the best person to talk to." His voice was hoarse, his tone recklessly hopeful. "And we'll get away, just the two of us. Drive to the coast. Fly to some island in the Caribbean. We'll figure things out. We will. Till death do us part, remember?"

She twisted on the bed until she was facing him, not bothering to mask her answer. Ray's eyes flickered, and it was a full five seconds before he said anything.

"Can we—" His voice broke, and he clutched her tighter. "Can we please just sleep on it?"

She didn't respond. She couldn't. Now that she had made her decision, the thought of another night in this house, in this bed, in this town, sent an army of insects skittering under her skin.

"One more night. That's all I'm asking."

She balled her hands into tight fists, buried her face in his wrinkled dress shirt and willed herself not to squirm. Ray Andrews had given her seven good years and three stepchildren she loved like her own. Surely she could give him a few more hours. At the very least, she owed him that much.

"Okay," she whispered into his chest. "But just one more night."

Ray's arms relaxed with the realization he'd just bought himself some more time. Ella Mae knew he'd spend all of it trying to come up with a way to make her change her mind, and she wanted to tell him not to bother, that it was too late for magic words.

Instead, she closed her eyes and allowed them both this little respite.

Tomorrow would be here soon enough.

Ella Mae had just drifted off to sleep when Ray gave her arm a little jiggle, his voice barely a whisper. "Did you hear that?"

She cleared the sleep from her head and listened to a feverish wailing outside, from somewhere over the hill in the direction of Bill Almaroad's farm.

"It's just a barn cat in heat." She allowed herself a little yawn, melted deeper into the mattress. "Go back to sleep."

"Not that." Ray lifted his head from the pillow. "It came from somewhere downstairs."

Ella Mae stiffened, her senses stirring to high alert. "Could it be Gia?"

"Shh." He sat up, swinging his feet onto the floor without a sound. "Gia's in North Carolina with the McCallisters."

Ray craned his neck, turning his ear to the door. That horny cat next door was still trying to summon every male feline in a fifty-mile radius, and Ella Mae struggled to hear around its wailing. And then Ray stabbed the air with a finger. "There! There it was again."

Alarm prickled her skin. Had she heard someone moving around downstairs? She thought so, but she couldn't be certain.

Ray, however, was. He rose, creeping on bare feet to the closet where Bo's old baseball bat stood propped in a pair of steel-toed yard boots. He clutched it in a fist by his side and crossed the room. He stopped at the doorway to the hall, turned and pressed a finger to his lips. "Stay here," he mouthed. And then he slipped into the darkness.

Ella Mae rose onto her elbows, straining to hear. The stairs creaked under someone's weight, and then the noise faded into nothing. The only sound was the rhythmic pounding of her heart. She lay there for what seemed like an eternity, willing herself not to panic, her eyes wide and glued to the bedroom door.

From somewhere downstairs, there was a yelp followed by a muffled thump. Blood roared in her ears, and she scrambled across the sheets to Ray's side of the bed, reaching for the phone with a shaky hand. It wasn't there. The phone wasn't there! For a brief moment, an irrational wave of anger replaced her fear. How many times had she told

Ray to return the handset to the charger? A million, at least. And now, thanks to Ray, she'd landed in the middle of a Stephen King novel without a phone.

And then she heard heavy footsteps on the stairs, and her breath caught in her throat. Because if there was one thing she knew with an icy certainty, it was that if the person approaching the bedroom door were Ray, he would have called out to her by now.

She cast a panicked glance around the room, searching for a place to hide. The closet—no, not the closet, that's the first place he would look. The footsteps grew closer, too close. Out of time and options, she slid noiselessly off the bed and crawled under it.

Two large feet stepped into the room, gleaming black Reebok runners under dark denim cuffs, and Ella Mae knew she was in danger. She knew it by the terror that rolled through every part of her, searing her chest and clawing at her throat and setting her skin on fire.

Ella Mae dug her nails into her palms hard enough to draw blood and willed herself to think. Think! But the only thing she could think of was please God let me get out of here. Please God don't let him see me.

The shoes moved to the closet—thank God she hadn't hidden in the closet!—and an arm swept aside the shirts and pants and dresses, arranged by type and color on matching plastic hangers. She shimmied across the carpet to her side of the bed, the side closest to the door.

And then she waited.

The shoes stepped around to Ray's side of the bed, not bothering to tread lightly anymore, and she heard a swishing of hand against sheets, she assumed feeling for warmth. She pushed herself out from under the bed on the opposite side from him, keeping a careful watch on the shoes.

When the feet turned toward the wall, she snatched the chance, scurrying on hands and knees toward the hallway. At the door, she broke into a sprint, not turning and not pausing at the stairs, which she took by threes and fours.

Somewhere about halfway down, a hand made contact with her curls and tugged, snapping her head back hard enough for Ella Mae to see stars. Her bare feet caught air and she landed with a sickening thud on her back, aware of a sudden, piercing pain in her left temple, right before her world went black.

Moments later, Ella Mae's world came flooding back at the bottom of the stairs, where she lay sprawled, her body steamrolled. Something warm and sticky—she knew viscerally that it was blood and that it was her own—pooled in the hair behind her left ear. She would have checked how much, but her wrists were bound and her arms had gone numb beneath her. She couldn't scream around the cloth in her mouth, turning her tongue to sandpaper and gagging her with its sour smell. She tried to work it out with her tongue, but there was too much of it, and it was in too tight.

Ray! Where was Ray?

There was movement to her right, a dark shadow coming at her in a snow mask, a long object in a fist. A fist covered with surgical gloves. When she saw what he was holding, a box of saran wrap, her blood pressure spiked and her pulse jackhammered in her ears. She tried to wriggle away, but he stopped her with a palm to the ankle. He gave it a jerk, and her head hit the floor with a gargled moan.

Her captor pulled a long strip of plastic from the roll and pressed the end against her mouth. She shook her head, frantic and flailing, and he slipped a palm under her neck, plowing his fingers into her hair and holding her there with a thumb across her windpipe. He wrapped the plastic, once, twice, three times, around her head. She struggled and his grip on her neck tightened.

And then his eyes flashed across hers, and her entire body went still. Ella Mae's captor was no stranger, and this was no random crime.

This was a crime of passion.

On the fourth or fifth time around her head, his work turned sloppy. A fat strip of plastic pressed across her nose. For one brief but electric moment, she thought this all must be a mistake. Surely he wasn't trying to suffocate her on purpose. She writhed on the floor at his knees, unable to breathe through either her nose or her mouth, desperate to make him understand. If only she could catch his eye, she could make him understand.

Their eyes locked, and what she saw there stopped time. For however long he watched her, nothing mattered but their silent conversation. Not his children or hers. Not what had happened before or what would happen next. Not space or time or reason. He pushed to a stand, and something ignited in her chest—her heart or her lungs or both—an explosion of acid and fire. And then he walked away.

That was when Ella Mae knew that for her, tomorrow would never come.

1

For aid workers, home can mean a lot of things. A two-bedroom ranch with a picket fence. A fourth-story walk-up in the city. A mud hut under a banana tree. A country listed on a passport. It can be big or small or anything in between.

One thing all these homes share, though, is that aid workers miss them. They long to go there. They are homesick.

Not me. I've spent the past sixteen years running from my home, and what happened there. Could have lived the rest of my life never returning to the place where I will always be known as the murderer's daughter.

And yet here I sit in my old driveway, in a rental parked behind a shiny new Buick. More than thirty-six hours into this new disaster—my disaster—and I've accomplished exactly nothing more than a crusty coffee stain down the front of my jeans and a mean case of jet lag.

Embrace the chaos, Gia. Over the course of the past seven thousand miles, it has become my mantra.

Uncle Cal climbs out of his car, and he's wearing his usual outfit: gleaming reptile skin stretched across pointy cowboy boots, Brooks Brothers suit of smoky pin-striped wool, black leather jacket worn soft and supple. Here in the hills of Appalachia, it's a look perfectly suitable for church, a fancy restaurant or a courtroom. As one of the highest paid criminal lawyers in Tennessee, Cal's worn it in all three.

I follow his lead and step out of the rental. It's mid-February and Rogersville—a tiny blip on the Eastern Tennessee map—is in the death throes of winter. My ancient fleece is not equipped to handle the Appalachian Mountain cold, and I long for my winter coat, still in mothballs in a London suburb. Cal opens his arms and I step into their warmth, inhaling his familiar scent, a combination of leather, designer aftershave and Juicy Fruit gum.

"Welcome home, baby girl," he says into my hair.

Home.

I twist my neck to face the house I've not seen for sixteen years, and a shudder of something unpleasant hits me between the shoulder blades. Once a place that instilled in me a sense of refuge and comfort, this house now provokes the exact opposite. Grief. Fear. Dread. This house isn't home. Home shouldn't give you the creeps.

Cal's hands freeze on my protruding scapula and he steps back, his gaze traveling down my frame. Thanks to a particularly nasty bout of food poisoning last month, it's a good ten pounds lighter than the last time he hugged me, back when I was already high-school skinny. "I thought you were putting an end to the famine, not succumbing to it."

"If you're ever on the Horn of Africa, you should probably stay away from the street stalls in Dadaab. Just because they claim their meat is fresh doesn't mean it's true. Or for that matter, that it's even meat."

"Good tip." He pulls the toothpick from his molars and

gives me his trademark squint, but there's a smile in his tone. "I'll try to remember that."

A lucky break Cal had called it when he finally tracked me down in Kenya. There was more, something about a perjury scandal and a diagnosis that required full-time, in-home hospice care, but by then I wasn't really listening. I was too busy wondering on what planet capping off sixteen years of high-security confinement by coming home to die would be considered lucky.

I swallow a sudden lump. "Is he in a lot of pain?"

Cal doesn't have to ask who I mean, and at the reminder of the cancer squeezing his only brother's pancreas, grief muddies his brow. "Not yet. But he will be very soon."

The lump returns and puts down roots.

"For an innocent man to end his prison term like this..." He sighs, and his breath makes puffy wisps in the February air. "I've got lots of choice words to say about it, none of them fit for your ears."

From the moment Cal arrived on the scene—before my father was a suspect, before he signed on as my father's attorney, even before Ella Mae's body had been photographed and bagged and carried away—his belief in my father's innocence has been unwavering.

For me, the situation was never that clear. If I thought my father was capable of murder, that he premeditated and carried out a plan to suffocate Ella Mae Andrews, his wife and my stepmother, I'm not certain I could forgive either him or his behavior. In fact, I'm not certain I would even be here, that I would have traveled all this way for a last goodbye.

But I came all this way because I'm not certain. In my father's case, the evidence is unclear, the testimony conflicted. The shadows of my doubt run in both directions.

I stuff my icy hands into my front jeans pockets and shiver, not merely from the cold.

Cal takes the gesture as his cue and reaches into his pocket, where a set of keys jingles. "Ready to get inside before you freeze to death?"

No. My heart races, and every tiny hair soldiers to attention on the back of my neck, commanding me to run. Never again. No.

"Ready as I'll ever be."

I follow Cal up the five steps to the wraparound porch, summoning the detached efficiency that's made me one of Earth Aid International's top disaster relief experts. I can't manage even an ounce of objectivity. This disaster is too close, its aftermath still too painful. I can't detach from its reality.

A reality that, according to the doctors, could last anywhere from three weeks to three months.

"The renters moved out about six months ago," Cal says without turning his head, searching through his key ring for the right one. The sisal mat under his feet mocks me with its cheery message: Welcome, Guests. As if anyone but me and Cal will be stepping on it, waiting to be invited in to pay their last respects. Not in a Million Years would be more like it.

"Good timing, I suppose."

"I've had the house painted. And all the furniture is new. Appliances, too."

"What happened to Dad's old stuff?"

"I donated most of the furniture and clothes to Goodwill after the trial. The rest is in a storage facility in Morristown. I'll get you the address and the access combination if you want to head over there."

"I doubt I'll have the time." Or the inclination. Digging through old memories sounds like torture to me.

Uncle Cal twists the key in the handle and the door swings open with a groan, a sound I find eerily appropriate. He steps inside like he owns the place, which I suppose by now he probably does, but I don't follow. I can't. Somebody switched out my sneakers for boots of lead. My knees wobble, and I grip the doorjamb to keep from falling down.

A strange thing happens when a home turns into a crime scene. Its contents are labeled, cataloged and photographed. Walls become scene boundaries, doors and windows, the perpetrator's entry and exit. Seemingly ordinary objects— dust bunnies behind the couch, scuff marks on the stairs, a tarnished nickel under the carpet—take on all sorts of new significance. And the people living there, in a place now roiling with bad memories and even worse juju, no longer think of it as home.

But what about that one spot where the victim took her last breath, where her heart gave its final, frantic beat? What do you do with that place? Build a shrine on top of it, wave a bouquet of smoking sage around it or pretend it's not there?

At the foot of the stairs, Cal stops and turns, studiously ignoring my distress. My gaze plummets to the fake Persian under his feet, and a wave of sick rises from the pit of my belly. Just because I can't see the spot doesn't mean I've forgotten what happened there.

Or for that matter, that I'm ever stepping on it.

"Shut the door, please, Gia."

I take a deep breath, square my shoulders and follow him into the house.

"My assistant Jennie did all the shopping," he says, gesturing with his keys toward the living room. Except for the unmade hospital bed in the corner, the decor—oversize furniture, silk ferns in dark pots, framed paintings of exotic landscapes on the walls—looks plucked from the pages of a Rooms To Go catalog. "I hope it'll do."

I finger a plastic pinecone in a wooden bowl on the dresser and peer down the hallway toward the kitchen. There's literally nothing here that I recognize. Probably better that way. "She did a great job."

"The bedrooms are ready upstairs. Thought we'd let the nurse take the master. You don't mind sharing the hall bath with me on the weekends, do you?"

I smile, hoping it doesn't come across as forced as it feels. "I've gone months with nothing but a bucket, a bar of soap and a muddy stream. I think I can handle sharing a bathroom."

One corner of Cal's mouth rises in what looks almost like pride. "You'd make someone a fine huntin' partner."

He motions for me to follow him into the kitchen at the back of the house, where he points to a credit card and iPhone on the Formica counter. "Jennie stocked the kitchen with the basics, but there's enough money on that account to buy anything else you need. You probably won't need it for a couple of days, though."

I peek into the refrigerator, check the cabinets above the coffee machine, peer around the corner into the open pantry. "There's enough food here to feed half of Hawkins County for weeks."

Cal smiles. "That's the great thing about Jennie. She always goes above and beyond." He plucks the iPhone from the counter and passes it to me. "She also programmed all the numbers you'll need into the phone. The lead officer assigned to the case will be calling to set up a meeting first thing tomorrow morning. The hospice nurse arrives tomorrow morning at eight, and the motorcade and ambulance with your father, sometime before noon. And the local doctors, hospitals and the funeral home have been notified."

"Sounds like everything's been taken care of."

He smiles, and his voice softens. "Just trying to make things as easy as possible for you, darlin'. I know you'd rather be anywhere but here."

I think of some of the worst places I've been sent. Overpopulated Dhaka, where if the water doesn't kill you, the air will. The slums of Abidjan after floods and mudslides have swept away too many of its children. The dusty streets of Dadaab, the world's largest refugee camp, where malnutrition and cholera compete for leading cause of death.

Uncle Cal has a point.

"And don't think you're completely out here on your own," he says after a long stretch of silence. "I'm less than an hour down the road, and so are your brother and sister. Do me a favor and don't let either of them off the hook, okay? This concerns their father, too."

I half nod, half shrug. When it comes to our father, Bo would rather bury himself in his work than admit the situation affects him, while Lexi prefers to pretend he's already dead. How can I let my siblings off the hook when neither of them are willing to acknowledge there is one? It seems as if the only person not getting off the hook around here is me.

Cal pulls me in for a hug, dropping a kiss on the top of my head. "Call me anytime, okay? Day or night. I'll pick up, no matter where I am or what I'm doing."

"Promise?"

"I promise." His tone is reassuring, but he's already backing away, already moving toward the door. "I'll see you Saturday morning."

He gives my shoulder one last squeeze and disappears

into the hallway, and I'm slammed with a wave of panic. Disasters and destruction of global magnitude I can handle. Facing my father alone, not so much.

I rush down the hall in his wake. "Uncle Cal?"

The desperate note in my voice stops him at the door, and he turns to face me.

"Explain to me again why you can't stay. Why you won't be here tomorrow when Dad gets here."

He scrubs a hand through his hair, now salt-and-pepper but still thick and shiny as ever. "Because I'm busy stalling the retrial. God willing and the creek don't rise, your father won't spend another second of his life in either a courtroom or a prison cell."

A casket sure seems like the ultimate prison to me.

A few seconds later he's gone, leaving me to wonder how I ended up here. In a town I vowed never to return to. In a house filled with ghosts and memories I'll never outrun. In a life I have spent the past sixteen years trying to escape.

But most of all, I wonder how I ended up here alone.

2

Back in the house, I put on a kettle and rummage through the cabinets for tea. Cal's assistant must be either misinformed or seriously delusional about the number of mourners we will be expecting because she bought us a 312-count, industrial-sized box of Lipton tea bags. If we get through even one row of them, it will be a miracle. I rip open the cellophane wrapping with my teeth, pull out a bag and drop it into a yellow ceramic mug.

The sharp, bitter scent reminds me of some of my British colleagues, who are convinced a spot of tea is the cure to all emotional ails. My boss, Elsie, a hard-nosed type, drinks enough of the stuff to poison her liver…thanks to the generous splash of bourbon she adds when things in the field get really hairy. If only life were that easy.

Unlike the satellite phone I carry in the field, Cal's iPhone has only a handful of contacts, most of them people I've never met and, after burying my father, will probably never think of again. It doesn't take me long to find Bo.

His cell goes straight to voice mail, so I leave what must be my fifth message in as many days, careful to keep my voice level. Five years older and light-years more serious, my brother has always preferred that people reserve their zeal for backyard fireworks and the Nature Channel, and he doesn't respond well to gushing.

I have better success with Lexi, who picks up on the second ring. I abandon my tea and squeal, "Lexi!"

Unlike Bo, my sister welcomes enthusiasm. Demands it, even.

"Is it true? Is it really true?" Lexi's familiar voice, the same gravelly one that used to give boys all over Hawkins County wet dreams. "Did my do-gooder little sister finally come home from Lord knows where?"

"It's true that I'm here, yes. But nowadays, home is in Kenya."

"Well, laa-tee-daa." She stretches out her words, loads them up with an extra serving of Tennessee twang. "Don't that sound fancy."

I snort at what I know to be a joke. Lexi is no dummy. She has a master's in finance from Stanford, runs a local chain of banks and could kick even Alex Trebek's ass at *Jeopardy.* Not only is she aware of my latest whereabouts, she knows Dadaab is pretty much the polar opposite of fancy. My chest seizes with a wave of sudden affection for my sister, who I haven't hugged in…six years? Has it really been that long?

"Where are you?" I say, switching gears. "Because I'm coming there right after I lock up the house."

"I'm going to need a little more time than that." Her tone takes a serious turn, matching mine, and her voice and vowels soften into the more generic timbre she perfected in college. Less country hick, more Southern belle. Unlike me, Lexi can turn her accent on and off like a faucet. "I'm about to head into a staff meeting, but I could meet you after for a late dinner. Say, seven-thirty?"

I check my watch. Three and a half hours I can fill with a nap and a shower, in that order. "Perfect. So where's the place to be on a Wednesday night these days?"

"It's Thursday, actually, not that it matters. And there's only one place to be every night, and that's the Roadkill Bar and Grill in town."

Roadkill? I make a face. "Do I have to bring my own rodent, or do they run it down for me?"

She laughs, a throaty, musical sound that makes me wish I'd called more often. "Don't tell me you've forgotten your roots, young lady."

"I haven't forgotten. My palate has just evolved to more refined creatures, like stray animals. And last month in the Philippines I tried this thing called balut, a fertilized duck embryo that's boiled alive and eaten shell and all."

Lexi makes a retching sound. "I think I'd rather starve to death."

Now it's my turn to laugh. Though I've always been adventurous with food and my sister the pickiest eater in Appalachia, Lexi does have a point. Balut tastes just as bad the first time as it does the second, on its way back up.

"A girl's got to eat. And besides, my rule wherever I travel is to eat or drink whatever is offered to me, even if it does end up turning my insides to gurgling water. Sharing a meal, no matter how vile, fosters trust between my team and the people we're there to help."

"Good Lord. Your job sucks worse than mine."

"Mostly, my job is pretty awesome, especially for a wanderer like me. I've flown around the globe more times than anybody on my team, and been to more than a hundred and twenty-five countries. The consulate has had to add pages to my passport now, twice."

"I thought your job was to make the world a better place."

"Well, duh. That goes without saying."

Lexi covers the receiver with a hand, muffling her voice when she tells a colleague she's on the phone, but will be right there.

"You've got to go?" I ask.

"Sorry. We'll catch up on all the rest tonight, okay?"

"Okay. And, Lex?" She pauses, but I hear papers shuffling around her desk, and even though I know I've probably already lost her, I say it anyway: "I've missed you."

"Same here. See you at seven-thirty." And then she's gone.

I plunk the phone on the counter by my mug and head outside to retrieve my suitcase, still in the trunk of my rental. In the past hour, the temperature plummeted and the air turned metallic, thick with invisible frost and crystals. I cast a glance at the darkening sky. No clouds yet, but I know what that scent means. I inhale enough of it to give my lungs freezer burn. God, how I've missed the smell of promised snow.

Up at the street, a silver Escort slows, tires crunching in the dirt and gravel on the side of the road. Any other day, any other place, and I probably wouldn't have paid the car a bit of attention. But I lived on Maple Street long enough to know strangers don't typically happen down this way by accident. I keep it in my periphery as I make my way up the concrete drive.

The car pulls to a sudden stop with a piercing squeal of brakes, and I freeze, gaze glued to the passenger side window. It whirrs and lowers to reveal a dark-haired man about my age. He leans across the seat, ducking his head to get a clear view through the window.

And though he may be wearing a friendly smile, I'm not.

"Sorry to bother you." His bangs flop over an eye, and he pushes them back with a palm. "But can you tell me where the closest gas station is?"

The breath I'd been holding makes a thick cloud before it dissipates into the air. I take two steps across the frozen grass to his car, keeping a careful distance, pointing him in the opposite direction. "You've got to go back toward town, but it's not far. Only two miles or so."

"Two miles?" He draws out the last word, stretching his mouth wide to fit the vowels. I get this a lot in the field, people trying to imitate my Tennessee drawl as if there's something funny or quaint about an accent. But their teasing only comes across as condescension, or at the very best, surprise that I'm not as dumb as I sound.

Which is why I lay it on thick now. "Two miles, yeah. Take a left at the four-way stop, and then it'll be on your right. You can't miss it."

"There wouldn't happen to be a decent hotel near there, too, would there?"

I take in his longish hair and battered leather jacket. Scruffy chic or penny-pincher? I can't tell. "There's the Hale Springs Inn in town, but it's pretty swanky. Take the highway either way, though, and you'll find some more affordable places a little farther out."

He gives me a smile of thanks, but I detect something more to it—there's something more than just fuel and shelter he's looking for. A chill that has nothing to do with the February air brushes my shoulders, and I think of my cell, lying useless inside on the kitchen counter. I glance behind me, eyeing the distance to the front door, my senses on high alert.

He points over my shoulder. "Nice place. You live here?"

"Only temporari—" I swallow the last syllable, realizing a second too late I shouldn't have admitted to living in a semi-deserted house at the end of a semi-deserted street.

He stretches his neck to get a better look, and then his gaze returns to mine. He smiles again, and I back up a step. "You're Gia Andrews, right?"

Something like relief that he's not a rapist or armed robber washes over me, quickly replaced by fury. A journalist. A goddamn journalist. You'd think after all my interactions with them in the field, I would have recognized him as one immediately.

I turn and stalk to my car. "I don't talk to journalists."

"Fine by me, because I'm not a journalist." I don't slow, and he bolts out of the Escort, his voice booming over its hood. "I'm a writer. I'm writing a book about America's most shocking wrongful convictions."

His words are electric, shooting a paralyzing current from my crown to the tips of my toes and melding my sneakers to the icy pavement. Wrongful conviction? I pivot my head to meet his gaze. "Excuse me?"

He bites off a mitten and digs around in a coat pocket, then crosses the driveway and hands me a card. "I'm Jeffrey Levine, by the way."

I blink at the paper between my fingers, thick white linen with raised letters and a crest embossed in blue. "It says here you're a professor of law."

He slides his bare hand back into his mitten and nods. "For Emory. I'm taking a semester sabbatical to work on my book. It's called *True Crimes, False Convictions: Crimi-*

nal Injustice in America." When I don't respond, he shrugs. "Yeah, it's a working title."

"And you think my father's case is one of them?"

His head bobs in a decisive nod, and those ridiculous bangs flop over one eye. "Let me put it this way—your father's case is a textbook on what not to do. How to ignore leads. How to sweep conflict of interest under the rug. How to miscarry justice and send an innocent man to prison."

"But there was a witness." I pivot now to face him, purposefully playing devil's advocate. It's one thing to say my father's conviction was wrongful, another thing entirely to believe it. There was too much evidence to the contrary.

"One who thought he saw him breaking and entering his own house two hours after the time of death, not standing over the body with a smoking gun."

"Ella Mae was suffocated."

He gives me a look. "It was a figure of speech. And between you and me and everybody else who's going to read my book, I think Dean Sullivan's testimony was coerced. Did you know the police held him for six and a half hours? That screams gross misconduct to me."

Six and a half hours? Is that even allowed? But still. "The judge and jury believed him."

"Of course they did. Mr. Sullivan was an upstanding, God-fearing citizen." He points past me to the ramshackle ranch where the Sullivans once lived. "Just look at him now."

I gape at the neighboring property, so neglected I'd assumed it was abandoned. Front steps, rickety and rotting, lead to a front porch littered with trash and a ripped brown leather sofa. The yard, a foul-looking patch of dirt and rock, has seen neither fertilizer nor lawn mower since sometime last century. Even Dean's prized rosebushes have hardened into brown and scraggly branches jutting up from the frozen earth, a tangle of sticks and thorns.

"People actually still live there?" I say.

"Dean Sullivan lives there. Alone. His family won't have anything to do with him. His only friend is Jack Daniel's. His house, his yard, his entire life is a mess."

A mess might just be the biggest understatement on the planet. Dean's house makes some of the shanties in Dadaab look like palaces.

"What do you think he's hiding from?" Jeffrey asks.

I don't know what to say to that. I'd never considered the possibility Dean was still living there, much less hiding from something.

I think for a moment. If everything Jeffrey said is true, then why not tell me this right away, when he stopped to ask for directions? Or better yet, why not tell Uncle Cal? I was barely eighteen when Ella Mae was murdered, and I've had practically nothing to do with the case since.

"What do you want from me? You should be talking to my uncle Cal. He's the one who handled everything."

"I'd love to talk to him, but unfortunately, he wants nothing to do with me." He gives me a wry smile. "It might have something to do with me telling him I'm devoting an entire chapter to his shoddy defense of your father."

His words echo in my ears, bounce around my brain, feel foreign on my tongue. I don't get it. Uncle Cal is known as the Tennessee Tiger, as tenacious and tireless in the courtroom as he is with his girlfriends, an endless string of gold diggers and social climbers. There's no way his defense of my father—his own brother, for Christ's sake—was shoddy. What is this guy talking about?

Jeffrey arches a brow, seeming almost amused at my reaction. "This surprises you?"

"Yes, this surprises me, and it also infuriates me. Cal is a brilliant lawyer, and he worked his ass off to put together Dad's defense. He barely ate, he didn't sleep and nobody—nobody—was more upset than Cal when his brother, the one he defended, went to prison."

He lifts his shoulders in a don't-blame-the-messenger gesture. "Then why didn't he try to appeal?"

And here, I think, I have him. Lawyer, my ass. He doesn't even have all the information. "You should check your sources, because I know for sure he did appeal."

"Once." Jeffrey points a mitten to the sky. "Just one time, to the Court of Appeals."

"And it was declined."

"Denied."

"Same thing."

"But why did he stop there? Why didn't he keep going?"

"I don't…" I take two steps to my trunk, pause and turn back. "He could have done that?"

"Of course he could have. He definitely should have, but he didn't."

My heart misses about five beats. Cal slacked on my father's case? I still don't believe it. Dad is his only brother. There's no way.

Jeffrey points to his card, still clutched between my fingers, and turns to go. "Think about it, and give me a call when you're ready to hear more. And I hope you'll be ready sometime soon, because in the spirit of full disclosure, you should know I'm writing this book with or without your family's input. You can help me write it, or you can sit back and wait for your copy."

He waves one last time, and I watch him climb into his car and drive away, my mind swirling, humming, tripping over his message. About Cal's shoddy defense, about

Dean Sullivan's coerced testimony, but mostly about Jeffrey Levine's steadfast belief in my father's innocence. How is it possible to have that much blind faith in a person he's never met? How can a complete stranger be so unequivocally certain Ray Andrews did not murder his wife, while I—his own daughter—can't?

Turning back to the rental, I slip his card into the front pocket of my jeans and push it with two fingers until it's as deep as it can go, flush against the bottom seam.

Maybe sometime soon I'll work up the nerve to call Jeffrey and ask.

3

Ella Mae Andrews, September 1993

Ella Mae thunked her empty mug onto the wooden floor planks and gave her porch swing another shove with the heel of a foot. The metal chains squawked in time to her movement. Back. Forth. Back...

Somewhere in the distance a lawn mower whined, and Ella Mae envied both its gusto and its purpose. With two stepchildren in college and the third headed that way next fall, she found herself with more and more time to fill in her already spotless house, in her increasingly aimless day. She checked her watch. Ten o'clock, and already she was bored as hell.

A green truck crested the hill, heading in her direction, and the sight of it made her feel like dancing. Even if the driver was merely turned around, maybe she could strike up a conversation. By the time she'd given him precise, detailed directions, she would have killed a good fifteen minutes, maybe more. Would it be completely pathetic if she offered him a cup of coffee?

Good Lord. When had life become so dreary? She should probably think about getting a hobby.

Ella Mae stood and walked to the edge of the porch, watching and waiting until the truck was close enough to read the letters above the cab: Golan's Moving & Storage. The new neighbors, and about damn time, too. The old Bennett house had been empty for over a month now, a month in which Ray had done nothing but complain about how the property was going to pot. Two hornets' nests under the gable, a milky film on the windows and a patch of crabgrass crawling dangerously close to Ray's prized fescue. As if Ella Mae gave a shit about grass.

But now. Now she sure could give a shit, and her heart dealt an extra, hopeful beat at the idea of new neighbors, a new girlfriend, new anything.

A black sedan with Illinois plates pulled to a stop at the curb, and a family of four clambered out. Two blonde kids—both lanky girls in their early teens—tore across the front yard, screaming and giggling with the sort of giddiness that can only come at the tail end of a long drive.

Their mother was considerably less merry. She unfolded herself from the car, smoothed her rumpled dress and squinted into the sun at her new home.

"It's pretty," she said. Her tone implied she didn't really care how it looked.

The husband, a tall man with his daughters' flaxen hair and the build of a former athlete, popped the trunk. "I know it's a little smaller than we're used to, but just take a look at that view." His accent was Northern and nasal, but in Ella Mae's ears it sounded electric, exciting, exotic. "That's not something we would've ever found back in Chicago."

Chicaaago.

The woman didn't seem to notice the rolling fields of grass and wildflowers beneath smoky mountaintops, a view that, the first time Ella Mae saw it, stilled her soul and nipped at her heart with its beauty. Instead, the woman sighed, her expression unchanged, her tone as mousy as her appearance. "Pretty."

"Come on," her husband said. He stepped around the car and swung an arm around his wife's hunched shoulders. "Can you at least try to want to live here?"

"I just told you it was pretty."

Ella Mae knew she was eavesdropping. She knew they would notice her soon, gripping the rails on the edge of her porch, and see she was hanging shamelessly on their every word, but she didn't go inside. She wanted to move even closer and hear everything, lean in and get a better view.

She didn't care if they saw her. This was the most excitement she'd had since last month, when she'd chased Bill Almaroad's cows out of her begonias with a broomstick.

The man looked down at his wife. "We agreed this move would be a good thing, remember? A new job, a fresh start." He deposited a chaste kiss on her cheek, and she shrunk even further into herself. He released her, sweeping a long arm toward the house. "Welcome to our new adventure."

And that's when he noticed Ella Mae. A jolt of something she hadn't felt in a good while shot clear to her toes and crackled and popped on her skin like a Fourth of July sparkler. Later, she would think back to this very second, and think it was appropriate their eyes met right as that last word rolled off his tongue. Adventure. But for now, she simply smiled and waved.

"Hi, y'all." Ella Mae started down the steps toward her new neighbors. "I'm Ella Mae Andrews. Welcome to Rogersville."

* * *

Later that evening, Ella Mae noticed that Ray barely smiled when he pulled up to find two strangers on his front porch, grinning and sipping wine from the good glasses, the ones they hardly ever used except for birthday dinners and at Christmas. He barely smiled when Ella Mae handed him a martini, extra cold and extra dirty, and told him she'd made his favorite supper—peppered beef Stroganoff with garlic bread. He barely smiled when Dean complained about the sad state of his lawn, and said he had a lot of work to do before it could measure up to the one he'd kept back in Naperville, which had won Cedar Glen's finest front yard five years in a row.

Oh, Ray was friendly enough. His manners were too refined to have been rude. He chatted about the town's history and the fine school system, and he asked after their girls. But he barely ever smiled, and that wasn't her husband's way with company at all.

After the main course, when Ray and Ella Mae were serving up dessert in the kitchen while their guests waited at the dining room table, his good graces went down the drain, along with the remnants of his second martini.

"It's a school night," he pointed out, a bit too loud for Ella Mae's taste.

Ella Mae was fully aware it was Wednesday and that the company was messing up his Wednesday night routine—supper, a mindless blur of sitcoms, bed. She was also aware that Wednesday night was like every other night in this house.

"Shh, keep it down, will you? I left a message for you at the pharmacy."

"I just wish you would've warned me ahead of time," he said.

"I tried." She began carving her famous rhubarb-and-strawberry pie into generous triangles with a butcher knife. "I had to make an executive decision, so stop fussing. It's not like you had anything important planned for tonight."

"The game's on."

This from a man who thought fumble meant sticking his hands down her pants. Ella Mae squinted and planted a fist on her hip. "Who's playing?"

Ray shrugged, his hesitation a beat too long. "Doesn't matter, now that I'm missing it."

Ella Mae returned to her pie. "I didn't think so."

"Besides, we don't know anything about those people. They could be sociopaths or serial murderers for all we know."

"Don't be ridiculous. He's the new vice principal at the high school, and she's a stay-at-home mother of two adorable girls. They're perfectly normal, everyday members of society. They're neighbors. We're being neighborly."

"Whatever. I don't like him."

Ella Mae wasn't surprised. She'd only known Dean a few hours, but already she could see he wasn't a man's man. Too groomed, his clothes too stylish, his looks entirely too playboy handsome. Oh, yes. Cherokee High's newest vice principal would certainly be a popular man about town, but not with the husbands.

"Let's get back to our guests, shall we?" Ella Mae slid the last piece onto a plate and pointed Ray to the forks. "And be nice. I'm looking to make a new friend."

Over the course of the next hour, Ella Mae tried. She honest-to-God tried. She asked Allison about her kids and if the girls played any sports. She asked about her favorite books and if Allison would be interested in joining the book club. She even offered to take Allison on a tour of the town and show her the best places to shop. Allison was painfully shy, said all of ten words over the course of the entire meal. By the time they moved outside for coffee and brandy on the porch, Ella Mae regretted her offer, and she dreaded those hours alone in a car with Allison.

Her gaze landed on Dean, sipping on a glass of Ray's best brandy and looking more comfortable in his skin than an out-of-town semistranger should. Talk about opposites attracting. Dean was gorgeous and funny and charming, and for the life of her Ella Mae couldn't figure out what a man like him saw in quiet, mousy Allison.

Three hours alone in a car with *him,* on the other hand...

Dangerous. Just thinking about Dean in that way was dangerous. Ella Mae flushed to the tips of her ears, and she gave herself a good scolding. Married women should not be thinking naughty thoughts about their equally married new neighbor, no matter how sexy he might be.

And then Dean laughed, a low and raspy sound that resonated somewhere deep in Ella Mae's belly.

Oh, God. She was thinking naughty thoughts about Dean Sullivan again.

"Thank you again for dinner," Dean said, his gaze lingering on Ella Mae a smidge longer than necessary. "I can't imagine a more perfect greeting on our first night in town."

"You're welcome anytime." Goose bumps tightened her skin, and Ella Mae looked away, out over her backyard, blinking into the inky blackness. There. Much better.

"And thanks for asking Gia to hang out with the girls tonight. I keep telling Allison they're old enough to—" Dean broke off at his wife's sharp look. "Well, we just worry."

"Our younger daughter was diagnosed with type I diabetes last June." Allison's voice was quiet as ever, but for the first time, Ella Mae heard footprints of fire in her tone. "Gave us quite a scare."

Ella Mae felt a familiar tug, like some sort of phantom limb in her uterus, at the mother's worry she saw in Allison's expression. She loved Ray's three kids fiercely, honestly she did, but it wasn't the same kind of love she had for her own flesh-and-blood child.

"That must have been terrifying," Ella Mae said.

"It still is," Dean said. "Every time we think we have things under control, Caroline gets the flu or has a growth spurt, and we have to adjust her diet and insulin." Dean turned to Ray, gave him a wry smile. "I have a feeling we're about to become the pharmacy's new best customers."

Finally, a subject that got Ray to smile, really smile, and he puffed out his chest. "Glad to hear it. Though lucky for you, the money won't be coming from your pocket. The school system recently overhauled their employee insurance plan, as I'm sure you know. I was an advisor to the task force."

"Then I should thank you, since their plan is one of the reasons we moved here. There aren't many plans out there robust enough to cover anything more than the bare minimum of insulin." Dean shook his head, made a sour face. "No matter what you think of her husband's politics, Hillary Clinton is right. The health care system in this country is flat-out broken."

Ella Mae winced. Uh-oh. Dean had said the *C*-word.

Ray grew about four inches in the wicker chair, and his tone took a turn for the nasty. "Now I know politics in Chicago are a whole lot bluer than down here in the South, but let me assure you in no uncertain terms. Hillary's plan is a disaster. Too top-heavy, far too regulated. Anybody who thinks it would work in the real world, isn't living in the real world."

Unlike his neighbor, Dean didn't seem to get the least bit riled up. He lifted his lips in a friendly smile, crossed his legs casually at the ankle. "I'm living in the real world, Ray. And my world has gotten a lot more expensive since our plan back home dropped the coverage for dependents. Do you know how expensive it is to find insurance for a kid with diabetes? I'm not saying she's not worth every penny. Just that her care is expensive and that clinics and hospitals seem to be in the business of making sure she stays sick, instead of caring about her health."

Ella Mae popped out of her chair. "Ray, honey, would you like some more Scotch?"

Ray raised his glass in the air, jiggled it around. Dangit. Still a good two fingers left.

She whipped her head around to Allison. "More ice water?"

But Ray wasn't to be distracted, and he turned back to Dean, his tone and stance on edge. "I'm not saying the insurance system isn't broken, Dean. Just that the health-care system is fine as it is, and the Clintons should concentrate on what's really ailing this country—the economy."

"Then what do you suggest for families like mine?" Dean's voice was as amiable as ever. "One whose employers drop the dependents from their insurance plan when one of their employee's family members is diagnosed with a chronic or life-threatening illness."

Before Ray could respond, Ella Mae stepped in front of him, blocking his view of Dean and reaching for his still full glass, and giving him a look that left no doubt as to how quickly he needed to stop picking a fight with the neighbor. "How about I refresh y'all's glasses?"

"That's all right, darlin'." Ray clenched his jaw and stood, snatching back his glass. "I'll go in and do it myself."

And then he went inside without another word, without catching the screen door so it didn't slam shut behind him.

Ella Mae sank back into her chair, and the three fell into an awkward silence punctuated by the angry cry of a cicada.

Allison broke it first, standing, smoothing her skirt. "I better get back to Caroline. Thank you for a lovely night, Ella Mae. Will you thank Ray for me, as well?"

Ella Mae cleared her throat. "Of course. I'll see you tomorrow."

At the bottom step to the side yard, Allison paused. "You coming, Dean?"

Dean pushed off the railing to go and then thought better of it. "I'll be over in just a minute. I want to wait for Ray, apologize for getting him so riled up."

"Oh. Okay, then." Allison glanced at Ella Mae, smiled stiffly and then disappeared, swallowed up into the shadows. "Don't be long," came her voice from across the yard.

"I won't." Dean's answer was distracted. His attention was elsewhere. On Ella Mae elsewhere.

Ella Mae went as still as an opossum on a country road. Across the lawn, a door squeaked, fell shut with a click. Inside Ella Mae's house, the low notes of a TV hummed. Ella Mae was breathless. Her heart might have even stopped beating. She was alone with Dean Sullivan on the porch, and something about the way he looked at her made her think he'd been waiting all night for this moment.

"Seems we chased everybody away," Dean said.

"Not that far away." Ella Mae's tone held a note of reckless warning, her eyes a flash of daring. Daring him, and maybe also herself.

A breeze kicked up on the front lawn, chilling Ella Mae's skin and tickling her nose with the scent of honeysuckle. This was the tipping point, Ella Mae knew. Dean could get up now and walk away, go home to his new house and boring wife and sleeping daughters, or he could send them both into a frenzy.

He turned and leaned his elbows onto the railing, staring off into the black night. "I love it here already. And that view is sure something else." He glanced at Ella Mae over his shoulder. "Too bad we can't see it now because it's pretty spectacular, don't you think? Especially now the leaves are about to change."

Ella Mae said nothing.

He straightened and whirled back around, and his dark gaze found hers immediately. "Principal Whitehead told me I've not lived until I've seen Great Smoky Mountains Park. Are the trees there as pretty as he says?"

Trees? He was really talking about trees? Disappointment spread across her skin like a bruise, and she reprimanded herself for it. "He's right. They are pretty."

"What's that, about a forty-five-minute drive?"

She bit her lip, nodded again.

And then his mouth rode up into a wicked smile. "Do you think that'd be far enough?"

Ella Mae's heart took off in a wild gallop.

Frenzy. Definitely frenzy.

4

In many respects, returning to Rogersville after all these years feels a lot like my life in the field. Families torn apart by tragedy. A disaster that's at best chaotic and unpredictable and far, far out of my control. And at the end of the day, an almost desperate quest for distraction from the doom brewing all around me, even if only for a few hours.

I squeeze my rental between an ancient Chevy and a mud-encrusted truck, wriggle myself out and peer over its roof at my destination. Square and stout, the building's restored bricks and a fresh coat of paint gleam under old-fashioned gas lamps and the fading evening light. My gaze travels to the thick white letters painted across the picture window to the right of the door. Roadkill Bar and Grill.

Distraction in the form of cold beer and flattened rodents.

The door swings open with a blast of country music and the scent of something delicious. Truffles, maybe. Truffles? A couple steps out onto the sidewalk, their jackets hanging open as if it were fifty degrees out instead of hovering somewhere just above twenty. At the edge of the sidewalk, the man stops to dig around in his pockets for his keys.

"But hasn't he already been punished enough?" his date says, picking up their conversation with a toss of her drug-store dye-job hair. "I mean, he is dying of cancer."

"Good," the man says. "He murdered that woman, and now he deserves to die. An eye for an eye and all that."

A high-pitched giggle. "This is America, not Afghani-stan."

I don't want to hear this conversation. I don't want to hear it, and yet I can't seem to stop listening. It's as if I'm rendered powerless by the spectacle unfolding in front of me, like staring into a black hole or accidentally discov-ering the hotel TV offers free porn. Curiosity takes over, and I have to stay until the very end. I duck my head and pretend to search through my bag, my ears practically flap-ping off my head.

I hear what can only be the sound of male spit hitting pavement. "Damn straight, this is America. And this here's American justice at its finest. That old man is getting ex-actly what he has coming to him."

"I don't think you can credit the justice system for giv-ing an old man cancer. Jesus Christ, maybe, but not the justice system."

"Freeing a convicted murderer ain't justice, that's for damn sure." Keys jingle, and their footsteps take off in my direction. "In my book, life in prison means dying in prison."

Another giggle followed by a playful slap. "Tommy Al-dean, since when did you write a book?"

"I'm the next Dan Brown, sweetheart. Guaran-damn-teed to be a bestseller."

By now they're coming up alongside me, and I bend and retie my tennis shoe even though the lace is still snug. None of my sneaky surveillance moves are necessary. They're not paying me the least bit of attention.

He loops an arm around her neck and pulls her close. "And if you lift that pretty little shirt of yours, I'll pull out my Sharpie and sign your chest."

She swats his arm and acts offended, but ten thousand Kenyan shillings say Tommy Aldean's Sharpie will be making an appearance later on tonight. They stop to make out on the sidewalk and I stumble off, their words ringing in my ears.

Small town. Big goddamn scandal.

Sixteen years is a long time to be away from anywhere, with the possible exception of Rogersville, Tennessee. The land that time forgot.

If only I could forget that time.

Murderer. Convicted felon. The taunts and accusations rattle through my brain and stir up old muck, suddenly as real to me as the sidewalk under my sneakers. Innocent until proven guilty sounds nice in theory, but it's a fairy tale. For the citizens of Rogersville, my father was a murderer long before the police put him in handcuffs. As far as they were concerned, the verdict was merely a technicality.

And now, Tommy Aldean and his bleached blonde just confirmed what I already knew. The Andrews family gossip rating is still at an all-time high. Our drama is still a favorite topic, our tragedy still local folklore.

I tell myself this time around will be different, that I'm older now. Older and wiser and toughened up by a job that has required me to grow a giant pair of testicles—not literally, of course, though I'm known to employ tactics in the field that make my colleagues wonder aloud at the contents of my pants. Regardless, I'm determined to handle things better. More maturely. Or at least, with not quite as much vomiting and public weeping.

I square my shoulders, pull open Roadkill's heavy oak door and step into my past.

The music doesn't screech to a halt when I walk through the door. Mouths don't hang open; eyeballs don't bug out; forks don't pause in midair. No one really notices me at all, an occurrence I find relieving and strangely anticlimactic at the same time.

I weave a path through the sleek wooden tables to a stool at the far end of the bar, picking out a few familiar faces along the way, trawling through my memory banks for matching names. I've kept in touch with no one here beyond my own siblings, and without old yearbooks (trashed) or high-school reunions (avoided) to keep the synapses connected, the endeavor is hopeless. I shrug off my coat, hang it on a hook under the bar and turn my attention to the drink specials on a chalkboard menu above the bar instead.

A loud thunk punctuates the music and I shift on my stool, twisting my torso to face the man pushing through the swinging door from the kitchen. Dark hair, three-day beard, ruggedly handsome enough to prompt an appreciative murmur from a gaggle of women behind me, but diplomatic enough to pretend not to notice. He sees me, and surprise flashes across his expression. I blink and it's gone.

"Sorry." He sets a crate of steaming wineglasses onto the bar and swipes his hands over his black apron. "Hope you haven't been waiting long."

"Nope, just got here."

He cocks his head and inspects me, and an icy shiver skates down my spine. It's this breathless moment I hate the most, that moment of waiting for recognition to hit, waiting on the verdict for a crime I didn't commit. His gaze travels over my curls and across my face, dipping even farther down to my vintage Rolling Stones T-shirt under an ancient wool cardigan. When his expression settles into one of resolute opinion, I reach for my coat.

"Beer," he says, "but only when there's nothing else better. An occasional cocktail, but not sweet. Vodka with soda and a lime or straight up. But first choice would be wine, preferably red and preferably imported."

Relief hits me like a Valium at both his innocuous message and his speech, deep and clipped with a generic accent. No nasal twang, no elongated vowels to tell me where he's from, except that he's not from around here. I drop my coat back onto the hook, settle back onto my stool.

But as far as drinks go, the man has me pegged.

"Well?" An undertone of mock uncertainty slips into his voice, playing bass to his lighthearted teasing. "How'd I do?"

"Pretty decent. Extra credit if you can actually produce the imported red."

The bartender grins like he just pulled the winning numbers for the Tennessee Mega Millions, and I feel myself relax the slightest bit. Flirting with handsome strangers in crowded bars? Now I'm back in familiar territory.

He slides a bottle of Bordeaux from the wine refrigerator behind him and sets to work uncorking it. "Did you know in Tennessee it's legal to take roadkill home and eat it, whether you're the one who creamed it or not?"

"I hope that doesn't mean you're planning to serve me skunk stew. Because I've tried it, and just between you and me, yuck. Ditto for opossum pie."

He perches on an elbow and glances over both shoulders in an exaggerated fashion, sending the tips of his hair brushing along the collar of his V-neck T-shirt. "Don't let the chef hear you. He's a little sensitive about his food. He once tossed a customer out for complaining his raccoon ragù was too salty."

"Which is, of course, ridiculous because everyone knows the only way to cook raccoon is by boiling it in salt water."

The bartender leans back, and a brow creeps upward. "And here I thought you were a Roadkill virgin."

"Virgin!" A familiar, throaty laugh tickles my ears, and I whirl around on my stool to face my grinning sister. "Not since Andrew Hopkins's parents let him borrow their brand-new station wagon sophomore year."

"Better than the bathroom at Burger King, where you lost yours."

"That was a vicious rumor." Lexi leans in, giggling, her breath hot on my neck. "And it was Kentucky Fried Chicken."

A laugh pushes up my throat followed by a hot sob, and I launch myself at my sister. I wrap my arms around her and bury my face in her hair, inhaling her familiar floral scent, blinking back the tears heating the corners of my eyes. I don't remember much of our mother—I was only five when she crashed her car into a tree—except for this feeling of love. Love so large I think my heart might explode. Love so fierce it hurts to breathe.

"Let go, Gi. You're suffocating me." Lexi wriggles her hands in between us and pushes me to arm's length. The skin around her eyes crinkles in a smile. "And besides, I want to get a good look at you." She surveys me up and down, her gaze settling on the denim hanging loose from my hips. "Good Lord, you're a walking advertisement for anorexia."

"And you are as gorgeous as ever." Honey hair that falls

perfectly straight down her back, bowed lips curved into a flirtatious smirk, sinuous limbs begging to be draped over the hood of a Corvette. My sister may be a little older now, her designer denim a little tighter, but Sexy Lexi Andrews is still every inch Miss Cherokee High three years in a row.

She turns and smacks a palm on the bar, demanding the bartender's attention. "Jake, you handsome devil, have you met my sister, Gia, yet?"

If Jake is surprised this is a family reunion, he doesn't show it. He flicks the towel over a shoulder and extends a long arm over the bar. "Jake Foster. Nice to meet you, Gia."

His grip is firm, his hand warm and smooth in mine. "Nice to meet you, too."

"Fire up your fry-daddy," Lexi tells Jake. "We've got to get some meat on my sister's bones, pronto." She winks at me. "There's not a soul within fifty miles who's not put on at least ten pounds since Jake opened this place five years ago. Wait'll you taste his food. You'll know why he's got girls all over town flinging their panties at his front door."

Jake gives her an appreciative grin and pours two generous glasses of wine. When he tells us about the special—seared duck breast and oven-roasted kale and sweet potato hash smothered in jus—my mouth waters and I smack my lips. Jake notices, and he gives me a cocky grin.

"Don't laugh," I say. "My last real meal was a watery stew with questionable chunks of what the cook swore was goat. The stray dog population took a hit that day, though, so I don't think he was being entirely honest."

"I don't know whether to be offended or relieved," Jake says.

Lexi snorts. "Try disgusted."

He throws back his head and laughs, a deep rumble that

vibrates through my bones, and then disappears into the kitchen with a twirl of his towel and our orders.

As soon as he's gone, I whirl on my stool to face Lexi, and the words tumble out of my mouth like stock cars at the Bristol Motor Speedway, racing to the finish line. "Did you know that vice principal Sullivan still lives next door—his house is a dump by the way—and is a raging alcoholic?"

"That's not exactly a 411, you know. By now that man's liver is so pickled, you could batter it, fry it and serve it on a platter."

"And his family? What happened to them?"

Lexi sips her wine. "Gone. Hightailed it out of here after what must have been his fourth or fifth DUI."

The professor's words—*What do you think he's hiding from?*—skitter through my mind, but I switch gears. Dean Sullivan's fall from grace, though intriguing, is the least of my worries.

I move on. "This law professor from Atlanta came by the house earlier, and you wouldn't believe what he said about Dad."

Lexi scowls and plunks down her wineglass, her gaze fishing over my right shoulder. "Why is it that every time somebody gets saved at Light of Deliverance church, they turn into a dowdy old frump? Surely that outfit can't be what Jesus intended for his fans."

I don't bother checking. My sister is the Carrie Bradshaw of Appalachia, and not many people can live up to her fashion standards. And besides, I know this tactic. By interrupting me with some ridiculous nonsense, Lexi is hoping to distract me from a subject she hasn't spoken more than a few words about in almost sixteen years: our father.

"I think they're called followers," I say, not backing down, "and we were talking about Dad's case."

"Whatever. That woman is a *What Not to Wear* episode waiting to happen. Oh, Lord. Now she's passing out flyers." She snorts and rolls her eyes. "Probably for their next snake handling."

"Could you focus, please? This professor is writing a book about wrongful convictions. He thinks Dad's is one of them."

And now, I think, I've got my sister's attention. Her gaze whips to mine, her good-humored expression fades and her brows slide into the ghost of a medically frozen *V*. She reaches for the wineglass and drains it, knuckles tightening ever so slightly around the stem. And then she dabs her glossy lips with a napkin and the storm on her face vanishes as quickly as it came, like a twister sucked up into a dissolving cloud.

"You'd think people would've heard by now that snake bites everybody." Her voice is a little too loud, and a lot too vehement. "Even holier-than-thou Bobby Humphrey. By the time they got him the antivenom, he was foaming at the mouth. Besides, I thought the whole point was prayer, not antivenom. Isn't that kind of cheating?"

"Lexi! We have to talk about Dad."

She leans across the bar, snatches the bottle of wine and fills her glass to within an inch of the rim. "The hell we do."

A familiar frustration ties a string of knots across my shoulders. My sister has always been a great believer in the power of denial. How else can I explain her staying in the one place where she will always be the murderer's daughter?

But what if what Jeffrey Levine said is true? What if all this time, I've been running from something my father didn't do?

"Did you hear me? This professor thinks Dad might be innocent. What if he's right?"

She shakes her head definitively, almost violently. "He's not."

"But what if he is?"

"He's *not!*" she shrieks, shrill enough that I jump. Everyone jumps, in fact. A young couple at a table to our left, three friends sharing a plate of fried calamari at our backs, two potbellied men in trucker hats three stools down. Even Jake looks up from the beer he's pulling at the opposite end of the bar, and hell's bells, I catch pity in his expression.

But Lexi has always preferred the part of sexy bombshell over damsel in distress, and really, who can blame her? Our life has been distressing enough. She tosses him a beauty-queen smile and reaches for her wineglass with a shaking hand, and all around us, conversations pick back up one by one.

I lean close, lower my voice. "Why do you refuse to discuss the possibility he may not be guilty?"

She glances over, and I see a flash of my sister. The real Lexi. The unguarded and devastated Lexi. "Because it's a whole hell of a lot easier than praying he's innocent."

And then she flicks her perfect hair over a perfect shoulder and real Lexi's gone.

5

When the kitchen door swings wide a few minutes later revealing Jake coming at us with two plates piled high with tonight's special, I realize I'm ravenous. Outta-my-way-and-let-me-at-it ravenous. He slides our dinners onto the bar, and I scoop up a bite and shove it in my mouth before he's pulled back his hand.

"Omigod," I mumble around the food, slicing off an even bigger bite of duck, stuffing it in with the half-chewed hash. I say more, but judging by the confused look on Jake's face, none of it very intelligibly.

He blinks at Lexi. "What did your sister just say?"

She watches me take another monster bite, and her pretty nose wrinkles. "I don't know, but you better back up."

When you live in an area mired in chronic famine, it's easy to forget how food is supposed to taste. Meals are freeze-dried and carried down dusty roads to distribution sites where nobody cares if they please the palate, as long as they nourish the body. After a while, you stop missing the tangy sweetness of a juicy plum, the prick of sea salt just before it explodes on your tongue, the way one bite of something delicious can be as satisfying as a sweaty romp between the sheets. Jake's food makes me remember all those things now.

I swallow, swipe a napkin across my lips. "I said, this is an orgasm on a plate."

A smile slides up Jake's face and settles in. It's a magnetic, no-holds-barred smile, a smile that's fierce and undeniably sexy, a smile that tugs and tingles somewhere deep and low in my belly.

Jake Foster would make a mighty fine distraction.

He refills our glasses and points to the far end of the bar. "I'll be down there if you need me."

After he leaves, Lexi and I don't return to our discussion of Dad. Not of the Emory professor, either. Skirting around the reason for our reunion is only a temporary respite, I know, but neither of us seems willing to risk another outburst. We scarf down our Thursday-night specials and tiptoe around each other, chatting and catching up on jobs and boys and Bo, who is about to put his name on yet another patent for Eastman Chemical Company, this time for a new and revolutionary mascara.

It takes a couple beats for her message to muddle through my jet-lagged brain. "Hold up. Bo hasn't called me back because he's working on a stupid mascara?"

"Excuse me, but just because you got all the dark lashes in the family—" she leans in, giving me a pointed look "—mascara is not stupid. Especially Bo's. His is about to change the way women put on makeup in the mornings."

"Again, we're talking about a cosmetic." My level tone abandons me now, as does my inside voice. "Not a cure for cancer. Not the key to world peace. A freaking cosmetic."

Lexi sniffs. "One that women all over the world are

going to pay a lot of money for. Good thing Bo promised me a lifetime supply."

I resist rolling my eyes, but just barely. "But not one that's more important than calling back his sister, who he hasn't talked to in forever. And I know I don't have to remind you what's happening tomorrow. I swear to God, if he ditches Dad's homecoming for a tube of face paint—"

She stops me with a manicured hand in the air. "Calm down. He's going to call you back."

"How do you know? When did you last talk to him?"

A frown tries to push up her forehead—a frown aimed at me, and not our errant brother. "Not for a few days, but Cal has. He told me Bo knows about tomorrow."

"Good." Though I may have been willing to back off—temporarily, at least—on the subject of Jeffrey Levine and his allegations, I bite down now. Dad's homecoming is a party I don't plan to host all by myself. "Because Dad's supposed to arrive at noon."

Her next words come at the tail end of a sigh. "So I hear."

"Lexi." My tone is weighed down with enough warning to sink a ship. "Don't even think about bailing."

She shoves away her empty plate with an elbow, opening her mouth for a response when she's distracted by Jake charging by, a sheet of paper half crumpled in a fist. Something about the way he comes around the bar, mouth set, shoulders determined, eyes not so much as glancing our way, silences her before the first syllable. She clamps her mouth shut and follows him across the room with her gaze.

I, however, have had enough of my sister's distraction maneuvers. "Just so we're clear, Lex, tomorrow is nonnegotiable."

But I'm talking to her back. Lexi is twisted around on her stool, watching Jake approach a woman with a droopy stack of flyers fanning over her arm like an accordion. The Light of Deliverance frump, judging from her outfit: a turtleneck sweater and pleated skirt that would give even Heidi Klum a fat ass.

The woman doesn't resist when he clamps a palm around her biceps and pulls her aside, parking her next to the cigarette machine by the bathroom hallway. She doesn't speak, either, mostly because Jake doesn't give her a chance. Not with his expression, which practically dares her to try. Not with his body language, which puffs his chest and makes him stand a few inches taller in his boots. And not with his scolding—for Jake is surely giving her a scolding—which continues unbroken for a good sixty seconds.

"Who's he talking to?" I say. "I feel like I should know her."

"You should. That's Tanya Crawford, formerly McNeal."

It takes me a minute to connect the long-forgotten dots. "The same Tanya McNeal who got suspended for selling hand jobs in the school parking lot?"

"That's her. Married one of those loony Pentecostals a few years ago, so I suppose it was inevitable she'd follow him over the hot coals."

Whatever Jake's message, Tanya doesn't like it. She scrunches her mouth and pushes past him without a word, barely pausing to snatch her coat from a hook on her way out the door.

Lexi returns to her wine, draining her glass and then reaching for mine.

"What do you think that was all about?" I say.

"Not about snake handling, that's for damn sure."

The back of my neck tingles at her ominous words, at whatever's written on Tanya's paper, now stuffed into the back pocket of Jake's jeans. And the undeniable hunch the episode has something to do with our father.

I steal another glance at Jake, but now he's swapping greetings with a man in head-to-toe Harley-Davidson gear, and I'd be hard-pressed to find any indication of his former aggravation without a blood pressure cuff. He slaps the biker on the back, sweeps up two empty plates from the table to his right and heads back to the bar as if nothing happened, as if he didn't just tell Tanya McNeal she was no longer welcome.

"Jakey." Lexi's voice is high and honey sweet, stopping him before he can slip into the kitchen. "Did you or did you not just toss that woman out of your restaurant?"

"Absolutely not." He shifts the plates onto a forearm, not quite meeting Lexi's eyes. Mine, either. "The choice to leave was hers entirely."

Lexi and I share a look, and then she reaches a hand, palm to the sky, across the bar. "All right. Hand it over."

He pauses a beat too long. "Hand what over?"

"Jake Foster, don't you play coy with me. Either give me that paper in your back pocket or I'll go over there and get a copy from Andy Jamison. Your call."

A faint furrow dips between his brows, but Jake slides the paper from his pocket with his free hand. He goes to pass it to her, then reconsiders. He pulls back his hand, and the wadded-up paper, just out of her reach. "Maybe you should wait till you get home to read it."

Lexi molds her lips into one of her beauty-pageant smiles. "Sweetheart, I wasn't born yesterday. By the way your eyes get all pointy just looking at me, I already have a good idea what this is about. But don't you worry. If that paper has something to do with that man, then it has nothing to do with me." She holds up her palm. "Now give it."

"What man?" I ask Lexi. "You have nothing to do with what man?"

Lexi doesn't answer, doesn't take her eyes off Jake, and he drops the wad into her hand. She uncrumples the paper, flattening it onto the bar with both palms. Her red-dipped fingertips swipe along the first three words: Guilty as Sin.

She thrusts the paper away like it's garbage.

"That hardly seems very Christian," I say.

"That's exactly what I told Tanya." Jake slides the dishes with a loud clatter onto the bar, his gaze hardwired to my sister.

Lexi ignores both of us. She reaches into her purse for a tube and a silver compact and sets about applying a fresh coat of pink gloss.

I slide the page closer with the tip of a finger and read further. My stomach twists at the image of my father, looking almost dashing in his trial suit, like he's on his way to the Barter Theatre rather than playing center stage in his own nightmare. But I can see why Tanya chose to feature this shot of him. His mouth is set in a crooked grin, his expression confident and cocky, as if daring the jury to find him guilty, which of course they did.

And now, according to the flyer, Tanya McNeal and her Pentecostal cronies plan to gather tomorrow morning at ten o'clock sharp on the street in front of the house. They will be armed with posters and banners and righteous indignation. And I predict they will be louder than a monster truck jam.

"Awesome." I throw up my hands. "Just awesome."

Jake tucks the flyer out of sight under a stack of menus, picks up the dirty plates and disappears into the kitchen. Later, I will thank him for not tolerating Tanya's propaganda in his restaurant, but for now, I'm too busy making plans. My training has kicked in, and I'm making plans.

Because if ever there was a disaster, then surely this is it.

I twist on my bar stool to face Lexi. "Okay, so here's what we're going to do. First thing tomorrow morning, I'll call Cal. I don't think we can stop them from protesting, but maybe we can come up with a technicality. A noise ordinance or loitering violation or something like that. And as soon as I get home, I'll look up the name for our contact at the police department. Maybe you can work some of your magic on him, get him to help us out somehow."

Lexi snaps the compact shut and glances over at me. "Why me?"

"Because he's a man, and you're Sexy Lexi."

"So?"

"So this is crisis mode. We are in crisis mode. A bunch of angry Bible beaters are about to take up residence on our driveway."

Her gaze fishes over my shoulder to the dining room behind me, and I know what she's doing: damage control. Mentally counting the number of tables Tanya managed to reach with her call to arms, checking expressions for pity or displeasure or hostility, taking a moral temperature of the room. And I can tell by the way she's folding her napkin, smoothing it over and over until it's a fat but small square, that the damage has already been done.

"That Cal has somehow guilted you into helping is your business," she says, her gaze returning to mine, her eyes narrower, sharper, "but I don't want any part of it. I never gave either of you any indication I'd help. In fact, I think I've made it pretty clear to everyone involved I washed my hands of that man long ago. I don't plan on getting them dirty again."

"Our father is coming home to die. To die, Lexi, and from what I understand, a pretty painful death."

"Oh, stop acting like such a goddamn martyr. Because I can assure you nobody in this town is going to feel a lick of sympathy for the murderer's daughter."

"Which is exactly what you are."

Lexi bristles like a cornered porcupine. "Not anymore, I'm not. The very second that man wrapped saran wrap around Ella Mae's mouth and nose until she suffocated, I stopped being his daughter, and he gave up any rights to call himself my father. And if there's any justice in the world, they'll call me when it comes time to pull the plug."

Her words zap me like a Taser, temporarily paralyzing my heart, my lungs, my conviction Lexi would do the right thing. No matter what Ray Andrews did or didn't do, he'll always be her father.

"You can't possibly mean that," I say.

Lexi holds my gaze with unperturbed eyes.

But bravado can be a real bitch. In order for it to work, you have to be able to sustain it long enough to make your audience swallow it. Lexi's wavers. She snatches her bag and bolts for the door, and I don't follow. I don't even turn my head to watch her go. Better to let Lexi wind herself down and try again later, in a less public venue.

I slump against the bar, staring with undisguised longing at the bottles lining the back wall. So this is my first night back. Cal deserted me, Bo ignored me, Lexi ditched me. My evening ends alone, in a bar filled with people I don't know or don't care to remember. I shrug off a surge of self-pity that threatens to knock me off my bar stool. My life is such a fucking fairy tale.

A figure steps up across from me with a slice of cake the

size of a double-wide. Jake, of course. He wags two forks in the air. "Chocolate always helps."

My stomach lurches at the thought of more food, and I wave his offer away. "Thanks, but no thanks."

He slides the dessert three seats down, offering it to a bearded man in flannel and denim. "Knock yourself out, Wade. On the house." And then he turns back to me, leaning across the bar on both forearms. "Bartenders are notoriously good listeners, you know."

I know he means well, but right now talking about my problems is the last thing on my mind. The very last thing. Not when a mighty fine distraction is standing right here.

"How about drinkers? Are y'all good drinkers, too?"

"I can't speak for all bartenders," he says, "but I've been known to tie one on when necessary."

One corner of his mouth lifts, and I watch for the other to catch up. Here it comes.

"Oh, it's necessary. Because I hate to drink alone, and I'm sure as hell not going back to that house sober."

And there it is. I free-fall into Jake's extraordinary smile.

6

I wake up the next morning in my bed, my tongue super-glued to the roof of my mouth and my head clanging.

No. Not my head. Cal's iPhone, on the pillow next to me.

I crack open an eye and squint at the screen. Both eyes fly open at the image of me and Jake, his arm swung over my shoulder, my head thrown back in laughter. I have no idea how it got on my phone. Hell, I have no idea how I got in my bed. On the fourth ring, I pick up.

"Good morning, sunshine." Jake's booming voice sets off a string of explosions in my head.

"Jesus." I jerk the phone away from my ear. "What time is it?"

"Seven-thirty. You made me promise to give you a wake-up call at seven-thirty and not a millisecond later, remember?"

I trawl through my memories of last night, but things start to get fuzzy after the second cocktail. "Not really."

"That bad, huh?"

I put a finger to my temple and groan. "A responsible bartender would've cut me off."

He laughs. "I tried. Honestly, I tried. Has anyone ever told you you're more stubborn than Curtis Cooper's old mule? But I drew the line when you reached for your car keys."

I would wince, but my face hurts. "Probably a good thing."

"I thought so, especially after you challenged Sheriff Briggs to a game of quarters. But just for the record, you took off your jeans all by yourself. I had nothing to do with undressing you. And I didn't peek, I swear."

Now, if I was any kind of good girl, I'd be embarrassed and horrified by what Jake just told me. I'd be worried about the wanton impression the drunken me made. But the truth is, I'm not exactly a good girl, and last night wouldn't be the first time I've tossed back one too many cocktails and shucked my jeans for a cute guy. At the risk of sounding like an oversexed trollop, I've kind of lost count.

Still. I really would've preferred remembering the experience. A quick check under the covers doesn't solve the mystery. I'm dressed, but just barely, in last night's panties and a white tank top. I chew my lip and wonder whether I should be relieved or disappointed I'm not naked.

Jake's voice drops an octave. "You just looked under the covers, didn't you?"

"Of course not."

"Uh-huh." I feel his smile clear through the line. "Nice tattoo, by the way."

His words scorch a trail of heat from my cheeks down to my tattoo, tucked away under the lace of my panties on my right butt cheek. A spot Jake wouldn't have seen, unless he'd been peeking.

"It looked like some kind of flowery tribal symbol," he continues. "What is it?"

"A flowery tribal symbol."

"No. I meant, what does it mean?"

"It means you were lying when you said you didn't peek."

He laughs, but he doesn't deny it. "Your keys are under the welcome mat," he says, right before he disconnects.

I throw back the covers, and the cool air in my bedroom practically hisses when it hits my skin. Jake neglected to mention where, exactly, he spent last night, and contemplating that answer makes me hot enough to fry an egg on my bare belly. Downstairs on the couch? Next to me in my bed? Almost certainly somewhere in this house. Town is exactly a two-point-seven-mile hike, mostly uphill, and Jake would be crazy to have walked back in the freezing dark.

I slither across the bed to the window and spot my car parked neatly in the driveway, its windows buried under a light dusting of snow, as is the driveway. No tire tracks either, which means my car has been there a good while. By the looks of things, most of the night.

At the end of the driveway, a red Jeep Cherokee slows to a crawl. The driver, a middle-aged woman with hair the color of traffic cones, stops to check the number on the mailbox against a piece of paper in her hand. She does a sloppy three-point turn and careens into the driveway, thrusting the gearshift into Park right before her bumper slams into mine.

I hop out of bed, scrounge around in my open suitcase for a pair of sweats and last night's sweater and pull them on. By the time I make it to the front door, she's standing on the welcome mat with a crate of medical supplies and a hurry-up-and-let-me-in grin.

"Lordy me," she says, "it's colder than a witch's tit in a brass bra out here."

"You must be the hospice nurse."

She doesn't wait for an invitation, just barrels past. "In the flesh."

And there's plenty of it. Her curves have been stuffed into clothes that almost fit her, and her permed and pigmented hair has been teased to unnatural heights and sprayed into submission. Add to that shiny blue eye shadow, watermelon lips and eyebrows that look as though they've been drawn on with a brown magic marker. The woman is pure Appalachia in yellow-and-lilac nurse's scrubs.

She thunks the crate onto the floor by the living room and takes a good look around. Her gaze lands on me, and she grins. "You must have had one wild night."

"Oh! Um, no, I… I mean, we…"

Her laugh is more like a cackle. "Honey, it may have been a good spell ago, but I remember that look. Wild hair, even wilder eyes. Plus, your tank top's on backward."

Yeesh. I wrap the sweater tight across my chest and thrust out a hand. "Gia Andrews."

"Fannie Miles." She waddles off as if the house is her own. "Sweet holy Jesus, I need a cup of coffee."

In the kitchen, Fannie gets the pot going with practiced efficiency. She digs around in the cabinets until she finds two mugs, then motions for me to follow her back into the living room.

"I'm gonna have to do some rearranging in here," she says, taking in the hospital bed pushed to the corner. "You don't mind, do you?"

"Not at all." This is clearly the Fannie Miles show, and I'm happy to let her lead.

"Great." She settles her ample behind onto the couch, casting an expectant glance around the room. "So where is everybody?"

"You're looking at them." I try not to feel sorry for myself as I say the words, or think about the knife of resentment I feel jutting out of my back, somewhere in the vicinity of right between my shoulder blades.

Fannie lifts a crayon brow. "I thought Cal said there would be three of you."

I nod. "There goddamn better be. But for now I guess it's just me."

She wraps a warm palm over my arm and gives me a kind smile. "Then right now, sugar pie, you're the only one who matters." Fannie pulls back her hand, sits up a little straighter. "Okeydokey, then. How much did Cal tell you?"

"He filled me in on the basics. That you're responsible for my father's care and comfort, that you'll manage his pain without prolonging his life, that you'll stay until the end."

The end. A growing ball of nausea takes root in my belly, one that has nothing to do with last night's liquor.

"But more important," I continue, "how much did Cal tell you?"

"I assume you're talking about your father's legal issues?"

I shake my head. "You'd have to be dead to not know about those. I'm wondering more what he could have possibly said to make you agree to take this job."

Fannie shrugs. "That's easy. He's paying me two dollars more an hour plus a whopper of a bonus if I stay until the funeral."

I don't respond. In my job, I've met plenty of people for whom money is a legitimate reason to do just about anything—dig a community well, disappear without a trace, murder a business partner. Tending to a dying man is as good a job as any, I suppose. And depending on the size of the bonus and how long Dad lasts, the amount could be substantial. Fannie doesn't look particularly hard up for cash, but who am I to judge?

"You're worried that money ain't proper motivation, aren't you?"

"I just want to make sure you know what you're getting into. We aren't the most stable of families, as I'm sure you can imagine. Quite honestly, though, our dysfunctionality is the least of your problems."

Fannie catches my meaning instantly, making me think she's already considered the consequences of taking this job. "You mean my being here isn't going to get me elected the next Miss Rogersville."

I nod.

She barks out a laugh, slaps a palm to a meaty thigh. "I hate to tell you, honey, but that train left the station 'bout twenty years ago." When she sees I'm not ready to join in her hilarity, her expression sobers to half-serious. "You must be the one living way off in Australia."

"Africa."

"Africa. I coulda sworn it was Australia…anyway, my point is you weren't here, so you couldn't have known folks are already blabbering about me on account of my rat bastard ex-husband. I swear, how I stayed married to Lester Miles for fifteen years without catching a venereal disease is one of God's great mysteries."

I can't help but smile, but there's a warning buried in the gesture. "This job is going to take gossip to a whole new level."

"Sugar, if I'da cared what people thought of me, I never woulda married that no-good snake back in '95, and I sure as hell never woulda told everybody he spent our retirement fund on cocaine and hookers after I left his sorry ass." She lifts her entire upper body in a shrug. "Not only do I need this paycheck, I also don't give a flying pile of pig shit what people think about my being here."

I sit for a long moment, trying to process what Fannie just told me. A lying, cheating, thieving spouse would certainly feed the Rogersville gossip mill. Not on the scale of a father who may or may not be a murderer, but still. She must be well-acquainted with how it feels to walk into a room and be greeted with silence, even though every person in there has plenty to say about you behind your back.

The bigger question is, how can she stand it?

"How do you do it?" I ask. "How do you not care?"

Fannie looks at me with kind eyes. "You just don't, sugar, that's all."

She pats my arm again and hoists herself off the couch, following the scent of freshly brewed coffee into the kitchen. Halfway there she turns back with a soft cackle. "Otherwise give 'em the line about the flying pile of pig shit. That one always works."

After a second cup of coffee, Fannie refuses my offer to help her rearrange the room or cart in her busload of medical supplies. She shoos me off, ordering me into a hot shower and something more proper than a backward tank top. Once upstairs, it's not the shower knob I reach for but my phone. Cal, Bo and Lexi, in that order.

Cal picks up on the first ring. "Good mornin', baby girl. How you holding up?"

"I'm okay. Fannie's here." I sink onto the foot of my bed and wait while Cal takes in my meaning behind those four words, which he does pretty much immediately.

"Where are Bo and Lexi?"

Nothing slips by the Tennessee Tiger.

The hurt comes flooding back, this time with the tears I managed to fend off last night with alcohol and Jake. Alone in my old room now, I don't bother to check them. "Lexi ditched me last night, and Bo still hasn't called me back."

Cal curses under his breath. "I'll call them on my way into court, and I'll use my lawyer voice. Don't you worry, darlin'. I'll make sure they get their asses over there pronto."

Part of me, and not a small part, wants to believe him— Cal's lawyer voice is certainly something to be feared—but the realistic side of me knows better.

"I'm afraid it's going to take a lot more than a stern talking-to to get Lexi over here, and same goes for Bo. But that's not why I'm calling. When I was in town last night, I heard about some protesters. A local group of Bible beaters, and it sounds like it's going to be a shit storm."

Cal half groans, half sighs. "I'm not particularly surprised. People in that town sure loved Ella Mae, and sixteen years isn't nearly long enough to heal their wounds. Especially with that damn garden to remind them every time they drive through town."

My uncle is right. If the Ella Mae Andrews Memorial Garden on all four corners of Depot and Main doesn't prompt folks to remember Ella Mae, the women of her former garden club, who make sure the plot thrives all year-round, will. Even in February, when the trees are bare like they are now, it's kind of hard to miss.

"Is there any way we can stop them?"

"Folks have a constitutionally protected right to engage in protests, assuming they're peaceful. As long as they stick to the street and don't disrupt traffic, we have to let them."

What traffic? I look out my bedroom window over the front yard and the empty asphalt that dead-ends into our driveway. With only a handful of homes on a stretch of almost a mile, Maple Street isn't exactly a major throughway.

"What about noise ordinances? I heard they'll have bullhorns."

"Noise amplifying instruments are a different story. They're not allowed without a permit. I'll have my assistant check if any noise ordinance waivers have been issued, but without those, they can sit out there all the livelong day if they want."

Cal's answer heaves and swirls in my stomach.

"Have you talked to the officer in charge yet?" he asks. "He should be able to tell you how much preparation the protesters have made, if any."

"Not yet. He's coming an hour ahead of Dad, so I'll ask him then."

"I knew I could count on you to keep things under control."

The absurdity bubbles in the base of my throat, and I want to laugh and cry and scream. Control? What control? Maybe Cal somehow got me confused with Fannie or his power-shopping assistant, because I have nothing—nothing!—under control.

"I should have this case wrapped up in a few weeks," he says, but the distracted quality in his voice tells me the only thing he's eager to wrap up is this conversation. "Once I do, I can move into the house with you. I sure hate that I can't be there today."

I don't respond. Seems to me if Cal had wanted to be here for my father's homecoming, he would've damn well been here. Surely he's not the only lawyer in the entire freaking state of Tennessee.

"But I'll be there first thing tomorrow morning, okay?"

I make a humming sound.

Cal takes it as his cue to go. "Keep me in the loop, okay? I'll do the same with you." He hangs up before I can agree.

My calls to Bo and Lexi are even less successful. Both their phones go straight to voice mail without ringing, not even once. The idea they've turned their phones off today of all days shoots a firestorm of fury through my veins. Instead of leaving yet another voice mail, I settle on a rather snarky group text.

No worries, I'm not alone. The protesters will be here soon to keep me company. You better not fucking be one of them.

I hit Send and fling my phone onto the pile of clothes erupting from my open suitcase, flop backward onto the bed and try—and fail—not to feel sorry for myself. In just a few hours, my dying father will walk through that door for the first time in sixteen years, and my siblings aren't here. Cal isn't here. My only buffer is a woman wearing too much makeup and scrubs smothered by tiny yellow ducks.

Something bangs and shakes the walls downstairs, and I picture Fannie heaving the couch onto her shoulders and hauling it clear across the room. The racket reminds me of all the things I should be doing. Helping Fannie rearrange the living room. Showering and unpacking. Hunting down my deadbeat siblings and dragging them back to help. Every single one of those options exhausts me.

I yank on my comforter, pull it across my shoulders and wrap it around me like a cocoon. A gust of wind whistles at my windowpane, and I burrow deeper into the down. Somewhere outside, a car door slams. By the time I reach the far side of a sigh, I've found temporary peace.

7

A clown.

That's my first thought when I open an eye. Why is there a clown standing above me, poking me in the shoulder?

"Go away." I pull the comforter tighter and roll toward a window I vaguely recognize as mine, but from a lifetime or two ago.

The clown gives me a two-handed shove in my back. "Wake up, 'fore I fetch me a bucket of ice water."

For a second or two, I get caught up on the way she said that last word—*warter*. And then it hits me. The thick accent, that frizzy orange hair can only belong to one person. I turn my head, blink up at Fannie. "Oh, sorry. I must've drifted off."

"Good Lord, child, I've been trying to wake you for the past five minutes. It ain't normal the way you sleep like the dead."

I push to a sit, swipe the heel of a hand across each eye. "In my line of work, sleeping is considered a job skill."

"What are you, a vampire?"

I would laugh, but I'm midyawn.

"Stick your head under a faucet or something, 'cause I

just parked one fine hunk of police officer on the couch downstairs. He says you were expecting him at eleven."

Her words are like a shot of caffeine to the jugular, and I spring out of bed so fast I see a rain of sparkles around the edges of my vision. "Shit. What time is it?"

"Sometime after eleven, I reckon."

I fall to my knees on the floor and rifle through my suitcase, flinging sweaters and T-shirts and underwear aside until I find my phone, lodged in one of my sneakers. "It's 11:19. Shit, shit, shit."

"How 'bout I fix him a cup of coffee while you get ready, lickety-split like." She heads for the door, but not before tossing a glance to the contents of my suitcase, now exploded all over the floor. "And, sweetie, if you don't mind me saying so, you may want to spend a little extra time searching through all that slop for a hairbrush."

By the time I make it downstairs seven and a half minutes later, my teeth brushed and my hair gathered into a messy ponytail high on my head, Fannie is holding court on the couch. She's brewed a fresh pot of coffee and scrounged up a plate of cookies from the stockpile in the kitchen. And she's seated suspiciously close to the police officer, giggling like a schoolgirl.

He stands when I come into the room, and with one last bat of her lashes, Fannie heads into the kitchen. Her definition of *hunk* is light-years away from mine. The policeman looks like an older version of Opie, that kid from *The Andy Griffith Show,* skinny and ruddy-complexioned. His receding hairline scoops two matching *C*s high on his forehead. He waits while I take in the patches and pins on his uniform, the heavy weapons at his belt, the stiff hat tucked under a biceps.

"For a Halloween costume," I tell him, "it looks pretty decent. How much did you pay for it?"

One corner of his mustache twitches. "I see you're still as much a smart-ass as ever."

"I'm sorry." I push two fingers at each temple and shake my head. "I'm just having trouble processing the fact that the boy who taught me how to funnel beer when I was fifteen has since sworn to uphold the law."

"Strangely enough, you're not the first person to tell me that."

I believe it. For the students at Cherokee High School, Jimmy Gardiner was a legend. Mastermind behind every school prank and organizer of every party. He was a straight-D student, an unapologetic pothead and a proven reckless driver who totaled cars faster than his broken bones could set. If it had been a category, he would have been elected Student Least Likely to Become a Police Officer.

"Holy crap, Jimmy!"

"I go by James these days." He grins, lifts a shoulder. "Had to pass on the name to the next generation."

"You have children?" I don't bother disguising my surprise, but I hope I manage to conceal my horror. Jimmy as a father, now there's a frightening image.

He nods and reaches for his wallet, flipping to a photo of four scrappy boys in front of a Christmas tree. "Jimmy Junior is six, Ronnie's four and the twins are two."

"Cute."

"They're the devil's spawn. Last night I caught the two older ones peeing on the living room ficus. Jimmy told me they were watering it."

I laugh. "Sounds like karma to me."

"Not the first person to tell me that, either."

The walkie-talkie on his shoulder hisses, jerking us out of our reunion with a harsh squawk. A man's voice fills the room. "Approaching Mooresburg, sir. ETA twenty-five minutes."

Jimmy slides his wallet back into his pocket, hits a button on the walkie-talkie and tilts his head toward the device. "Roger that."

My heart lodges in my throat. Twenty-five minutes.

At the reminder of why he's here, Jimmy's expression sobers. He offers me a neutral smile, his posture assuming that of police officer rather than old school friend. "As much as I'd like this to be a social visit…"

He doesn't have to finish for me to get his sentiment. I nod, pointing him to the couch. "Please. Have a seat."

He drops his hat with a soft thunk on the coffee table and sinks onto the couch. Fannie appears with a fresh coat of coral lipstick and two mugs of coffee, plunking them with an admiring grin at Jimmy onto the table. He thanks her, waiting until she's slipped back into the kitchen before continuing. And then he ignores his coffee, turning on the couch to face me.

"I just want to make sure we're all on the same page here since the paperwork lists you as the defendant's sponsor."

Silence settles over the room. That I am sponsoring my father is news to me, and a brief flare of resentment for Cal and my siblings bursts in my chest. I don't recall being asked, and I certainly don't recall volunteering to be anybody's sponsor.

"What does that mean, exactly, that I'm Dad's sponsor? I thought he was being released."

Jimmy blinks at me in obvious surprise. "Your uncle didn't tell you?"

"Tell me what?"

"That your father is not a free man. This arrangement is a home arrest, not a release, and the prisoner is not to leave these premises under any circumstances. As your father's designated sponsor, you agree to this, as well as to take care of all his business and personal needs until the time of his new trial."

I give Jimmy a get-real look. "We both know my father won't make it that long."

He hands me a stack of papers. "These are the conditions and terms of your father's home arrest confinement. He will arrive here in less than a half hour. He's not constrained, but as soon as he enters the house, I'm to secure a monitoring device onto his ankle. Once that's on, his movements will be monitored 24/7 by satellite through a chip in the electronic bracelet."

Jimmy's voice doesn't carry even the slightest trace of farce, and his hardened brow sets off more than a few of my internal alarm system bells.

"If I see your father has left these premises without explicit written permission from the Hawkins County Criminal Court, I will assume he is violating the terms of the home arrest. This place will be swarming with officers before he can make it to the corner. And they will be armed and instructed to shoot to kill."

"Shoot to kill." I nod, not quite able to meet Jimmy's eyes. "Got it."

He takes offense at my casual tone. "I'm not playing around here, Gia. Every department within a ninety-mile radius is on high alert. If your father tampers with the ankle bracelet or leaves this house without permission, he will be arrested and returned to prison, or worse. Do you understand what I'm telling you?"

I nod again, letting my gaze sweep over the paper in my hands. "It says here you make exceptions for life-threatening emergencies. What if Dad needs medical care?"

"I know what hospice care means, and so do you. It means if you're going to play the life-threatening-emergency card, I'll expect to come out here and find the house on fire."

I bristle at his thinly veiled threat. "My father is almost completely bedridden, so I hardly think he'll be making a run for it. And besides, why would he bother? The doctors give him a few months at most."

I don't add that Cal intends to make sure those few months are spent here at home, and not sitting trial in the county courthouse.

"Still." Jimmy hesitates, as if to choose his next words carefully. "You should be aware there are more than a few cops who don't agree with the judge's ruling. If given the chance, some of them wouldn't hesitate to put one of their bullets in your father's body."

More than a flicker of irritation seeps into my voice. "Then maybe they should speak with Cal or the judge, because releasing him wasn't my idea. I had nothing to do with this."

He sighs. "Look, Gi, I'm not trying to get you riled up, but I want you to be aware of what you're in for here. The law's the law. People don't agree with the judge's ruling that one of the witness's testimonies was perjured. They don't like watching a convicted killer, even if he is an old friend's father, walk away on a technicality."

"Do you include yourself in that statement?"

"Are you askin' me as an old friend or a police officer?"

"Whichever one gets me the answer I want to hear."

Jimmy scrubs a palm over his face, and the set of his mouth softens. "Your dad was my Little League coach until I was twelve. He taught me how to make a stink bomb, and he didn't go blabbin' to my mama whenever I bought condoms at the pharmacy. I hate every goddamn thing about this case."

"That's not technically an answer."

"The hell it ain't." He gives me a sheepish grin that reminds me of the younger Jimmy, the same one who was suspended for switching out all the school's videotapes for porn. "And I'd appreciate it if you don't ever ask me that question in public."

I smile to let him know we have a deal. "Oh, and one more thing. I hear there will be protesters. Do you know if anyone's applied for a permit for noise amplifiers?"

Jimmy shakes his head. "Don't think so. But Americans have the right to peaceful protest, and until they step over your property line, I can't do one doggone thing to make them stop. And I hate to tell you, but they're already here."

"They are?" I crane my neck and sure enough, a swarm of people is gathered at the far end of the driveway. Judging by their homemade signs and high-tech cameras, it's a mix of media and protesters.

"Your father's not going to be the only one who feels like he's under house arrest."

It takes me exactly one millisecond to realize Jimmy's right. A chill slithers up my spine at the same time my internal thermometer shoots into the danger zone. Every time I step outside the front door, every time I so much as pass by a window, someone will be watching.

Jimmy pulls a card out of his breast pocket, scribbles a number and passes it to me. "My cell. I don't care what time it is. You call me the minute something happens, okay?"

"Thanks, Jimmy."

He points to the papers in my lap. "I'll give you a few moments to read and sign those. I need to make sure the house is secure and the landline is working, so take your time." He stands, checks his watch. "ETA, ten minutes."

Ten minutes.

But as Jimmy sets off to patrol the house and I return my attention to the papers in my hand, it occurs to me he didn't say *if something happens*.

8

Ella Mae curled her legs underneath her on the porch chair and began reading the *Kingsport Times News* article for a third time. Something about Representative Quillen and East Tennessee State University's medical school, but she couldn't seem to concentrate on the words. She was too focused on watching the house next door, watching for signs of Dean.

As new neighbors, Dean and her husband tolerated each other, but just barely. The men waved from behind lawn mowers and swapped small talk in the driveway, but their civil smiles deteriorated into scowls as soon as the other's head was turned, and their attempts to hide their mutual dislike from the rest of the neighborhood were halfhearted at best.

Dean and Ella Mae, however… They tolerated each other just fine.

From the moment the moving truck backed out of the driveway, Dean had been circling Ella Mae with the single-minded determination of a mountain cat. The more he pursued her, the more she welcomed the attention, and lately even encouraged it, sending smoldering looks across flower beds and timing trips to the mailbox to coincide with his.

There was definitely something wrong with her. Something that made her brain-dead where Dean was concerned. Something that allowed her to consider casting aside everything she thought she believed about marriage and loyalty.

But Dean made Ella Mae's heart beat a little faster and her head feel a little lighter when he gave her so much as a casual wave, and when he smiled at her, a crooked close-lipped grin that promised all sorts of naughtiness, she had to remember to breathe.

Like now, for example.

Now she forced air into her lungs, a swift series of whispered gasps, and pretended to concentrate on the stupid article. The letters do-si-doed on the page in time to her heart, because on the other side of her *Times News,* Dean was coming up the porch steps.

And he was smiling that smile again.

"Pretty enough to be an ad," he said.

Ella Mae looked up with feigned surprise, and the newspaper fluttered to the porch floor. In his tight gray T-shirt, white linen pants and suede slip-ons, Dean was sexy and citified in a way folks around these parts found uppity. Ella Mae found him positively delectable.

"Oh, hi, Dean. I didn't hear you come up. What did you just say?"

"That you looked so pretty just now." He pointed to the rumpled paper on the ground. "I wish I'd taken a picture. The *Kingsport Times News* could plaster it on every billboard within a hundred miles. Would make themselves a fortune."

Ella Mae's blood fizzed in her veins.

He leaned a hip against the porch railing, his eyes intent on hers. "Allison and the kids are in Knoxville, shopping. They won't be back until tonight after dinner."

"Oh." One word, said on an exhaled breath, was about all she could handle. His family was ninety miles away, Gia at cheer practice, Ray at the pharmacy. Ella Mae and Dean were alone.

Alone. The thought flipped and kicked in her belly.

A corner of Dean's mouth rode upward. "It seemed like perfect timing."

"Perfect timing for what?" Ella Mae fought to keep her voice level around her heart pounding in her throat.

"To ask your thoughts." He moved closer, stepping over the crumpled paper and pointing to the wicker chair next to hers. "May I?"

She nodded and he sank into it, his knee brushing against hers.

"I was thinking of getting the girls a dog. They really miss their friends back home, and well, I was hoping a puppy would help, or at the very least distract them enough to make new friends. What do you think?"

Ella Mae pictured it, a tiny tornado of fur and floppy feet, barking and bounding around the yard, digging up flowers and turning the lawn into a virtual minefield. Ray would detest both the noise and the mess. But Ella Mae was thrilled. She'd always wanted a dog.

"I think a puppy is a marvelous idea."

"Really?" His face lit like the rising sun, a smile so unself-conscious she couldn't help but return it. "You don't have pets so I was worried…well, I'm glad you like my idea."

"I do."

"Excellent." He leaned forward, propping his elbows on his knees, and the chair creaked under his weight. "I was also hoping you could give me some advice on where to get one."

Ella Mae thought for a moment. "You could go to a pet store, but it'll be expensive. Otherwise, I have a friend over in Mount Carmel who breeds Maltipoos."

"What the heck's a Maltipoo?"

"A mix between a Maltese and a poodle. They're precious. Your girls will adore them." Ella Mae tried not to think of Dean's wife when she said the word *girls,* but Allison popped into her mind anyway. She quickly returned the conversation to the puppies. "So what do you think?"

Dean cocked his head and gave her a look that tingled all the way down to her toes, a look so suggestive it might as well have been adulterous. "Are we still talking about puppies?"

Puppies?

Dean laughed at whatever he saw on Ella Mae's expression. "I think a Maltipoo sounds perfect."

Ella Mae stood and motioned for Dean to follow her into the house. She didn't speak, but she held her back a little straighter, her shoulders a little squarer, her head a little higher, all the way through the living room and down the wallpapered hallway into the kitchen. Only her hips swayed loose and free, putting on a show, she knew, underneath the ruffles of her white tennis skirt.

A show she knew he was watching. His gaze was as good as leaving a trail of blisters down her entire backside, as if she was being chased through the house by a bonfire.

In the kitchen, Ella Mae reached for the phone on the wall and dialed Shelley's number, leaning against the counter and twisting the cord around a finger while Dean watched from the doorway. It was an all-consuming, toe-curling scrutiny that made something deep inside her belly buzz and hum.

When Shelley answered on the third ring, Ella Mae gave her friend a brief rundown of Dean's request.

"Shelley says she has two female puppies available," Ella Mae told Dean, dropping the mouthpiece to her shoulder, "one black and one cream colored. Both are weaned and ready to go."

Dean's smile was white-hot, and her knees caved a little. He took three long strides across the checkered linoleum. "Tell her we're on our way."

"We?"

He gestured to her tennis outfit. "Unless you have something else you need to do."

Other than a tennis lesson she could just as well skip, Ella Mae didn't have anything else she needed to do. She didn't even have anything else she wanted to do, other than spend the rest of her day playing with Dean Sullivan's fire.

She should say no. Say no and show him the door and avoid any more contact with Dean. Did they make blinders for wives with wandering eyes and handsome neighbors? Then again, blinders only help if you were willing to turn your head, and Ella Mae was not.

Nor was she willing to turn him down.

Ella Mae pressed the phone back to her ear. "We'll be there in about thirty minutes."

If Shelley answered, Ella Mae didn't hear. By now Dean was close, so close. Close enough for her to feel his heat. Close enough for him to touch her. He slid a palm to her waist, and she let him. He pulled her up against his body, hard and lean and ready, and she practically fainted with relief.

Finally.

He lowered his mouth to hers, and at the very last second, she somehow came to her senses.

"Shell, it may take us a teeny bit longer." The words tripped and tumbled in a hurry off her tongue, right before Dean took the phone from her hand and dropped it onto the cradle.

9

Prison has not been kind to my father.

How ridiculous is my first thought upon seeing him through the living room window? Of course prison hasn't been kind; that's why they call it prison. I push my face into the glass to get a better look, and something sharp and spiky twists in the pit of my stomach. Riverbend Maximum Security Institution has stripped my father down to a ghost of an unrecognizable stranger. A hard, angry, bitter stranger.

Then there's the cancer eating away at his insides. His face and neck have grown gaunt, his eyes sunk deeper into their sockets. His chest no longer fills out his shirt, which is now concave down to his protruding hip bone. And thanks to the tumor squeezing his pancreas and shooting sprouts into his liver, his skin has turned an awful yellow-orange like he's been dipped in carrot juice.

Two armed and uniformed men settle him into a wheelchair. They tuck a heavy wool blanket around his scarecrow frame and then stand guard on either side, which is, of course, ridiculous. If there's a working muscle under those state-issued scrubs, it's not strong enough to win a race to the end of the driveway, much less a getaway chase through the woods.

And running looks to be the last thing on my father's mind. He tilts his face into the sunshine and puffs out a breath long enough to have been saved since 1994.

Has it been that long since he last felt the sun's warmth?

One of the guards, a stodgy man with thinning silver hair, pushes the wheelchair up the ramp Cal built. The guard whistles a country tune, but not loudly enough to drown out the protesters at the end of the driveway.

"Ray Andrews is guilty. We want justice."

A news van pulls up, scattering the protesters like cockroaches, and a camera crew piles out. They find a spot on the front lawn and begin taping, the house as their backdrop. Two seconds later their newscast is interrupted by a noisy procession of trucks and SUVs, their drivers laying on their horns. The cameraman abandons the broadcast and swings the lens around, focusing in on the lead truck where a bearded man leans out the open window. He lifts a bullhorn to his mouth. "Wife killer! Die, wife killer!"

His evil words echo through the valley and slice, as sharp and deadly as a Buck knife, into my gut.

My gaze darts to my father, now almost to the top of the ramp. He chomps down on his lips and burrows farther under the blanket, but not before I catch his expression. The sixteen years' worth of outrage and indignity have slashed lines on either side of his mouth, his eyes, his forehead, but there's still plenty of room in between for this afternoon's mortification.

Fannie tsks, stepping up behind my left shoulder. "Crackpots. No matter what your father did or didn't do, darlin', he doesn't deserve that. Everybody deserves to die with dignity and respect."

"He used to be respected." My voice is thick, and it cracks on the last word. "He was a member of every service club, raised money for every nonprofit, served on every board. Just look at him now." I swipe a cheek with the back of a hand. "He's pathetic."

The guard makes the last turn onto the porch, and Fannie pats a palm on my shoulder. "Get ahold of yourself, sugar. 'Cause here he comes."

She leaves me sniffling into the curtains, waddles to the door and pulls it wide. Through the window I see Dad's gaze land on her with an expectant thud.

"Welcome home, Mr. Andrews." She lifts a hand. "I'm Fannie Miles, and I'm gonna take real good care of ya."

Disappointment is written across Dad's forehead as clearly as the Tennessee Department of Corrections painted in big blazing block letters on the van behind him. He cranes his neck toward the side of the house, searching. Searching for Bo and Lexi. Searching for me. I step into the shadow.

The protesters increase their volume, marching back and forth on the road while the news crew films their angry chants. Dad returns his squint to Fannie. "I see you called the welcome wagon."

Fannie motions for me to come to the door. "Your lovely daughter Gia is here. We were just getting acquainted."

His eyes flash to the window. "Where is she?"

I don't move. I barely breathe. Last month our convoy was almost ambushed by four armed bandits, and I sped the Rover away without breaking a sweat. Now I'm about to hurl my coffee onto the burgundy Rooms To Go carpet.

"Gia's right here. Come on inside and say hi."

He shakes his head. "Hold it right here, fellas."

Dad doesn't wait for the silver-haired guard to stop the wheelchair. He grips the chair's metal arms and tries to push himself upright, but his feet are still propped onto the metal flaps and his scrawny body can't get more than four or five inches of air. After a few clumsy tries, he sinks back into the chair, his face ashy-orange beneath his whiskers. "Somebody get me out of this goddamn chair."

The second guard, a stocky man with a bottom lip bulging with tobacco, plants his feet and palms his billy stick. "Sir, my orders are to escort you into the house and tether your ankle monitor before allowing you out of that chair."

My father flops one slippered foot onto the ground. "I aim to walk."

For the first time I notice Jimmy standing guard at the bottom of the porch. He gives my father a disciplined smile and climbs the ramp, his equipment chinking at his belt. "Afternoon, Mr. Andrews. You remember me?"

Dad glares up at him. "Of course I remember you, Jimmy. But right now I'm trying to walk through my own goddamn door, so our little reunion'll have to wait until I get inside."

Jimmy's mustache doesn't even twitch. He motions his silver-haired colleague aside and stomps on the wheelchair's brake. Fannie rushes to help, tucking the foot supports out of the way and planting my father's feet onto the cold concrete. Together, the two heave him out of the chair.

Dad grumbles he doesn't need any goddamn help and then grips their sleeves until he's found his balance. He eyes the distance to the door, four feet at best—so close, but it must seem like a country mile for this dying man.

Fannie and Jimmy hover at either elbow, waiting, watching. Dad takes his first wobbly step. His knees knock through his state-issued pants, and he holds out both hands for balance. Three halting steps, and he's at the door. He falls against the frame, punching a victory fist into the air.

My heart flips right over. One more step, and he'll be inside.

Fannie's cheers are cut short at my father's first tee-ter. She pushes his wheelchair forward and scoops him up with it right before he crumples to the ground. Behind her, Jimmy looks relieved. The guards look bored.

Fannie wheels Dad inside the house and fusses over him. I sink farther into the curtains.

But it's too late. My father looks over, and our eyes meet for the first time in sixteen years.

I drop my gaze, and I have the sudden urge to cry. Eyes burning, throat squeezing shut, sob pushing up my chest. I want to fall into a ball at Dad's knees and feel his skinny arms around me, and I want to run away from him, from this house, from this town, as far and as fast as I can. But mostly, I want to believe my father without a sliver of a shadow of a doubt when he says he didn't harm Ella Mae Andrews.

I take a breath, haul air deep into my lungs and blow it out slowly, once, twice, again and drag my gaze to my father's. If I can't give my father my unwavering belief in his innocence, the least I can do is look him square in the eyes. Around him the room fades and spins.

"Where's everybody else?"

His voice cuts through the ocean roaring in my ears. I try to answer but my mouth won't work. Neither will my lungs, which are burning a hole in my chest.

Jimmy catches my eye, and a frown blooms between his brows. He says my name, low and slow as sorghum syrup, and that's the last thing I notice before everything around me goes black.

* * *

I awake on the couch, something cold pressed over an eye, and Fannie hovering above me. The ceiling fan frames her head like an asterisk, its blades jutting out from her overteased hair like whirling exclamation points. She's wearing her nurse face again, but this time it's directed at me.

"Lucky me. Two patients for the price of one." Fannie gives my arm a little pat. "Though I gotta say, I sure didn't take you for a fainter."

"I'm not." My voice scratches my throat, my breath scraping over sandpaper.

She cackles. "Tell that to the coffee table."

Which would explain my throbbing brow. I reach for the bundle of freezing cloth pressed over the left side of my face. Fannie stops me with a hand to my wrist before I can wreck her makeshift cold compress. "Leave it. The ice will help the swelling."

Swelling? I think, or maybe I say it.

"Swelling," Fannie repeats. She pushes to her feet and grins at Jimmy, standing stiffly at the foot of the couch. "You can call off the rescue squad, Officer. She's conscious."

Jimmy hooks his thumbs in his pants pockets and leans back on his heels. "Don't reckon I've ever seen anyone go down that fast without a bullet."

"My head feels like it took a bullet." I push myself upright, holding the ice pack in place over my eye. "But I'm fine."

Or I will be, as soon as the room stops spinning.

Crisis over, Fannie receives the last of the house-arrest instructions from Jimmy and walks him to the side door. He tells her he will check in daily by phone or in person, a promise he manages to make sound more like an assurance than a threat, and turns to wave one last time before slipping into the icy afternoon air. Fannie clicks the dead bolt in place and disappears into the kitchen, muttering something about the restorative merits of tea with extra honey.

"You always did have a particular talent for upstaging everyone, didn't you?" Dad says.

A rhetorical question if I've ever heard one. I twist on the couch to face my father, reclined on his hospital bed behind me, but don't respond.

"Things are about to get a lot hairier, you know." Prison has hardened his easy drawl into a sharp twang. "Can't wait to see what kind of tricks you have in store for us then."

"Well, you don't have to worry. I'm not a fainter."

He points to the floor by the coffee table. "Then what do you call that?"

"Jet lag and last night's tequila."

Dad snorts, his gaze darting to the front window. "Did you get a look at the lynch mob? They're a rowdy bunch."

"Sorry about that. Cal and I tried to run them off."

He barks a mean laugh. "I've seen worse. A whole helluva lot worse. Those stories you hear about men in prison? They don't even come close."

There's really nothing I can say to that.

"Well," he drops his head back onto the pillow and stares at the ceiling, "as much as I'm enjoying this little family reunion, you can go now." His hand fans the air above a sharp hip bone, dismissing me.

I drop my hand, and the ice pack clatters to my lap. "Go…?"

"Yes, go. Frannie'll keep me company."

"Fannie."

"Fannie will keep me company, so git."

The edge of self-pity in his voice doesn't mitigate his message. I'll admit I saw my coming here as some sort of half-assed atonement for not visiting Dad in prison. Not once, though, did I ever think he wouldn't want me here.

"Where am I supposed to go?"

"Back to saving the world. Back to acting like I'm already dead."

His message knocks me silent. Is that what I was doing? Acting like he was already dead? A barbed ball of guilt pitches and rolls in my belly.

"Sixteen years, seven months and twenty-three days. That's how long I've had to put up with people looking at me like I'm guilty of murder. I'm not going to have it in my own home, from my own daughter."

"I don't—" I begin, then stop myself. There was more than anger and accusation buried in his words. There was also an unmistakable question.

I don't look at you like you're guilty is what I was going to say, but that's not quite the same as *I don't think you're guilty,* is it? My father would recognize the difference. He's a man who misses nothing, including, according to his scowl, the reason behind my silence.

Dad's face goes slack. "That's what I thought."

Still. I don't budge from the leather couch.

"Goddammit, Gia! Either get out or stop looking at me like I killed Ella Mae, because I didn't. The only crime I ever committed—the only one—was loving that woman more than she loved me."

I hold his gaze and my breath, not moving, not speaking, not capable of lying. Not about this. Not without him seeing right through me.

My father looks away first. "So go on back to those

brown babies you love to save. There's nothing for you here. I've got cancer. I can't be saved."

"I know."

"If you hurry, you might be able to leave this afternoon."

"I'm not going anywhere."

"Would you listen to me? I don't want you here."

"Too bad, because I'm not leaving!"

The force of conviction driving my words surprises him, surprises both of us. After all, why shouldn't I leave? My siblings wouldn't notice, and my father says he wouldn't care. Nobody would miss me, except perhaps Cal. As far as I can tell, I'm not bound here by anything but guilt and a warped sense of duty, so why not simply leave?

The chants outside crescendo into an offensive clamor, a sick sort of anticheer. I turn to the window and beyond it the protesters, an army of bodies wearing puffy jackets and woolen hats and angry expressions. Judging by the gear they've lined up on the lawn—a dozen camping chairs, multiple hot plates, a portable butane heater— they're here to stay.

As am I.

I can't leave. Not yet. Leaving now would be the equivalent of packing up the camp in Dadaab and moving on to the next bigger, better disaster before eradicating famine in the Horn of Africa: unfinished. My father would still be dying, my siblings would still be hiding behind their busy, busy, busy lives and I would still be tackling everyone's disasters but my own.

Dad says I can't save him, and in a way, he's right. Not even the doctors can reverse the cancer coaxing him into a quick grave.

But saving a life is not the only way to rescue a person. Sometimes the only thing left to do is make peace.

Suddenly, I know what I have to do. I grab my tattered messenger bag, my coat and my keys and go to the door. "Dad, I'm leaving now."

His eyes are closed, his breathing steady. If he hears me, he doesn't respond.

"But I'll be back."

And even if it means slipping them a roofie and dragging them in chains, I'll be back with Lexi and Bo.

The reporter comes out of nowhere, a short, weasely looking guy with squinty eyes, twenty feet or so before I reach my car. A bored cameraman hovers on the driveway behind him. I've been interviewed enough to know what that blinking red light beside his camera lens means. It means I give them both my best no-comment face and pick up the pace to my car.

One of them yells to get my attention. "Ms. Andrews!"

The protesters are lined up by the road like a row of tobacco plants, a pack of unabashed rubberneckers at the scene of an accident.

But I'm not about to become anyone's victim.

"Ms. Andrews!" This from the reporter, who is now jogging alongside me, close enough to shove his microphone in my face. "What do you think about your father's release from prison?"

Seriously? He risks trespassing on private property, and that's the best he can do? I answer with an eye roll only he can see.

"The D.A.'s office claims to have new evidence. Were you aware of an affair?"

That almost stops me. Almost. No way Dad was sleeping with anyone but Ella Mae. I may have been eighteen and self-absorbed at the time, but an affair I would have noticed.

"Is that why he murdered Ella Mae? Because she was leaving him for another man?"

I scramble into the rental, strategically swinging my head so my curls block the cameraman's view of my face, which must register shock. Ella Mae was the one having an affair? A whisper somewhere deep in my gut says not to dismiss the possibility.

I throw my car into Reverse and hurl it backward, scattering the protesters at the end of the driveway, not without glee. As I'm shifting into Drive, my gaze slides to the left and lands on Tanya, the Light of Deliverance frump, silent and still as a statue in the middle of the road, her expression this side of smug. She holds up a homemade poster: Guilty as Sin, Lock Him Back In in angry black letters.

The nicest thing I can say about it is at least she can rhyme.

I punch the gas and peel away.

"Motherfucker!" I scream into my empty car, searching for the recipient of my curse in my rearview mirror. By now Tanya has rejoined the group and I can't pick her out, but I still know she's there. And with any luck, she heard me. "Motherfucking fucker!"

My back tire slides off the asphalt and spins in the dirt and grass at the edge of Mr. Wheeler's lot, and I snap my gaze back onto the road. I jerk on the wheel and swerve, straightening. And then I floor the gas and fly up the hill a little faster, to Bo and Lexi and anywhere but here.

10

I roar in my rental up Lincoln Street, along the edge of Eastman Chemical Company, a maze of more than nine hundred acres straddling Kingsport's Holston River. To my left, a messy row of smokestacks pokes up beyond the plant's corroded shop buildings and twisted metal pipeline.

The business center is a massive building of brick and glass and one of the few I don't need a pass to enter. I park my car and sprint across the lot, hiking up my coat collar against an icy mist. I burst into the lobby and shake the moisture off my hair and skin.

A row of uniformed personnel sits behind sleek computer screens at an information desk. One of the employees, a woman with eighties' hair and an impressive under chin, does a double take when she catches sight of me.

"I need to see Bo Andrews right away," I tell her. "It's a family emergency."

Her wooly brows dip in a frown. "Oh, my."

"Exactly." I thunk both hands on the marble countertop and lean in, trying to keep the duh from my tone. "Which is why I need to see him. Can you tell me where to find him?"

The woman shakes her head, cheeks quivering in time with the wattle under her chin. "I'm afraid it's not that simple. All visitors must be approved beforehand by the head of the department. What department does your brother work in?"

I lift a damp shoulder. "He's working on some kind of supermascara. That's all I know."

"Research, maybe?" When I don't immediately nod, she reaches for her mouse. "Let's just look him up, shall we?" She clicks around on her computer screen.

I plunk both palms onto the shiny marble counter, a fresh surge of urgency rolling up my chest, and check the name on the woman's plastic name tag. "Look, Ms. Greer, I'm in a bit of a hurry here. How long will this process take?"

Her hand stills, and she looks up from her screen. "Well, assuming I can reach the head of your brother's department, get you the proper paperwork and an escort, it shouldn't be much longer than an hour or two."

My eyes bulge. "Two hours?"

"At the most."

I chew my lip and consider my options. If this woman alerts the head of Bo's department, there's a good chance she'll also be alerting Bo, giving him up to two hours to burrow farther underground. He'd be halfway across Virginia by the time I got through the gate. No, knowing my brother, my best course of action is still an ambush. A quick ambush and a teeny-weeny white lie.

I point to the woman's fancy desk phone. "Can that thing call my brother's extension?"

"Of course." She presses a few keys on her computer keyboard, punches the number into the phone and hands me the receiver. Two rings later and bingo.

"Bo Andrews speaking."

"Bo, it's Gia."

"Gia? What...? Where...?"

"Listen up, because here's how this visit is going to go. You can either wait for me there, surrounded by all your friends and colleagues, or—"

"You can't get in without a pass." There's an unmistakable tone of relief in his voice, but buried underneath a heaping helping of satisfaction and big-brother mockery.

His taunting feeds an easy fib. "Got one, as well as the lovely Ms. Greer, who's about to escort me over there." Bo squeaks, and I swallow down a serves-you-right victory call. "So you can either sit tight and wait for me to come to you, or you can get your sorry ass out to the business center—"

"Building 280," my fictitious escort interrupts, not uneagerly.

I thank her with a quick smile. "—to building 280. Your choice."

"But I'm clear across the plant!"

"Then you better hurry, because you've got five minutes—" I check the time on my cell "—starting now. I'll meet you at the door."

I drop the receiver into the cradle before he can form a reply. "Thanks for your help," I say to Ms. Greer.

Now, finally, she gives me a smile, a real smile, not one she learned in customer service training. "Oh, honey. It was my pleasure."

Bo pulls up in his silver Honda Element a little over four minutes later and springs the locks, motioning for me to get in the passenger's seat. The sight of him through the tinted window, looking so much like the Dad I remember, the Dad before the trial, before this morning, flips a bittersweet loop in my stomach. Same straight brown hair, same square forehead, same thin lips that would sooner set in a solemn scrunch than a smile.

And right now, Bo's scrunch is aimed at me.

"What the hell?" he says before I'm halfway in the car.

"I got pissed, that's what." I slam the door, twist in the seat to face him. "You should've called me back."

He points to my left temple. "I'm talking about your eye."

My fingers fly to the spot, prodding into too spongy skin, and my mouth twists in pain. I flip the visor and check my reflection in the tiny mirror. A lump, angry and mean, pushes up under the arch of my left brow and dips into a bruise, covering the skin around my eye like a puddle of port wine.

"Good Lord. I look like a circus freak."

"You'd need a biological rarity, like a horn or a tail or a third eye, to qualify you as a circus freak. A simple bruise isn't going to do it."

His correction is classic Bo. Even sarcasm must be factually accurate.

I flick the visor into place and flop back onto my seat. "Is it too early to start drinking?"

"Yes." Bo puts the car into Drive and releases the brake, his hands at ten and two. "Put on your seat belt, please."

After a bit of discussion we settle on Pal's, one of a local chain of fast-food shacks decorated with a giant plastic burger, hot dog, box of fries and fountain drink on its tiered roof. At the drive-through window, I order all of the above, and Bo asks for a sweet tea. We get our goods and find a spot in the tiny parking lot.

"So can we maybe just start all over?" I say, digging through the bag for a handful of fries. "This time without all the ignoring and threats?"

Bo rests a wrist on the steering wheel, his posture relaxed and unperturbed. "I wasn't ignoring you, Gi. I've just been really swamped with this new pentaerythrityl hydrogenated rosinate we're working on."

I try not to roll my eyes and fail. Bo thinks the entire world speaks his lingo. He always has. Even before he figured out how to make baking soda explode or the best ingredients for a smoke bomb, he was always going on and on about mutant turtles or deck graphics or some place called Eternia. The only person in the house who understood him was Dad, especially once he started talking in periodic table. For Lexi and me, our brother might as well be speaking in tongues.

"I know, I know, your mascara is going to change the world. But I hardly see how that matters, in light of what's going on with Dad. You do know he came home this morning, right?"

Bo sucks on his straw, three giant gulps. "Of course I know. But we're on a tight deadline and working eighteen-hour days at the lab. Where, I might add, there's a meeting going on without me right now."

A familiar jolt of rage at my brother's self-absorption shoots up my spine. I clench my teeth, my stomach, my fists. "I have a job, too, you know. One that supports almost a half million displaced people. One I took a leave of absence from to come here."

"What's your point?"

My answer is loud enough to rattle the windows. "My point is, get your ass over to the house and see Dad."

"Jesus, calm down. You don't have to yell. And besides, I plan to."

"When?"

"Soon."

Frustration fizzes in my veins but fuels my determination. I am not getting out of this car before I've extracted a solid promise from Bo.

"Well, how about tonight? I'll pick up something for dinner."

Bo inclines his head, manages to look sorry. "The client's in town with their entire product development team. We're taking them to Troutdale."

"Okay, tomorrow morning. Cal's coming at ten."

"Tomorrow is Amy's birthday, and we're going to the Grove Park Inn. We won't be home until late Sunday morning."

Until I met Bo's wife, a prominent orthodontist's daughter who's as petite as she is prim, I thought there couldn't be a more serious person on the planet than my brother. Amy has him beat by a couple billion brain cells. I can just imagine their afternoon in Asheville now—discussing Native American history, visiting Civil War sites, cataloging local flora and fauna.

But still. I refuse to let myself get sidetracked from my goal. "Sunday afternoon, then."

"Maybe. Let me talk to Amy."

A maybe! I grab on to it, sink my teeth. "I'm sure Amy will understand. Sunday will be perfect. I know, why don't I pick up some—"

"Will you just back off?" Now, finally, Bo loses his neutral expression, as well as his temper. His brows ride down, crashing into a sharp V, and he matches my snappish tone, which I imagine must cost him a substantial effort. "I know Dad's home. I know you and Cal want me there. But I also know our rosinate is still testing as a confirmed irritant and the Bare Beauty guys are breathing down my neck to fix it, and my wife is nagging me to spend time I don't have with her, so believe me. I've got enough guilt as it is. I don't need any more from you."

"I'm not trying to guilt-trip you, but he's your father, too."

Bo drags a long inhale over his lungs, blows it out through his mouth and voilà, he's composed. "I'm perfectly aware he's my father, and I already told you, I plan to visit as soon as I can find a minute."

"When?"

"As soon. As I. Can find. A minute."

Clearly, stubbornness is a family trait.

I soften my voice, my posture, try another tack. "Will you at least promise me you'll talk to Amy and let me know?"

Bo takes a long pull from his tea, stares straight ahead into the twisted branches of the hedge flush against his front bumper. His mouth twitches around the straw, but he doesn't answer.

"Please." I know I'm begging, but I no longer care. "I just need to know I'm not all alone here."

He twists the key in the ignition, revs the engine and sighs like I'm the one who's being difficult. "You're not alone. I'll talk to Amy and let you know."

"You'll let me know tomorrow?"

"Yes, tomorrow," he repeats.

I relax into the seat. His answer is not the one I came here to get, but I tell myself it's progress. Progress in the form of promised peace. I loop my arm around his neck and pull him close, sneaking a thank-you kiss onto his cheek before he can shake me off.

But Bo has never been one for physical contact. He swipes a palm over the spot and busies himself with shifting the gear into Reverse and double-and triple-checking his mirrors. "Can I please go back to the lab before I get fired?"

"Of course."

I reach into the bag for a celebratory burger and rip open the waxy paper wrapping. "Oh, and while we're on the subject, maybe you could talk to your contacts at Bare Beauty about alternatives to animal testing."

Bo twists in his seat to look out the back window, his eyes sweeping across mine for only a split second. "Should've stopped while you were ahead, Gi."

11

I jog up the few steps to First Appalachian Bank, an imposing two-story brick building worthy of Rogersville's Colonial history. A marble plaque to the right of the double doors tells me it's been here since 1837, and it's a good thing. That means the structure is sturdy enough to bear my sister's wrath when I confront her here, at her place of business.

Inside, pairs of cherry desks are organized in shiny clusters, and three teller windows line the far right wall. One of the tellers, a brunette I recognize immediately, sees me and whoops. Missy Parker. Class motormouth and school know-it-all, now sixteen years older and sixty pounds heavier.

"Gia Andrews! I heard you were in town. Oh, my goodness, you look exactly the same." She giggles into a pudgy hand. "Well, except for that black eye. What on earth happened?"

I try to wave it off. "Oh, it's nothing. I'm fine. Is my sister here?"

"She sure is." Missy crosses her arms and leans on her elbows across the counter. Her posture suggests she's about to reveal a confidence, her volume loud enough to alert all of Hawkins County. "So d'you hear Scott and I got divorced last year?"

"No, but...what a shame."

Her strawberry-stained lips push even wider. "Oh, you don't have to play nice. Everybody in town knows he was a big ol' horn dog. I suppose the bigger mystery is why nobody thought to tell me."

"I suppose so. So could you let Lexi know I'm here?"

"Yes, but first I'm gonna tell you what I told her." Her expression sobers and she clears her throat, straightens her neck and shoulders. "For whatsoever is born of God overcometh the world. And this is the victory that overcometh the world, even our faith. Who is he that overcometh the world, but he that believeth that Jesus is the Son of God?"

Am I supposed to answer that question?

I look around for the other tellers, who all seem to have disappeared. "That's...that's very interesting. Thank you."

"I'm praying for you both."

"Thank you. Again. Um, about Lexi..."

Missy starts at the reminder, punches a button on her desk phone. "Oh, good golly. Of course. Silly me."

She prattles on while over the speaker the phone rings once, twice and then: bingo.

"Lexi speaking."

Missy grins. "Hey, Lexi. I got you on speakerphone. There's somebody down here wants to say hi."

"Hi." I lean closer to the phone. "And surprise."

Lexi hesitates, but only for the briefest of seconds. "It sure is a surprise, and a lovely one, too. What are you doing here?"

"I came to see you. Thought maybe I could kidnap you for a bit, take you for a drive."

"Is that right? Where to?"

I glance at Missy, who's hanging shamelessly on every word. "Oh, I have a place or two in mind."

"Well, then. I can't think of anything I'd rather do than take a ride with my favorite sister." The sincerity lacing her voice almost convinces me she means every word. "Give me ten minutes to finish up here, and then I'll be right down."

We disconnect, and I take a seat on a chair by the back wall, too far away to get caught up in Missy's endless babble. I flip through an old copy of the *Economist* while I wait. And wait. Ten minutes tick by. I wait some more.

I toss down the magazine and stand, making my way across the bank floor back to Missy's window when I catch a flash of someone in my periphery. Someone curvy and blonde, hurrying in the opposite direction. I blink. Look again. Perfect honey hair, tucked inside a navy wool coat, disappearing out the back door to the lot.

"Lexi?"

The door clicks shut behind her.

I tear through the bank, banging shins and stubbing toes against chairs and desks, and fly down the little hallway after her. The door doesn't slow me. I shove it open with both hands and search the still lot. A van, some sedans, a lineup of trucks, their windows dark and empty. No Lexi.

An engine cranks at the far end, and seconds later a red sports car peels out, a sunglasses-clad blonde at the wheel. I rush down the concrete stairs and onto the asphalt, sprint up the middle row of the parking lot.

"Lexi!" I wave my hands, trying to get her attention. "Are you shitting me?"

Her car takes a sharp right and disappears up the alley,

motor screaming, tires squealing. By the time I reach the edge of the lot, she's halfway up Main Street.

Disbelief explodes into fury, tightening every fiber in my body and pumping adrenaline through my veins. I stomp up the length of the lot, shrieking every cuss word I know, and there are a lot. I stop just long enough to give the wooden fence at the back end a few solid kicks before whirling back around and stomping the other way.

My sister left. She goddamnitalltomotherfuckinghell left.

At the mouth to the alleyway, I lean against the building and unzip my coat. I stay there forever, waiting until the cold brick and icy wind cool my neck, my torso, my temper.

Finally, I push off the wall, pull my coat back around me and drag myself back in the direction of my car, wondering the entire way how I'm supposed to make any sort of peace when no one—not Bo, not Lexi, certainly not my father—wants peace but me.

I emerge from the bank's alley onto Main, where a man in jeans slouches against the trunk of my car. His head is ducked, his face half-hidden under mirrored shades and a faded Braves cap, but I recognize him immediately. Jake Foster is not a man easily mistaken.

My chest fills with tingly air. Even though I've spent more time with Jake while under the influence of alcohol than without, even though I know pathetically little about the man beyond that he can cook, the sight of him standing here, waiting for me, gives me a bubble of lightness in my chest. I close my eyes and savor it, feeling it puff and inflate, pulling me up and out of this disaster of a life to which I've returned.

How can a virtual stranger make me feel as if I can breathe again? Impossible. And yet, somehow, he does.

I jaywalk across the two-lane street, stepping into non-existent traffic in front of the Main Street Realtors, an icy breeze stirring my hair. "Did you see which way Lexi went?"

He looks up, hooking a thumb over a shoulder. "That way, and like a bat—" He stops when his gaze lands on me. He rips off his sunglasses, squinting against the sudden light. "Jesus! What happened?"

I park my sneakers at the edge of the sidewalk. "I'm fine, it's just a bruise."

He pushes off my trunk and leans close. His light finger brushes across my brow, only a flutter, but enough to tingle my skin.

Not for the first time, I notice his bone structure is perfect, angular and strong and utterly masculine. His cheeks and chin are covered in a perpetual three-day beard, and his neat sideburns are just the right length, trailing alongside his ears like perfectly clipped tassels. And his lips, when they're pursed in contemplation like they are now, are highly kissable.

Surely I'd remember if I'd already kissed those lips. Wouldn't I?

He makes a low but impressed whistle between his teeth. "That's one hell of a shiner. Care to elaborate?"

I shrug, trying to think how to tell him I fainted without getting into all the reasons why, without the weight of my life settling back around me like a lead blanket. I can't come up with a plausible story quickly enough, so I settle on a half truth: "I fell, and a coffee table got in the way."

"You fell."

I nod. "Into a coffee table."

"Right. Okay, Rocky. Let's get some ice on that thing before it swells up any further."

I tell myself I should be getting home, but my feet refuse to listen. When Jake steps onto the sidewalk, gesturing for me to follow three doors down, to Roadkill, I do.

Inside, the place is empty. It's still too early for the after-work crowd. Light from the kitchen spills through the window in the swinging door, and reggaeton music thumps from within. The prep staff, I assume.

Jake helps me out of my coat, dumps it on a bar stool and rummages around behind the bar for a bit, coming up with a bag of ice wrapped in a checkered towel. Once he's satisfied I've got it pressed to the exact right spot on my brow, he leans a denim-clad hip on the bar and winks.

"I'm guessing no tequila."

I smile. "You're guessing right."

We settle on a cup of Earl Grey for me and a smoothie for Jake, which he whips up in a blender from fresh fruit and almond milk until it's pink and frothy. He walks around the bar and sits on the bar stool next to mine, swinging his long legs around until he's facing me, and I have a sudden and overwhelming sense of déjà vu. An empty bar, facing bar stools, same half-cocked grin. I've done this before. Here. With him.

"I have a question," I say. "Or actually, a whole string of questions, pretty much all of them involving what occurred between ten-thirty last night and seven-thirty this morning."

"You really don't remember?"

I shake my head, and the bag of ice rattles and shifts against my forehead.

"Then you're a total lightweight. You only had two margaritas, and they were more lime juice than tequila."

"Seriously?"

He nods. "And you didn't even notice when I switched you over to virgins."

"Wait a minute. What about the sheriff and the game of quarters and me reaching for my car keys?"

He lifts a shoulder. "Tiny embellishment."

"And yet you still drove me home."

"It was either that or let you sleep on my bar. I don't think I've ever seen anyone pass out quite like that before. You put your head down and boom. Lights out."

"I guess the two days on a plane finally caught up with me. I just hope I didn't scare off your other customers."

Jake gives me a get-real look. "Last week two guys decided to use the dartboard for a tobacco spitting contest. You're going to have to do something a lot more drastic to shock anyone in this place."

How about caring for your maybe-murderer father in the house where he maybe-murdered your stepmother? Is that shocking enough?

I flush the thought from my brain before it sucks me under. "So then what?"

"Then I threw you over my shoulder and took you home. Good thing you weigh nothing, because you weren't very helpful. If you hadn't been snoring like a fifty-year-old fat man, I would've checked your pulse."

"Oh, God." I cringe. Literally cringe. "I'm sorry you had to witness that."

Jake gives me a grin that tells me he's not the least bit sorry. "Seeing your tattoo more than made up for the snoring."

I blush, dammit.

Jake takes in my pink cheeks and laughs. "Don't look

so horrified. It was easily the highlight of my night. Of my month, even. Don't you want to know what happened?"

I wave a palm in the air between us. "Some questions are best left unanswered. Questions like How fat would you have to be to be bulletproof? and Where is Elvis, really? and How did my jeans end up on the floor last night? Sometimes it's better not to know, because the answer would only be a disappointment."

One eyebrow rises in silent question at my last word, but he doesn't offer it up. Instead, he points to the hand holding the ice pack in place. "Like the truth behind how you really got that black eye?"

"And other questions are best left unasked because they lead to subjects too depressing to talk about. This——" I pull the cold compress from my eye, and Jake's expression confirms my shiner is still there, and still bad "——is one of those questions."

"Fair enough. I won't ask again."

I give him a grateful smile, but a familiar weight is already settling over me, pushing at the edges of my heightened spirits, threatening to drag me down. *Quick, swim to the surface.*

"I got the tattoo a few years ago in Thailand," I say, almost tripping over my words in my rush to change the subject. "The artist there used bamboo, which he assured me hurt less than a traditional machine. Quite frankly, I find that hard to believe. He must have stabbed me a million times, in what I don't need to remind you is a very sensitive spot. It was torture."

"For you." Jake grins. "But I'm betting not so much for the guy holding the bamboo needle."

I laugh, and the sound catches me off guard, light and

twinkling and unforced, the way a laugh is supposed to sound. The way my laugh used to sound.

"And anyway," I say, "I don't need you to tell me how you saw my tattoo, because I'm pretty positive nothing happened between us last night."

"Really." His teasing tone is mirrored in his eyes. "How can you be so certain?"

"Three reasons. First of all, my tattoo is neither floral nor tribal, so you didn't get that good of a look. Two, my jeans were on the floor of the bathroom, which leads me to believe I was the one who took them off."

"Excellent sleuthing, Sherlock. And the third?"

"That you don't seem like the type to lay a finger on me without my consent."

Jake tilts his head and looks at me. Really looks at me. His phone buzzes on the bar, but he ignores it, acts like he doesn't even hear it.

"So, are you?" he says finally.

"Am I what?"

"Disappointed in the answer." He hesitates, bows his head in mock bashfulness and smiles. "That nothing happened between us, I mean."

My sensory system feels like someone popped me in the toaster oven, warm and glowing. In that minute, I forget everything. My family. My responsibilities. The tsunami of shit that is my life. All I know is right here, right now, with Jake.

There's only one thing to do at a moment like this, really. To celebrate the euphoria of my escape. To mark its significance. To thank Jake for being its cause.

I kiss him.

12

Ella Mae should have felt ashamed. After what Dean Sullivan had just done to her in her own kitchen, contorting her body every which way and heating her up from the inside out until she begged him for it—twice!—she should have felt embarrassed and regretful and goddamn ashamed.

But she didn't.

She glanced over at Dean, slumped casually in the driver's seat, thumbs tapping the wheel in time to the R.E.M. tune on the radio. Dean didn't look like he felt any of those things, either. As a matter of fact, he looked pretty damn proud of himself.

"Take a left up at the intersection."

Dean simply nodded.

Maybe that canary in his mouth was making it hard for him to talk, because fifteen minutes ago he wasn't so quiet. At first, Ella Mae had been shocked by and more than a little self-conscious of his graphic descriptions of how he wanted her to stand and all the places he wanted to put his fingers and his mouth, but before long she was talking back and screaming like a porn star.

Porn. What Dean and Ella Mae just did was pornographic. The kind of sex that required a good hamstring stretch beforehand. The kind of sex that was likely illegal in a handful of states. After seven years of mostly missionary with Ray—in the dark and under the covers—Ella Mae's body came alive under Dean's hands, contorting and responding in a way she didn't know was possible.

But now, Lee Highway's wastelands had given way to Mount Carmel's businesses and fast-food shacks, and Dean still hadn't said more than two words. What did his silence mean?

"Bear left here, and it's the second house on the right."

Dean responded only by turning the wheel with the heel of a hand, and Ella Mae chanced another glance. His cocky grin had dimmed, and the skin around his eyes was creased with an emotion she couldn't place. She gave herself a mental eye roll. Of course she couldn't place it; she barely knew the man.

But she knew what he looked like naked.

"Dean, what happened back there at the house, I..." Ella Mae cleared her throat and started again, swallowing down the panic beating in her throat. Was he having second thoughts? Did he have regrets? The possibility sent something unpleasant skittering over her skin. "I don't..."

Dean pulled into Shelley's gravel drive and parked, pivoting his upper body to face her full-on. "You don't what?"

"I don't know what happened back there, with us."

"I do." His voice was teasing, his tone lighthearted, and Ella Mae relaxed just a tad. "I have every second of it burned onto my retinas. Would you like me to give you a quick recap?"

Now she did roll her eyes. "There's nothing wrong with my memory. I'm just trying to figure out what happened to my common sense. I don't normally lose control."

"That's too bad." He gave her a lewd grin, igniting a spark in her belly. "Because when you lose control, you're incredibly sexy."

Ella Mae was flattered, but she forced herself to remain focused. "I'm trying to be serious here. I've never cheated before. Ever. Have you?"

One of Dean's brows shot skyward but he didn't answer, a response Ella Mae took as an affirmative.

"Well, I haven't. For the past seven years, I've been faithful to Ray. Completely faithful. And then you come along, and I go and lose my mind."

Ella Mae waited for the wave of remorse and regret that should have rolled in on the tail of her message, but it didn't come. It didn't come because Dean was looking at her in that way again, that way that made her nerve endings tingle and her body temperature shoot up a good ten degrees. Maybe that was the problem. All that internal heat was scrambling her brain.

Dean's hand skipped across the gearshift and landed, butterfly soft, just above her knee. Ella Mae's gaze dropped to Dean's long fingers, sliding up the inside of her leg, ducking under her white tennis skirt. Her thighs parted as if by magic, without conscious command. Open sesame.

"I make you lose your mind?" he said.

Her answer was barely a whisper. "You make me certifiable."

"Good." His pinky crept higher.

Ella Mae bit her lip to keep from moaning.

"Do you like losing your mind?"

Ella Mae nodded.

"And would you like me to make you even crazier?"

A finger brushed over her sweet spot, and she threw back her head. "Oh, God, yes."

Dean's touch disappeared—poof!—and Ella Mae felt its absence like a sharp slap. She didn't care that she'd almost let Dean feel her up in broad daylight. She didn't care that they'd almost been caught by Shelley, coming up the drive. Ella Mae didn't even care that she didn't care.

The only thing she cared about was getting Dean's touch back.

Dean flew out of the car, scooping up both puppies and cradling them against his neck while Ella Mae watched through the car's front window. The puppies really were precious, she had to admit. Like those stuffed animal prizes the girls used to bring home from the Gray Fair, a tiny round tuft of fur filling up each of Dean's hands. Ella Mae would get out of the car, too, but she was still composing herself. Weren't men the ones who were supposed to need a moment?

Shelley turned and waved, and Ella Mae knew she couldn't sit here any longer. She ran her fingers over her ponytail, smoothed down her tennis skirt and reached for the door handle. Her legs were still weak, but her heart rate was almost back to normal.

"Ella Mae!" Shelley swept her into a hug. "I'm so glad y'all are here."

Ella Mae looked over at Dean. Only two minutes ago he'd had his hand up her skirt, about to make her even crazier. Now he had his hands full of two puppies, and he was grinning like a little boy. Grinning and ignoring Ella Mae.

She turned back to Shelley. "I see you met Dean."

"How am I supposed to choose?" Dean said, holding the

wriggling puppies up to his face. "They're both so damn cute."

"Take as long as you like." Shelley looped an arm through Ella Mae's and tugged her toward the front door. "Let's go in the house and get caught up while he decides. How's Ray?"

Ella Mae tore her gaze off Dean. "What? Oh, Ray's fine. Working all the time, as usual."

"Two kids in college will do that for you. And isn't Gia a senior this year?"

Ella Mae nodded.

"Things are about to get a lot more expensive in your house, that's for sure."

Ella Mae followed her friend up the stairs to the front door, looking one last time over her shoulder for Dean. Still ignoring her.

Seriously? Ella Mae was seriously jealous of puppies?

"You know Ray," Ella Mae said, turning back to Shelley. "For him the pharmacy isn't only about money. It's his life."

Shelley led Ella Mae into the living room, parked her in a love seat by the picture window and disappeared into the kitchen for refreshments. While Shelley was gone, Ella Mae watched Dean through the glass, playing on the front lawn with the puppies. He let one of them, the white one, gnaw on a knuckle while the black puppy slept in the crook behind his left knee.

God, that man was gorgeous.

Shelley appeared with a tray of iced tea and cookies, placed it on the coffee table and handed Ella Mae a glass. "Okay. Now spill."

"Spill what?"

Shelley sank onto the couch next to Ella Mae, her eyes

going a little squinty. "Ella Mae Andrews, you know exactly what I'm talking about."

Panic zinged up Ella Mae's spine, exploding in a burst of pinpoint sweat beads across her forehead. What had Shelley seen?

"No, Shell, I really don't know."

Shelley hitched her chin toward the scene on her front lawn. "Dean, of course. Lordy me, that is one fine male specimen."

Ella Mae couldn't help but agree.

"How on earth do you get anything done with that man living next door? Please tell me he mows the lawn shirtless."

Ella Mae didn't know how she managed, but she pushed up a breezy laugh from real deep, from somewhere around her left big toe. "Only when it's ninety or above."

Shelley puffed a dreamy sigh. "You'll call me next time that happens, right?"

Ella Mae frowned. Hell no.

That's when Dean looked up, and Ella Mae's skin barely had time to tingle before his eyes found hers. It was like her body knew it was coming—that look of his—and Ella Mae responded like one of Pavlov's dogs.

But Dean had caught the backwash of her frown, and he raised his brows, just slightly. Ella Mae smiled, and he pushed himself off the grass, cradling the puppies in the crook of his arm, and headed for the door.

And she knew by the set of his brow he was coming for her.

Shelley met Dean at the door with a smile and a glass of tea. "Well? Did you decide which puppy is the lucky one?"

"The white one." And here he gave Ella Mae one of his naughty grins. "She's a wild little thing. I like wild."

Ella Mae shifted out of the ray of sunshine beating through the window. Hot. This living room was too damn hot.

Shelley gathered up the black puppy, asleep next to his squirming sister, and pointed Dean to the couch. "I'm going to give this little one back to his mama in the barn, and then I need a few minutes to draw up the paperwork. You two can entertain yourselves in the meantime, right?"

Dean glanced at Ella Mae. "Oh, I'm sure we can find something to do."

Two seconds later, Dean and Ella Mae were alone.

"She's cute," Ella Mae said, gesturing to the puppy in his hand. "What are you gonna name her?"

"I don't know." Dean scooted closer. "I thought I'd let the girls decide."

"Are you giving her to them tonight?"

Dean slid the puppy to the floor, and it pawed and whined at his feet. "Hush."

Ella Mae didn't know if he was talking to her or the puppy.

His hand dipped to her breast, and she had to fight to keep from panting. "Dean, we can't...not here. In Shelley's—" his teeth nipped Ella Mae's neck and she gasped "—house. She'll be back any minute."

"Then we'd better hurry."

Somewhere in the very back corners of her mind, Ella Mae knew she was screwed. She was so goddamn screwed. Letting Dean have his way with her on Shelley's living room love seat was not the smartest thing she'd ever done—not even close—but Dean Sullivan was like a magician. One with conjuring tricks and alchemic charms far, far beyond her human understanding. And Ella Mae was completely under his spell.

No, the bigger problem was, Ella Mae couldn't figure out if he was using his powers for good or evil.

13

Normally, this would be the part where I slink out. Pluck my panties and T-shirt and jeans from wherever they're strewn about the floor, pull them on as quickly and noise-lessly as possible and tiptoe out of the room, preferably while he's still asleep. No apologies, no "I'll call you later" or "Let's do this again sometime," no note saying…what exactly? Because honestly, what is there to say after you shag a near stranger silly, other than Gee, thanks? I know the rules of a one-night stand, and they call for as little talking afterward as possible.

But this is no normal one-night stand.

For one thing, it's not night, only barely dusk, and no one's sleeping. In fact, who can sleep with all the noise, a steady thumping that alerted us hours ago to Roadkill's happy hour in full swing below us? Jake didn't seem to no-tice when it started, and when I asked him if he needed to go, he pushed me up against the wall and kissed me, and before I knew it that thumping noise was coming from us. Again.

For another, slinking indicates shame, and I feel none

of that, only the euphoria that comes after really, really spectacular sex. Hands down the best ever. Sex that bears repeating—often and a lot—which basically negates the one-night part of one-night stand. I want tonight to happen again and again. Now that I know Jake's tricks, what those hands of his can do, I want a more-please-night stand.

I swing a leg over his, twist onto my right side on the bed. "Having your place above the bar must be very convenient for you."

"It certainly cuts down on my commute."

I laugh. "I meant with all the girls tossing you their panties."

Jake rolls his head on the pillow to face me, and yowza, he's gorgeous. "What are you talking about?"

"According to Lexi, girls all over town are throwing theirs at your front door."

"No offense, but sometimes your sister is full of shit."

No kidding. My mind skitters to last night, how she ran out before we'd really talked, and to today at the bank, how she ducked out the back door before I could catch her. "No offense taken."

And then I think of something even worse, something even more distressing. Something that—knowing my sister—is highly possible. "How well do you know Lexi?"

Jake squints at the ceiling and thinks. "Well, I've known her about as long as I've lived in Rogersville. She helped me with my loan for this place, and she's in here a couple times a week. I guess you could say I know her fairly well."

"Half the boys in town know my sister fairly well. Can you be more specific?"

"Are you asking me if I've slept with your sister?"

I shake my head. "Of course not. And please don't make me ask it again."

His hand slips up my thigh to my waist, his thumb thrumming my hip bone. "Just in case I didn't make this clear earlier, I'm on team Gia. Your panties are the only ones I care about at this particular moment. I like the way they look on your ass." He pushes me onto my back and rolls on top, fingers twining through my hair. "But I'd like them even better—" he pauses to plant a row of kisses from my ear to my breastbone "—on my floor."

"You don't..." I gasp as his mouth dips lower, then lower again. My fingers slide through his thick hair, guiding him, feeling the rough scrape of his three-day beard on my skin. "You don't have to go?"

Jake lifts his head, and his brow creases. "Go where?"

"I don't know." Lust, thick and hot in my veins, is drowning out all rational thought. *Don't stop.* I wriggle a little underneath him. Why did he stop? "Wherever."

"You're not trying to get rid of me, are you?"

There's something dubious and unsure in his tone that brings me back. I run my hands down the hot skin of his bare back and arch up into him, making him groan a little. "No. No, not at all. Carry on."

He does, and I throw back my head and sigh.

"In fact," I say between gasps, "if you leave me now I'll have to kill you."

After that, neither of us asks any more questions.

By the time we come up for air a second time, it's good and dark outside, and the thumping below us has escalated into a downright roar. Lexi wasn't kidding when she said Roadkill was the place to be. Half the town must be down there, judging from the steady din of voices and laughter and music vibrating the walls and floorboards. It's a good thing Jake lives above his own bar, because there's not an-

other renter on the planet who would put up with all that
racket every night.

He checks the clock on the bedside table—8:23 p.m.
"Dilemma time." His voice and expression are suddenly
serious.

"Oh." I push up onto an elbow, trying to pick my clothes
out of the shadows on the floor. "Okay."

He stills me with a hand to my biceps. "Not you. Me.
I'm starving."

But I've already swung one leg out of the bed. There's
somewhere else I need to be, should have been hours ago.
"That's okay. I need to get home."

"Come on. At least let me feed you first."

I sit up, shaking my head. "I really should go. Dad and
Fannie are probably waiting up, and Cal's coming early
tomorrow morning. This weekend is going to be a little
crazy."

He sits up, too, wrapping both arms around my waist
and tugging me tight up against him. "Stay," he whispers
into my hair. "Just a little while longer."

I think about Fannie and my father at the house, wondering where I went, if I'm ever coming back. I think about
the protesters, wielding their vile signs and chanting their
even viler slogans. I think about Cal and Lexi and Bo, all
of whom are probably snuggled on their couches with a
glass of wine and the remote, and who haven't given me a
second thought since the last time I talked to any of them,
hours ago.

I'm homesick, I realize suddenly, only I mean that in the
most literal sense of the word. I mean the thought of going
home makes me physically ill—queasy and dizzy and like I
can't breathe. I don't want to go there. Not yet. I don't want
to go back to how that place makes me feel.

Jake's breath tickles my neck while he waits for me to decide.

But then, it's really not a difficult decision, is it?

I twist around to face him. "Dinner better be good."

He grins, and my belly gives a hot squeeze. Jake really does have a great smile, an amazing smile, one that's big and open and makes his whole face shine. One that's impossible not to return.

"So I was thinking we could go downstairs and grab a bite," he says, "or I can bring us something up here. Up to you."

Quite frankly, after my tequila-inspired performance at Roadkill last night, I'm not exactly anxious to show up there again, with or without a black eye. Plus, one look at Jake's just-got-laid grin and the purple love bite below his right ear, and everybody in the place will know. People in this town are already talking enough. I'd rather not add fuel to their gossip fire.

"I vote for takeout."

Jake squeezes my hand like it was the answer he'd hoped for, then hops out of bed and plucks his jeans off the floor. I watch as he slips them back on, admiring the way his muscles ripple and pulse as he buttons his fly and reaches for his shirt.

Who needs crack cocaine when there are men like Jake Foster walking this planet?

After he's gone, I snatch my panties and bra from the floor and pull them on as I head into the bathroom, doing a double take at my reflection in the mirror. Good Lord. My curls are a wild tangle around my head, my lips look like they've been stung by a bee and there's a streak of bright red beard burn on my neck. Oh, and the shiner. Let's not forget the shiner. I don't look like I've been well bedded. I look like I've been raped.

I splash water on my face and run wet fingers through my curls until they're semipresentable, and then I flick off the lights and make my way back into the dark bedroom.

Better.

I'm just getting settled back on the bed when Jake returns, a black cast-iron pan in his hands and a bottle of wine tucked under biceps. "Coq au vin," he tells me with such perfect pronunciation I think he must speak French. He deposits the pan in the middle of the bed, drops the bottle onto the mattress beside it, and fetches a few things from the kitchen. A bottle opener, cloth napkins, two glasses and a pair of forks.

"No plates?" I ask. "What kind of dump is this?"

Jake shucks his shoes and sinks onto the mattress beside me. "The best kind."

He removes the cast-iron top with a flourish. The aroma hits me, and I close my eyes and breathe it all in. The garlic and onions and chicken and wine sauce and Jake, pulling his long legs around on the bed next to me. He picks up his fork, tears off a large bite of steaming meat and blows on it before offering it to me. "Now shut up and eat."

I do, and it's completely and totally delicious. I reach for the fork and rip off another chunk of meat, dragging it through the sauce, not bothering to blow before stuffing it into my mouth. Jake fights a smile, watching me do it another three times while he uncorks the wine.

"Why is your restaurant in Rogersville?" I ask him between bites. "You could make so much money somewhere else. New York or L.A. or Paris. Your food is that good."

He pours, hands me a glass. "I'm not here for the money."

"Why, then?"

He shrugs, reaching for his fork. "I don't know. I like the scenery. I like to cook. I like the people I'm cooking for, especially when they're as enthusiastic about my food as you are."

"Yeah, well, we've already established I'll eat just about anything, so I'm not sure you should use me as your litmus test."

His hand scorches a trail up my bare thigh, and he drops his voice. "I prefer to use you for other things."

I give him a playful swat on the biceps. "Be serious. No one just up and moves to Rogersville without having roots here."

His teasing expression sobers. "I do have roots here, or at least close to here. My mom grew up in Church Hill. She met my father when he was stationed at the Holston Army Ammunition Plant. After that they lived all over the place, but we came here every Christmas and summer. This area was the closest thing I had to home."

"Home never felt like home?"

He stabs another bite. "Dad was in the army. We never stayed long enough in one place for it to qualify." He cocks his head, like he's just thought of a new revelation. "Wow. This is the longest I've ever lived in one spot."

"And you're still not bored as hell?"

His eyes get big and round. "How could anyone be bored in Rogersville?"

"Because there's nothing to do. No shopping. No museums. Back when I lived here, there wasn't even a movie theater."

"What about all the outdoor stuff? The hiking and biking and rafting."

I make a face. "Too many bugs."

"But what about the nature? You can't deny the beauty of this place."

I laugh. "You sound like a commercial for the Tennessee Board of Tourism."

Jake puts down his fork and swivels his torso toward mine, adjusting his legs until they're alongside my right thigh. "It's more than all those things. It's this place, my restaurant and the people who come here to eat my food. I feel connected to them somehow. They're like family, some of them, and Roadkill feels like a place I've always wanted to be. I can't imagine ever living anywhere else. Which is why I bought the whole building last year."

I bury my nose in the pan, something vaguely unpleasant swirling in my stomach. After traipsing all over the world as a child, Jake finally finds the one place he wants to settle, the one place he thinks of as home. That it happens to be the same home I fled when my world fell apart feels like a strange kind of irony. His home will never again be mine, not after what happened here. Not even after my father's funeral, when I plan to be on the first plane out of here.

But then again, this isn't a relationship. Jake Foster is temporary, a mighty fine distraction while I whittle away my days here in Rogersville.

Jake nudges me with an elbow. "Okay, now you."

I look up. "Now me, what?"

"I told you something about me, now you have to tell me something about you."

"Oh, I don't know." I duck my head and smile at him through my curls. "My life has been really boring."

He laughs. "Tell me about all the places you've been. I know about Kenya and Thailand, but where else?"

"A better question would be, where else not? The famine in the Horn of Africa and the tsunami in Japan and the earthquake in Haiti and the refugee crisis in Ivory Coast. The list of disasters goes on and on, unfortunately."

"Impressive."

"And you haven't even seen my frequent-flyer statement."

"I'm not talking about the travel. I'm talking about all the people you're helping."

"Come on, Jake." I push a laugh up my throat, shove a flippant note into my tone. "It doesn't take a genius to figure out my intentions are not purely altruistic. It's mostly just to get away from here."

Jake doesn't joke or laugh, doesn't even smile. He puts down his fork and reaches forward, tucking a stray curl behind my ear, brushing a butterfly finger across the skin of my black eye, watching me with not pity, but tenderness.

And then, slowly, slowly, he leans in and touches the bruise with his lips, as if kissing it better. The gesture undoes me, more than a little, and my throat tightens at the same time something deep inside my chest whispers and stirs.

On impulse, my voice barely a whisper, I tell him what only a few hours earlier, I managed to evade. "I fainted. My father came home this morning, and he was so changed. So thin and frail and sick I barely recognized him, would've passed him on the street without a second thought. And the protesters…" I shudder, shake my head. "It was just awful. I fainted and hit my head on the coffee table."

Jake slides a hand onto my knee. "I'm so sorry, Gia."

I nod, pity for my father comingling with pity for myself, blending into a bitter brew that seeps into my voice. "And I could just kill Bo and Lexi. They weren't there, and they haven't been returning my calls and texts. This afternoon, Lexi snuck out of the bank so she wouldn't have to talk to me. I don't think I'm going to be able to talk either of them into coming by to see Dad before he dies."

"That situation would be too much for anybody. Not everybody would've agreed to come back to that kind of hell."

"Turns out coming back was the easy part. Actually staying is so much harder."

His hand curls around my thigh and squeezes. "I'm glad you did both."

"I'm a mess. My life is a mess." I draw a deep breath, clear my throat. "If I were you, I'd run as fast as I could in the other direction."

As if in answer, he scoots a little closer on the bed.

"I mean it, Jake. I'm the last thing you need right now. Ask anybody. They'll all tell you not to get involved with one of Ray Andrews's daughters. We're bad news."

"You're not bad news. What happened sixteen years ago to your family was tragic, but that doesn't make you bad news. It has nothing to do with you."

I lift my head and meet his gaze. Jake Foster just said the best thing I could ever imagine, that I am not my circumstances, and I can think of only one thing to do. I pounce, kiss him hard, maybe too hard, sliding one hand through his hair and gripping his head and holding him close, my tongue reaching right into his mouth and kissing the stuffing out of him. It's the kind of kiss that makes my entire body hum with energy, the kind of kiss that leaves no doubt of what happens next.

Jake pulls back, panting a little, and gives me a look of mock confusion. "Does that mean you don't want dessert?"

"Oh, yes." I yank his T-shirt up and over his head. "I want dessert right this instant."

14

When I awake, the morning sun sits high in the sky and paints slanted patterns across the bed through the blinds. Blinking, I will my eyes to adjust to its golden light and turn to look at the man still asleep on the pillow next to me. Jake Foster is delicious. His cheeks are flushed, his thick hair rumpled, one arm thrown above his head. Delicious enough to be on a billboard somewhere. Delicious enough to scoop up and eat for breakfast.

Breakfast?

I shoot upright in bed, reality stinging my skin like a swarm of horseflies. Shit. I glance at the clock—11:07 a.m., double shit—and throw back the covers. "Shit."

Jake presses a palm to my lower back. "What's wrong?"

I spring out of bed, snatching pieces of my clothing from the floor. "We weren't supposed to fall asleep. I wasn't supposed to fall asleep. I was supposed to be home hours ago. No. I was supposed to be home last night."

Jake yawns and sits up, reaching on the floor for his jeans. He takes his sweet time sticking one leg in, then the other, pulling them up over his bare ass.

I shove my legs through the holes of my panties. They're all twisted and wrong and get caught halfway up my thigh, and I stomp back out. "Goddammit!"

"Calm down." He comes around the bed to where I'm standing, picking up my bra along the way. "I'll help you."

"You don't understand." I yank my panties to my hip, inside out now but I don't have time to care, and snatch my bra from his hand. "I'm over an hour late—scratch that, over a day late. What am I going to tell Cal? What am I going to tell my father?" Jake pushes my T-shirt over my head, holds it so I can ram my arms through the sleeves. "That I was too busy getting fucked every which way to remember I'm supposed to be taking care of him?"

He raises a brow at my choice of words but remains silent.

I find my jeans in the hallway, spot my sneakers and jacket on the floor by the front door. "This is bad. This is really, really bad." I shove my feet into my shoes and yank my coat onto one arm, pivot to the door, then stop. "My bag. Where the hell is my bag? Oh, Jesus. I think I'm going to throw up."

"Not exactly the sensation I was going for when I was fucking you every which way."

The harshness of my words on Jake's tongue hits me like an electric jolt, paralyzing my limbs and bolting my untied sneakers to the floor. "Oh. I didn't mean it that way."

Jake reaches an arm into the kitchen, plucks my bag from the table, drapes it over my shoulder. "How did you mean it, then?"

I can tell he's trying to keep his voice neutral, and my thoughts skid into Reverse, my mouth backtracking. "I just meant…" My gaze drops to his chest, thinking it would be a safe place to park my eyes, but he's still shirtless—deliciously shirtless—so I drag my gaze back up to his face.

"My little temper tantrum back there had nothing to do with you. Honestly it didn't. I'm just really angry I let myself get so distracted."

His mouth dips like it wasn't the answer he wanted to hear. "I'm a distraction."

"Yes. Put a shirt on so I can think straight."

He smiles then, and good Lord, it hits me like a narcotic. Without my permission, my palm slides against his bare rib cage, up to his chest. He captures my hand, his fingers threading through mine, and pulls me up against him.

"But I do have to go," I remind him as well as myself.

But if I'm in such a hurry to go, why am I not more eager to leave?

Jake nods, brushes a kiss on my lips, yet doesn't release me. "When will I see you again?"

"I don't know. Cal's here all weekend."

"This Cal person you keep mentioning. Is he my competition?"

"What?" I laugh. "Ew, no. Cal's my uncle, and my father's attorney. I just meant it will be hard for me to get away while he's here."

"Ah."

"So I'll kind of need to stick close to home, especially after bailing on everyone last night."

"Ah," he says again, and the disappointment in his voice makes me want to stay until next week. Jake steps back, threads the zipper of my coat, drags the pull until it stops under my neck. "Just don't forget about me, okay?"

I give my head a little shake. Like that's possible.

After one more kiss he opens the door, waiting in the doorway while I make my way down the stairs. At the bottom step, I turn to wave one last time. "Go back to bed."

"I will, and I'll be thinking about you the entire time."

* * *

Returning to the house is the mother of all walks of shame. Past the protesters, stunned for once into wide-eyed silence when they get a load of me, wild-haired and black-eyed, puttering past them in my rental. Across the lawn and up the stairs to the door, while reporters speculate story lines for my less-than-wholesome appearance and their cameras follow my every hurried step. Into the living room, where Cal and Fannie sit on either side of my father, their expressions a combination of displeasure and surprise. I might as well be wearing a sign: Three Orgasms in One Night, Y'all. A New Personal Record!

"Good Lord, Gia." Uncle Cal looks pissed. "What on earth happened to you?"

Fannie gives a snort of laughter and returns to her blood pressure cuff.

At her right elbow, my father flops his head back onto the pillow and glares up at the ceiling. Balloons bob in the air above his bed, their cheerful colors and message—Welcome Home!—a burning contrast to the bitter man dying beneath them. I don't have to wonder who they're from. Anyone who cares enough to have sent them is already here, for Dad's first night home.

The same night I just missed.

The breath hitches halfway down my throat. "It's just a bruise. I'm fine."

"I'm more concerned with where in God's name you've been all night," Cal says.

I give him an I'm-thirty-four-so-don't-even-go-there look. "Out."

"Out?" The question carries a ton of weight. Accusation, disappointment, blame. "Out where? Stop. Don't you dare answer that. I may be an old man, but I'm not that old."

I unzip my coat, shucking it along with my bag onto the chair by the door, and head into the kitchen. I don't have to turn to know the person I hear following me is Cal.

"You could've at least called. What if you'd been in a car wreck, or floating facedown in the Holston River? One more minute and I would've filed a missing persons report."

"My phone died."

Technically, I'm not entirely certain my answer isn't a fib. I heard my phone's incessant buzzing while I was… er, otherwise occupied. Somewhere around ten o'clock last night it stopped, I assume because of the battery.

"You should've checked in."

I pour cold coffee into a yellow mug and pop it in the microwave. "I didn't have a charger."

There. That one was for sure the truth.

Cal crosses his arms, leans a hip against the countertop. "Your priorities are messed up, baby girl. Last night was your father's first night home in sixteen years, and you missed it."

His words ignite a slow burn deep in my belly, and guilt combines with my anger and resentment to make a fast flame. I step a little closer, stand a little taller.

"Excuse me, but as I recall, I was the only one who didn't miss his homecoming. So don't talk to me about priorities, and don't you dare try to guilt-trip me. I put my life on hold to be here, and as far as I can tell, I'm the only one."

"You knew I'd only be here on the weekends until I've wrapped up my case."

"But where are Bo and Lexi? Did either of them tell you they'd help?"

Cal doesn't shake his head, but he doesn't nod, either.

"Figures." The microwave dings, and I reach in for my coffee. "A little advance notice would've been nice."

"I was hoping you could help me talk some sense into those siblings of yours."

"I'd have to catch Lexi first." A splash of resentment for my sister pools on my tongue, and I chase it down with coffee that's just as bitter. "But Bo promised he'd call sometime today with plans for tomorrow."

"Good. Let's just hope he can muster up enough contrition for your father to forgive him for not getting his sorry ass over here sooner."

Not for the first time, I wish I had Cal's sense of conviction as to my father's innocence. What about Dean Sullivan's testimony and the lack of foreign prints, when my father insisted there were intruders?

What about his injuries, bruises on his forearms and a lump on the back of his head, which the medical witness testified could have been self-inflicted?

And what about the little nuggets of new information I received from Jeffrey Levine and that reporter, both of which only added fuel of doubt to an already smoldering fire? After all, if Ella Mae was having an affair, that gives my father the one thing the D.A. couldn't sixteen years ago: motive.

For all these years, I've held on to my questions. Now it's time I finally get some answers.

"Did you know Dean Sullivan still lives next door?"

Cal dips his head in a curt nod.

"Then you also probably know he turned into the crazy town drunk. But why? What happened to him after the trial?"

He lifts a shoulder. "I'm not exactly on his Christmas card list."

"I hear his statement took six hours to extract. Isn't that a little suspicious?"

"Six hours is on the long end, but it's not unheard of in a murder case."

"Six hours would be long enough to coerce someone into a lie."

My last word jolts him like a poke with a live wire. He stiffens, snatches me by the biceps, and pulls me deeper into the kitchen, past the table and into the hallway by the back door. And then he whirls around to face me so suddenly I startle, and a swell of coffee sloshes onto the linoleum floor.

"This is one heck of a fishing expedition you're taking me on, and I surely don't like the hook you're trying to sink in my side. So why don't you just spit it out? What is it you want to know?"

"Did you ever hear any rumors of Ella Mae having an affair?"

My question clearly shocks him. His eyes widen, and his coloring fades more than a few shades. "Who told you anything about an affair?"

"A reporter asked me about it yesterday, and if jealousy was the reason Dad killed her. He said the D.A.'s office had evidence."

"What did you say?"

"Nothing. I got in my car and drove off."

He nods once. "Good. That was good. I don't want you talking to any reporters."

"I'm not stupid, Cal. I interface with the media all the time, and I know how they can twist your words to suit their purposes. What I need to know from you is, is it true?"

"Of course it's not true. The D.A. who inherited this case has vowed your father will die in prison. But his allegations of an affair aren't backed with even one lick of evidence. Ella Mae and Ray were fine. Happily married fine." He leans back and crosses his arms. "Are we done here?"

Not even close. "Do you know Jeffrey Levine?"

Cal's eyes darken, just for an instant, but long enough for me to see that he knows Jeffrey, and that he doesn't like him. And then his face melds back into his courtroom mask.

"Yes, I know of Mr. Levine. Why?"

"Because I hear he's writing a book about Dad's case. One that proclaims he's innocent, and that his trial was a gross miscarriage of justice."

"He's right. Sending an innocent man to prison for life is a gross miscarriage of justice."

"He meant your defense. He called it shoddy."

Now Cal doesn't bother hiding his surprise, or his fury. His neutral expression mushrooms into something livid and then clenches. Slammed brows, squeezed lips. He leans close and lowers his voice, a gesture I know is meant to intimidate his witness.

"Listen up, darlin', 'cause I'm only gonna say this once. Mr. Levine is a fool, and you would be, too, to think even for one second I didn't do everything in my power to keep your father out of prison."

Though he didn't phrase it as a question, I know Cal is waiting for my answer. Did I think, even for a second, that his defense might have been shoddy? Maybe. Jeffrey certainly knows more about the law than I do, and I was eighteen at the time of the trial. I didn't understand half of what was going on, and I was too traumatized to remember the rest.

"I'm just trying to figure out why you didn't fight the verdict."

Cal looks away, purses his lips, looks back. "That's not really an answer, now, is it?"

I bury my nose in my mug. My memory is good enough

to remember Cal's courtroom moves. His unblinking poker face. The way his moods ricocheted from businesslike to derisive to cordial and back. This is just the first time I've been at the receiving end of his interrogation tactics, and I can't say I like playing the role of Cal's witness.

He grows tired of waiting for an answer I'm not willing to give. "I did fight the verdict, dammit. I filed an appeal with the Tennessee Court of Appeals, but it was denied."

"I meant after that. Couldn't you have kept going, all the way up to the Supreme Court if you had to?"

Cal all but rolls his eyes. "You watch too much TV, child."

"I'm being serious."

He fills his lungs with enough air to strain the buttons on his starched Brooks Brothers shirt, then huffs it out, loud and long. "It's not that simple."

"Humor me here, Cal." I lower my coffee cup and soften my expression, my tone, my attitude. "Please. Please explain it to me."

"Your father's case took me over four months to try. It generated tens of thousands of pages of transcripts, hundreds of exhibits and a stack of pleadings higher than Mount Le Conte." Cal's voice has risen at a steady climb, booming on the last word hard enough to shake the windowpanes in the door behind me, and he pauses to regain his composure. "The Appeals Court looked at everything we had, and they still denied us. Based on their reasoning, none of us, including your father, who was rigorously involved in every aspect of his case, had any reason to think filing another appeal would result in a reversal of the verdict."

I know I should feel convinced by Cal's words—I so want to feel convinced—but Jeffrey's allegations keep nipping at my memories of that awful time. I lean against the back door and gaze at the floor.

"I remember those months better than you think I do, you know." My voice is quiet, barely a whisper, and sounds as exhausted as I suddenly feel. "How you practically moved in here, didn't eat or sleep or go home for weeks at a time. How you hired a team of lawyers, put them up in the Quality Inn on the interstate, covered all of the costs. How after the verdict you picked up where Dad couldn't, footing the bills for college, buying us books and clothes and cars, inviting us for birthdays and holidays. I remember everything."

I look up now, and Cal is watching me intently. His courtroom mask has softened around the edges but is still guarded, and he remains silent. I wonder if he already senses the words that are building in my throat, threatening to choke me.

"But you still stopped after one lousy appeal."

Anger flickers over his expression, followed closely by something else, something I can't quite read, as well as the undeniable spasm of pain. Is Cal hurt and angry that I don't understand? Or are his emotions more self-inflicted, fueled by guilt at letting his only brother languish in prison? Either way, I don't think I want to know the answer.

We stand in silence for a long moment, an endless moment, and then he turns to leave.

But a few minutes later, as I'm climbing the stairs to my room, I can't help but wonder what Jeffrey will say when I tell him he was right.

15

Cal and I spend the rest of Saturday tiptoeing around one another, neither of us willing to bring up Jeffrey Levine or allegations of slutty behavior. Mine or Ella Mae's. When, late that afternoon, he asks me to run a few errands, I take his request for what it is—a test. I shuttle to the stores without so much as a passing thought about a detour down Main Street.

Well, maybe a teeny passing thought. A fleeting fantasy. But how could I not? Jake said he would be thinking about me, and what girl would not obsess about that?

But the point is, I don't go to Roadkill. I don't even do a drive-by. I push my carts through Walmart and Winn-Dixie, schlep the merchandise to the trunk and steer my car straight back to a house that is starting to feel more and more like a prison.

One woman's prison, another man's escape from the same.

Cal meets me at the door, motions for me to follow him into the kitchen.

"I finally got ahold of your sister."

"Congratulations." I dump the bags on the counter and

turn to face him. "Because she's apparently not speaking to me."

"She is tomorrow. She's expecting the two of us after church."

"We're going to church?" I might even make a face as I say it. Quite frankly, I can't imagine anything worse. I prefer my services in churches where I can remain anonymous, where the congregation's judgmental stares don't taint the air until I choke on every breath, where the sermon of Christian values of forgiveness and acceptance isn't contradicted by the congregation's whispered allegations.

"Of course not. But when somebody tells you to drop by after church, they mean around 12:30."

"Then why don't they just say around 12:30?"

Cal shakes his head like I just asked him why Tennessee is called the volunteer state. "You really have been gone a long time, haven't you, baby girl?"

"What about Bo? He still hasn't called, and his cell keeps going to voice mail."

A long sigh. "I swear, that boy. If he doesn't get his ass over here soon, I'm—"

"Hey!" Dad's voice, fueled by anger and something more desperate, something that shoots through my veins like ice water, cuts Cal off midthreat.

For an old man, Cal is pretty spry. He rushes to Dad's bedside, beating me by a good four seconds.

"What does somebody have to do to get attention from you people, keel over and die?" Dad's face is squinty and drawn. "I've been hollering for the past ten minutes."

"What's wrong?" Cal uses his lawyer voice, now laced with worry.

"My goddamn back is on fire, that's what's wrong. Where the hell is Frannie?"

"Fannie," I whisper.

"I don't give a shit what her name is, just go get her." Dad's face contorts, and he twists on the bed like a garden snake. "Hell's bells, it's like somebody stabbed me in the kidney."

I watch my father, thinking of all the death I see in the field. Rows and rows of injured and dying alongside mass graves. Wailing mothers mourning a lost child. Soldiers far too young to have died holding guns. I've learned to somehow distance myself from their suffering, to not succumb to the emotions of their tragedy, to rescue the survivors without stopping to grieve for their dead.

But now my training fails me, utterly and completely. My dying father writhes around in agony and I stand here, sneakers stuck to the living room carpet, stiff with indecision.

Because how do I distance myself from my own tragedy?

"Gia, get Fannie." Cal's order doesn't register around the emergency-broadcast-system siren blaring in my ears.

My father clutches his side, practically folds himself double on the bed. "Son of a bitch!"

Cal jiggles my arm, and I startle to attention. "What?"

"Go get Fannie. Drag her out of the shower if you need to. Tell her we need her right away."

He gives me a less-than-gentle shove in the direction of the stairs, and my body responds. Ninety seconds later I return with Fannie, in her bathrobe and panting, who handles Dad's complaints with good-natured competence. She assesses his pain level and administers liquid morphine, and within a few minutes the muscles in his face unscrew and his body melts into the mattress.

Disaster averted—for now. No thanks to me.

Cal draws a bottomless breath, scrubs his face with

his hands. "Can the three of us have a little huddle in the kitchen real quick?"

My stomach drops into the crawl space under the living room floor. I follow them into the kitchen, bracing myself. Cal's deep scowl tells me I'm not getting away without a good tongue-lashing.

But before Cal can launch into me, Fannie intercepts him. "Well, this sure changes the game."

I don't dare meet Cal's glare, focusing my eyes on Fannie's instead. "I know, and I'm really sorry. But I'm better trained than what just happened back there. I swear I'll do better next time."

Fannie blinks at me once, twice. "Sugar, I was talking about your father. His pain level. I wasn't expecting things to get so volatile so soon."

"Oh."

"What does that mean?" Cal says.

"It means things are progressing a whole lot quicker than any of us expected."

"Oh," I say again.

Not for the first time, Fannie looks at me like she does Dad. Like I'm someone to be taken care of. She gives my arm a few pats. "Don't you worry, sugar. I come armed with a butt load of morphine. I aim to keep your father comfortable and pain free for whatever time he has left."

Cal clears his throat. "The doctor said up to three months."

"I'd ballpark it more at three weeks. That's if we're very lucky."

Cal and I suck in a simultaneous breath. Three weeks? When I filled in the paperwork for my leave of absence five days ago—has it only been five days?—I requested a minimum of three months. Now Fannie is telling me I might only need one?

A new and unpleasant sense of urgency nips at my conscience and leaves a sour taste on my tongue. One month to prove to everyone I can handle any disaster, including my own, and forge some sort of peace with my dying father. One month—and we're already a week in.

I check my watch, turn to Cal. "I'm thinking Bo may need another little shove."

"I was just having the same thought."

I wriggle my phone from my back pocket, push a few buttons and wait for Bo's voice mail to kick in, which I knew it would as soon as he saw my number.

"Bo, it's Gia." My voice is relaxed and singsong, as if I'm calling to wish him a happy birthday. "Hey listen, I just wanted to invite you to my Nancy Grace interview tomorrow night at the house. You know Nancy, right? That blonde on Headline News? Anyway, I told her I could probably get her a few choice quotes from you. And, oh, I almost forgot."

I pause for a breath, enough to fuel every ounce of menace I can force into my tone. "Cal and I are hosting a family get-together at Lexi's tomorrow after church. Attendance is mandatory. Don't test me on this, Bo, 'cause you won't win."

I hang up.

Cal's face clears, and he gives me a smile that lets me know my previous blunders are forgiven. "Baby girl, are you sure you don't wanna be the next Tennessee Tigress? Because that was one kick-ass bit of prowling."

My sister lives in a charming brick cottage with shuttered windows smack in the middle of Rogersville's historic district. I follow Cal up the narrow walkway, looking longingly in the direction of Roadkill, only a few blocks up the road. I imagine Jake upstairs in bed, sleeping off what was surely a busy Saturday night, and I wonder if he's alone. For a man who promised to spend the weekend thinking about me, he could have at least texted.

"Looks like we beat your brother," Cal mutters without turning, right before he stabs the doorbell.

"He'll be here." My voice is thick with authority I don't own. Bo better show. Nancy Grace is a beast I'd really rather not face.

Lexi answers the door in sweatpants and the remnants of yesterday's makeup, her normally perfect hair is a greasy knot on top of her head. I haven't seen her like this in, well, ever. Even in the privacy of her own home, she was always trying. Now, her pretty lips don't even smile.

"Interesting look for church," I say.

She points to my left eye. "I think you went a little overboard with the purple shadow, Tammy Faye."

I would roll my eyes, but it would hurt. Lexi motions us in, shuffling across the hardwood floor in giant Sponge-Bob SquarePants slippers. Cal and I step inside, clicking the door shut behind us.

My sister's house is, to put it politely, a pigsty. Crap everywhere. Blankets and pillows strewn about, a scattering of papers and magazines and books, three days' worth of dirty dishes and food wrappers on every horizontal surface. Not like my sister at all.

"What's wrong with you?" I say over the flat screen blaring from the living room wall. "Are you sick or something?"

"Peachier than ever." Lexi digs under a blanket for the remote and punches the mute button with a chipped thumbnail. "What's this I hear about you perched on Jake Foster's bar stool again yesterday?"

Good Lord. The gossips in this town. I give her my most casual shrug. "He fed me."

"I hear he did a whole lot more than that. I hear he took you upstairs and closed the blinds."

I flash a glance at Cal, who chomps down on his toothpick. "Maybe we should go ahead and get started."

"Why don't we give Bo a few more minutes?" Cal shrugs off his coat, folding it in half and draping it neatly over a chair by the window. "His church service must've run long."

I check my watch—12:43 p.m.—and a new wave of dread twists in my stomach. Why couldn't I have threatened with something less hard-hitting than HLN, something like wine hour with Hoda and Kathie Lee?

Cal moves a jumbled stack of newspapers from the couch to the floor and sits, crossing his legs and looking like he's getting comfortable enough to wait all day. "I'm sure he'll be here by the time coffee's made."

Cal's reminder of Lexi's manners seems to snap my sister out of her sloth. She nods, snatching up as many plates and cups from the coffee table as her hands will allow, and gestures for me to follow her into the kitchen, where she dumps them unceremoniously into the sink. When she crosses her arms and leans a hip against the countertop, I sigh, reaching for the coffeepot.

"I don't know what you're trying to prove with this helpless act, Lexi, but I also don't care." I dump the used grounds into the sink, drop in a fresh filter. "Not after you ditched me this weekend."

Lexi grins. "Sounds like you found something else to occupy your time, you big ole slut. So what is it? Eight, nine inches?"

"Can you be serious for ten seconds?" I flick on the

water, hold the pot under the stream. "Things with Dad are going quicker than anyone expected."

"For such a slut, you certainly are a prude."

"Fannie says if we're lucky, he might live only three more weeks."

"Fannie Miles? The one whose husband spent their retirement fund on drag queens and meth?"

"It was cocaine and prostitutes, but yeah, that's her."

"What a disappointment. My version is so much more interesting."

I whirl around to face her so fast, water from the pot in my hand sloshes down Lexi's sweatpants and onto the floor. "I need you to focus here. I've been thinking about what that lawyer said about Cal's defense, and about Dean Sullivan. And the fact that he's an alcoholic now."

"So?"

"So what if it's because he can't live with himself since the trial? What if it's because he feels guilty for something he did or didn't do?"

"Like what? Dean saw him, Gi. He saw him pretending to break into his own house the night Ella Mae was killed. You do the math."

"I did the math, over and over for sixteen years. But what if the math was right, but the equation was wrong?"

"I have no idea what that means."

"It means, what if this professor is right? What if all this time we were adding up evidence that didn't exist, basing our judgments and beliefs and guilty verdicts on a shoddy defense and coerced testimony? Don't you get it? If this professor is right, Dad might not have been found guilty. He might never have gone to prison."

Lexi presses her lips together and drops her head, mopping the spilled water with a slipper. I've seen that expression before, right before she threw up on a Sunday drive over Grandfather Mountain. Still. I don't back down.

"I think we should talk to this Jeffrey Levine," I say.

Her head pops up, her eyes wide. "Oh, no. No, no, no, no, no."

"Come on, Lex. Ten minutes. Let's just hear him out for ten minutes, and then—"

Cal interrupts with a loud harrumph, and his expression tells me he heard more than I would have liked. "Your brother's here."

16

Ella Mae drove up Main, snapping off the car radio with a flick of her fingers. If she heard one more song about the holly, jolly season, Ella Mae swore she would slit her wrists. Those damn carols reminded her too much of the one thing she wouldn't be getting this Christmas.

Dean.

Oh, she got him every now and then, stolen moments when their families were out or when Dean and Ella Mae could get away for an hour or two. Cheap motels along the interstate, gas station bathrooms a few towns over, a secluded parking spot by Burem Lake Dam. Dean wasn't particularly choosy, and neither was Ella Mae. But their time together was never enough, their trysts too sporadic and infrequent, and Ella Mae found herself obsessing over the next when, where, how.

Nine days. It'd been nine whole days since Dean had surprised her during one of her morning walks down by the river, pulling up next to her with a grin and a hard-on.

But now that the kids were out for Christmas break, she didn't know when either of them would be able to get away again. The uncertainty niggled and poked, especially in her quieter moments. Had Dean already had his fill of her? Ella Mae hoped not, because she was nowhere near done.

She found a spot a few doors down from the pharmacy and squeezed her Jeep in. Almost closing time, and Rogersville's late-afternoon, last-minute shoppers clutched lists and paper bags as they hurried from shop to shop. Ella Mae waved to a few of them as she jaywalked across Main to the pharmacy.

Louise Moore, a blue-haired woman who couldn't be a day younger than a hundred and thirty, poked at the register with gnarled fingers. She glanced up when Ella Mae pushed through the pharmacy door. "How-do, Ella Mae. Happy birthday."

Ella Mae figured birthdays wouldn't be so bad if people didn't keep reminding her she was forty-five today, a number she couldn't quite believe and would really rather forget. Lately birthdays felt more like she was counting down instead of up. Counting down until the end.

She pushed up a smile. "Thanks, Louise. Is Ray here?"

Silly question. Ludicrous, really. If Ray wasn't at the house, he was sure enough at his beloved pharmacy, counting pills and filling prescriptions and reminding whoever would listen to take their multivitamins.

Louise gestured to the back wall, where Ray's workstation overlooked the store from an elevated platform. "You know where to find him."

Ella Mae wound her way through the aisles, past the scented candles and collectible figurines and sugar-free candy. She rang the bell, an old-fashioned silver desk version Ray insisted added ambiance, and his head appeared above the counter.

"There's my birthday girl." It was Ray's pharmacy voice, animated and singsong and loud enough they could hear him clear up by the register. "I was worried you were going to stand me up."

"I had trouble finding a parking spot."

Ray leaned way over the counter and winked. "'Tis the season for holiday shoppers. This place has been jam-packed with 'em all day, isn't that right, Elroy?"

Ella Mae turned to find Ray's assistant stocking a display of reading glasses. "Only two more shopping days left, thank you, Jesus."

Ray laughed, shedding his white pharmacist coat and draping it neatly over a hook. He was such a completely different person in his pharmacy—cordial, lively, often even funny. Ella Mae was no longer surprised by this fact, but she found herself wishing he could make more of an effort at home. Like just about everybody else in town, she rather liked Pharmacy Ray.

After a few hasty instructions for Elroy, Ray turned to Ella Mae. "You ready for your big night on the town?"

Was she ever.

When Ray had asked Ella Mae what she wanted for her birthday, she couldn't come up with a single thing. She didn't need clothes or makeup or a new appliance, and other than a plain wedding band, she hardly ever wore jewelry. All she wanted was a night out. Dinner, maybe a movie in Kingsport afterward, mostly so they wouldn't end up marking the occasion by watching old *Baywatch* reruns in the den.

The pair set off for the door, fifty feet or so at best, but a trek that took at least ten minutes. Ray stopped about a million times, to straighten a display of greeting cards, to point Otis Olsen to the cough syrup, to inquire about Mrs. Crigger's bunions. Ella Mae waited patiently, and as she watched her husband socialize with his customers, she almost remembered why she'd fallen in love with him, coming up on a decade ago.

"Where are you taking me?" she asked once they were finally on the street.

"I thought we'd start with a drink at Hal's, then head over to Main Street Grille. How does that sound?"

"Heavenly." Ella Mae actually meant it.

At Hal's, Ray's pharmacy mood continued. He swapped greetings and clapped backs and shook hands, and he even bought a round of drinks and led the place in a loud and off-key rendition of "Happy Birthday." Afterward, he dipped Ella Mae in a kiss that felt strange and familiar at the same time. By the time he led her two doors down to Main Street Grille, Ella Mae was flushed and giddy and more than slightly tipsy. Why didn't they go out every night?

At the restaurant, they ended up in a candlelit booth in the back, Ella Mae on the seat facing the bar and Ray directly across.

He cocked his head and studied her. "Did you do something to your hair?"

Ella Mae brushed her fingers through a curl at her temple. "Just touched up the gray. I guess now that I'm forty-five, I'll be spending a lot more time down at the Hair Loft."

"Well, tell Diane to keep doing whatever it is she's doing, because it's working. You really do look beautiful tonight."

Ella Mae was flattered and surprised, pleasantly so, at the compliment. "Thanks."

The waitress stepped up with a basket of bread and their drinks. She began listing off the night's specials, but somewhere right around the chicken-fried steak, Ella Mae became distracted by a slow burn that sparked deep in her belly. Automatically, she began searching the crowd, craning her neck to try to see over the edges of the booth.

"And for you, ma'am?"

The burn exploded up her chest, and Ella Mae's heart thundered hard enough to shudder the fabric of her new birthday blouse. She ordered the first thing she read from the menu. "I'll have the chicken marsala."

"What would you like for your side?"

Ella Mae could barely hear her through the bells—ear-piercing bells, warning bells—clanging in her ears. She leaned a little to the left, craning her neck, but the waitress's backside blocked Ella Mae's view of the room. "I'm sorry?"

"Mashed potatoes, cheese grits, sautéed mushrooms, creamed spinach, corn on—"

"Creamed spinach will be fine."

The waitress moved on to the next table, and Ella Mae understood the roaring in her head and the fire in her veins. Time skidded to a stop, and so did her heart. The entire room around her went about its business. A man laughed, a woman knocked over her wine, a kid shrieked, but Ella Mae barely noticed. She barely noticed, because Dean Sullivan was right there, standing by the bar with the high-school football coach and a beer, his gaze glued to Ella Mae.

A wave of longing seized her so strongly she almost swooned. Almost hopped out of the booth and sashayed across the bar, shedding clothes along the way. Her body craved Dean Sullivan like her lungs craved oxygen, like her cells craved nutrients. Like her heart would bleed out without his touch on her skin.

"Are you okay?"

Ella Mae dragged her gaze back to her husband. "What? Oh, yes, I'm fine."

"Are we?"

"Are we what?"

"Okay." For the first time Ella Mae could remember, Ray looked uncomfortable, and worry crawled up his face. "You just seem so… I don't know. Distant. Like you're always somewhere else, thinking of something else. Even when we're, you know," he leaned forward, whispered, "intimate."

Ella Mae reached for her chardonnay with a shaking hand. "Don't be silly." She forced a smile. "There's nothing the matter with me. With us."

After an endless moment, Ray nodded and reached for the bread, and that was that.

Somehow—Ella Mae didn't know how—she made it through dinner. She choked down her meal and held up her side of the conversation, but just barely. After his third glass of wine, Ray was too tipsy to notice. Dessert came, loud and conspicuous, a slice of candled cake brought by a procession of clapping waitstaff. Dean sipped his beer and watched from his bar stool the entire time.

"I know you said you didn't want a gift," Ray said after he'd paid the bill, reaching into the inside pocket of his jacket for a tiny box, "but I got you one anyway. Happy birthday." He pushed it across the table.

Jewelry. That much was clear from the box, small and square and tied with a red bow, and Ella Mae's stomach flipped and kicked. She didn't want to open it, not with Dean watching. And she knew Dean was watching. Her skin sizzled wherever his gaze roamed.

Ray grinned, hitched his chin at the box. "Go on. Open it."

She tugged at the bow, peeled off the lid and peered inside. A golden heart pendant and chain gleamed from a white cotton cushion. Her heart turned over, but not in a good way, twisting something painful behind her breast.

"Oh, Ray. I…"

"Does that mean you like it?"

Ella Mae glanced over at Dean. Since that first afternoon when he reached for her in her kitchen, she'd seen plenty of lust and longing and desire on his face. But now she saw something she'd never seen there before. She saw jealousy.

"Put it on," Ray said. "Let me see how it looks."

Ella Mae did as she was told, clasping the necklace behind her neck while Ray beamed and Dean scowled. She was suddenly desperate, breathless with the need to escape. Escape Ray. Escape Dean. Escape the guilt that seared her insides and clogged her throat and blurred her vision.

But Ella Mae couldn't do any of that. Not without telling Ray. Not without losing Dean.

So she did the only thing she could think of. She slipped out of the booth, reached for her husband's hand and went home.

And later, when Ray took her upstairs for happy-birthday sex, she closed her eyes and pretended he was Dean.

17

Bo's here.

Relief hits me, as hard and fast as Dad's liquid morphine, at the same time another wave of frustration flushes my skin. Cal and I may have orchestrated the four of us under one roof, but it's the wrong roof. My father is still dying in a bed four miles away, without his three children by his side. I shove the coffeepot into place, stab the on button and follow Cal into the living room.

He points us to the couch with a look none of us would dream of disobeying and pulls up a chair directly across. Once we're all settled, he leans forward, elbows planted on his knees, fingers steepled before him, and lasers us with a glare.

"Okay, this is the way it's gonna go. The three of you are gonna get your asses over to your father's bedside this afternoon. You're gonna cry and carry on about how glad you are to see him, and how sad you are he's dying. I don't care if you mean it or not, but you're gonna goddamn well act like you do."

I think about my conversation with my father only yesterday, how he wanted me to leave when I couldn't tell him, assuredly and unequivocally, that I believed in his innocence. I glance over at Lexi, her face a mixture of mockery and contempt, and suck in a breath at the words I suspect she has for our father. Cal's lawyer-voice commands aren't going to make her mince them, and she's certainly not going to plead the fifth like I did.

Bo coughs into a hand. "Amy's waiting for me at home."

"Your wife will understand." Cal turns to Lexi. "And, you. You're gonna apologize for not visiting, for not writing, for not being there yesterday when he came home. And when he asks you if you believe he's innocent, you're gonna lie your little heart out good enough to earn you an Academy Award."

Lexi crosses her arms and legs and leans back, but she doesn't respond.

Bo shifts on his seat. "And I still have a ton of work to do at the lab. I'll probably be there all night."

"I can call the chairman of the board and explain the situation if I have to." Bo opens his mouth to protest, but Cal doesn't give my brother the chance. "Don't think I don't have his number on speed dial, 'cause I do. The Tennessee Tiger knows everybody worth knowing. Are we clear?"

Bo blinks, a rapid-fire of a few dozen flutters, and then he nods.

Satisfied, Cal turns to Lexi. "Go get in the shower. You're riding with me."

Lexi uncrosses her legs, plants her feet. "I'm not going anywhere."

"Oh, yes, you sure as hellfire are." Cal stands, puffing his chest with an intensity that makes me shrink a little farther into the couch. "Now go fix yourself up."

My sister seems less impressed. She juts her chin and

lifts a casual shoulder. "Fine, I'll go, but I'm not gonna cry, and I'm sure as hell not gonna lie. I didn't miss him for a second, and I'm not sorry he's dying. And when he asks me if I think he killed Ella Mae, I'm gonna look him in the eye and say I know he did, and that it's about damn time he's finally getting what he deserved all those years ago."

"Don't you say it." Cal steps around the coffee table until he's standing right in front of her. The air stretches tight between them. "Don't you dare say it."

Lexi looks up, looks him straight in the eye. "A death sentence."

The oxygen leaves the room with an audible whoosh. Or maybe that sound came from me, I don't know. Either way, my lungs are deflated balloons, empty and useless. My sister's words just knocked me breathless.

Cal scrunches his face into a scowl, and his voice takes on an ominous edge. "I'm gonna pretend you didn't say that."

"Pretend away." Lexi pushes herself off the couch, pushes by Cal toward the back hall. "Y'all help yourself to coffee while I hop in the shower." At the edge of the room she turns back, trains her beauty-pageant smile onto Cal. "I'm actually looking forward to this visit. Will finally be able to get a few things off my chest." She disappears down the hallway. A few seconds later, a door slams and the shower starts.

Bo and I turn back to Cal, both of us shocked silent. Cal mutters something under his breath, then points a long finger at Bo. "Gia will drive your car. You're riding with me."

"What about Lexi?" Bo asks.

Cal doesn't respond, just snatches his coat from the chair and stomps toward the door. By now he's been up against enough hostile witnesses to know they're as unpredictable as a black bear, and can be just as vicious. Bo shrugs, passes me his keys and follows silently behind.

From what I can tell from the driver's seat of Bo's Honda, my brother doesn't say a word the entire way home. Then again, Cal doesn't give him much choice. Bo sits, staring straight ahead, his back ramrod straight the entire drive, while Cal spouts what can only be a lecture. An arms-flailing, fingers-pointing lecture. It continues unbroken, for all the five minutes it takes for us to pull onto our street.

And no. I don't feel the least bit sorry for Bo.

Ahead of me, Cal's Buick brakes, then banks a sudden and sharp left, executing a tight U-turn over the road and a big chunk of Bill Almaroad's lawn. I follow suit and swing Bo's car around, trying not to make eye contact with any of the protesters stationed along the edge of our lot with their banners and posters and slogans. What have they done now?

At the four-way stop, Cal pulls onto the grass and hits the hazards. I park behind him, yanking on the hand brake and leaving the motor running, and race to Cal's car. Breathless and confused, I slide into the backseat.

"What?" I lean my head between Cal and Bo, who looks like he's about to throw up. "What's wrong?"

Bo twists around, his eyes wild. "What's wrong? What do you mean what's wrong? Every goddamn thing is wrong. Didn't you see what they did?"

I shake my head. "What who did? The protesters?"

Cal slams the steering wheel with the heel of a hand. "Goddammit!" He points a finger at Bo, then at me. "Not one word of this to your father, do you understand?"

"I don't understand anything. What's going on?"

"I can't." Bo thrusts both hands in his hair and pulls, his voice lifting into a wail. "I can't do this."

Cal clutches a palm over Bo's shoulder, gives it a hard squeeze. "Son, I'm gonna need you to buck up, all right? You buck up and don't let those people see you hurt, because that's exactly what they want. Don't you give them the satisfaction."

Good grief. If I'd known Bo would be so squeamish about crossing the protest line, I would've brought a blindfold and some earplugs. I settle on a little white lie. "Once you get inside you can barely hear them."

Bo looks at me like I'm crazy, and then he looks at Cal.

"Your father needs you, Bo."

My brother shakes his head swiftly, almost violently. "Sorry, Cal."

It's not Bo's apology that sways Cal, I suspect, but his tears. Bo never ever lets anyone see him cry. Not when Ella Mae was killed, not when our father was taken in for questioning, not even when the gavel came down on the side of guilty. When my brother reaches for the door handle, Cal doesn't try to stop him.

After Bo's gone, Cal puts the Buick into gear and swings the car around, and the two of us head back to the house.

As soon as we crest the hill for the second time, I know something's off. The protesters are lined up on the asphalt in the middle of the road, but they're turned the wrong way, facing out instead of aiming their angry chants at the house behind them.

And speaking of chants, there are none. A scraggly man in a red scarf coughs into his hand as we pull closer, but otherwise, no one makes a sound. They simply watch.

Cal sets his mouth and stares ahead, steering straight for the driveway. The protesters hustle back, parting to let our car through, and that's when I see it. Two words, spray painted in thick, capital letters across the front siding of the house, a bloodred reminder of why I've come home.

Die, Murderer.

Dread punches my stomach like a fist and shoots fire through my veins. Fire so red-hot I can barely see, breathe, think. What greater power did I offend to deserve this shit? A dying father, deadbeat siblings and now a house defiled with the most hurtful words I could ever imagine. I dedicate my life to helping others, and this is what the universe does to thank me?

I clamber out of the backseat before Cal has pulled to a full stop, gesturing with a wild arm to the house behind me. "Which one of you assholes is the graffiti artist?"

By now the protesters are huddled at the end of the driveway, Tanya dead center. No one responds.

"Which one?"

Behind me, I hear Cal step out of the car. "Let it go, baby girl," he says softly. "This is a police matter now."

"That's right," I shriek, not turning, not backing down. "The police. Because we're calling them as soon as we get inside."

Somebody clears their throat, and a few others look away.

I ignore the cell phones and news cameras capturing my tantrum in full color, high definition and march down the driveway. "What is wrong with you people? A man is dying in there. A man who discounted your prescriptions when you couldn't pay and made midnight medicine runs when your kids were sick. Why can't you let him die in peace?"

Tanya lifts her bullhorn, points it directly at my head and chants, "Life in prison means dying in prison. Send the murderer back!"

One by one, the others join in.

In that instant, I understand the phrase *crime of passion*. Because right now, I am passionately seething. At the scraggly man in the scarf and a bearded mountain man in a ten-gallon hat and a woman in Coke-bottle glasses and a guy with ridiculous fur earmuffs, all repeating Tanya's words as if by rote. But especially, I'm seething at Tanya.

Because anyone who would desecrate a man's last weeks with hate-filled protests in the name of God wouldn't think twice about defiling that man's property with graffiti.

I step right up in front of Tanya, screaming above her chant. "Do your Pentecostal pals know about you?"

She cuts off midword, putting a screeching stop to the "angry protest" record, and the hand clutching the bullhorn drops to her side. "Don't you dare."

I turn to the first camera lens I see. "Tanya McNeal wasn't awfully popular back in high school, but her right hand sure was."

Cal steps up behind me, reaches for my sleeve. "Let's go."

I wrench my arm from his grip, speak loud and strong into the camera. "Until she and her hand got expelled, that is, for prostitution."

"Gia." It's Cal, and his tone is urgent. "Inside. Now."

I pluck the bullhorn from Tanya's hand, flip it around, punch the button and holler into the mouthpiece loud enough they hear me clear to Church Hill. "That's right, y'all. The preacher's wife was a whore."

The protesters give a collective gasp.

"Oh, man." A guy with a puffy coat and an iPhone aimed at my head nudges the person next to him. "I'm gonna upload the shit out of this."

I flip him a bird. "Upload this, asshole."

Tanya's mouth scrunches into an ugly squiggle, and she

draws a deep breath. "Let the wicked forsake their ways and the unrighteous their thoughts. Let them turn to the Lord, and He will have mercy on them."

I snort. "Whatever that means."

"It means I've been born again." She smiles kindly, sweetly, but I'm not fooled. I remember the real Tanya, and she wasn't half that nice. "It means Jesus Christ has washed away my sins, and I've been forgiven."

I speak into the bullhorn. "Good for you, Tanya, but tell me. How does Jesus Christ feel about your inability to forgive others?"

She blinks, and her smile plummets.

"That's what I thought." I shove the bullhorn into her arms, turn and stomp past a chuckling Cal back up the drive.

"That wasn't the dumbest thing you've ever done, baby girl," he says, catching up to me on the top step of the porch, "but it was pretty damn close."

"I know, I know." I stop at the door and lean against the siding, shoving my fists into my coat pockets. "But some things needed to be said."

He pulls a toothpick from his molars, twirls it between his fingers. "Like that bit about the preacher's wife being a whore?"

"Especially that part."

Cal pops the stick back into his cheek and grins. "And here I thought Lexi inherited all the Andrews family spunk."

I wriggle the phone from my back pocket and slide a thumb across the screen. "Well, then, stick around. Because I'm calling Jimmy, and somebody goddamn well better be arrested."

From inside, Dad's laugh, a dry *heh-heh-heh,* floats through the windowpane. "She can stay."

As it turns out, no one gets arrested. No one gets so much as a slap on their spray-paint-wielding wrist. Until I can prove someone trespassed on private property to commit vandalism, Jimmy claims his hands are tied.

"I kind of assumed the graffiti was proof of the trespassing and the vandalism." I don't bother to disguise the sarcasm seeping from my voice. My veins are still hot with adrenaline, and I have to take my frustration out on someone.

"Did you identify anyone trespassing on your property?"

I don't answer, which Jimmy takes as one.

"Look, Gia. I'm sorry they're there, I really am, but call me back as soon as you see anyone crossing the property line. I'll be there with sirens blazing."

"That'll sure be helpful when the Molotov cocktails start flying." And then I think of something else. "Arrest Tanya McNeal, then. She has a bullhorn."

Jimmy sighs, long and deep. "C'mon, Gia. You know I can't arrest her for a bullhorn, but I can come down there and give her a stern dressin'-down. Would that make you feel better?"

"I guess," I tell him after a long moment, even though I don't. I don't feel any better at all.

Cal isn't much help, either. After an hour-long soliloquy about the difference between direct and circumstantial evidence, he wheels his weekend suitcase out the door and heads back to his flavor-of-the-month in Knoxville.

After he's gone, Dad asks Fannie for more morphine then promptly conks out. With nothing more to do, I collapse on the couch.

"Now what?" I say to Fannie. It's sometime past seven, and the best thing I can say about the day is that the rain has finally chased the protesters home.

She twists to face me, her face suddenly solemn. "Now we have some serious issues to discuss."

I catch her meaning instantly. All weekend long, I've been tiptoeing around her, bending over backward to help around the house, offering her coffee or cookies or a smile. Now, though, she deserves an apology.

"I feel so crappy for ditching you Friday night, for leaving you here to deal with Dad all by yourself. It was selfish of me, and I won't do it ever again, I swear. I'm here 24/7 from now on."

My heart kicks at what my self-imposed house arrest means for Jake and me, but I reprimand myself. Spending time with my dying father is far more important than with a man I barely know, no matter how talented his hands.

But Fannie doesn't seem to think so. She makes a face like she just bit into a June apple. "I'm gonna say this as nice as I know how, sugar, but you gotta go."

It takes me a few beats to realize she, like Dad, doesn't want me here. "What?"

"I don't know how much longer I can stand you moping around this house. It's about to make me lose every last bit of my stuffin'." When she catches the look of offense on my face, she pats my hand. "Nothing personal, sugar. But this girl needs some alone time every now and then."

"But where would I go?" I say, even though I know the answer. Even though I'm already thinking about where I left my keys.

Her strawberry lips curl up in a grin. "I'm sure you'll find somewhere."

I think both of us know I already have.

And then I remember what started this conversation. "What were the serious issues you wanted to discuss?"

Her face fills with confusion. "The serious...? Oh, that." Fannie gestures to the TV, still dark and silent on the wall unit across from us. "*Amazing Race* or *Celebrity Apprentice?*"

I smile, push to a stand. "That's easy. *Amazing Race,* even though I could kick every one of their asses. I once made it from Cairo to Cape Town, over land by the way, in a month and on a hundred dollars."

Fannie punches a button on the remote and shoos me toward the door. "Just bring me back some of that venison chili, wouldja?"

18

The next few days progress something like this: Bo blocks my number and Lexi tells me she liked me better when I lived in Africa; Jake and I explore the challenging world of bar-stool sex. Dad wakes up moaning and Fannie ups his morphine to nearly fatal proportions; Jake and I are almost arrested for public indecency while parking at Burem Lake Dam. My YouTube fame peaks at a hundred thousand views; Jake and I duck into a roadside Arby's bathroom for a particularly rough go that ends in bruises and scratch marks and love bites. It's like the worse things get at home, the more I can't get enough of Jake.

For me, Jake is like a minivacation from the stress of Rogersville. When floodwaters rise or locusts attack or volcanoes threaten to spew lava and ash, he is a welcome distraction from the impending doom. He makes me forget the end is near. He gives me a bubble of happiness in my chest that I think will never burst, until it does, when I walk through my front door.

I will admit that the dichotomy of my life here feels a little schizophrenic, like there are two distinctly different

Gias. Dad Gia feels trapped and claustrophobic, like she's hiding in a place she doesn't want to be, being hunted by people who hate her for something she didn't do. Jake Gia is the polar opposite—the puppy hanging her head out the car window, ears flapping, tail wagging, not caring where she's going, as long as it's away from here.

The only question now is, which Gia is me?

On Thursday night, I awake to a swishing sound.

The house is dark and quiet. The kind of dark and quiet it can only be in the middle of a winter night in the middle-of-nowhere, Tennessee. Somewhere in the distance, a train rattles and rumbles through the frozen hillside, but otherwise the silence is piercing.

Except for the gentle swish, swish, swishing.

I crawl across the bed to the window and peer onto the front yard. The protesters are gone, but there, under the streetlight at the very end of the driveway, is Jake's truck. Empty and dark. I stuff my feet into my fake Ugg boots, wrap the down comforter around my shoulders and sneak into the hallway.

Even after all these years, creeping down the stairs without waking my sleeping father feels like second nature. Hug the wall at the top. Avoid the squeaky spot halfway down. Take a giant stride over the Persian at the bottom. I glance into the living room, where my father softly snores, and slip out the front door into the night.

Jake's face glows under a supermoon and a zillion stars. He looks surprised to see me, but no more surprised than I am at the paintbrush in his hand. He gives me a guilty smile, and then he shrugs.

I step back and check the house, still shiny and wet where he painted it pale, creamy yellow. The exact shade of the siding. Beneath the gleaming paint, those awful words—Die, Murderer—are now only a vague shadow.

"How did you know the color?"

"I stopped by earlier for a chip." His voice is a wisp of a whisper, but I hear him just fine. He dips his brush in the can by his boot and returns to the siding. "I think it's going to need a few coats. There's water if you want it."

I shuffle to the edge of the porch by the stairs, pluck a bottle from the paper bag, twist it open. The cold liquid does nothing to wash down the sudden lump. A lump so sweet it hurts, literally aches, in my chest. Not the same ache I have when my father writhes in pain, or when Lexi told me she'd given up on wishing he were innocent. This ache is the good kind. Buoyant, like there's a secret smile tucked just behind it.

"They'll only paint it again tomorrow." Thank God I'm whispering, because I'm certain my voice would fail me.

"Then so will I."

I slide my back down the railing until I'm sitting, tucking the comforter around my bare legs. "But why? You don't even know my father."

Jake turns and smiles like it's a silly question. Like I should know the answer. And then he goes back to painting.

I watch him work for a while in silence, thinking back to the last time someone offered me a gift so beautiful. A gold locket from my father and Ella Mae on my sixteenth birthday. A bouquet of wildflowers, mismatched and wilted but handpicked by my first love. A homemade card from a four-year-old boy I pulled—literally and with my own hands—from the rubble. None of them come even close.

Jake's gift sinks into my brain and my heart, imprinting both. It is the single most generous thing anyone has ever given me, and Jake, painting in the dark with no witnesses, gave it to me without even trying.

The universe works in tricky ways. Maybe Jake is its way of throwing me a bone.

"Jake?"

He glances at me over his shoulder, his brush never missing a stroke.

"If I forget to tell you later, thank you."

Jake turns now, brows dipped. "Why would you forget to tell me?"

"Because once I get you in that truck of yours, I plan to forget all my manners."

He nods thoughtfully. "Promise?"

"I do."

"Well, then." He turns back to the wall, but not before I catch a flash of white teeth. "I better hurry."

Somehow we make it all the way to the four-way stop before Jake slams his truck into Park, shoves the seat back as far as it will go and pulls me onto him. As far as hottest places to get it on go, Jake's cab is not the most comfortable, but there's something about the image of his truck, steamed up and rocking in the middle of a country road, that's wildly erotic. Jake seems to think so, too, judging by the way he barely pauses to recover before guiding my hips into another steady rhythm, slower this time.

Afterward, he pushes back my hair, planting a row of kisses along my jawline. "I had a secret fantasy you slept nude, but that little tank top of yours is a damn close second."

I glance down at my thin white shirt, now twisted and damp with sweat. "Does that mean you want me to take it off?"

Jake shakes his head. "I want to take it off. Slowly, and preferably in a place where there's central heating and a bed."

I blow out an exaggerated sigh. "You'll never be a good country boy if you don't learn to love your truck more."

"I love my truck." He pulls me to him for another quick kiss. "Especially with you in it."

I giggle and roll off, reaching for the comforter and my panties, both in a heap on the cab floor. Jake fastens his jeans and cranks the engine, and the vents spew frigid air at my head. I bounce around for a bit, shrieking for him to turn it off. He drapes the comforter over both of us instead, pulling me tight up against him, and guns the gas until the heater kicks into gear. A few minutes more, and the cab is warm and the windows clear.

"So now what?" I ask. I'm so not ready to go back to the house.

Jake reaches around my shoulder for the gearshift, works it down a few notches. "Now we go for a ride."

I check the clock on the dash. "But it's after three in the morning."

"So?" He flicks on the radio, pulls into the intersection, swings his truck away from town. "You have anywhere else you need to be?"

"No." I don't even have anywhere else I want to be.

"Good. 'Cause it seems like a nice night for a drive."

I slip my hand across his waist, snuggle against his shoulder. "I take it all back, Jake. You are an excellent country boy."

For the next few hours, we drive aimlessly over dark streets, winding up hillsides and coasting down into valleys, over train tracks and potholes and dirt roads. We talk about everything and nothing, about weather and food and our childhoods. Jake tells me, in between a story about his first real girlfriend and a new supplier of venison he found in one of the Carolinas, about some of the places he's lived, and I intersperse my anecdotes about Bo and Lexi with how I lost my mother and found another in Ella Mae. Jake points out the house he's thinking of buying, a fixer-upper by the river, and I show him where I crashed my first car, Ella Mae's hand-me-down Chevy Citation, into a tree. Neither of us seems in a hurry to get anywhere special, and neither of us seems to mind the occasional silences.

At sometime around seven, when the first of the morning pink slashes the sky, Jake steers the truck into a fast-food drive-through. If the attendant finds anything unusual about the half-dressed girl wrapped in a comforter attached to his hip, she doesn't show it. She simply smiles, hands us our coffee and a ridiculous amount of food in exchange for just under twelve dollars, and wishes us a nice day.

"Seriously?" I peer into the giant bag on my lap, stuffed full with paper-wrapped sandwiches and breakfast platters stuffed into cardboard containers. "Twelve dollars for all this? This can't all be food."

"Sure it is." Jake pulls into a parking spot at the far end of the lot and digs a sausage biscuit out of the bag. "Genuine processed animal parts mixed with artificial fillers and genetically manipulated corn sugars. Try it. It's the food equivalent of crack cocaine, so good."

I open one of the larger containers and gape at the steaming mound—pancakes buried under scrambled eggs, sausage patties and hash browns. Enough to feed a dozen kids for an entire day in Africa.

I poke the eggs with a plastic fork, a familiar frustration flaming in my belly.

"I know these fast-food chains do good work with their

charities and all, but with their buying power they should really be tackling world hunger. I bet if they pooled together, they could feed the entire third world for half of what it costs us to feed Dadaab alone."

Jake swallows, wipes his mouth with the back of a hand. "I think they're too busy exploiting those third world countries to care about their starving population."

"Exploiting how?"

"Cutting down their forests, using their land to grow grain for cattle, depressing their wages for cheap labor." Jake swipes a hash brown from my container. "Those charities are only a distraction tactic."

My stomach turns, and I flip the lid on the container and lower it, uneaten, back into the bag.

Jake notices, and he looks down at his half-eaten sandwich. "Oh, Jesus. I'm one of those clueless Americans who's part of the problem instead of the solution, aren't I?"

"It's not your fault. I've just seen too much, watched too many people die of starvation." I sigh, try to shake it off. "I'm sorry, I don't mean to preach. It's sometimes hard for me to balance the poverty of that world with the wasted wealth in this one."

"No, no. I'm a dick, and you're totally right." He rewraps what's left of his sandwich, crumples it into a ball and drops it back into the bag, and then he swings the truck out of the lot and into early-morning traffic.

"Where are we going?"

"You'll see."

When he whizzes past my neighborhood a few minutes later I'm a little surprised, even more so when he pulls onto a dirt road almost completely overgrown with brush.

"Hold on," he says, and it's a good thing I do. The cab plunges into darkness, then hurtles and jostles us around like a county fair ride. I cover my ears at the piercing squeals of branches and sticks tearing down the sides of his truck bed. Moments later we emerge, in a clearing just big enough for the double-wide parked in its middle.

Jake winks at me, reaches for the bag of food. "Be right back."

I watch him jog to the door and dig under a cinder block for the key, which he uses to slip inside. The cab feels cold and empty without him, and I pull the comforter higher over my chest. Less than a minute later, he slides back into the cab and hurls the truck into Reverse, tossing me another wink.

"When old Otis wakes up, he won't let that food go to waste. He's skinnier than a telephone pole, but the man can eat."

I look over at Jake, and something squeezes, warm and tight, in the pit of my stomach. Painting my house, bringing old Otis and who knows who else food. This man is a blue-ribbon prize, and I feel like I'm the winner.

We're barely at the edge of the clearing when I wrap a leg over his lap and climb on. Jake hits the brakes, skates his hands from the wheel to my waist.

"I like you, Jake Foster. I like you a lot."

Maybe even more than a lot.

"You're likely to have me starve to death, Gia Andrews, but the feeling is mutual."

I lean forward, touch the side of his neck with my tongue and whisper, "Do you think old Otis is awake yet?"

Jake's fingers tighten around my middle. "If he is, he'll be more interested in the food."

"Okay, but this might take a while." I nibble on his earlobe, slip my fingers under the hem of his T-shirt. "And I'll probably be loud."

I feel his grin against my shoulder and his right thigh shift underneath me, and the truck eases ten feet forward, until it's completely swallowed up in the brush.

It's close to eight by the time Fannie pulls up along-side Jake's truck in the Sulpher Springs Primitive Baptist Church parking lot, grinning like she's the one who just got serviced.

"Well, good mornin', sunshines," Fannie says through her open window. "I would ask how y'all are doing, but judging by the looks of Gia's hair I think I already know."

"Your hair is hot," Jake whispers from the side of his mouth.

Fannie lifts her hand for a high five from Jake, who flashes me an amused-apology smile before he taps her palm with his.

I slump against the seat, a hot blush blooming up my chest. Asking Fannie to meet us here this morning ranks right up there with requesting a transfer to war-ravaged Somalia. But when Jake and I pulled onto my street a half hour ago, the protesters and press were already stationed at the end of the driveway. The image of me and my bed head, hopping in my blanket and skivvies out of his truck, was something neither of us wanted to see flashing across the 65-inch plasma above Roadkill's bar.

Jake leans an arm out the open window like it's mid-June, and not February and freezing outside. "How are you, Fannie? Haven't seen you in Roadkill for a while."

"On account of I've been working like a dog, trying to recoup what that rat bastard Lester stole from me. But I tell you what. I'd quit tomorrow for some more of that wild boar ravioli."

Jake smacks a palm on the outside of the driver's door. "I'll talk to the chef, see what I can do."

"You do that, sugar. Now if you two lovebirds don't mind, I'd like to get down to business. There's a sweet old man waiting on me back at the house."

Fannie hands him my jeans and coat, and he passes her the comforter. The instant frigid air hits bare skin, I snatch my jeans from Jake's lap and pull them on at the speed of sound.

"Th-th-anks."

"No problem," Fannie says. Her car inches forward, then stops. "Oh, and, Gia?"

I grit my teeth into a smile, peek at her from around Jake's shoulder.

"Your tank top's on backward."

Dammit. My arms fly to my chest, covering myself.

And then she guns the gas, and not even her tires peeling off the pavement can drown out the sound of her cackles.

Less than ten minutes later, Jake kills the engine on the street behind mine, a mere fifty-yard trek through the trees to my backyard. Even though the protesters and reporters will almost certainly see me coming up the back hill, at least this way I'll be decent, and they'll never know about Jake.

I turn on the seat to face him. "Can I ask you something?"

"Shoot."

"I realize you weren't here when Ella Mae was killed, but you have a bar. You hear things, right?"

He nods. "Mostly gossip and conjecture, but sure. I hear twenty versions of everything."

"Did you ever hear anything about an affair?"

He nods again.

"Did you ever hear a name?"

Something shutters on his face, like he heard one but doesn't want to say.

"Just tell me. Please."

"I heard a couple names, but they're all along the lines of old Otis back there. But from everything I know about Ella Mae, she was good-looking and charming and irresistible, right?"

I nod.

"Any way she could have had a fetish for a guy like Otis, a two-toothed old man with more earwax than sense?"

I giggle. "Not that I know of."

"Then I wouldn't worry too much about the crazy names I've heard. Instead, think about the men in town who were just as good-looking and charming and irresistible as Ella Mae."

Without thinking, without stopping to ask myself why, my gaze travels toward Dean Sullivan's property, to his house half-hidden behind the trees. I'll never forget the first time he walked down the halls of Cherokee High, how the entire female population—and even a few of the males—swooned. How all anybody in town could talk about was Dean's movie-star looks, Dean's northern accent, Dean's stylish city ways. Dean was good-looking and charming and irresistible. He was all of those things, and he lived right next door.

And then I remember something else. Something that shoots a shiver up my spine and slams my heart to a standstill.

I remember looking out my bedroom window one weekend afternoon, watching Dean Sullivan scurry across the lawn from our house to his, tucking in his shirt. I remember Ella Mae's frantic fluster at finding me ten seconds later in the upstairs hallway, when she'd thought I was at the movies, not napping in my room. I remember her furtive, almost feverish looks that night at supper, searching me for knowledge I didn't know I had.

I was too young and naive and self-absorbed then to see the signs.

But now. Now I see them. Now I understand.

Jake says something, jiggles my arm. "Did you hear me?"

I shake my head. I didn't hear anything.

"I need to tell you something. I wasn't completely honest with you before, when I told you how I ended up here in Rogersville." He scrubs a hand over his cheek, hauls a breath deep enough to reach his toes, blows it all out. "Jeez, this is so much harder than I thought. Okay, so the thing is… I didn't come here by accident. I came because…well, what I haven't told you is that I was—"

"Jake, I want to hear this, I really do." I'm already scooting to the passenger door, yanking on the handle. "But I gotta go."

And then I'm off, tearing out of his cab and through the trees and up the hill, bursting through the front door and past Dad and a grinning Fannie, flying over the fake Persian and up the stairs to the scrap of paper I know is tucked in the inside pocket of my suitcase.

The one with Jeffrey Levine's number.

I don't need a professor of law to tell me what my memory could mean for Dad's case. That if it's true, if Dean was having an affair with Ella Mae, that gives him motive. Motive to lie on the stand. Motive to point the finger at my father.

Maybe even motive for murder.

19

Ella Mae Andrews, December 1993

The morning after Ella Mae's birthday night on the town, she stared out the kitchen window at Dean's dark house while she waited for the coffee to brew. The sky was barely pink with the new day and the rest of her family was still tucked in their beds upstairs, but Ella Mae couldn't sleep. Hadn't slept at all last night.

She couldn't stop thinking about Dean.

Ella Mae hadn't been particularly surprised at seeing him at the Main Street Grille—the bigger surprise would've been not running into him in a town as small as Rogersville—nor at her body's reaction to him. They'd been sleeping together for over two months now, and she'd almost gotten used to the way heat shot through her veins whenever he was near. Last night was only the first time her body had been quicker than her eyes.

But the reason she hadn't slept was because last night was also the first time she'd felt even the slightest stab of guilt.

The only problem was, Ella Mae didn't know who her guilt was for. She'd done wrong by Ray, that much was certain, but as she took her husband's hand and sailed past her lover at the bar, Ella Mae couldn't shake the feeling that the person she was cheating on was not Ray but Dean.

A light flipped on across the frozen lawn, and Ella Mae's skin began to tingle. She gripped the counter and waited. Two seconds later Dean appeared in his living room window, just as she knew he would. A look of surprise flashed across his face when he saw her, then dissolved into something dark and far more serious, something that made Ella Mae's chest feel even heavier.

He put a hand to his ear, the universal sign for telephone, and she nodded. A phone call this early in the morning might wake the entire house, Ella Mae knew, but she also didn't care. As of today she'd gone ten days without hearing Dean's voice, and withdrawal was making her reckless.

She answered halfway through the first ring. "Dean."

His reply was sharp, his voice low and angry. "Did you fuck him?"

Ella Mae's breath left her body in a rush, and her caffeine-deprived mind struggled to catch up.

"Did you fuck him?"

"Who, Ray?"

"Yes, Ray. Or are you fucking someone else now, too?"

"What? Of course not. Only you."

"So did you fuck him?"

"I..." Panic zinged up her spine. Of course she'd had sex with Ray. He was her husband, and yesterday was her birthday. She didn't have any other choice. "I had to, Dean."

A long silence while Dean took that in. "Did he make you come?"

Ella Mae closed her eyes, and her voice was barely a whisper. "No."

"Good." He paused until she opened her eyes, his gaze

lasered onto hers across the frozen grass. "I'm the only one allowed to do that."

She nodded.

His voice softened into a croon, smooth and low and so damn sexy, and good Lord, lust for him hit her like a pharmaceutical. She would do anything to please this man.

"I want to make you come now."

Ella Mae nodded again. She wanted that, too.

"Do it."

"Do..." She thought she knew the answer, but still. She had to ask. "Do what?"

His answer made Ella Mae gasp, as much from shock as from desire. He told her to loosen the tie on her robe, and she did. He told her to push aside the fabric so he could see, and she did. Dean's instructions were exact and explicit and erotic, and she followed them to the very letter while he watched from thirty feet away.

Apparently, she would even please herself in order to please this man.

"Good girl," he said when she was done.

Ella Mae tightened her robe back around her body. She didn't feel like a good girl. What if Allison had looked out the upstairs window and seen her? What if Ray or Gia had picked up the phone? Ella Mae felt shocked and guilty and kind of dirty.

And then he said something that thudded her heart to a standstill.

"You're mine, Ella Mae. You belong to me."

Christmas came and went. Lexi and Bo returned from college in a flurry of Christmas presents and dirty laundry, and the phone didn't stop ringing. Every time Ella Mae heard its incessant trill, her heart thudded to a stop, held there for a bit, then kick-started into overdrive. Surely Dean wouldn't risk calling with this many people in the house? And surely she didn't want him to?

Oh, but she did. She so did. Every time the phone rang, Ella Mae held her breath, waiting, hoping. She told herself she didn't want Dean to call, but she couldn't deny her disappointment when the caller wasn't him. And that made her feel guilty, which in turn made her angry. The emotions looped and curled in her belly until she made herself sick, literally sick, with worry.

And then, finally, on the very last day of the year, he called.

Ella Mae was at the kitchen sink, her hands elbow-deep in soapy water when the phone rang. "Get that, would you?" she said to Lexi, who was painting her nails at the kitchen table.

"But my nails are wet."

Ella Mae turned back to her dishes. By now Lexi had alerted every friend in a fifty-mile radius she was home, and they'd been calling all damn day. If Lexi didn't care enough to answer, then neither did Ella Mae.

"Ella Mae!"

She scrubbed at a plate. "What? It's for sure not for me."

Lexi made a frustrated sound in her throat and lunged at the wall phone. "Hello?" She paused to give Ella Mae a told-you-so look. "Yes, she's right here. One sec." She stretched the cord over to the sink and rolled her eyes. "Thought it wasn't for you."

Ella Mae took the receiver with a dripping hand and cradled it under her ear. "Hello?"

She knew it was Dean by the way her cheek burned before the first word came down the line. "Pretend I'm Brad from the Historical Association."

"Oh." Her heart plunged to her toes at the same time her nipples peaked. Damn that man, and damn her body's reaction to him. She glanced over her shoulder at Lexi, starting in on a second coat of hot pink on a thumbnail, and turned back to the window. Thirty feet away, Dean looked back at her from his living room. "Hi, Brad."

"That red sweater is hot. I want to rip it off."

"Um, thanks."

"With my teeth."

She squirmed against the counter, but not from nerves. "Merry Christmas to you, too, Brad."

"And I can think of all sorts of fun things to do with that soapy water."

She gasped a tiny breath, her insides tingling. "Like what?"

He told her what, and she had to grip the countertop to keep from falling into a puddle on the kitchen floor. "You like that, do you?"

Ella Mae hummed out a yes. She liked it. She liked it a lot.

"I'm going crazy over here. I have to see you. Now."

Ella Mae still had a million things to do before the Rotary party tonight. Straighten up the house, wash her hair, iron her little black dress and she promised Gia she'd help with her makeup. None of that mattered, because Ella Mae was going crazy over here, too. "Where?"

"Meet me at the hotel at exit 23 in twenty minutes. Can you do that?"

Ella Mae yanked on the plug to drain the sink. "I sure can."

"Good girl. And, Ella Mae?"

She looked out the window, sought out his gaze. "Yes, Brad?"

"If you wear that necklace Ray gave you, I'll rip it off your neck and flush it down the toilet."

Less than three minutes later, Ella Mae and her bare neck were flying up the hill in her car, an addict in search of a fix.

20

It takes more than one person to make a lie—one to say it, and another to believe it. But when the person who says it is well-known and respected, more than one person listens. When that same person lays his hand on the Bible and swears before judge and jury that his lie is nothing but the truth so help him God, more than one person believes.

Sixteen years ago, Dean Sullivan, high-school vice principal and most-talked-about man in town, pointed a finger at my father in a court of law and accused him of breaking into his own house the night Ella Mae was killed. The small-town, small-minded citizens of Rogersville hadn't seen that much excitement since 1916, when the idiots over in Erwin hung an elephant, and they gobbled Dean up. The hand-selected members of the jury took one look at his résumé and believed his every word. Dean might as well have testified he saw Dad wrap the saran wrap around her mouth and nose himself. Even Dad's own kids were willing to accept the possibility he killed Ella Mae Andrews, just because Dean Sullivan said so.

Only now I know Dean had reason to lie. Did he lie because he was a jealous or scorned lover, to punish Dad for someone else's murder? Did Dean lie to protect his own marriage, to keep his wife, Allison, from discovering the affair? Or were his reasons more sinister? What if Dean was the killer? What if he murdered Ella Mae because she wanted to break things off, or confess the affair to their spouses? Pointing the finger at an innocent man would serve as an excellent alibi.

My stomach feels like there's a fist in it. Jake may have sparked my memory, but he did so sixteen years too late. Too late to save my father from all the finger-pointing and allegations, from losing his job and family and position in society, from sixteen years in prison. Because Dad never, never would have been found guilty if even a wisp of a rumor of improprieties between the victim and the prosecution's star witness had come out. Sixteen years—what a fucking waste.

New questions roll through my mind. How long had Dean and Ella Mae been sleeping together? Were they in love? Was Ella Mae planning on leaving Dad for Dean? Or did Ella Mae choose to stay with Dad? Did she try to break things off with Dean? Did Dad ever find out about the affair?

No. There's no way Dad knew Ella Mae was cheating on him with Dean. Cal would have destroyed Dean on the stand, and Dad would have never been convicted.

But I knew. Somewhere deep in the tucks and folds of my brain, I knew. I just didn't ever understand until today.

The most important question now is, what am I going to do about it?

I begin with Uncle Cal. I perch on the edge of my bed, scroll until I find his number in my phone and pray a call this early doesn't give me another funeral to plan.

Cal picks up on the second ring, his voice croaky and thick. "What's wrong? Is Ray all right?"

"Dad's fine. Well...not fine, but he's not any worse, either."

He releases a sharp breath, then clears the sleep from his throat. "You scared the living daylights out of me, child."

"I know, I know, and I'm sorry. But what I have to tell you couldn't wait." I pause to make sure my next words carry the appropriate weight. "Ella Mae was sleeping with Dean Sullivan."

The line goes still for so long I wonder if Cal has passed out from shock.

"Did you hear me, Cal? She was sleeping with Dean."

Cal's voice turns from concerned brother to businesslike lawyer fast enough to leave skid marks. "And you know this how?"

"Because I remembered something. Something that didn't really make sense to me at the time, but it sure does now. I remember Dean leaving the house, in the middle of the day when I wasn't supposed to be home. Ella Mae freaked when I came out of my room ten minutes later, and she looked at me funny for days."

"What else?"

"What do you mean, what else?" I turn and look out my window, the same window as all those years ago, and the scene replays itself in my memory. Dean hustling across the yard, straightening his clothes in the middle of the afternoon. The look of guilty surprise on Ella Mae's face upon finding me in the hall, only minutes later. What other reason could there be? "They'd just had sex. I'm positive of it."

"Was either of them naked?"

"No. But their clothes were mussed."

"Did you overhear them talking about anything inappro-

priate?" Cal's using his lawyer voice on me again, a voice
I'd hate to have to face on the stand.

"No, but—"

"Did you ever catch them kissing or holding hands?"

Frustration heats my skin, and I pop off the bed. "Cal,
stop interrogating me! I saw what I saw. Dean was buck-
ling his belt and fixing his shirt, and Ella Mae was all wild-
eyed and flustered. What else could it be?"

"Well, it could be a million different things." Cal's tone
has cooled by a thousand degrees, and I hear a new note
in it, one that sounds strangely like relief. "Maybe he'd
just used the bathroom, or ate a big lunch. The point is, we
don't know for sure."

I sink back onto the bed, and my gaze travels to the
run-down hovel across the lawn. "Dean Sullivan knows."

"There's not a soul in all of Hawkins County who'd believe a word that man says nowadays."

The irony hits me in the gut. When Dean lied, he was
Rogersville's VIP, and we all believed him without doubt.
If he told the truth now, now that he's become the crazy
town drunk, who would listen?

"Okay, then—I know." I sit up straighter and square my
shoulders, certain. "I know that Ella Mae and Dean were
having an affair. I'd lay my hand on a Bible and swear to
it. Think what that would mean for Dad's case."

Cal makes a scoffing sound in his throat. "What case?
My office has buried the D.A. in so much paperwork, he
can't see the forest for all the red tape. By the time he digs
himself out, it'll be too late for another trial."

"But the star witness was sleeping with the victim, which
meant he had about a thousand reasons to lie on the stand.
To deflect attention from himself. To get revenge. To keep
his own ass out of jail for murder. What if he pointed the

finger at Dad because Dean was the one who came for Ella Mae that night? Dad spent sixteen years in prison for nothing!"

Cal heaves a swollen sigh. "Look, baby girl, I understand your frustration. It's the same frustration I've been feeling for all these years. But honestly, the sudden return of your memory doesn't change a goddamn thing. There's not going to be another trial, and people are still gonna think your father is guilty of a crime he didn't commit."

"But they wouldn't if they knew the truth."

He grunts. "What are you gonna do, go door to door?"

"No, but what if I went to CNN? They'd—"

"No, Gia! No reporters. Your father only wants to die in peace, and I won't have an even bigger media circus adding to the chaos already on the front lawn. You will not go spouting off to any reporters about this. Do you understand?"

I pluck Jeffrey Levine's card from between a fold in my comforter. "But what about—"

"No! I mean it, Gia. No reporters." When I don't respond, he adds, "I want to hear you promise."

I look at the card in my hand and puff a breath. "Fine. Whatever." I brush my thumb over the words under Jeffrey's name. Professor of Law. "No reporters, I promise."

"Good. And I don't want you putting the possibility of an affair in your father's head, either. The idea of Ella Mae stepping out on him would break his heart."

I suddenly remember Dad's words to me the day he came home—*the only crime I ever committed was loving Ella Mae more than she loved me.* If Dad doesn't know about Dean and Ella Mae, I'm certainly not going to be the one to tell him.

Cal misreads my silence as rancor. "Do not go putting

ideas about Ella Mae's infidelity in your father's head. Okay?"

"I won't. I won't say anything."

"Look, baby girl. The only people who need to know the truth are the ones who should've known Dean Sullivan was lying on the stand in the first place. You, and your brother and sister. Everybody else in Rogersville can go to hell as far as I'm concerned. You kids are the only ones who matter."

I hear the hidden accusation behind his words, that I shouldn't have needed proof of Dean's lie to believe in my father's innocence, and it strikes me that Cal is right. How could I have believed Dean Sullivan, a man I barely even knew, over my own father? Dad never raised a hand to me or my siblings or Ella Mae. He loved us, and he worshipped Ella Mae. How could I have ever thought him capable of murdering her?

A new certainty melts through my body and solidifies, and something inside me clicks. That's the only way I know how to explain it, that it clicks, and becomes unstuck. I may not ever know why, exactly, Dean Sullivan lied to police, but I am positive of one thing.

My father did not kill Ella Mae.

Four hours later, I'm seated across from Jeffrey Levine at a Perkins all the way over in Colonial Heights, a sleepy little town thirty-five miles from the prying ears of Rogersville. The restaurant is packed with a blue-haired, dentured lunch crowd, but on a positive note, Jeffrey and I don't have to worry about lowering our voices. The folks in this place couldn't hear us with a bullhorn.

"Did you ever hear anything about Ella Mae having an affair?"

Jeffrey looks up from his Kickin' Chicken special and nods. "Sure. Who hasn't?"

"I would've thought you'd be more worried. An affair couldn't be good for the case."

Jeffrey lifts his shoulders in a no-big-deal shrug. "Depends on who it was with. But the point, as they say, is moot. The D.A. is posturing. If he had any evidence at all, he would've flooded the media by now. Not even the gossip rags are buying it."

My stomach twists but not from the last bite of my burger staring at me from my plate. I take a sip of my Coke and swallow it down, along with the guilt pushing up my throat. "But what if I told you I remembered something?"

He snorts like he thinks I'm joking. "I really wish you wouldn't. My editor will go through the freaking roof."

I sit silently, waiting while he drags a French fry through a puddle of ketchup on his plate, pops it in his mouth and chews. That's when he notices I'm not laughing, and the realization hits. He swallows with an audible gulp, and everything about him falls still. And then he leans back in the green vinyl seat and scrubs a hand through those silly bangs.

"Okay." He blows out a long breath, pushes away his plate. "Well, the sudden return of your memory would mean a hellish amount of revisions on my end, but honestly, my problem is the least of your worries. An affair would also be really, really bad news for your father."

"Because it would give him motive."

Jeffrey lets my last word buzz in the air between us like a swarm of agitated yellow jackets for a moment, then nods once. "Exactly. Which would make me have to re-examine the entire premise of what I'm trying to say about this case. No matter what, Cal's defense would still be a debacle, but

I guess the number of revisions would depend on who the affair was with. Do you remember that, too?"

I squirm on my seat. "Yes."

"I see." Jeffrey leans an elbow on the table and thinks for a bit. "Well, your evasiveness tells me one of two things. Either you want something from me in return for this information, or Ella Mae's lover must have been a doozy." His eyes widen to almost comical proportions, and he grins so hard I think his lips may crack. "Holy balls, if you tell me it was Cal, I might just get down on one knee and propose."

Given the context, I try not to smile too broadly at either his expression or his exclamation. Why couldn't my college professors ever be this entertaining?

"Put your ring away. It wasn't Cal."

"Who then?"

"I believe you called him a doozy."

Jeffrey thunks both forearms on either side of his plate and leans so far over, the table teeters under his weight. "The judge? The prosecutor? A witness?"

At his last guess, a jolt of something electric sweeps through my veins. I produce the barest lift of a shoulder.

Jeffrey is smart, I'll give him that. It takes him all of a millisecond to do the math. The realization slams him back onto his seat and sobers his expression more thoroughly than ten double espressos. "Sweet Jesus," he whispers, his face flush with astonishment. "Dean Sullivan?"

I don't move, not even to breathe, and I don't blink for a good five seconds.

Unlike Cal, Jeffrey believes me immediately, and he understands what my uncle didn't even attempt to grasp. "You can't blame yourself, you know. We don't always have control over what we remember when. Especially if that memory is painful, which this one clearly was."

The sympathy softening his voice slams me like a mallet, snatching my breath and flooding my eyes with tears. Cal was too busy trying to talk me out of my memory to think what I must be feeling—guilt and pain and regret and anger, coiling and tangling in my chest until I can barely breathe. But not Jeffrey. I bite my lip and look away, my gaze falling on the geriatric couple at the next table.

Jeffrey reaches across the plates and gives my hand a gentle squeeze. "Gia, listen to me. Don't beat yourself up, okay? The mind is a complex and tricky thing, and sometimes your unconscious uses memory as a coping mechanism. You don't remember things you're not ready to face, so stop blaming yourself."

I think of Ella Mae, a woman I loved as a mother, sleeping with a man who was not her husband. I think of Dean, and how his repulsive lies sent a man to prison. And I think of how somewhere tucked away deep inside, I knew all along that Dean was lying.

How can I not blame myself?

I swipe at a tear and turn back to Jeffrey, willing myself to refocus. We don't have that much time. "I appreciate your concern for the sorry state of my conscience, but what I really need is your help."

He manages to look genuinely surprised. "Apparently, you've forgotten the gist of my book. It's about wrongful convictions, remember? What other help could I possibly offer?"

"The faster kind. Dad's not going to last much longer, and I want him to be around when this story hits."

Jeffrey leans back, resting an arm over the back of the booth, and studies me for a long moment. "Let me get this straight. You're giving me the affair with Dean in exchange for a quick turnaround?"

"On one condition. You can't mention news of the affair came from me. Dad doesn't know, and he'll be devastated. I can't do that to him on top of..." My words dissolve into a shrug. "But feel free to snoop around, ask people. Maybe somebody else will remember something."

"I'll start with Allison Sullivan."

I half nod, half shrug. "You'll have to find her first. She disappeared after the trial."

"I'll find her. And after your father's death?"

It doesn't take me long to consider my answer. After Dad's gone, nobody, not even Cal, will care about Ella Mae's cheating, only the implications of who it was with. "Then I'll tell you everything I remember, and you can quote every word. Just keep me updated in the meantime, okay? And hurry."

He reaches an arm across the table, and we shake.

The waitress appears at the end of the booth, sliding the check onto the table between us. When I reach for my wallet, Jeffrey shoos my hand away.

"Oh, hell no. This one is on me." He slaps two twenties onto the table, weights them down with his empty glass. "Can I ask you something?"

I nod.

"There are about a hundred hungry journalists circling your house right now. Why me? Why not someone flashier, someone with a major news network behind them?"

"That's easy." I grab my coat and bag, slide out of the booth. "Because you were the first person other than Cal to tell me my father should have never gone to prison."

21

Even asleep, my father looks angry. Brows knitted, eyes squeezed shut, teeth clenched. His lips are scrunched into a hard line that drives both corners downward, and his hands clutch the wool blanket in tight fists atop his chest. Even his dark brown hair, now thinning above the temples, sticks out in wild, almost feral peaks on his head. He doesn't open his eyes when I approach his bed.

Neither does Fannie. Snoring softly in an armchair next to him, she naps with the wild abandon of a toddler, or perhaps a disaster aid worker on a ten-minute break. Her arms and legs are flopped wide, her mouth is hanging slack and open, and her head is thrown back against the cheap chenille fabric. Yet somehow, she makes her awkward position look comfortable.

I give her arm a shake. For someone so sound asleep, Fannie awakens with surprising clarity. She sits up and smiles.

"Why don't you go take a break," I whisper, gesturing toward my father. "I'll sit with him for a bit."

She nods, reaching fluidly for her clogs, and pushes to

a stand. "Of course, darlin'," she says in a stage whisper. "I'll just be in the kitchen, making us some tea." And then she stretches her arms to the ceiling and waddles off.

I sink into her still-warm chair and look at my father, feeling my stomach flip. I've had sixteen years of wandering the globe to distance myself mentally from him, from his constant cries of injustice and from my guilt at not believing his innocence, but for my father, the anger and resentment must still feel as fresh as when he was carted away in handcuffs.

"Oh, Daddy," I whisper. His skin is still so orange, and his body barely makes a bump under the blanket. "I'm so sorry."

"Huh?" He snorts, then cracks open an eye. "Oh, it's you."

"It's me!" I say brightly. "I thought I'd keep you company for a while."

Now both eyes open, but neither of them look particularly happy to see me. "Where's Frannie?"

Fannie, I think but bite my tongue. "Making tea in the kitchen. Doesn't that sound good?"

Dad doesn't respond, other than to look at me like he can see right through me to the wall. His narrowed gaze gives me an extra jolt of nerves. I feel my face reddening.

"You must be thirsty."

"I'm not."

I lean forward to straighten a nonexistent fold in his blanket. "When's the last time you had something to drink?"

Dad's reply is to clamp his lips, close his eyes and turn his head. He stays like that for so long my gaze drops to his chest, just to make sure his lungs are still filling and falling with breath.

"Okay, then. How about something to eat? I picked up

the ingredients for beef Stroganoff for tonight. That was always one of your favorites, right?"

"I can't eat meat," he says to the wall.

"Vegetarian stroganoff it is." I look around the room for a magazine or book. "Can I get you anything to read? Or another blanket, maybe? Are you cold?"

Now Dad opens his eyes, but only to glare at me.

"What? I'm just trying to make conversation."

"That's not conversation." He twists his lips into a sarcastic grimace. "That's triage."

"Sorry," I mumble, flushing again. I know I'm trying too hard, plugging every moment of silence with inane chatter, filling the already fraught air with my overly enthusiastic voice. Dad is clearly becoming more and more annoyed with me. His fingers twist and yank on the blanket.

But ever since that moment in the truck with Jake earlier this morning, when he jiggled loose a long-forgotten memory, I've been struggling with how to form an acceptable apology. All day long, my emotions have been dangerously close to the surface because really, what words are adequate enough for sixteen years' worth of silence? What words can convey the guilt and sorrow I feel at presuming my own father guilty? What words could possibly make him forgive me?

"Why don't you just spit it out already?" he says as if reading my thoughts.

"Of course." I straighten on the chair, my insides squirming like a bucket of night crawlers. "Okay, so here's the thing. I'm here to tell you that I'm sorry. For taking off after the trial, and for not writing or visiting you while you were in prison. And I'm sorry for disappearing the first night you were back, and all those other times since. Me not being here was more about me than about you."

Dad all but rolls his eyes. "Can I ask why this sudden change of heart?"

I chew on the inside of my cheek, stalling as I come up with a response. I gave Cal my word I wouldn't tell about Ella Mae's infidelity, which basically negates the I-know-Dean-lied portion of my argument. Besides, I'm not entirely certain a confession of my returned memory would even help my case. Dad would see right through me, would think it an attempt to take the pressure off myself and put it squarely and conveniently on Dean. No, I decide, better to keep things honest but diplomatic and vague.

"Because I feel like we have a lot of time to make up for, and not enough time to do it in. I know I haven't been here for you these past sixteen years, but I want to be here for you now. That is, if you'll let me."

"That depends." He dips his chin to his chest, looking at me through his frown in a way I remember well from childhood. "Who do you think killed Ella Mae?"

I hesitate and chill bumps sprout on every inch of my skin, but not for the reason Dad thinks. It's because before my brain can form a calculated response, my gut screams, Dean Sullivan. I think Dean Sullivan killed Ella Mae.

"Because twelve of my so-called peers thought I did," he continues, "and so did pretty much the rest of Rogersville, including my own children. Including you."

"I never, not once, said I thought you were the killer."

Dad snorts, and his hands fist tighter around the blanket. "You didn't have to. Your silence, as they say, was a helluva lot louder than those words could have ever been. Words which, by the way, you're doing a darn good job going out of your way to avoid saying now."

The way he watches me, with eyes that are both furious and hopeful at the same time, is too much. Tears burn in my eyes.

"There was a witness," he says as if I need reminding, "one who saw me breaking into my own house the night Ella Mae was murdered. Who else could it have been? Nothing was stolen. There were no valuables missing. Even Ella Mae's wedding ring was still on her finger when the police got here."

Stop, I think.

"Maybe I panicked. Maybe that person breaking in really was me, trying to cover my tracks."

I shake my head insistently, almost violently. "Stop."

Dad doesn't stop. He pushes up onto an elbow, curling his entire face into an ugly sneer. "Ella Mae was cheating on me, you know."

I startle at both his hateful tone and his revelation—so Cal lied? Dad knew about the affair? But Dad doesn't seem to notice my widened eyes, doesn't hear my pounding heart. Does he know it was with Dean?

"How Cal managed to keep that little tidbit under wraps during the trial is a goddamn miracle," he says, "but Ella Mae was cheating, and she was planning to file for divorce. So maybe we fought, and maybe things got out of hand. Maybe I would have rather seen her dead than with another man."

A shot of outrage at his goading bolts through my veins, catapulting me to the edge of my seat. "Daddy, stop! Okay? Just stop."

"Why? I'm just repeating what everybody else is saying."

A sudden lump takes root in my throat, one that takes three or four tries to swallow down. By this time next month, my father will in all likelihood be dead, so screw vague and diplomatic. Screw my promise to Cal. I opt instead for honesty. Honesty, and the words that have been sixteen years in the making.

"Because I know Dean lied, and I know with every ounce of me that you didn't do what everybody says you did. And I'm so unbelievably sorry it's taken me this long to tell you I believe you. You didn't kill Ella Mae. It's simply not possible."

It's not pure relief that swallows up his face at my words. Some relief, certainly, but so diluted with another emotion—regret, maybe?—that it's almost unrecognizable. Still, he doesn't say anything, so I plow on.

"And I shouldn't have left you like I did. Without saying goodbye or telling you where I was going. Without ever writing or visiting you in prison. Of all the things I have to be sorry for, that's the one I regret most."

His brows dip, and he searches my face for a long moment. "You're most sorry for leaving?"

I nod, a little surprised by the lack of aggression in his voice. It's the first time since I've been home he hasn't sounded bitter or resentful. In fact, his voice is devoid of any emotion at all, a development I think cannot be good.

He purses his lips and looks away, his gaze drifting to the milky sunlight streaming through the window, and my stomach twists with a wave of ill. I've waited too long. My apology is too late. And honestly, who can blame him? I wouldn't forgive me, either.

"Do you remember the first time you saw the ocean?"

Ocean? His sudden change of subject nearly knocks me off balance. I sift through my memories and manage a jerky nod. "Kind of."

"Took you to Myrtle Beach, the summer after your mother died. You'd've been about six or so. You'd seen pictures by then, of course, but none of them prepared you for that first real look." He turns back to me, his gaze locking on mine, his tone still in neutral. "You 'bout near fainted. Bo and Lexi splashed around in the waves, and you stood there with your little mouth hanging open, feet rooted in the sand, just staring and staring at the water. Do you remember what you said?"

I shake my head.

"You asked me what was on the other side."

I don't remember saying those words, exactly, but I can easily summon up another memory—of my stunned silence, of profound fascination with that great expanse of water. "That sounds like something I would've said."

"Anyway, the point I'm tryin' to make is that's when I knew. Of the three of you kids, you were always going to be the one to leave. Your sister and brother don't have that kind of curiosity. They never did. But you…" He puffs out a breath that's almost a laugh. "I swear. What six-year-old asks what's on the other side of the ocean?"

I don't share in my father's sudden levity. I can't. I'm too busy trying to sort out what Dad's anecdote might mean for my choice of career and nomadic lifestyle. "I always thought I left because of what happened."

Dad gives me a look. "What was the first thing on your Christmas list every year?"

I don't have to think, even for a second, about my answer. "A subscription to *National Geographic*." Still the best seven bucks I spend every month.

"What did you beg us for that summer Bo went to college, and every summer after?"

"An exchange student." I lift a shoulder, resurrect my age-old argument one last time. "His room was just sitting there, empty."

"And when all your friends were getting cars for their sixteenth birthday, what did you ask for?"

"A backpack and a round-the-world ticket. It took me waiting tables all through college, but I left the day after graduation."

"See?" He points a bony finger at my face. "No use fighting that kind of wanderlust. So stop beating yourself up for not staying, because I don't blame you for leaving. Especially not after..." He sighs, rolling his head back toward the window. "Besides, at least you came back."

His mouth doesn't finish the sentiment, but everything else about him does. His pinched lips, his squinty eyes, the way his entire body tenses, then goes slack and haggard. He's clearly struggling with his emotions, anger and disappointment and sorrow, barely holding it together because I came back, and Bo and Lexi didn't.

A familiar well of indignation toward my siblings bubbles up inside me at the same time I'm slammed with a giant fist of pity for my father. How can I tell him Bo and Lexi aren't in their cars around the corner, speeding this way? How can I tell him I've given up on my siblings?

But Dad must read the message from my silence. He puffs out another sigh, then closes his eyes. Before long, his breathing beats out a steady rhythm. This time, I let him sleep.

Outside, the chanting fades to a low rumble of conversation, and I walk over to the window and peek out. A car is stopped on the road, hazard lights flashing, and an overweight man in a puffy coat and mittens is passing out Starbucks cups. Funny how I've gotten so used to the chanting that I don't notice until it melts away to nothing.

Kind of like what Bo and Lexi are doing with Dad.

22

The new me doesn't leave the house for days. I channel Fannie and her efficient but caring touch, helping to assess Dad's vital signs and pain levels and record them onto a chart, trying not to notice how they seem to be moving in opposite directions. I dole out pain medicines and cajole Dad into one more bite, or when that doesn't work, refuse to let up until he sucks up every last drop of his Ensure. I wash laundry and sweep floors and do windows when Dad's asleep, and I watch TV and sweet-talk him into stilted conversations when he's awake. Neither of us bring up Bo or Lexi. Neither of us talk about Ella Mae. He doesn't tell me I'm forgiven, and I'm too afraid to ask.

Cal comes for the weekend, and Fannie and I spend most of it in the kitchen, covered in flour and butter and sugar. She shows me how to make rich yellow pastries stuffed with creamy white filling. Giant cranberry pecan muffins with clumps of raw brown sugar. A sticky sweetbread roll filled with crushed nuts and honey that was so good I ate half of it in one sitting. Between her and Jake, I've already gained seven pounds, and my jeans no longer need a belt.

We work mostly in silence, and I must admit, something about the work is soothing. Maybe it's the rhythm. The crack of an egg, the swish of a brush, the chink of a sugar shaker. Or maybe it's the way baking allows my thoughts to flow freely, like they're suddenly let loose from their cage to fly from Dad to Jake to Dean back to Jake. I think about Jake a lot these days.

And I barely ever sleep.

Jake drives over every night after closing up Roadkill, slipping like a shadow through the trees edging up to the backyard and texting me as he's coming up the porch. I let him in and lead him past a snoring Dad and up the stair-case, demonstrating how to hug the wall in order to silently step around the Persian, and which treads to skip so the squealing boards don't give us away.

Upstairs in my room, he undresses me with slow but sure hands, letting my clothing—first my sweater and T-shirt, then my jeans, followed by thin scraps of cotton and lace—flutter to the floor, each piece followed by a whisper of how much he wants me, that he's been waiting all day for this, that I'm beautiful and sweet and funny. His fingers make me forget all about Dad's fever that fluctuates any-where from nonexistent to terrifying, his violent attacks of hiccups that last for up to four hours, his increasingly hard, bloated stomach. About the escalating symptoms and de-creasing appetite and comfort levels. About the worry and dread. He loves it all away.

He lays me on the bed and cradles me in his arms, kiss-ing my forehead, the hinge of my jaw, the spot underneath my right ear, my collarbone, dipping lower and lower. I think about my job, waiting for me back in Kenya or wher-ever disaster strikes next. I think about Dad dying on his bed downstairs, tomorrow or next week or next month.

Who knows how much time Jake and I have left? I want to savor every millisecond.

"Now, Jake. Now. I need you now."

Jake complies.

Afterward, in whispered conversations under my comforter, I tell him everything. About my resurfaced memory and my guilt and the secret meeting with Jeffrey Levine. About how I've pretty much given up on Bo and Lexi. About how Cal lied about the affair, and how my father knew. About Dean Sullivan, and how I suspect his face was the last Ella Mae ever saw.

Jake seems more disgusted than surprised about Dean. "Have you told the police?"

"What for? They're not going to do anything about it. As far as they're concerned, Ella Mae's case is closed."

"Well, then, maybe your uncle can help."

I lift a noncommittal shoulder. When I confronted Cal for denying Ella Mae's affair, he spat out a brusque apology and then launched into a lengthy argument about how Ella Mae's infidelity can only make Dad look more—and not less—guilty. Even if that affair was with Dean Sullivan.

So, since I can't ask Ella Mae, I don't dare ask Dad, and I figure Cal would just as soon lie again than tell me the truth, that leaves me with just one person.

"Stay away from Dean Sullivan," Jake says, reading my mind. "If what you think happened really happened, then that man is dangerous."

"From everything I've heard, he's too drunk to be dangerous."

The pillow shifts as Jake shakes his head. "Alcohol makes people dangerous, because it makes them unpredictable. I've been around enough drunks in my life to know that booze will just as soon turn a man into a lion as a pussycat, but you can never tell which one it's going to be when you pour that first drink."

I brush his warning off with a breathy laugh. "What's he going to do? Besides throw up on my shoes, that is. Lexi says if he's not stumbling drunk, he's not conscious."

"Even so, you never know what a drunk is capable of. Do not confront the guy. It could push him over the edge."

An icy chill skitters down my spine at his warning, mostly because I've already begun to think about how, exactly, I am going to do just that—confront Dean. I'll have to somehow sneak by the circus on the front lawn to do it, but what if Jake's right? What if Dean is a violent drunk? In that case, the protesters and cameramen might serve as a good safety net. At the very least, there would be witnesses.

But Jake is still watching me, and waiting for an answer I'm not ready to give.

"Stay away from him, Gia."

Though I'm flattered by his concern, I'm not particularly swayed. I've already decided that the route to my father's redemption begins and ends with Dean Sullivan. I just haven't figured out how to get a confession out of him yet.

"I can't do that," I whisper. "Dean is the only one who knows what really happened the night Ella Mae was killed."

"Do you really think he's going to tell you?"

"Yes. No." I sigh. "I don't know, maybe if I catch him drunk enough. All I know is that for all these years, everybody's been blaming my father for Ella Mae's death. But now I remember the prosecution's star witness was sleeping with the victim. His testimony sent my father to prison for a crime he didn't commit. I have to at least try."

Jake lets my argument sink in for a bit. "When do you want to go?"

"Well, if I wait until the protesters leave, he'll have all

day to get good and loaded. So I was thinking about right before they show up, usually around seven or so."

He nods once. "We'll go as soon as it gets light."

That Jake is including himself in this adventure does not escape me. "Won't you make him nervous? What if he thinks we're ganging up on him?"

"Dean doesn't have to know I'm there. I'll hide behind a bush or something. Because think about it. If Dean's already killed once, he's certainly capable of doing it again. I don't want him coming after you without me there to stop him."

I pull back and look at him, a tiny bit miffed. "My job is one of the most dangerous jobs in the world. I've been robbed at knifepoint and gunpoint and every other point you can come up with. I've come this close to being kidnapped, raped or murdered more times than I care to count. I've faced down terrorists and militants and bandits and natural disasters of global magnitude. I think I can handle a drunk old recluse."

"Not if he comes at you with a gun."

I fall silent because, despite all my posturing, the man has a point. I've been shot before, in the upper right shoulder, and besides the experience being terrifying, it hurt like a motherfucker. It's hard to win any argument when you're on the wrong side of the barrel.

"Then I'll just have to hope he doesn't, because I'm still going."

"Then I'm going with you."

My blood pressure surges at his overprotectiveness, and my muscles and teeth clench in response. In the ears of someone who's been on her own since 1994, his statement comes across sounding much more like a requirement than a request. I scrunch my lips and look away.

Jake notices. He wraps a palm around the back of my head and brings my gaze to his, and his tone softens. "I know you're more than capable of taking care of yourself, but I would feel so much better if you would let me go over there with you. Not because I think I'm bigger or faster or stronger, but because I want to know that you're okay. Because I need to know. Please?"

My heart turns over at both his words and the message I hear behind them. He wants to protect me. He needs to know I'm safe. And I have to admit, it feels kinda nice. I decide to let him.

But first, I decide to reward him.

I sweep a finger down his bare stomach. "I don't know. How much heat do you carry?"

"That depends." Jake sucks in a breath as my hand dips lower. "How much heat do you need?"

I roll him onto his back and show him how much. After that, Jake seems to forget all about Dean Sullivan.

And honestly, so do I.

23

The next morning, Jake and I sneak back down the stairs and out the door. The sun is barely up, the sky just beginning to streak with pink and orange, and a good two inches of snow fell while we were…well, not sleeping exactly, but tucked upstairs in my warm bed. The snow acts as a muffler, dulling our voices and smothering the neighborhood's early-morning noises. At least now we'll hear the protesters coming from miles away.

"Whatever you do, don't provoke him," Jake tells me, head down, boots crunching as they make tracks across the yard.

"I know."

He looks over. "If he gets belligerent, just back off, okay?"

"I know."

"And if he comes at you with a weapon—"

"Jake." I pull him to a halt at the edge of the lawn. "I know all these things. I'll be careful, I promise, but I'm also not going to coddle a confession out of him. Stop lecturing me."

"I'm sorry. I guess I'm just nervous."

"Well, stop, okay? Because you're making me nervous."
I give him my best calm-in-the-face-of-disaster face. "I'm
trained to handle people who don't want me there. I know
what to do if they start threatening or turn hostile. I'll be fine."

Jake watches me for a moment, and I can see he wants
to believe that Dean won't harm me. But it's not skepti-
cism I read on his face. It's concern, and a rush of delight
skitters down my chest and flutters around in my belly. I
curl a finger around one of his and smile, and silently, re-
luctantly, he nods.

We continue our trek across the snow to Dean's house.
We pause at the stairs leading to Dean's rickety front porch,
and I check to make sure my iPhone is recording. Satisfied,
I slip the device carefully back into my front coat pocket,
and Jake motions to the left of the door, where we agreed
he would stand just out of sight. Once he's in place, I suck
a deep breath, climb the stairs and punch the doorbell.

Which doesn't make so much as a peep. No surprise
there. I go old-school and knock.

Nothing.

I pound on the door, hard and with the side of my fist, and
press my ear against the wood, straining to pick up movement inside. The only thing I hear is my own hammering
heart and steady breathing. I thump on the door a few more
times, then go to the side window and peer through. Nothing but shapes and shadows behind the dingy lace curtains.
I go back to the door and pound again and again and again.

Still nothing.

I reach for the handle and twist—and then, oops, with
a click and a creak and maybe a teeny tiny shove, the door
swings open and I'm peering down Dean's dark hallway.

"Hello?"

The smell hits me, an overpowering combination of

vomit and whiskey and unwashed skin and shit. My stomach recoils and I cover my nose with a hand, trying not to breathe as I lean my head inside. The stairs and hardwood floors are almost completely covered with dirt and junk, ratty shoes and papers and trash, and there's something moving—please let it only be a mouse—in the corner.

But no Dean.

"Mr. Sullivan?"

I glance over at Jake, who is shaking his head. "Don't do it," he mouths.

I take a few tentative steps inside, ignoring the creepy feeling slithering through my bones. "Mr. Sullivan?" I step over an empty bottle and make my way farther into the hall, my scalp tingling, my spine flagpole straight. "It's Gia Andrews, from next door."

A dull thunk on the floorboard behind me sends a sharp jolt kicking through my muscles. I stifle a shriek and whip my head around to find Jake, close enough to be a human shadow.

"This is breaking and entering," he whispers.

I shake my head and whisper back, "This is a concerned citizen, checking in on her neighbor." Louder, I call, "Mr. Sullivan, is everything okay in here?"

Nobody answers. An icy wind blows through the front door, stirring the papers on the floor and intensifying the chill in my spine. I just pray Dean is passed out and not something worse, something like dead. Coming upon a corpse was so not on my agenda for today.

Jake and I continue down the hall to the living room, where we find a motionless Dean on the couch, naked but for a pair of grubby tighty-whities. If I weren't standing in his living room, if I didn't know for certain this was his house, I might not have recognized him. There is literally nothing left of the handsome, charming Dean Sullivan I once knew. He's scrawny skinny, and his skin is gray and pasty. Dark scabs cover his chest and legs, and his entire body is sunken in and purplish in places, like the skin of a bruised fruit. His formerly flaxen hair is long and dull and sticks to his head in greasy clumps. An empty bottle of Jack Daniel's is clutched in one of his hands, the one resting on the floor.

But praise your God of choice, he's still breathing.

"He's alive," Jake says, his voice swollen with relief.

I step closer. "Mr. Sullivan?" I stab a finger into his chest. It's like poking a cadaver—cold and stiff and unmoving. "Are you all right?"

Dean doesn't stir.

I turn to Jake. "It's freezing in here. Look around and see if you can find the thermostat."

Jake disappears into the hall and returns two seconds later. "His gas must be shut off, because the heater isn't coming on. I'll see if there's a blanket somewhere."

I nod and Jake heads upstairs. While he's gone, I go into the kitchen, find a semi-clean glass and fill it with water. By the time I make it back into the living room, Jake is draping a blanket over Dean's unconscious body. Either the noise or the movement causes him to stir and awake.

It takes a few beats for Dean's eyes to focus in on Jake. "Who the fuck are you?" Not even Dean's slur can soften the nasal twang of his Chicago accent. Who da fuckah you?

"I'm Jake Foster, sir. When's the last time you had something to eat?"

"None of your goddamn business, that's when." Dean tries to sit up, but the most he can manage is to push up onto a shaky elbow. "Now get the hell outta my house."

I step around Jake. "Hi, Mr. Sullivan. I'm Gia Andrews, from next door. Remember me?"

Dean squints, and his face pales to an even deathlier shade. "I know who you are."

"Jake and I were worried about you." I hold out the glass of water, but Dean doesn't move. He's too busy staring at me with glassy, panicked eyes. "It's only water. It'll make you feel better."

He throws off the blanket and bolts upright with surprisingly little effort. And then he clamps a hand around my wrist, sloshing most of the water over the couch and onto my shoes. "Did Ella Mae send you over here?"

I glance at Jake, but I can't read his face. His jaw is set in a hard line, his brow dipped in a frown, his body ready to pounce if Dean makes so much as one false move. I try to reassure both men with my calm response.

"No, sir. Jake and I came here today because we were worried about you. We wanted to make sure you were okay."

His fingers press painfully into my arm. "I need to see Ella Mae. I have to tell her I'm sorry."

Every hair on my body springs to attention, and suddenly, I'm no longer cold. "Sorry for what?"

"She said that she forgave me. She said that she still loved me." He shakes my arm hard enough to rattle my teeth, and there goes whatever was left of the water. "Where did she go?"

Jake and I exchange a quick glance.

"Mr. Sullivan, were you having an affair with Ella Mae?"

Dean's eyes bulge, and his fingers dig harder into my arm.

I take his reaction as confirmation. "Were you in love with her? Did she threaten to break off the affair?"

"It was an accident. I didn't mean to do it."

A surge of electricity straightens my back and heats the skin of my cheeks, and my heart pounds in my ears. "Didn't mean to do what?"

And suddenly, Jeffrey's words to me a few days ago

flash across my brain—your mind won't remember things you're not ready to face. The more I think about it, the more it makes sense. Dean said he didn't mean to do it. He talked about forgiveness. These two puzzle pieces make me think the hallucinations are trauma rather than alcohol induced, and a not-so-subtle sign Dean feels guilty for something his subconscious is not ready to confront.

Something like murder.

"Didn't mean to do what?" I ask again.

His only answer is a nod, leading with his head and neck, lurching forward then back, quickly picking up speed until his entire upper body rocks back and forth. The whole time, he chants, "It was an accident. I didn't mean to do it. It was an accident. I didn't mean to do it."

"Did you murder Ella Mae Andrews?" My voice is high and pitchy, my tone urgent.

It's like I didn't speak. Dean pitches and rolls and chants, jerking on my arm, almost pulling me down with him.

Jake, who's clearly had much more experience than I in dealing with incoherent drunks, steps forward. He loosens Dean's grip on my arm with one hand and pushes me gently behind him with the other.

"Mr. Sullivan, how about I help you into a shower while Gia rounds up something to eat?" Without waiting for Dean's response, Jake pulls him away from the couch, guiding him firmly toward the hallway stairs. "You look like you could use a little protein, if you don't mind me saying so."

Protein? Not until I've gotten my answer. That thought overrides everything else.

"But—"

"A shower will help," Jake says, giving me a look that leaves no doubt his words are meant more for me than for Dean. "And so will some scrambled eggs."

For a moment or two, I consider following the men up-stairs. I don't like the thought of Jake talking to Dean with-out the voice recorder, still humming away in my pocket, and I'm eager to hear more about Ella Mae, even if it is only gibberish. But that would mean facing Dean Sullivan naked, so I decide to wait a few more minutes. Hopefully Jake is right, and the shower and food will sober Dean up.

There are no eggs in the kitchen, and even if there had been, I wouldn't have touched them. The entire inside of the refrigerator is covered with a fuzzy green layer of mold. I shut the door and scrounge through the cabinets until I've found a package of unopened Oreo cookies and a can of peanuts. I refill the glass with water and take it, along with Dean's breakfast, back into the living room.

Upstairs, the shower shuts off, and Jake's voice floats down the stairs. "Gia, get up here."

I drop everything and race up the stairs, following the sound of movement to Dean's bedroom. From the looks of him, the shower didn't help. Dean is curled on his side under a filthy bedspread, his body shaking violently.

Jake stands by the window a few feet away, hands shoved in his front jeans pockets. "Tell Gia what you just told me," he says to Dean. "About Ella Mae."

Dean's tremors intensify, and a spring in the bed squeals in protest. "She's p-p-pregnant."

The last word hits me like an ice bath, freezing my limbs and heart. I shake my head at Jake. "She wasn't pregnant. He's hallucinating."

Jake steps closer, lowers his voice to a whisper. "That's what I thought at first, but what if he's not? A pregnancy would have forced an already tense situation."

"But something that major would've come out in the autopsy."

"But what if… I don't know, all the worrying about Ray and Dean was too much? What if she miscarried? What if she'd already lost the baby by the time she was killed?"

It makes me dizzy to process his words. If Ella Mae had been pregnant, the baby could have just as easily been Dad's as Dean's. She'd be forced to come clean. One man—and after everything I've heard here this morning, my money is still on Dean—was furious enough to murder. He may not have admitted it, not technically, but that doesn't mean I don't believe that Dean, not my father, was one to commit murder.

"Holy shit," I whisper.

Jake nods. "In a nutshell."

Outside, a trio of car doors slam, announcing the arrival of the first protesters. Jake jerks his head toward the back of the house. "Time to go."

I nod. By now I've heard all I needed to hear. Besides, one glance at Dean, passed out cold on the bed, tells me he's beyond any further answers.

Jake and I make our way down the stairs and out the back door, not stopping until the tree line where Dean's backyard ends.

"I'll add Dean to my list for food delivery," Jake says, his face grim, "though I'm not sure he'll eat any of it. As far gone as he is, he's probably not getting any of his calories from solids."

"Will I see you again tonight?" I push up on my toes and give him a kiss on the lips. "I'll be naked."

And for the first time since we left my bedroom this morning, Jake gives me one of his smiles. "Try and keep me away. But first, I have to go home and disinfect myself."

24

When Ella Mae threw up her breakfast for the fourth day in a row, she knew. She didn't need a doctor or a bunny or one of those fancy pee-on-a-stick tests Ray sold down at the pharmacy to tell her a little something had slipped by the diaphragm. She'd felt this way once before, more than eighteen years ago, complete with the nausea and exhaustion and tears and panic and cussing, lots and lots of cussing. She had known it then and she knew it now, blast it all to hell. Ella Mae knew she was pregnant.

The one thing she didn't know—the one thing, the most important thing—was who the father was.

Good Lord. Knocked up at forty-five, and by someone who may or may not be her husband. She felt like one of those poor, pathetic, white-trash girls on *Jerry Springer,* except Ella Mae was no girl. She was an old lady. Old enough to know better, and too old to be having a baby, that was for damn sure.

Ella Mae contemplated her options on the drive to the

hotel. Ray would be furious at the prospect of a baby, even if it was his. But what if the baby came out a spitting image of Dean? Ray would be furious then, too, both at her betrayal and at being made a fool.

And Dean wasn't stupid, either. He would do the math, know the baby could just as easily be his as Ray's. Would Dean even acknowledge his maybe-baby? Would he still want Ella Mae when she was swollen and fat, her belly filled with the fifty-fifty possibility of another man's child?

Then again, neither of them needed to be told. She could hope for a miscarriage, or take a trip to one of those women's clinics over in Knoxville. If she left early enough, she could make it back before Ray got home for supper. It would be like nothing ever happened. Nobody would ever have to know but her.

Only problem was, none of those options sounded particularly appealing.

At the hotel, she parked around back and climbed the short flight of stairs to room 223. Dean answered the door before she'd even finished knocking. He grabbed her by the waist, pulled her inside and gave her a kiss, a deep, long, titillating kiss that showed her how much he'd missed her. By the time he released her, they were both panting.

He pointed to her red sweater, the one he loved so much. "Take off your clothes."

Ella Mae smiled, dropped her purse on the table by the door. "You certainly don't waste any time, do you?"

"Not when I've been waiting all day for this." Dean shucked his shoes and shirt and sat on the edge of the bed. Ella Mae peeled off her sweater, and he reached for a bag on the floor.

"What's in there?"

"Toys."

"Toys?" She giggled. "Like Matchbox cars and model trains?"

"Not quite." Dean gave her one of his extra naughty smiles. "These toys are for girls."

Ella Mae knew better than to make a Barbie reference.

"For you." He held the bag in her direction. "Take a look."

Ella Mae's heart sped up, at the same time her mouth went dry. Dean's toys excited her and terrified her at the same time. She took the bag and dumped its contents on the bed. Some of the toys were obvious, creams and vibrators and tiny strips of lace and leather. Others were more perplexing and, quite frankly, more than a little disconcerting.

"What if I don't want to?"

He gave her a wounded look. "Why wouldn't you want to at least try?"

"I don't know. I just…" She pointed to a giant pink contraption, shuddering at the thought of where that thing was supposed to go. "That one looks painful."

"It's not. I guarantee you'll love it."

"But what if I don't?"

He shrugged, tugged on her belt loop, pulled her onto his lap. "We'll start small, work our way up. How does that sound?"

Ella Mae's gaze went back to the pile of plastic. She thought it sounded insulting. He was that bored with her already? "Why toys all of a sudden? Where's all this coming from?"

Dean didn't give her an answer. Instead, he nibbled on a spot behind her right ear until she felt like she might combust, then whispered, "Come on, baby. Do it for me. Do it for us."

There was a note of desperation in Dean's persuasion he

didn't bother to disguise—he needed this, and he needed it with her—but that wasn't what swayed Ella Mae. What swayed her was that last little word.

Us.

For the next few hours, Ella Mae let Dean push her to the edge of every inhibition she had, to edges of inhibitions she didn't even know existed. More than once she asked him to stop, begged him to stop, cried out in pain mixed with pleasure mixed with something that felt awfully close to humiliation. Every time, he caught her right before she fell over the brink, pulled her back at the very last moment, only to start pushing her closer and closer to the next limit.

"Dean, wait," she said when he picked up the scary pink contraption. "Stop."

Dean didn't wait. He didn't stop.

Ella Mae scooted up the bed, moving away from Dean and his torture toys. "I don't want to do this anymore."

"What? But we were just getting started."

"You were just getting started. I was done hours ago."

The dismayed look that passed over his face—as sad and disappointed as a child who didn't get his way—was appropriate, Ella Mae thought. He was acting like a baby. Next he'd be throwing a tantrum.

Which was exactly what he did. He flung down the toy, grabbed her by the ankles and jerked her back down the bed. "*We* were just getting started." He pinned her legs under his and clamped an iron palm around both her wrists, pinning them together above her head. "Don't make this harder than it has to be."

She squirmed, tried to break free, but Dean was too strong. "Dean, this isn't funny. Let me go."

His hand came out of nowhere, connecting with her

cheek with a sharp smack that shocked the fight right out of her. Her eyes watered, and she whimpered into the mattress.

With his free hand, Dean grabbed her roughly by the chin and jerked her head so she was looking straight up at him. His expression was angry, his words ones she thought she'd never, ever hear from a lover. "I don't want to hurt you, Ella Mae, but when you don't behave, you force me to do things I don't want to do. Do you understand what I'm saying?"

Ella Mae blinked, and she gave the slightest nod.

"And will you still understand if I let go of your arms and legs?"

Another nod.

His palm loosened on her wrists.

She adjusted her arms but left them heavy on the bed.

"Good girl." He released one ankle, then the other.

She didn't move, barely breathed.

"Very good girl." His naughty smile said otherwise. He reached for the pink toy with one hand, grabbed a handful of her hair with another. "Now be still and this won't hurt a bit."

For the next however long it lasted, Ella Mae squeezed her eyes shut and let Dean have his way. Sometimes she felt pleasure. Mostly she felt pain. After a while, she stopped feeling anything at all.

The next morning, Ella Mae threw up her breakfast again. Afterward she wiped her mouth, pulled herself up on the sink and gave herself a good long look in the mirror.

And this time, she knew exactly what she had to do.

25

I spend days obsessing about Dean's words. That he needed to tell Ella Mae he was sorry. That he didn't mean to do whatever he did. That Ella Mae was going to have his baby. No matter how I twist and turn his comments around in my mind, I can't come up with any other explanation than that he did something awful to Ella Mae, her baby or both. Otherwise why would he be looking for her forgiveness?

After dinner on Friday I call Cal with the news, who insists Dean has officially lost his whiskey-chuggin' mind and commands me in his lawyer voice to cease and desist any further contact. I call Jeffrey, who tells me he's about to board a plane to Chicago, where he tracked down Allison Sullivan's latest address, and asks me to email him the recording of Dean's confession. And I call Lexi, who apparently still isn't talking to me. After two rings, she pushes my call through to voice mail. I punch End and settle for a text.

Aren't you supposed to be the older, more mature sister? Whatever happened to conversation? You know what that is, right? A verbal back and forth?

Two seconds later, my cell phone chirps.

Do you have anything to say that's not about the wife killer?
Because otherwise I'm not interested.

My fingers tick out a reply.

Yes. As a matter of fact, I do. Dean Sullivan says he's sorry
and that he didn't mean to do it. And then he told me Ella
Mae had been pregnant with his baby.

And then I stare at the phone for a good three minutes,
waiting for her reply. Finally, it comes.

Wait. Whaaat?

I roll my eyes and text her back.

Everything Dean told me points to him being the killer,
not Dad. If you want to know any more than that, you're
going to have to talk to me in person.

Lexi doesn't text back. She doesn't call. When the screen
darkens and then goes black, I slip the phone into my back
pocket and head downstairs.

"Just in time," Fannie says, looking up as I come into
the living room. An episode of *The Bachelor* blares from
the TV against the wall. Beyond her, Dad stirs from the
racket but doesn't wake. "The bleached-blonde airhead is
about to have a meltdown."

I drop onto the couch beside Fannie, kick off my shoes
and prop my bare feet up on the coffee table. "Shocking."

She cackles, gesturing to the TV with the remote. "As

soon as they start referring to themselves in third person, you just know they're gonna lose it. Oh, here it comes. Crazy train's 'bout to go off the rails."

The airhead doesn't disappoint. Her meltdown is both spectacular and ridiculous. After a half minute of her blubbering I lose interest, concentrating instead on the still-silent hunk of metal and glass in my back pocket. Should I go out and hunt my sister down? Tackle her and sit on her chest until she listens about Dean? I quickly dismiss the thought. After this evening's text war, I would probably need a homing device and a tranquilizer gun to catch her.

A retching noise jerks me out of my thoughts and launches Fannie off the couch. She's at Dad's side in an instant, rolling his head to the side with one hand while she lifts his entire upper body, pillow and all, with the other.

Whatever he heaves up cannot be what he ate. It's greenish brown and slimy and looks nothing like digested food, and much more like something I've seen come out the other end of a choleric infant. Fannie gets a surge of it over her forearm and belly, not that she seems to mind.

"That's right, sugar." Her voice is low and soothing, her expression almost pleasant. "Get it all out. You'll feel so much better when you do."

"I'll go get some towels," I say, already halfway to the hall. There's a fresh pile of them in the laundry room, as well as an empty bucket on top of the dryer. I snatch both and tear back into the living room, shoving the bucket under Dad's chin just in time for him to gag up another greasy wave.

Between retches, without looking up, he snaps a hand in my direction. "Go 'way."

His words bounce around the bucket and my brain. I

shoot a glance at Fannie, thinking I must have misunderstood. "Who, me?"

He looks up then, looks straight at me. His pinched eyes leave no doubt.

Yes. Me.

The room pitches and rolls.

Dad spits, then retches again, followed by a belch so vociferous, any other night it would have sent me into a fit of giggles.

Not tonight.

Tonight I clutch the towels to my suddenly tight chest and frown. "Where am I supposed to go?"

Fannie winks at me over Dad's head. "Be a sweetie and fetch me some clean sheets and blankets, would ya? And there's a fresh pair of pajamas hanging in the laundry room. Then after you bring all that, I'm gonna need you to get everything ready for his sponge bath. The container is in the bathtub, fill it about halfway with lukewarm water. Dip your elbow in to make sure it's not too hot, okay?"

By now Dad seems to be winding down. His heaves are fewer and shorter, and the last handful have produced more air than vomit. Still, he doesn't lift his face out of the bucket.

"Think you can help me out, sugar?" Fannie pastes on a smile and gives me her best nurse face, making me think Dad's not the only patient here.

I nod, dropping the towels on the back of the couch without another word. As I trudge down the hallway toward the laundry room, a rush of resentment swirls in my chest. After my first unforgettable fuckup with Dad, when I stood frozen while he writhed around in agony, I've been waiting for another chance to prove myself. Now, finally, I get one, and my father doesn't want me anywhere near him.

And just like that, the anger fades, leaving behind a stout, pulsing ache in the center of my chest.

My father doesn't want me anywhere near him. Even though I apologized. Even though I told him I believed him. I don't know what else to say. A quick and bone-deep exhaustion settles over me, sapping my strength and making each step feel like I'm wading through wet cement. If nothing I say or do is enough, why am I even here?

In a haze, I fetch the clean linens. I prepare the sponge bath. By the time I bring the last load into the living room, Dad's stomach is empty and he's quiet. I come closer, and he looks away. Sighing, I pick up the giant pile of towels by Fannie's feet and haul them down the hall.

Fannie finds me twenty minutes later in the laundry room, watching soapy water churn behind the little window and feeling sorry for myself. "You okay, sugar?"

I swipe my cheeks and glance over. "I'm fine. Can I do anything else?"

She pats my arm, ignoring the question. "Aw, sweetie, try not to take it so personally. Your father's a proud man. He didn't want you to see him like that, is all."

I give her a whatever shrug, not because I believe her but mostly so she'll stop talking. At this point, all I want to do is go upstairs, have a good cry and sleep for a week. No, a month. Fannie takes the hint, and after another gentle arm pat, slips down the hall and into the kitchen.

My bare toe has barely touched the bottom step when I hear him.

"Gia."

Shit.

It takes every ounce of self-control to force my body to stop. To paste on a neutral expression and lean around the corner. The living room is mostly dark, but Dad is lit up by a floor lamp, shining golden light from behind his left shoulder. "Yes?"

"Kids aren't supposed to be cleaning up after their parents, you know." His breathing is labored, but his eyes are clear. Clear and wide and focused on me. "It's not right. You should be out living your life, not picking up the pieces of mine."

Fannie was right. My father is a proud man, and I know this is as close to an apology as I'm going to get.

I could tell him he wouldn't have been the first to puke on me, or that I've lived in plenty of cultures where caring for your elders is not only an obligation but an honor. I could even lie and say I don't mind cleaning up, am happy to pick up his pieces. Instead, I tell him the reason that matters most. "I only want to help."

"I know you do." He says it like he thinks it's a good thing. Baby steps, I tell myself.

"Can I get you anything?"

He shakes his head, and I'm about to continue my trek upstairs when he stops me again.

"You know the other day, when I said I knew you'd be the first to leave me?" He pauses to receive my nod. "What I forgot to tell you is, I also knew you'd be the first to come back. You're just built that way. Loyal and true. I only wish there was something better for you to come back to."

I think about the protesters' constant cries outside our window, about my missing-in-action uncle and my deadbeat siblings, about Dean Sullivan drowning in his lies across the frozen yard. About what's left of Dad's wasted life, and his less-than-warm welcome home. My father is right. There's so little left for me here.

And then I think about Jake, and my heart gives a happy kick. In a few hours he'll be sneaking up the porch and slipping into my bed, kissing away my worries, loving away my sorrow. "It's not all bad," I say, and it's the truth. When did Jake become the anchor holding me here?

Dad falls silent for a bit, but I can tell there's more. Everything about him—his intense stare, his parted lips, the way his body fidgets under the blanket—indicates he has more to say. Is he searching for the right words? Is he working up the nerve for a heart-to-heart? I'll never know, because he seems to give up. His face falls and his shoulders slump, but he gestures to the chair. "Come sit with me for a spell?"

They're not the words he was gearing up to say, but they're good ones nonetheless. I make my way across the Rooms To Go carpet, biting back the beginnings of a smile. "I'd like that."

The way Dad nods makes me think it was the answer he wanted to hear.

As soon as I'm settled, he clicks off the lamp and closes his eyes, and he doesn't say anything more. He doesn't have to. Knowing my father wants me sitting here in the dark, curled up on a chair beside him while he sleeps, is enough.

26

My phone doesn't light up again until sometime after ten as Fannie and I are washing the last of the day's dishes in the kitchen. My heart flutters when I see the name on the screen.

I hand Fannie the dish towel, excusing myself to the hallway.

"Hey, gorgeous," I say to Jake. "Don't tell me you're already done."

I can barely hear him over Roadkill's bar crowd. "No, but can you get away for a little bit? It's Lexi."

My heart thuds to a stop, then goes from zero to sixty in less than a second. "Did something happen to her?"

I hear a puff of air as Jake sighs. "Tequila happened to her. Not mine, for the record. She was loaded when she got here. I've cut her off and confiscated her keys but…" There's a shrill shriek I recognize from my sister's pom-pom days on the edge of the football field, then a burst of raucous laughter followed by another sigh from Jake. "Oh, Jesus. I think you better hurry."

And then the line goes dead.

I give a quick update to Fannie, who finds the situation a whole lot more amusing than I do. She smacks a meaty thigh and cackles. "That sister of yours sure is a firecracker."

"Dynamite is more like it. I just hope she's passed out in a corner by the time I get there. She's a lot more pleasant lately when she's unconscious." I slip on my coat and dig around in the pocket for my keys. "I'll be back as soon as I can. Call me if you need me."

"I'll do that, sugar." She stops me with a holler as I'm running out the door. "Oh, and bring me back some more of that chili."

When I push through the door at Roadkill ten minutes later, I don't immediately spot the blonde, ex-beauty queen I'm looking for, but I know she's there. I know this from Jake, who looks up from the beer he's pulling, makes a face and gestures with his head to the far back corner. And I know this from the wall of backs to my right, at least fifty of them in everything from Levis to dark suits to dirty work clothes, sucking on beer bottles and grinning, watching the show.

I shove my way through the crowd, not bothering to apologize for jabbed elbows and stomped toes, not stopping to respond to the snickers and whispers and murmurs of "Hey look, there's her sister." I force my way through the bodies until I come out the other end, into a semicircle clearing of twenty feet or so with, at its center, my sister, standing in her favorite place on the planet: the spotlight.

Her back is to the crowd, both hands propped high on the flashing jukebox, her designer-denim hips swinging to the beat, her high and honey-sweet voice singing along, loudly and off-key, to "Friends in Low Places."

How appropriate.

"Lexi."

She pivots on one of her pumps, losing her balance and

almost falling over in the process. "Gia!" She holds out a sloppy arm in my direction. "Dance with me, sistah friend. I think they're playing our song."

Next to me, Terri Lynn Williams snickers. I toss her a glare that freezes the grin on her lips.

I reach for one of Lexi's hands, jingling her arm full of bangles. "Come on. Time to go."

"What?" Her face falls, and she wriggles her fingers out of mine. "No, I don't wanna go. This party's just getting started."

It takes all my willpower to not clamp a hand over her mouth, throw an arm around her neck and drag her out of here by her bleached-blond hair. But Lexi has a good five inches and almost twenty pounds on me, and I know she could extricate herself with very little effort. Besides, this evening is embarrassing enough without turning it into a girl fight.

I step closer, giving her a stern look I copied from Cal, and lower my voice to an insistent growl. "This isn't a party, it's an embarrassment. You're embarrassing me, and you're embarrassing yourself. And now I'm taking you home, before you make it any worse."

"Worse!" Lexi pitches her upper body forward, doubling over at the waist and clutching her stomach, and I take a hasty step backward to avoid puke spatter on my shoes. It's only when she peeks up at me through her hair that I see she's laughing. Laughing like she smoked an entire joint, all by herself.

She straightens, and everything falls effortlessly back into place. The sharp part in her stick-straight hair, the perfect folds of her silk blouse, the trio of silver necklaces hanging around her neck. If she weren't my sister, I would hate her for it.

"Please tell me how this could possibly get any worse.

Because I'm already living in a fucking nightmare." Her last two words shoot out in a hysterical shriek, and conversation in the room all but falls away. "Don't look now—" she giggles and points over my shoulder "—but I think we have an audience." She waves like she's just been crowned prom queen.

I hear a few giggles to my rear, but I don't turn around. I know they're there, watching us like we're some kind of fairground attraction. My back burns with the force of their stares, sharp as swords slicing into my shoulder blades.

"It's because you're giving them a goddamn freak show."

Lexi rolls her eyes so hard she staggers. "Me? I'm the freak show? No, darlin', I'm the daughter of the goddamn freak show. Which is exactly what you are, too."

Jake saves me from a response by coming up behind me, pushing through the crowd. "Why don't you two ladies continue this discussion in my office? It's a lot quieter back there, and you won't be disturbed."

Lexi curls her lips into one of her beauty-pageant smiles. "Pour me a smidgen of something good and strong, hot stuff, and I'll consider it."

"I don't think you should—"

"Pour it!" Lexi shrieks, then glares until he fetches her a glass with a good three fingers of clear liquid. Lexi swipes it from his hand and throws it back, chugging more than half of it. "Water, Jake? I expected better of you."

But she doesn't seem to consider giving up center stage. "So tell me all about dear old Dad. How is the old buzzard?"

Fresh humiliation shoots a surge of blood to my cheeks and adrenaline through my veins. "Seriously? This is how you choose to finally have this discussion?"

Her forehead crumples in mock confusion. "Why not?

You said if I wanted to know any more I had to talk to you in person, so let's talk. What was it you told me about Ella Mae?" She snaps her fingers and sways, then plants her feet wide to keep from falling. "Oh, that's right. About how Dean Sullivan knocked her up."

There's a collective gasp from behind me, and I wince at our audience of blabbermouths. This was not how I'd imagined dropping that little bombshell on the world—I'd prefer a more conventional channel than by way of Rogersville's rumor mill—and this was certainly not how I'd imagined discussing the details of my conversation with Dean with my sister.

"Only I don't understand how that's supposed to make me believe Dad didn't kill her. You do realize Ella Mae's affair makes him look even guiltier than he already is, right? It doesn't change anything."

I step closer and lower my voice. "Can we please talk about this somewhere else?"

"Tell me!" she shrieks, right as the Garth Brooks song ends. The room plunges into silence. Silent enough to hear my sister's hitched breathing and the hum and whirr of the jukebox as it makes the next selection.

I toss a glance at Jake, who gives me a might-as-well shrug. I consider the implications of telling Lexi amidst a roomful of gossips, and it doesn't take me long to decide he's right. They've already heard the part about the baby, and better to go ahead and give them all the information than to let their imaginations run wild. Besides, I'm pretty sure at least one person behind me is filming this fiasco, so what do I have to lose? Certainly not any more of my dignity.

"Think about it, Lex. Ella Mae's lover was also the prosecution's star witness. Nobody would have believed a word he said if they'd known he was sleeping with the victim. Dean Sullivan had just as much motive as Dad, and just as much reason to lie about what happened the night Ella Mae was murdered."

My sister's face turns to parchment, pale and stretched tight, and she closes her eyes for a few seconds.

"I'm sorry," I tell her, my voice softer now. "I didn't want you to find out like this."

Her eyes pop open, and they flash with an emotion I hadn't expected—fury. She steps forward, jabbing a finger between my breasts. "You can't do this to me. You can't jet out of here all those years ago to God knows where and leave me here to deal with all the mess. And you can't come back here now, feeding me some bullshit story about Dean and Ella Mae. It's too late. I'm not buying it."

"It's not bullshit," Jake says. "I heard him. I was there. And Gia and I will be happy to tell you all about it, if you'll just come with us into my office."

Lexi's gaze bounces from me to Jake and back, landing, finally, with an almost audible thud on Jake. "Gia sure has worked some kind of spell on you, hasn't she, Jakey? She's got you wrapped up so tight around her pinky finger, I'm thinking she must really put out good."

Someone behind me chuckles. Someone else mutters, "Runs in the family."

"Oh, shut up, Steve. Do you want me to tell everyone here that's really a cucumber in your pants?" Lexi's revelation drops the smile from Steve's face like the blade of a guillotine. She holds up a hand, thumb and forefinger an inch apart at best, and looks at me with a snort. "Cocktail sausage, and that's being real generous."

A snicker runs through the crowd, and Steve turns an alarming shade of purple.

And then she turns back to Jake. "My advice to you, hon, is don't get too attached to this little sister of mine. Because as soon as the old man kicks the proverbial bucket—" she makes a sweeping motion with her right arm, sloshing a good swell of her water onto the floor "—she'll leave you so fast you'll get whiplash."

A flush of fury at my sister's personal shot snakes through my body and explodes out the top of my head. "What is your problem?"

Lexi holds up a finger, making me and everyone wait while she drains her glass. She wipes her mouth with the back of a hand, then smacks the glass onto the top of the jukebox hard enough to leave a dent.

"You're my problem, because you don't stick."

"What do you mean I don't stick?"

"Oh, pardon my hillbilly French—you don't stay. You didn't sixteen years ago, so why would you now?" Her gaze flicks to Jake, and I know what she's implying. Everyone knows what she's implying. That not even Jake can make me stay.

As one, the heads in the room swing to me, waiting for my reply. Jake included. He gauges me like only he can, and he must not like what he sees because his shoulders fall and he looks away and I know, without either of us saying a single word, that my answer has let him down.

"I never said I would stay," I say to the room, but mostly to Jake. "I have a job on the other side of the planet, where people are dying from starvation and disease. Where people need me."

As usual, Lexi thinks this conversation is all about her. "I need you! I need you here, and you keep leaving."

I don't know what to say. Lexi has never needed anyone. Besides, she and Jake know how I feel about this town, and that my return here has always come with an expiration date.

Before I can tell either of them this, Lexi plucks a bottle of Jack Daniel's from a server's tray, jerks off the cap, sends it skidding across the floor and takes three long swallows straight from the bottle.

And then she pitches forward again. This time she's not laughing. This time she heaves her liquid dinner over Jake's boots, and then again and again, into a puddle on the wooden floor. When her stomach is good and empty, her legs give way, and Jake scoops her up before she can hit the ground. She's a rag doll, limbs flopping, head lolling, in his arms. Her eyes are closed, and hallelujah and praise the Lord, so is her mouth.

Jake swings them both around, gestures with his head for people to move out of his way. "Show's over, people. Let us through."

The crowd parts, and Jake whisks Lexi through the bar and into the kitchen, past a couple of cooks and runners who look up from their dishes with a double take. He hangs a right into a narrow hallway without a word, without looking back, without checking that I'm following right behind him.

"Jake, stop," I say, scurrying to keep up.

He doesn't stop. He doesn't even slow. He rounds a curve and begins the steep climb to his front door. On either side of him, Lexi hangs from his arms, a human deadweight.

I rush up after him, wishing he would turn around so I can see his face, see if he's angry or not. Then again, the way he's stomping up the stairs is probably a clear giveaway as to his current emotional state.

"Are you mad at Lexi or me?"

He hits the top of the landing and whirls on his heel.

One of Lexi's arms whacks sharply against the wall. My sister doesn't flinch. I do, though, at the look of undisguised fury on his face.

"What do you think?"

Me. I think he's mad at me.

"This isn't exactly fair, you know. Tonight's the first time we have this discussion, and it's in front of the whole freaking town. You've never even so much as hinted you wanted me to stay until Lexi—"

"Stay." His anger fades into desperation, wild and raw, and his expression eats at me. "There are plenty of people here who need your help. Plenty of communities in Appalachia where the poverty is just as staggering as Africa and Asia and all those other places you work. I don't... I don't want you to leave."

His words churn something unpleasant in my stomach, and I grip the handrail to keep from swaying. "Stay in Rogersville?"

"Why not? Dean practically confessed. Once word of that gets out, you won't be the murderer's daughter anymore. Things'll go back to the way they were for you here before Ella Mae was killed."

I look at him like he's crazy. "You weren't here during the trial, so you don't know. You didn't hear what people said, didn't see the way they looked at me. My best friends, my teammates, my teachers. People who treated me like family suddenly wanted nothing to do with me, acted like I was the one holding the saran wrap when I was more fucking traumatized by Ella Mae's death than anyone!" By now, my voice has risen to an alarming decibel, but I shove even more power behind it. "I will never forgive them for what they put me through, and things can never, ever go back to the way they were for me here."

"So Lexi was right? When your dad dies, we do, too?"

"No!" At the thought of no more Jake, a ball of nausea mushrooms in my belly. "No, of course not."

He shifts Lexi in his arms, and I know his biceps must be burning. "What, then?"

"I… I don't know." I open my mouth to say more, but what is there to say? My sister is right. I won't stick. No matter how much I don't want to lose Jake, I'm on the first plane out of the country as soon as Dad's in the ground.

Jake nods, once, and his expression turns to stone. "Then neither do I." Before I can respond, he swings back to face the door, then curses. "You're going to have to get my keys."

"Oh," I say, turning to head back down the stairs. "Are they in your office?"

"No. They're in my front pocket."

Before tonight, I would've slid my lips in a sultry smile and said something like "Are those keys in your pocket or are you happy to see me?" or "You know you don't have to work this hard to get me in your pants."

Instead, I say, "Which one?"

"The right one." Jake grunts and lifts Lexi higher, shifting her torso farther up his chest. "And hurry up, will you? I can't feel my arms."

I climb the last few treads and reach into his front pocket. Lexi's head flops back and her mouth falls open, and she gives a loud snort. My fingers make contact with his keys, but not before they accidentally make contact with something else.

Jake sucks in a breath, and his voice becomes strained. "Careful down there."

"Good God." Lexi chooses that moment to come to. "Would y'all please get a room?"

27

Jake deposits Lexi carefully onto his bed and shucks his boots, dropping them on the balcony to air out until he can clean them later. Music and voices from downstairs rattle the floor and walls, and I picture the town's greatest scandalmongers posting a play-by-play of tonight's action on Facebook and Twitter. I fire off a quick heads-up text to Cal, who's going to be livid at my sister's Great Reveal, and one to Fannie to let her know I'm spending the night with Lexi and that I'll keep my phone on in case she needs me.

Jake breezes by, and I follow in his fumes down the hallway. "Jake, wait."

He stops, but he doesn't look like he plans to stay stopped for long. He tosses a glance at his watch and points his body toward the door, anxious to escape.

"She can sleep it off here. I won't be back up for another few hours, and then I'll take the couch. Lock the door on your way out."

I step closer, trying not to dwell on the fact that Jake suggested I leave, while my sister sleeps in his bed. "Don't go yet. I feel like we haven't finished—"

Jake cuts me off with a swift shake of his head. "I can't do this now. I've got at least fifty customers downstairs, and I don't know how much longer before they trash the place and run out on their bills. If I hurry, maybe I can prevent Lexi's performance from trending on Twitter."

"Oh." Right now I don't care about his bar or the stupid internet. The hard edge is still in his tone, slicing into my skin, my stomach, my heart. "Okay. Do you want me to come with?"

"Not a good idea." He turns back to the door, reaching for the knob without a kiss, without even a goodbye.

"Wake me up when you're back."

He turns long enough to make a gesture somewhere between a nod and a shrug, and then disappears down the stairs at a half jog. A knife twists in the pit of my belly. Jake's running, and it's away from me.

I fetch a glass of water from the kitchen and make my way to the bedroom, where moonlight filters through the sheer curtains and casts a pale glow over Lexi's form on the far end of the bed. She's kicked off her shoes and her eyes are now open, staring unblinking up at the ceiling.

I'm suddenly furious at her—for embarrassing me and Jake, for throwing up on his floor, for slicing into our relationship with talk of what we don't discuss. I don't know whether to hand her the water, or throw it in her face.

And then she sits up and reaches for the glass with a shaky hand. "Thanks."

I watch her drink the liquid down, then make a disgusted face as it hits her empty belly. "You're not going to throw up again, are you?"

"It's entirely possible." She edges the glass onto the nightstand and flops back onto the pillow. "I feel like shit."

"Serves you right for that fiasco downstairs. Thanks a

lot for including me and Jake in that, by the way. He's really pissed."

"I'm sure he is. Especially after the way you pretty much agreed with every word I said."

"I just… I don't… What? I didn't agree with anything."

She rolls onto her side, and her bleary eyes focus on me in the dark. "How can you be so smart and so dumb at the same time? He's not mad at me for saying you're leaving. He's mad at you for not denying it."

Her words sting, but only because I know she's right. "Then he's the one who changed the rules, not me."

"So it's true? You really are leaving?"

"Of course I'm leaving." I huff and cross my arms, frustration pushing at my skin. "Jake knows this. He always knew."

"Maybe at first he did, but by the looks of his face downstairs, I think he was hoping you'd changed your mind."

I shake my head, sink onto the mattress. "I haven't."

"Silly rabbit. That man is crazy about you, and you don't have any idea how remarkable that is. Jake doesn't date. He doesn't let anyone in. He doesn't bring anyone up here, into his home and his bed, ever. And believe me, there's not a woman in town who hasn't tried. Myself included."

"Really?" I rear my head back, look at her down a crinkled nose. "You like Jake?"

"No, but after all those nights I spent parked on one of his bar stools, flirting my fine ass to high heaven, the least he could've done was shove his tongue down my throat." She smiles to let me know she's at least partly kidding. "But my point is, are you really just going to walk away from the man you love without a fight?"

I fall backward onto the pillow. Even after all these years, how can my sister still peg me so perfectly? How can she still sense the one thing I'm unwilling to admit even to myself?

Because for days I've been telling myself the bubbling in my chest whenever Jake reaches for me isn't love. I tell myself it's relief to be away from the sick and dying, or a pleasurable distraction from the escalating protests on my front lawn, or simply a case of old-fashioned horniness. I tell myself I'm not in love with him, I just love the way he helps me to forget my guilt and anger and heartbreak for little bits of time.

And also, I love him. I've tried not to, struggled to keep my stomach from tightening and my heart from quickening whenever he's around, but I can't. I am in love with a man who will never leave where I can't stay, and I don't know what to do about it.

Lexi sees my distress. She pushes a curl off my cheek, tucks it behind an ear. "Aw, sweetie. I'd give you advice, but good Lord, that would be like the traumatized leading the traumatized, wouldn't it?"

I laugh, but her face goes blurry on the other side of my tears.

"And besides, I'm biased. I want you to stay here forever."

"I can't stay." Three words, and their truth sinks sharp teeth into my heart. "I'm not strong enough."

Lexi smiles. "This from the sister who parachutes into the eye of the storm for a living."

"You know what I mean. You're the strong ones, you and Bo. You didn't take off with your tail between your legs like I did."

"Yeah, well, the jury's still out on which of our methods is better. Bo has the emotional depth of one of his petri dishes, and need I remind you? I just puked in public. We're not exactly the picture of mental health."

My heart twists at the look of resigned martyrdom on her face, and I suddenly know why Lexi stayed all these years. She stayed because, as much as she despises being defined as the daughter of the murderer, attention is attention, even if it involves humiliation and vomit.

But the Rogersville grapevine is long and hardy, and by now gossip of Dean and Ella Mae will have galloped as far as the county lines. I don't know what that means for the quality of Lexi's attention, but as far as quantity goes, I have a feeling it's about to explode.

Which is why she needs to know the whole story. I roll onto my side, facing her. "Can we please talk about Dad now?"

She closes her eyes for a long moment, and then nods.

So I tell her. I begin with the morning Jake jiggled loose my memory and keep going from there, landing on a detailed account of each of my subsequent conversations with Dad and Cal and Jeffrey. I tell her Dad knew about an affair but not who it was with, and that Cal had tried to deny any knowledge of both. I tell her I'm waiting on word from Jeffrey, and his visit with Dean's ex-wife. The rest I want her to hear firsthand, so I wriggle the phone from my back pocket, pull up the recording from earlier this morning and push Play.

At the first nasal twang of Dean's slurred voice—*Who da fuckah you?*—Lexi's face goes as still and hard as steel. She doesn't move. She doesn't blink. I'm not certain she even breathes. She just lies there, staring with wide, dry eyes at my iPhone until I reach the part where Dean passes out, and I punch Stop.

Lexi is the first to speak. "That man's crazier than a

loon, and he was completely sauced. Why would you believe a word he says?"

"Because he was sleeping with Ella Mae. I remember. I know. And if he was sleeping with her, then not only did he have reason to lie about what he did or didn't see the night she was murdered, he also had motive. What if he found out about the baby and was angry it was Dad's? What if Dean was a jealous lover who was trying to cover his own tracks?"

She shakes her head, tight and dismissive. "That's an awful big stretch."

"Maybe, but didn't you hear him? He said he's sorry, and he didn't mean to do it."

"But do what? He didn't mean to sleep with the neighbor's wife, cheat on his own, run over Ella Mae's black-eyed Susans with his car? Take your pick. It could be anything."

"How about he didn't mean to kill her?"

"Dean didn't kill her." She says the words in slow motion, and I know what her next ones will be from the hatred I see in her eyes. "Dad killed her."

But hatred can be a horrific weight, dragging you down to cold, murky depths, or it can be an anchor, holding you steady in a storm. For Lexi, it's been both. Letting go of hers for Dad will be freeing and terrifying at the same time, and it won't be easy.

"And—" Lexi points a finger at the ceiling "—there was no baby. Ella Mae wasn't pregnant when she died."

"Anymore. Ella Mae wasn't pregnant anymore. Maybe she got an abortion, or miscarried."

Lexi chomps on her lips and considers the possibilities.

"Don't you see, Lex? The affair with Dean creates reasonable doubt."

"Exactly, doubt. Reasonable doubt is still doubt."

"It's okay to have doubt. But what I'm trying to tell you is no jury member would have convicted Dad if they'd known about Dean. And no daughter would have, either."

She makes a face like I just slapped her. All these years, my sister has been so convinced of Dad's guilt, she's been like an angry Baptist preacher, spewing hellfire and damnation from her pulpit to anybody who would listen. Now I've given her doubt, and it crawls over every inch of her expression.

"I'm not saying I've changed my mind or think he might be innocent, but what if? What if all this time, I spent all my energy wishing him dead for something somebody else might have done? How would he ever be able to forgive me?"

"He already has, Lex. He doesn't want to die without you and Bo and me by his side."

Moonlight illuminates her eyes, wide with fear and guilt. "I don't think I can face him."

I connect with her reluctance, because I felt it, too. The house, our father, the memories are all so painful. But I also know she doesn't have much more time.

"We'll go together. We'll face him together. First thing tomorrow morning." I hold up a hand between us, pinky finger extended. "You and me."

She watches me for an eternity, body stiff, eyes unblinking. Finally she relaxes, and I can see how much it costs her. A tear rolls down her perfect nose, drips onto the pillow, but she curls her pinky around mine. "You and me."

I smile, and we lie there for the longest time, until the moon disappears behind a cloud, until the voices from downstairs fade away one by one, until our eyelids grow thick and heavy. Finally, I give in, let them fall shut.

"No offense," Lexi whispers, pulling me back from the

edges of sleep, "but this wasn't exactly how I imagined my first time in Jake Foster's bed."

I give her finger a squeeze, let myself start to drift once again, holding on for the words I know are still coming.

"It's so much better."

28

It's quarter to four by the time I awake, a good two hours since Roadkill's last call, and other than Lexi's light snoring on the pillow next to me, the building is quiet. The house is dark.

And there's no sign of Jake.

Careful not to wake my sister, I slip out of bed and down the hall. At the doorway to the living room I pause to take in Jake, bare-chested and asleep on the couch, an old blanket tangled around his legs. His hair is mussed and sticking up on one side, and one of his arms is thrown above his head in abandon. Something about his expression—recklessly unreserved and so beautifully male—steals my breath, and my heart does an unexpected backflip. Without meaning to, without even being awake to do so, Jake Foster just dealt me a sucker punch.

I can't stay, yet I so don't want to leave this man.

He awakens, his eyes find mine, and heat surges in me from somewhere deep, from some place I've not felt heat before. I shimmy out of last night's jeans and T-shirt, dropping them with a whispered thud onto the floor on my way across the room. Jake doesn't move. At the couch, I trace a light finger down the inside of his forearm, following a vein from his elbow across his skin to his hand. When I get to his wrist, his fingers twine through mine.

"You said you'd wake me up," I whisper.

"I wasn't in the mood to talk."

"That's okay." I give his hand a squeeze and release it, reaching behind my back for the hook of my bra. "I'm not in the mood to talk, either."

Jake doesn't drop his gaze, not even when I push the straps from my shoulders, first the left, then the right, and my bra falls to the floor. The entire time, he keeps his eyes on mine, and I love him even more for it.

He lifts a corner of the blanket. "Come here."

I slide in and he pulls me to his chest, all warm skin and hair and muscle. His fingers skitter down my spine, featherlight but searing my skin like tiny licks of fire. He pauses at the top of my ass, pulling me tighter against his naked body, and then hooks a finger under my panties and slides them down my legs. My heart pounds out an anxious rhythm. A hopeful rhythm.

"Jake. What are we—" I gasp as he slips one finger inside me. "What are we doing?"

Another finger teases its way in. "If I have to tell you that, then I don't think I'm doing it right."

"Not that." I reach for his wrist, and his fingers still. "I meant, what are we doing? Why is this so difficult?"

Jake watches me steadily. "I thought you said you didn't want to talk."

"I want to fix this. Whatever happened to us tonight. I want to fix us."

His hand moves up my thigh and settles on my hip, and

he heaves a sigh. "Look, I'm sorry for the way I reacted earlier. I know I'm only a distraction for you while—"

"No! No, you're not a distraction at all. Well, maybe at first you were, but lately..." I snake my arm around his neck, twist my fingers through the hair at his nape. "You're more."

"I'm more?"

I nod. "A whole lot more."

"Good, but what I was going to say is that I'll take it. I'll pull all-nighters and play hooky from work and drive you all over Appalachia anytime you need a distraction, because that means I get to spend time with you."

His last few words, especially those, light me up from inside. I don't answer. I can't speak.

"I knew what I was getting myself into when we first started up, and I let myself fall for you anyway. But I'm a big boy, and I'll be fine. When it comes time for you to leave—" he smiles, and it's the saddest thing I've ever seen "—then I'll just have to let you go."

His words, the tenderness in his voice, twist in my chest. "But I don't want you to let me go."

There's the slightest of curves to his lips, an infinitesimal lift of his shoulders, the tiniest puff of breath.

Deadlock.

And then I have a thought. I look into his eyes for a moment, letting the idea sink into my brain, feeling it float around my skin and flutter at my heart, spinning around and around me until I'm dizzy with something I can't deny feels a lot like hope.

"What if you came with me?" I blurt, at the same time my heart takes off running. I ask people for favors all the time. Presidents, politicians, deep-pocketed donors, they don't intimidate me. When it comes to feeding starving people, to saving someone's life, I'll ask anybody for anything. But I can't remember the last time I asked someone for something for me.

Jake blinks, three staccato flickers. "Wow. I didn't see that one coming." His expression is solemn, unreadable.

"It doesn't have to be Kenya if that's too far. Just any place where people need help." Jake doesn't smile or nod or respond in any way, so I keep going, a bit frantically, trying to ignore the pitchy sound of my voice as it backpedals. "You don't have to answer me now. You can think about it for a bit."

"I'd have to sell my restaurant."

"Well, yeah. But you could open another one. The where is up to you. Big city, small town, middle of nowhere, it doesn't matter to me. I could live just about anywhere on the planet but here."

"And my house." His expression is so serious that my heart thuds to a stop. "I doubt I could get much for either."

My gaze drops to his chest, and my eyes blink back tears. Now I know how he felt earlier. Jake won't leave either, not even for me. "I understand," I whisper. How could I not?

He traces a thumb down my cheek, hooks a knuckle under my chin and nudges my gaze up to his. "I wasn't done yet. What I wanted to say is, I'll do whatever it takes, because my heart is with you. Africa or Asia or the moon, I don't give a shit. My home is wherever you are."

Up until this very second, I thought those singular moments of clarity—when angels sing and bells sound and lightbulbs pop to life—were the stuff of cartoons and comic books. But not anymore.

Home isn't a place. It's not found behind the door the killer broke through or at the top of the staircase Ella Mae was dragged down or in the foyer where she took her last breath. Home is this man lying next to me, and this feeling beating through my veins whenever I'm with him, like my whole body just took its first breath. It's whispered conversations under comforters and midnight rides in his truck and take-out dinners for two in his bed. Jake is my home.

"I can't believe I've been so stupid," I say. "All these years I've spent traipsing around the globe, never staying long enough for whatever place I was in to feel like home, because in my mind, home was where disasters occurred. And I chase disasters for a living! Omigod, I'm a walking cliché."

Jake starts to object, but I press a finger to his lips.

"But that's not my point. My point is I was too busy running to notice that no one was behind me. The only person chasing me was myself. And now that I've gotten nowhere but exhausted, I refuse to run any longer. My home is wherever you are, too."

"Even if that's right here in Rogersville?"

I swallow a lump the size of Bays Mountain.

He sees my hesitation and clarifies, "It wouldn't be forever. Just until I can sell this place, get things settled. After that, I don't care where we go. We'll figure it out."

"But…but what if I can't?" My voice breaks on the last word, not from sorrow but from terror. A bone-chilling, breath-choking terror at the thought of staying in Rogersville long enough to put down roots, even temporary ones.

"We'll take road trips," Jake says, and his voice is so hopeful my heart wants to settle, if only for him. "Lots of them. Together. Just you and me and the truck, going wherever. We'll see every town and tree and blade of grass in a two-hundred-mile radius. And we'll take things one day at a time. I'll check in with you every night before we fall asleep. If you say you're done here, we'll leave the next morning, no questions asked."

Even through my panic, I can see the flaw in his plan. "But you can't just up and leave."

"Why not?"

"Because you need to recoup what you put into this building. You must have spent a fortune in renovations alone. And then there's the goodwill you've built up in the restaurant. How much is all this worth?"

He brushes off the question with a quick shrug. "You're more important to me than money. I'll go whenever you say it's time."

Jake's proffered sacrifice stuns me silent. I've spent my entire adult years drifting wherever the road led, whenever the impulse hit. Now Jake is offering to do the same, not because he's consumed by the same wanderlust, but for me. In order to be with me. My heart races with joy at the same time it twists with something less pleasant. I can't let him walk away from his restaurant, his friends, everything he's worked so hard for to become like me—a person with a life small enough to fit in a single duffel bag.

But more important, I don't want to be that person anymore. I want life with Jake to be big and wide and filled with possibilities, not limitations. Even if that means staying, just a little longer, in the one place I vowed never to return to.

"You have to stay, Jake. At least until you've found a buyer." I draw a deep breath, tug up a shaky smile. "And I'll stay here, too, with you. For however long it takes."

But the relief I hoped to see on Jake's face doesn't come. The smile I love so much doesn't show. Instead, I see something that looks very much like remorse.

"Gia, I... I have something I need to tell you before you make that promise."

My stomach does a slow flip-flop that's not entirely pleasant. "Is this the part where you tell me you're married, or that you used to be a woman?"

"This is the part where I tell you why I came here...to Rogersville. I..." He falls silent.

Lexi's message—Jake doesn't let anybody in, ever—combines in my mind with his obvious struggle for words and forms an answer. I think I know where this confession is headed, and I decide to help him out a little.

"Did you come here chasing after a woman?"

He nods, once.

"Did she break your heart?"

A sharp puff of astonishment. "You could say that."

"And has your heart recovered?"

"Yes, but it's not what you think. She—"

I stop him with a shake of my head, soften the gesture with a smile. "The only thing I need to know is, has your heart recovered?"

My question takes the edge off his expression. He picks up one of my curls, twists it around a finger. "It has now."

Relief mingles with his answer to coil a tight spiral around my heart. I wrap my arms around his neck and pull his body closer to mine.

"Then that's all I need to know. As long as you can assure me you're not still harboring feelings for this woman, I don't feel threatened by her. At all."

"But—"

I silence him with a kiss, long and sweet and tender, putting everything I have into it. I want him to feel my heart pounding in my chest, breaking open and spilling out everywhere, but I am also not above admitting I want him to forget about her, whoever this woman was, as long as he's holding me in his arms. And by the way Jake kisses me back, I think I might have succeeded on both counts.

And then his hand is on the move—skimming my waist, cupping a breast, traveling back to the spot between my legs—and I can't think anything but more, more, oh, God yes, more. I throw back my head and moan, and my stomach and thighs start to clench.

"Jake." I arch my back, push up against his hand. My body is on fire, my senses humming like they're electrically charged. I'm so close. So goddamn close. "Please."

"Please what?"

"Please…" Please what? I can barely think, I'm so dizzy with arousal. "Please hurry."

He smiles against my mouth but he obeys, his fingers pushing me within only a few more strokes to the brink. I call out his name as my body lights up from within, and then after that, as the orgasm spirals up and out and everywhere, I can't say anything at all.

Jake says it for me, so quietly I think I haven't heard him. That I dreamed it.

"I love you," he says.

"I love you, too."

It's a long time before either of us falls asleep.

29

"Oh, good God. Would y'all please cover that thing up?"

I open my eyes, but all I see is the morning light and Jake's chest and arms, clutching me to him. I twist my head around and focus in on Lexi. She's standing in the doorway to the hall, one hand shielding her eyes.

"Cover what thing up?" I say.

As Jake and I are both stark naked, our bodies twined around each other on the couch, Lexi could be talking about one of many things, mine or Jake's. But judging by her bit-back grin and the way her fingers are spread just wide enough to peek through, I assume she's not offended by his. He stirs beside me, and the last remaining corner of the blanket covering us drops to the floor.

Lexi waves her hand in our direction, giving up all pretense of not peeking and taking a healthy look at Jake's goods. "All of that. And here." She thrusts out my iPhone. "This thing won't shut up."

Shit. Wide-awake now, I spring off the couch, hop over the blanket and coffee table and sprint across the room to Lexi and my phone.

I snatch my phone from her fingers and check the messages and missed calls. Seventeen total, all of them from our brother.

"It's Bo," I say, flicking through the texts. "Looks like he heard about last night."

"Figures." Lexi peeks around my bare shoulder. "Mornin', Jakey. Hope you don't mind, but I borrowed your toothbrush."

There's a long pause, then Jake's controlled voice. "Now why would I mind you using my toothbrush?"

"I didn't think so." She points a finger toward the kitchen. "Coffee?"

"Help yourself."

Lexi shuffles off to the kitchen, and I switch to the voice mails, listening to them one by one. For someone who's learned to rein in his emotions tighter than Lexi's favorite pair of jeans, Bo's messages are downright histrionic— on a scale of one to ten, clocking in at somewhere around forty-seven. His mood ping-pongs from shocked to furious to despaired to elated and back to shocked. In some of them, the only sound I hear is his sobbing.

Even through all the blubbering, it doesn't take me long to figure out that for Bo, Dean's adultery is equivalent to Dad's redemption. Unlike Lexi, Bo sees the affair as indisputable proof of Dad's innocence. Dean slept with Ella Mae means Dean lied means Dad didn't commit murder. It's as simple as that. Maybe I should get him to explain his theory to Lexi.

I call him back, and he picks up on the first ring. "Is it true? Was Ella Mae sleeping with Dean?"

Jake comes up behind me and cocoons us both in the blanket, and I lean into his warm chest. "Yes."

A loud thump booms down the line, then, "Fuck!"

"What happened? Are you okay?"

"No. I'm not okay, dammit. I'm about as far away from okay as you can get. I believed the motherfucking next-door neighbor over my own father!" Another crash, followed by a good ten seconds of racking sobs. "How could I have been such a *shit?*"

"I'm going to have to get back to you on that one, sweetie, because I did the same thing. Look, calm down, okay? I'll come over there, and we'll figure this out. Are you at home?"

He sputters out something that sounds like yes.

"Where's Amy?"

"At a medical conference in Florida."

I don't know if that's a good thing or bad. Though Amy might be able to stop Bo from tearing up their house, she would probably not know what to do with all his new emotions. I look around for my clothes.

"Stay put, okay? I'll be there in thirty minutes, tops."

"Everything all right?" Jake says after I've hung up. His breath tickles the skin behind my ear.

I think about the mess Bo is making of his house and puff out a dry laugh. "Depends on who you ask."

"I'm asking you."

The vulnerability in his tone slices into my skin, and I know what he's asking. I twist around in his arms and snake my hands around his neck, pulling his warm body to mine. "I'm still staying. Even though right now I have to go."

"Let me know how it goes?"

I'm about to nod when there's a loud crash from the kitchen, then Lexi's sugar-sweet voice. "Sorry, Jakey. I'll buy you another one."

"Please," Jake whispers into my hair, "take your sister with you."

* * *

By the time Lexi and I make it all the way over to Church Hill, Bo has pretty much demolished his living room. Books and papers and magazines litter the carpet next to the overturned couch, its pillows flung clear across the room. Lamps and pictures lie in pieces on the floor next to a sniveling Bo, just as messy, just as broken, in a T-shirt and yesterday's work pants. Lexi shoves him under the shower while I clean up as best I can, and then we load him in the backseat of the car and head off for home.

As soon as we crest the hill on Maple Street, I notice two things are off.

First of all, Cal's here. On a Tuesday morning, when he's supposed to be sweet-talking the judge and jury in a courtroom a hundred miles away. My heart hammers out a beat in triple time until I remember I just checked my phone, and then it thuds to an ominous stop. No get-home-now messages from Fannie means Cal's not here because of my father. I mentally prepare myself for a tongue-lashing.

The second thing is the street is empty. No cars, no media vans, no people. The protesters are gone. The only sign they were ever here is a patch of stomped-down grass, a few stray Starbucks cups scattered over the asphalt and a scarlet *A* spray painted across the front of Dean's house.

On the passenger seat beside me, Lexi snorts. "Do you think whatever idiot did that thought it stood for *asshole?*"

I park behind Cal's Buick and twist in my seat to face Lexi and Bo. "Okay, so a couple of things before we get in there. Dad looks awful. His skin's orange and he's really skinny, so don't freak out when you see him. He sleeps a lot because he's doped up on morphine, and when he's awake, he's not always lucid. If he gets confused, the best thing to do is just remind him where he is and who you are, okay?"

Bo's eyes go wide. "He's not going to remember me?"

"He remembers all of us, just not all the time. Now I need both of y'all to take a deep breath and put on your game faces, okay?" I reach for the handle on the door and swing it wide, not waiting for either of them to disagree. "Let's go."

Bo and I climb out of the car, but Lexi doesn't move. I lift both hands in an are-you-coming? gesture through the front windshield. She rolls her eyes and gets out, but she takes all the livelong day, lagging behind Bo and me with heavy steps as we make our way to the front door.

And then on the porch, her feet grow roots.

"Go on in," I say to Bo. "We'll be right there."

He nods, sucks in enough oxygen to pop a lung, then steps inside and breaks down. Through the door I hear him bawl something in loud, unintelligible bursts, but Dad must understand at least some of it because he says, "It's all right, son. Come here."

"I liked our brother better when he was on emotional lockdown," Lexi jokes, but her heart's not in it. Her voice is off by a good octave, and her mouth is sloped in a way I recognize from last night, right before she threw up.

"Lex, you can do this."

She looks at me, and her eyes are wide and wet. "I don't think I can."

"I swear to you this is the hardest part. After you get that first hello out of the way, it's all smooth sailing from there. I promise." I offer her a hand. "Come on. We'll go in together."

She doesn't nod, but she clamps her fingers around mine. "Don't let go."

I don't tell my sister she has my hand in a death grip and I couldn't let go even if I wanted to. Instead, I smile and squeeze back. "I wouldn't dream of it. You and me, remember?"

I give her arm a little tug and push open the door. Lexi makes a squeaking sound when she spots the fake Persian, but she doesn't stop moving, mostly because I don't give her the chance. I lead her into the living room, where Bo is weeping on the chair next to Dad's bed. My brother's back is hunched, his forehead pressed to the mattress, and Dad's bony hand rests on top of Bo's head. And judging from Dad's expression, Bo's sins have been…well, if not forgiven, then at least forgotten.

"See?" I whisper to Lexi. "Piece of cake."

In fact, if I were Lexi I'd be more afraid of Cal, glaring at us both from the armchair by the window. I swallow down my smile when he doesn't return the gesture. Jeez. You'd think he'd at least thank us for the lack of protesters on the front lawn.

Dad motions Lexi closer. Her viselike grip on my hand tightens, but she complies.

"Law, if you aren't the spittin' image of your mother."

His speech is a little slurpy around the edges from the morphine, but he couldn't have chosen better first words. Lexi's mouth curves upward, just a teeny bit, but enough to let him know she sees them as a compliment, and that she's pleased.

"Sit down, girls. Now that you're all here I have something to say."

Bo looks up, blinking. Lexi and I shed our coats and sink onto the couch.

"I'm not stupid. I know what you kids thought of me these past sixteen years, and I know there's a not-so-small part of you that still thinks it. But nothing puts matters into perspective like dying. I'm not looking for your trust or belief or anything else you can't give. I'm just grateful you came."

I don't know if it's the pain meds talking, or if Dad's really had a change of heart. I look over at Cal for a clue, but his face is stone, his lips thin and tight, and his gaze is lasered onto Lexi.

She leans back on the couch, crosses her arms and legs and purses her lips. Her silence speaks volumes, but so does the fact that she stays put. Though she's not ready to apologize for presuming Dad's hand in Ella Mae's death for the past sixteen years, she's no longer certain enough to leave, either. What was it she said to me last night? Reasonable doubt is doubt all the same, and Lexi is still holding on to hers.

Dad notices, and so does Cal. He stands and points to the back of the house. "Lexi, can I get a quick word with you? Bo and Gia, you, too."

Lexi and I exchange a glance, and her expression matches mine. Whatever Cal has to say, it's going to be neither quick nor pleasant. He marches us into the kitchen, and Fannie grins at us from the sink, where she's washing dishes. Her smile plummets at Cal's expression, and she drops the sponge onto the counter and skedaddles out the other door. God bless her, the woman has a particular talent for knowing when to slip away.

As soon as she's gone, Cal whirls around to face us, and his anger is directed at me. "What part of don't go around talking about the affair didn't you understand?"

"Don't look at me. I only told Lexi."

And Jake, I think, but that's beside the point. The point is, Lexi is the blabbermouth and I'm not taking the blame.

Cal swivels his head to Lexi, and his brow lifts in a silent *Well?*

She hikes a casual shoulder. "I don't see the problem. People would've found out sooner or later. There's not a soul in this town who can keep a secret for more than five minutes. Except maybe Ella Mae, but look where that got her."

"How? How would they have found out, if it wasn't for the two of you barroom busybodies?"

Lexi grows a good three inches under his condescending tone. "I hardly think being the victim's stepdaughters qualifies us as barroom busybodies, Cal. We are Dad's children. We have every right to talk about his case, whether in a barroom or my own living room. What I don't understand is why you haven't. From what Gia told me, you've not only withheld information from judge and jury, but also from the three of us. We deserve to know what you do, even if you don't think we'll like what we hear."

"This isn't about you. It's never been about you. The only reason I didn't tell you or anybody else about Ella Mae's affair was to protect your father."

"Sorry, but how is that protecting Dad, when Ella Mae was sleeping with the star witness?"

Cal loses what has always been a short supply of patience. "Keep your voice down, dammit. Ray doesn't know who the affair was with. Hell, I didn't know until Gia told me last week. But now, thanks to the scene you two made last night, the whole dadgum town knows."

"Not the whole town," Bo corrects, ever the realist.

Cal gives him a look.

"So now what?" I ask. "We go in there and tell Dad about Dean?"

"No. No one tells. What do you think that would do to him when he realizes Dean Sullivan stole more than sixteen years of his life?"

Bo and I bob our heads, but Lexi shakes hers. "Somebody keeping secrets is what got us into this mess in the first place. Dad deserves to know the truth."

"In a perfect world I might agree, but this situation is about as far away from perfect as you can get. My baby brother is in there on his deathbed, and I'm not about to tell him something that will push him over the edge any quicker."

"I can't keep this a secret, Cal. It's not fair to—"

"You will not mention Dean Sullivan's name in this house again. Are we clear?" When she doesn't respond, Cal leans forward, clamping down on his lips so she knows he's serious. "You broke your daddy's heart sixteen years ago. Do not, I repeat do NOT, break that dying man's heart again. Do you hear?"

After an eternity, Lexi sighs and rolls her eyes. "Fine. Whatever. I don't agree, but I'll keep my mouth shut."

With Cal satisfied, we file back into the living room, where Fannie has supplied us with homemade lemon pound cake. Outside the window, a procession of cars pulls into view and slows to a stop by the mailbox. One by one, the protesters file out. I flick a watchful glance at Bo and Lexi, worried at how they'll respond to the hateful cries of death and justice, but the cries don't come. Outside, silence hangs heavy in the air.

And then Fannie does a double take out the window. "Well, I'll be. Would you take a gander at that?"

I crane my neck and follow her gaze to a colorful mound on the front lawn. "What is that?"

"I do believe it's flowers."

"Flowers?" I pop off the couch and move closer to the window, squinting to get a better look at the pile of red and yellow and pink and green bouquets wrapped in shiny cellophane. A group of creamy cylinders lines the edge of the driveway, their soft lights flickering in the March morning. "And are those candles?"

"That Rogersville grapevine is powerful stuff," Lexi says, shaking her head.

Just then, a silver SUV slows at the edge of the drive. Shawna Kerney slides out of the passenger seat with a bouquet of yellow and white flowers, places them atop the pile, nestles a creamy envelope between the buds and hoists herself back into the car.

Bo takes off for the door, not bothering with his coat. "Be right back."

We watch through the pane as he roots around in the flowers, returning moments later with a handful of papers and a wide grin. He spreads them out across Dad's lap and legs, and then one by one, reads the messages aloud to the room.

With the same feverish fervor they concluded him guilty all those years ago, the people of Rogersville have now switched sides. The collective tides have turned. The general consensus now is that the most heinous crime was our father serving time for a murder he didn't commit, and for that, the people of Rogersville are deeply, truly, fervently sorry. For the assumed guilt, for all the wasted years, for the cancer now eating away at his insides.

While Bo reads, Fannie and Dad cry, Cal bows his head, Lexi bites her lip and studies her nails, and I wonder how I ever worried about the opinions of the people of Rogersville. Sometime in the past few weeks, my worry has dissolved into apathy, filling up every inch of me. I no longer care what they think.

Am I the only person in the room who sees the pile of flowers and candles on our front yard for what it is? An awfully hollow place for people to bury their guilt.

30

Whether it's the town's renewed faith in Dad's innocence or Bo and Lexi's homecoming, something seems to revive Dad. His face clears and his cheeks flush and his lips turn up into a smile and set. His bony shoulders, until now perpetually hunched up to just under his ears, relax and drop, and that bottomless crease between his eyebrows unfolds into a pink line. And there's no disguising the way his eyes light up, especially when Lexi pulls up a chair at his right elbow.

He insists we eat lunch—grilled cheese sandwiches and a chunky tomato soup I help Fannie serve up in the kitchen—huddled around his bed. Fannie even hands Dad a bowl, though more for form than function. These days he does more picking at his food than actual eating.

Once everyone is settled, we dig in. Spoons scrape. Lips slurp. Crusts crunch. The air is thick with the cloying scent of salted tomatoes and buttered bread and words none of us know how to say.

Dad clears his throat, and everyone looks up from their plates, waiting. The sound is, I suspect, purely practical, since he doesn't follow it up with words. Or maybe he simply changed his mind. Regardless, he swirls his spoon around in his bowl until one by one, everyone returns to their lunches.

Everyone but me.

I look at Bo, who's shoveling food into his mouth faster than he can chew. I recognize the strategy from his high-school days, when Dad would use dinnertime to interrogate us about sliding grades, missed curfews, a fresh dent in the fender. If Bo's mouth is full, he doesn't have to talk. I eye his dwindling food supply and think he'd better slow down, if for no other reason than impending indigestion.

I glance at Lexi, tugging off the crusts and nibbling at her sandwich's gooey center. Though she certainly seems subdued, she doesn't look the slightest bit contrite. Actually, maybe it's even worse. Maybe she's trying not to look contrite.

My veins hum with unreleased frustration. "Fine."

Across Dad's bed, Cal sits up straight and glares. I give him a look that says chill the hell out. I'm not planning to mention Ella Mae and Dean, but with Dad lying here—literally—on his deathbed, now is not the time for eating or mincing words.

"Fine," I repeat, dropping my spoon maybe a tad too hard onto my plate. "If no one else is going to do it, how about I begin?"

Fannie must hear something in my voice, because she pops out of her chair and disappears with her plate into the kitchen.

I turn to Dad, who clearly doesn't know what's coming. The crease between his brows is back, and his shoulders are climbing up his neck again. I smile, softening my expression, my tone, my tactic.

"Do you remember when Ella Mae bought us that home-waxing kit? The one we warmed up in the microwave?"

Dad's shoulders drop a good inch, and he almost smiles. "I came home, and y'all looked like mummies. You were covered in long strips of fabric, and the whole house smelled like tar."

I laugh. "I think it was tar, because we couldn't get it off. Our legs were sticky for months. Anyway, neither of us dared to yank off our own strips, because what none of those packages will tell you is waxing hurts like hell."

"Word," Lexi says around a soft snort.

"After forever, Ella Mae stuck her foot up on the counter, squeezed her eyes shut and told me to just rip them off. She said fast and clean was the least painful way, and she was right. So that's what I'm gonna do now. I'm gonna rip off the Band-Aid."

Bo swallows his food with an audible gulp. His eyes bulge, then rapid-fire blink. Beside him, Lexi puts down her sandwich and crosses her arms, and her face closes up. Neither of them speak.

Rip the Band-Aid off.

I set my plate on the floor and turn back to Dad.

"All these years, I've been waiting for proof you didn't do this horrible thing everybody said you did. I thought if someone supplied me with even a shred of reasonable doubt, this whole nightmare would be over and you could be my dad again. And then I got it. I got my reasonable doubt, and you know what? Turns out you were always my dad. I was just a shitty daughter."

I hear a hiccup, then Bo sucks in a thick breath. He is on the verge of tears, I know, and I don't dare look at him for fear his tears will instigate mine. Instead, I focus on a fold in Dad's blanket, how it lifts and falls with each breath.

"Because sixteen years is a long time to be searching for doubt," I continue, "when really I should have been more focused on trust. I don't know why I didn't trust you. I don't know why I couldn't trust you. What I do know is that sometime in the past sixteen years, my suspicions broke me. I am broken because for so long, I thought my own father was capable of murder. And I don't think I will ever be able to accept how much that must have hurt you."

Silence settles over the room, swollen and heavy as a lead blanket. There's a certain anguish in Dad's face, a faint twist to his mouth, and he's frowning. He stares at his hands for a long moment then, finally, clears his throat.

"You're here now. That's all that matters."

His answer both disappoints and annoys me—not because I am waiting for absolution, but because I was hoping for more. More acknowledgment of his obvious pain, more blame for my hand in it, more anger and disdain and hostility.

And speaking of more, why are Bo and Lexi so silent? What good is ripping off this family's Band-Aid if I'm the only one?

I lean forward, shake my head. "It's not all that matters. We thought you were a liar and a murderer. We were actually relieved when you went to prison. And we never, not once, wrote or visited you there, because it was easier to pretend you didn't exist than to admit to having a father who was a convicted murderer. How can you not hate us?"

Dad startles at the word *hate,* as if he'd never once considered it.

"Of course I don't hate you. Y'all are my blood, mine and Rosalie's, and I couldn't hate you if I tried." He looks at me, then to Bo and Lexi. "Once you have kids of your own, you'll understand."

Lexi thunks her plate on the tray table beside her, her gaze skittering to the window. "I'll never understand," she whispers, and I know she's not talking about a parent's unconditional love.

Dad seems to know, too. He reaches for Lexi's hand, and she lets him, though she won't quite meet his eyes.

"No one says you have to understand why things happened the way they did, or even that you have to accept them. Your mother died, your stepmother was killed, your father was taken away. I think it's safe to assume you kids have been in your own kind of prison for the past couple decades."

I fall back into my chair, my anger fizzled. Dad's right. We have been in prisons of our own. My stomach twists at the thought of all the years I've spent wandering the globe, burying myself in someone else's drama in order to forget my own. It didn't help. I didn't forget. And since Bo and Lexi were reminders of that awful time, it was easier to ignore them, too.

"I'm so sorry," I say, this time not to Dad.

Bo looks up. His gaze goes from me to Lexi, and I can see he has the same regrets. "Me, too. I wish I'd been a better brother."

There's a long silence, one that expands and fills the room until it becomes almost tangible. A strained silence.

Lexi glances at both of us, defensively, as if by asking forgiveness, we have accused her of something. She opens her mouth, closes it, then shakes her head, just barely, but enough that I understand. She wants to apologize, but she can't. Something—doubt? her pride?—is holding her back.

Dad closes his eyes, and he makes that face again. "I forgive you anyway."

Lexi stares at her lap. "No you don't," she whispers.

"I do." His eyes are too dehydrated to well up, but even without tears, he looks like he's crying. "I forgive you."

"But why?"

"Because I love you kids. Because I've missed you. Because I don't have time for grudges."

At the reminder of why we're here, at Dad's bedside, my sister begins to cry. Not the silent kind of tears, the ones slipping noiselessly down her cheeks and falling with a muffled splat onto her lap, but the heaving, blubbering, sputtering kind. The kind that convulse her entire body with choked-out sobs and turn her pretty cheeks snotty and splotchy. She doesn't hold back or try to hide it, either, just screws up her face and howls.

A jagged pain ripples up my throat, aching with tears I can no longer hold back. For all my sister's posturing, she's always been the fragile one. Up until this very moment, she's just been better at hiding it than the rest of us.

"It's not fair," she wails, loud enough to hurt my ears. "It's not fucking fair."

Dad shushes her. "I know it's not, darlin'. Believe me, I know. But now that I've got you kids back, I'll die a happy man."

"But I don't..." A shuddering sob racks her body and steals her breath before she begins again. "I don't want you to die yet. Not when I just got you back."

Lexi's words are not an apology, but judging by the way they light up Dad's face, they're even better. I know for Lexi, they were just as difficult to say. He closes his eyes and opens his arms, and Lexi falls into them, holding on for all she's worth.

I take a moment to let it sink in. This is what I've been fighting for—this moment—for Lexi and my father and our family. I can't save Dad, but at least I've saved what's left of us, of me and Bo and Lexi. Especially Lexi. Something inside me unravels, that tight knot around my heart finally comes untied, and an unfamiliar feeling spreads across my chest like warm honey. It takes me a few beats to recognize it for what it is. Happiness. For the first time in what feels like forever, I am more happy than sad.

Dad smooths down Lexi's already smooth hair with a palm and smiles, actually smiles at me over the top of her head.

"Thank you," he mouths.

Over the course of the next few days, we fall into a comfortable rhythm. After breakfast around Dad's bed, Bo and Lexi head off to work while Cal commandeers the dining room table, spreading his papers and laptop all over its shiny surface and screaming into his cell phone from one of its chairs all day long. Fannie and I spend the day puttering around the house and caring for Dad, who sleeps more than not nowadays. While he dozes, the two of us watch a mindless string of sitcoms and talk shows and eighties movies, bake enough pastries to fatten up all of Appalachia and chat about pretty much every subject under the sun.

And somehow, every day, all day long, I end up talking mostly about Jake, counting down the seconds until the house goes dark and quiet and he tiptoes up the porch.

Upstairs alone in my room, we make love, and then we make plans. What Jake and I jokingly refer to as my Rogersville Test Drive will begin the day after the funeral, when I will call my boss to extend my leave. Jake suggested I ask for another month. I said he needed at least six to get a good price for his place. We compromised on three.

And every night, he asks me if I'm certain I want to stay. So far the answer has always been yes.

I still don't entirely know how I feel about remaining in Rogersville after Dad's gone, but I am certain about one thing: I cannot, cannot leave Jake. He assures me every day and in no uncertain terms that he feels the same. Somehow knowing he would pick up and leave whenever I say it's time softens the edges of my panic at staying. I know I have an out, one Jake has unconditionally included himself in, and that knowledge gives me strength. Strength to face the Rogersville gossip mill, strength to put up with their whispers and half truths and misguided assumptions, strength to stay in a place where I will always be, before anything else, Ray Andrews's daughter.

When I tell all this to Fannie, she clutches a pillow to her chest, leans back onto the couch and sighs dreamily. "That there's the most romantic thing I think I ever did hear."

"It is pretty sappy, isn't it? Too much?"

"Gracious, no." She pats my knee and grins. "Let this old lady live vicariously, will you? What else you got?"

"Well…" I think for a moment. "The other day he told me he wants to take me away for a weekend after…well, you know. He won't tell me where, only that it's his second favorite spot in the world."

"Why not his first?"

"That's exactly what I asked. He said we were already there, because his first favorite spot was wherever I was."

Fannie smacks her thigh and whoops.

I make a moony face. "I know. Gross, right?"

"Oh, no, honey, not gross. Not coming from a man as fine as Jake Foster. That boy is one smooth talker. And right smitten, too, sounds like."

I can't deny I am just as smitten, and content in a way I never dreamed I could be when I boarded the plane in Kenya. Or maybe *content* isn't the right word. Maybe what

I'm feeling is something more like blissful. Blissful because my family is back, the protesters are gone and Jake is warming my bed at night. What more could I have wished for, considering?

Even Lexi seems to have come around. As soon as she gets home from the bank, she plops into an armchair at Dad's right elbow and stays there until bedtime, coaxing him into conversation when he's awake, sitting quietly at his side while he sleeps. I don't much mind that she's hijacked my chair and his attention. Bo and I have already had our moments with Dad, and I want her to have hers, as well.

Dad's bitterness and anger seem to have evaporated, as well, replaced by a calm acceptance of what is to come. I guess his brain has finally accepted what his body already knew, and by some unspoken agreement, he's decided to make the best of whatever time we have left together.

This new normal makes it almost easy to forget why I came, why we have all gathered here, in our former home, at Dad's bedside. And then Dad thrashes about on the bed or screams in his sleep, and I remember. Remember what was lost—Ella Mae. Dad. Rogersville. What is about to be lost all over again—Dad, this time around irrevocably.

How is it possible to feel so perfectly happy and so heartbroken at the same time?

31

On Sunday, the hallucinations begin.

One minute Dad is just fine, the next he's going on about spiders in the TV and giant pills dressed as clowns. I can't help but find his mistakes mildly amusing, until his hallucinations target us. First Fannie, whom Dad mistakes for his mother, and then Lexi.

"Sweetheart!" Dad says, smiling broadly at Lexi when she walks into the living room with a beer and a plate of spaghetti. "You're back, and lookin' so beautiful, too."

"See?" I cross my arms and lift an I-told-you-so brow at my sister. "He totally missed you."

Lexi doesn't look convinced. "No, I think he thinks I'm Mom."

I'm about to disagree, when Dad's expression of pleasant surprise curls into a leer. "Get over here, Rosalie. I got a hard-on with your name written all over it."

My sister raises the bottle to her lips, drains it, then looks at me and shakes her head. "Nope. Still not drunk enough."

The next morning, it's my turn. I've just come out of the

kitchen, where I'd been dawdling while Fannie gave Dad his sponge bath, when he calls out to me.

"Where you been?" Something about his tone, suspicious and thick with disdain, sends a rash of chill bumps exploding up my arms.

"I was just cleaning up breakfast." I point in the general direction of the kitchen, wishing Fannie hadn't already disappeared upstairs to the shower and Cal hadn't chosen this morning to meet up with a former client in Kingsport. "Can I get you anything?"

"I see the way you look at him." His mouth twists in pain, but something in the squint of his eyes tells me it's not the physical kind. "It's the way you used to look at me."

I step closer to his bed and into his line of vision, an icy chill hijacking my spine. Who does he think I am?

"I don't know what you're talking about, Dad. Nobody's looking at anyone."

"I won't have it. I won't have you runnin' all over town like a whore, makin' a goddamn fool of me. People are starting to talk."

The realization rips through my veins and chills my very core. He thinks I'm Ella Mae.

"Dad, it's Gia, remember?" I clamp a hand onto his wrist, give it a little jiggle. "I'm your daughter. Gia."

"Huh?" His eyes focus on me and he blinks rapidly, eyelids fluttering. "Did you count out the feathers, or did the penguins eat them?"

Good grief. I've had less confusing conversations in Swahili.

Dad slumps back onto the bed, falling unconscious before I can form an answer, leaving me to wonder which part of that conversation was real, and which part was nonsense.

Later, when Fannie and I are folding laundry, I find

we have a new subject to talk about. "Dad's hallucinations seem to be getting worse, and he doesn't always make sense."

She folds a bath towel in thirds and tucks it under her chin. "That's pretty normal with cancer patients, sugar. It's all part of the dyin' process."

"But is it normal he thinks we're people who are long gone? First Grandma, then Mom, and this morning he thought I was Ella Mae. I mean, I have dark hair and curls, but that's kind of where the likeness ends."

Fannie settles the folded towel atop a neat pile of matching ones and turns to me, her expression filled with compassion. "Sweetheart, your father's in the active stage of dyin'. Part of his confusion is from the morphine, but it's also because his body is filling up with toxins. His organs can't clean the poisons out of his body because they're too busy shuttin' down."

I swallow hard, my heartbeat heating into a roiling thunder. "How much longer do you think he has?"

"Hard to say." Fannie lifts her massive shoulders in a shrug. "Everybody's different."

"Give me your best educated guess."

She purses her carnation lips into a sympathetic pout, blinks her crayon eyes. "I'd say two or three days, at the most. I'm sorry, sugar." She pats my arm, snatches up the pile of towels and waddles off.

In the morning, I'm leading Jake back down the stairs when Dad's reality takes another turn for the imaginary.

"You sneaking off again, Ella Mae?"

His tone seals my slippers to the carpet runner halfway down. Jake raises a questioning brow, and I hold a finger to my lips with one hand, point him down the hallway toward the back door with the other.

"Don't you dare ignore me, woman. I know you're there. I hear you breathing. Did you bring that man into my house again? Did you fuck him in my bed?"

By now Jake and I have reached the bottom of the stairs. I catch him by the shoulders, turn him a sharp left and give him a gentle push in the small of his back. He takes a reluctant step into the hallway.

"I'll kill you for it, you dirty whore."

Dad's words skid Jake to a stop on the hardwood floor. He swivels his upper body to face me, shock and something else I don't have time to think about pushing at the edges of his mouth.

"Dad!" I double back, leaning my head around the corner into the living room, and yell-whisper, "It's me, Gia. Not Ella Mae. Now go back to sleep before you wake the whole house."

"Don't lie to me, bitch! I know he's right there behind you. If he was any kind of man, he'd not be running out the back door. That's what he's trying to do, isn't he? Goddamn chickenshit."

I dart a glance to Jake, still frozen on the other side of the Persian. "The morphine makes him hallucinate," I whisper.

"I'll kill him, Ella Mae. I'll kill you both."

I turn back to Dad. "Dad! I'm Gia, okay? And the only other person here is Jake. My boyfriend."

I motion for Jake to come into the doorway, but he doesn't comply. His feet stay rooted to the floor.

It's like I didn't even speak. Dad throws off the covers, arms and legs thrashing, and tries to push to a sit. He tilts dangerously to the left, and I rush across the room to keep him from flailing himself off the bed.

"Stop, before you fall and snap a hip bone." I try to snatch one of his arms out of the air, but his movements are jerky and, for such a sick man, still pretty forceful. After a few tries, my palm finally makes contact with his wrist, right before a fist lands in my cheek. His three other limbs are still on the loose, wild and writhing him closer and closer to the edge, and I only have one more hand.

"Jake!" Short of throwing my body over Dad's and weighting him down, I don't know what else to do other than call for help.

Jake doesn't come. "Should I go wake up Fannie?" he suggests instead.

Dad uses my grip on his arm for leverage, pulling and pushing to get himself higher off the bed. A knee comes out of nowhere and thonks me on the temple, hard enough to make me see stars.

"Ow! Shit. Jake, I need help now."

After a moment, hasty footsteps come up behind me, and Jake steps around the head to the other side of the bed. He clamps a palm onto Dad's right shoulder and the other onto his thigh and pushes, pinning his right side to the bed. I think there might be something off in Jake's expression, judging by his pinched mouth and the red flush rising from the collar of his North Face fleece.

Jake's appearance works on Dad like a stun gun. His muscles unclench and he collapses back onto the bed, blinking up at Jake with an expression of delighted confusion, or maybe it's confused delight.

"Brian! Well, I'll be. When...? How...?" Dad shakes his head, and his face breaks into a grin. "So good to see you again, son!"

Now there's definitely something off in Jake's expression. He goes completely still, and he won't quite meet my eye.

"No, Dad. His name is Jake Foster. He owns the Road-kill Bar and Grill in town."

Dad grabs a hunk of Jake's shirt and clutches it into a ball. "Tell her, Brian. Tell her I didn't kill Ella Mae."

"Who's Brian?" I say, more to myself than anyone else. So far, Dad's hallucinations have been filled with real people from real pieces of his past, and I don't recall any Brian. Maybe he was one of the summer stock boys down at the pharmacy?

Dad turns to me, his face lit up like the July sky. "This here's Ella Mae's boy. This is her son."

"But Ella Mae didn't have a so—" I swallow the last letter at the look on Jake's face, and a bitter taste pools on my tongue.

"Gia, please." He reaches a hand across the bed, but I step back before he can touch me. "Let me explain."

People who say the world is small have never traveled to La Rinconada in Peru, or Motuo County in China or to the Kerguelen Islands in the southern Indian Ocean. When your destination has no airports or trains or even roads, when the journey is just as long and treacherous as the land is untouched by the modern world, our planet feels enormous, its farthest flung corners infinite.

But as I stare across my dying father at Jake, I realize the world will never be large enough for me to escape my past.

"Is this a joke?" It's my voice, but the tone is all wrong. Quiet and controlled and strangely detached, like I just asked him if it's supposed to rain tomorrow.

"No."

"Am I being punked? Is somebody going to pop out any minute with a hidden camera?"

"No. Gia, I—"

I stop Jake with a palm in the air. Dad's arm, now freed from my grasp, drops to the bed with a muted thud.

"Is it tr—" My voice almost breaks from the sob trying to sneak up my throat, and I gulp it down before it can escape. "Is it true?"

My heart already knows the answer. Of course it does. But that doesn't mean my brain doesn't still need to hear Jake say he's Ella Mae's son. I clutch the edge of the mattress and brace myself for his reply.

He closes his eyes briefly, and I think he sways, but that might have been me. "Yes."

The sourness on my tongue explodes in a rush of bile, and I press a shaky hand to my lurching stomach. So far it's the only one of my organs to fully grasp the meaning behind the truth. My brain and heart are still struggling to catch up.

"I don't understand. Ella Mae never said anything about a child."

"My birth wasn't exactly a joyous occasion. At least, not for her. My adoptive parents thought differently." His fingers clench harder into Dad's shoulder. "Please don't look at me like that."

But I'm still having trouble processing. "Like what?"

"Like you've never seen me before. This doesn't change anything. I'm still me, and I still mean every single word I've ever said to you."

"Right now I'm more concerned with the words you didn't say."

He makes a face like I punched him in the stomach. "I tried to tell you."

His excuse strikes me somehow as perversely funny, and I bark out a laugh. "When? By mental telepathy?"

"I tried, at least twice. I just… I didn't know how."

"You should have found a way."

My adrenaline suddenly spikes, smashing my anger instinct out of its paralysis. A cold ball of fury forms in my belly, pushing at my throat, putting down roots in my organs, snaking through my veins, growing and pulsing with life. I feel it swirl inside me, and somewhere in the very back closet of my mind, I acknowledge relief that it's rage, rather than grief, gripping me by the guts. At least my anger, even as sharp as it is, feels like it's holding me together rather than ripping me apart.

"Okay," I say, my voice rising loud enough to wake Dean Sullivan from his drunken stupor next door, "so let me get this straight. Your mother fucked my father, and now you're fucking me? Is that about right?"

"Watch your language, young lady," Dad says, lifting his head and his brow in a warning look.

I make a get-real sound in the back of my throat. My father hasn't scolded me since I was eighteen, and I'm not about to let him start now, sixteen years too late. I fix my glare steady on Jake, waiting for his reply.

"That's not how I see it."

His nonanswer sends me over the edge, and gives my volume knob another sharp twist. "Jesus, Jake! Her son? That's kind of an important detail, don't you think? You should have told me that very first night I climbed onto one of your bar stoo—" And then I think of something else, and my body fills with ice. "Oh, God. Does Lexi know?"

"Does Lexi know what?" my sister asks, blinking at us from the hallway. Despite her rumpled T-shirt, mussed hair and last night's smeared mascara, she looks like a Victoria's Secret pajama model.

Jake doesn't even notice her. Not for one millisecond

does he shift his gaze away from me. "No. No one knows. I didn't even know until a few years ago."

"Know what?" Lexi asks again.

"Yes. Know what, Jake?" I lift a brow, signaling I'm not going to be the one to tell her.

Jake's shoulders slump in defeat. He blinks, then looks beyond my shoulder to Lexi. "Ella Mae Andrews was my birth mother."

I hear my sister's gasp behind me, then another louder and deeper one that can only have come from Fannie.

Awesome. An audience.

"Tell them I didn't do it," Dad says, reaching excitedly for Jake, who steadies him with a distracted hand on his shoulder. It's a comforting but familiar gesture, and a new realization slams me with the force of a Mack Truck. These two men are not strangers.

My gaze lifts to Jake's. "Dad recognized you. He knew your name. How?"

Jake drops his head, but not before I can see his wince. When he looks back up, his gaze is anywhere but on me. "There was a letter. From Ella Mae to me, written less than a month before she died. I showed it to your father, when I visited him in prison."

His message punches me in the gut, deflating my lungs and stealing my breath and leaving me gasping for air. "You visited? When?"

"Just once. It was a long time ago, a few months after I moved to town. Long enough ago I didn't think…"

Jake doesn't have to finish. I know what he was about to say. Long enough ago he didn't think Dad would recognize him.

"Could this letter have gotten him out of prison?"

Jake pauses to look over my shoulder. He is, I think,

about to nod, when from behind me booms a loud, emphatic "No."

One word from Cal, spoken with the doggedness of a thousand lawyers.

I don't know how long he's been standing there, lined up along with Bo and Fannie on either side of Lexi, but I assume he was the recipient of Jake's pointed look just now. I can also give an educated guess as to why he doesn't look as shocked as the rest of the spectators.

Because Cal's read the letter, too.

"No," he asserts again, stepping into the room. Even in his bare feet and slept-in pajamas, he somehow still manages to carry a commanding courtroom air. "What you're forgetting is that your father's case wasn't that simple. There were mountains of different facts and circumstances and evidence to sort through for the appeal. A one-page letter wasn't going to make a dent in the transcripts, which were over ten thousand pages. So let's not go around making assumptions about things we don't understand, all right?"

No one agrees, not even Dad. I turn back to Jake, and his expression confirms what I'm thinking. That Cal is bullshitting us. That this letter could have made a dent, and a significant one. That I understand a lot more than the Tennessee Tiger would like.

"Where is this letter?" I say to Jake.

"At my house."

"I want to see it."

Behind me, Cal sputters loud sounds of protest, but I ignore him. Jake does, too. He digs a hand in his pocket for keys and moves toward the door.

I turn and motion to Lexi to follow me upstairs. "Get dressed. You're going with us."

"Wait." Bo latches onto my sleeve, almost jerking it off

my arm. His hair is a mess, and he's in bad need of a razor and a toothbrush. "What about me?"

"There's no room in Jake's cab. If you want to come, you'll have to follow behind. We're leaving in two minutes."

"Now let's all calm down, folks," Cal says. "This is just a silly piece of paper we're talking about. A letter from Ella Mae to a man she never knew. If it had been anything more than that, don't you think I would have jumped all over it? This letter has no legal significance whatsoever in your father's case."

I hear more than just pride and a patronizing bite to his voice. There's also the tiniest edge of panic.

"Then you won't have a problem with us seeing it," I say.

Cal tucks his thumbs in the elastic waist of his pajama pants, leans back on his heels and uses his best good-old-boy drawl. "It's not the seein' that worries me, darlin'. It's the believin' this letter has some kind of magical powers. I already told y'all it's not going to change a thing."

All at once I am even more suspicious. The longer Cal tries to talk me out of wanting to read this letter, the more magical I think it may be.

But if the Tennessee Tiger has taught me anything at all, it's how to give good poker face. I wipe all traces of hope and distrust I'm feeling from my expression and blink up at him.

"Then maybe you should come along so you can explain it to us."

After a long moment, Cal gives me a thin smile. "Fine. Because you're sure as hell not leaving me behind."

Two and a half minutes later Jake and I are flying up the hill to town in his truck, my sister wedged between us on the seat, Bo and Cal on our tail.

32

In my job, I've been put in more impossible situations than I can count. I've watched cultures be destroyed by the people who were supposed to protect them, their citizens murdered, their artifacts looted. I've come face-to-face with spectacular evil in the form of genocidal regimes and aid-resistant bureaucrats and reckless idiots with semiautomatic rifles. I've stood before thousands of people with rations meant for half that number, and turned away weeping mothers as they chose which child to feed, and which to let starve.

But never, never have I felt as helpless as I do now.

Helpless because I can't seem to distinguish my fury at Jake from my confusion and heartbreak at his lie of omission. I want to scream obscenities and pummel my fists into his chest at the same time I want to throw my arms around his neck and beg him to rip off my clothes. I detest his lie, and yet I think if I try really hard maybe I could learn to live with it. I love him and I hate him.

Outside the windows of Jake's truck, the neighborhood's scenery rushes by in the early-morning glow. Makeshift twig and electric fences snaking along the edges of frozen farms and yards. Golden light glaring from windows shut against the cold on houses and cabins and double-wides. A row of brown and white cows pressed together for warmth, their tails whipping as we pass.

"I don't understand." Lexi's honey hair is gathered high in a ponytail, and she borrowed a pair of my NYU sweats that sit a tad too snug across her thighs. "You never knew you were adopted?"

Jake shakes his head. "Not until a little over five years ago, after Mom—my adopted mom, that is—died." He leans around Lexi to look at me. "I was cleaning out her house when I found the papers."

My heart gives a painful squeeze for the betrayal he must have felt at discovering the papers, at the same time another part of me, and a not so small part, thinks the experience should have taught him better. Surely he remembers the ache he felt that day strongly enough to want to never inflict it on another person, especially one he claims to love.

I turn my gaze to the street.

"Okay," Lexi says. "So let's just assume for the sake of argument that Jake isn't lying."

I snort. "Which time?"

"That he didn't know anything about Ella Mae until he found the papers." She drapes a palm over my knee and turns to Jake. "That must have been devastating."

He tosses her a humorless smile. "And confusing. And maddening. And ultimately, damn disappointing. Thanks to Google, it wasn't very difficult to figure out what happened to her."

"Why did you come to Rogersville?" I say, more accusation than inquiry.

"Because the internet only gave me the facts. I needed

to know who she really was, where she was from, why she made this place her home. I needed to feel closer to her somehow." Jake's voice is calm, patient, placating in a way I wish offended me more. "I thought maybe if I came here, even a decade after her death, I could get to know her better somehow, so I packed up my stuff and moved here the next day."

"Makes sense." Lexi's tone is filled with a sympathy I resent her for. Where's my sympathy? I'm the one who just got her heart ripped out of her chest. My sister takes in my glare and shrugs. "What? It does. I would have wanted to know, too." She returns her attention to Jake. "So do you?"

He glances at her. "Do I what?"

"Feel closer to Ella Mae."

"I did for a while, but..." He looks over with hangdog eyes for long enough that Lexi gives an alarmed squeak and yanks on the wheel. Jake straightens the truck right before we land in a ditch. "Not anymore."

My eyes burn with unshed tears. I close them and focus on finding my anger, letting it swirl all around me until my teeth and thighs and fists clench, heating my blood until it boils, consuming every inch of me. And then I open my eyes and attack the first person I see, the one sitting directly to my left.

"Why aren't you pissed?" I ask Lexi. "He lied to you, too."

"I know, but honestly, I don't blame him."

My mouth falls open in indignant disbelief.

"Think about it, Gi. You know how people in this town talk, how they make assumptions about you based solely on your kin. It would have taken Jake all of five seconds to have figured out that as soon as he mentioned Ella Mae, they'd be making assumptions about him, too. So no. I can't work myself up into a lather, because I would have done the exact same thing in his position."

The silence that follows stretches a good thirty seconds, maybe even a minute, and for however long it lasts, I feel something inside me cracking open, letting in light, filling me with understanding I don't want to grasp.

Folks come to small towns like this one for their promised peace. All the years I spent tromping down Rogersville's two-lane roads, I'd felt the serenity, too. There's something safe and secure in knowing all your neighbors, in recognizing every face and voice and gesture. And then Ella Mae was murdered, and the tranquility grew teeth. The calm thrashed and crushed. Behind all the fences and windows and doors flashing by my window, I know it still does. If Jake's secret gets out, it will for him, too.

In so many ways, his reasons for not telling parallel mine for not staying.

"But you should have told me. Especially after…" My voice trails as I stare out the passenger window at the brick buildings that line Main and think, *after we kissed, after we made love, after you told me you loved me, take your pick*.

Jake slams the brakes, and the truck skids to a crooked stop in front of Roadkill. When he turns, his eyes are filled with so much anguish I want to turn away, but then his gaze locks onto mine and I can't.

"I know I should have told you. I know that. I had it all clear in my head, too. Exactly what I was going to say, how I was going to tell you. And I tried, dammit, at least a million times. But then you'd look at me and my mouth refused to cooperate."

"So tell me now."

His gaze flicks to Lexi. "What, here?"

"Yes here." My sister starts to squirm over top of me toward the passenger door, but I stop her with a hand to her biceps. "Stay. This involves you, too."

Jake thrusts both hands into his hair and pulls, making it stick up on the sides. My palms itch to reach over, run my fingers through it until his dark waves fall back into place, but I make two hard fists on my lap instead. Finally, he blows out a resigned sigh and then leans around Lexi to fix his gaze onto me.

"Do you believe that some greater force controls what will happen to us in the future? Because I used to think that was a load of crap. Everybody has free will, right? We all make choices, good or bad. We all cross bridges or burn them. And then I found out that the woman I always thought of as my mother wasn't the same woman who gave me life, and I started to wonder how I got so lucky. How did I end up with two parents who loved me so much I never questioned our bond was anything less than blood? Dumb luck. Fate. Destiny. Whatever you want to call it. That's what brought me to them. It's also what brought me to you."

"Oh, Jakey." Lexi brushes three light fingers across his sleeve. "That's beautiful."

I don't respond.

"I thought I came here searching for Ella Mae, but the truth is, I was looking for you. I knew it when I offered you that slice of chocolate cake the first night we met, and I know it now. You are the reason I felt drawn to this place. I was supposed to come here to find you. Not Ella Mae."

In my mind, I crawl over Lexi and onto his lap, grab him by the ears and cover his lips with mine. I feel his tongue in my mouth and his hands on my skin and his heartbeat beating strong and sure against my chest. I hear his flurry of apologies and his vows of forever in my ear, and the sympathy in my voice when I tell him all is forgiven. In my mind, I do all of these things.

In real life, I don't crawl or grab or cover. I don't feel or hear anything.

Because in real life, I don't forgive. My too-scarred, too-scared heart won't let me.

"Destiny isn't preordained, Jake. It's the sum of all the millions of choices we make, not the reason we make them. Your parents chose you out of all the babies born that day, and that was a good thing, for them and for you. But when you chose to lie to me about your identity—"

He shakes his head almost violently. "See, that's where you're wrong. I never lied about me. I'm Jake Alexander Foster, a name given to me by my parents, Sandra and Lieutenant Colonel Joseph Foster, both deceased. They changed my diapers and helped me with homework and tossed a football with me in the backyard. They taught me about the birds and bees and cried at my graduations and worked overtime to pay my college tuition. We didn't share the same DNA, but they were the only parents I ever knew, the only ones I ever loved wholly and unconditionally. So I never lied about who I am, because all my life I've only ever been Jake Alexander Foster."

"A lie of omission is still a lie."

I might as well have punched him. His face dissolves from stubbornly hopeful to painfully resigned. When he doesn't say anything, I go on.

"But what I was going to say is, when you lied to me, that was your choice. Now it's my turn. I get to make a choice, and I choose not to forgive you."

He lets out a sharp breath, and the look of devastation that settles on his face is too painful to watch. I turn away and reach for the handle, shoving open the door, stepping into the cold, pulling my sister out of the cab with me.

"Now let's go get that letter so we can go home."

The second we file into Jake's living room, I know I've made a mistake. I should have waited in the car. I should have sent Lexi in for the letter. I should be anywhere but here, in a place haunted by memories of me and Jake, because I know, I know, I know they're going to make me cry.

Jake tosses his keys onto the table by the door and heads into the hallway toward the bedroom. "Make yourselves at home. I'll just be a minute."

The couch, the carpet, the windowsill, the corner of the countertop by the kitchen sink, the kitchen sink. There's nowhere to look that doesn't give me visions of me and Jake. The room darkens, the air thins, the claustrophobia squeezes until it feels like too much to bear. I move into the hall, sink onto the floor by the wall, bury my face in my hands and squeeze my eyes shut. How long does it take to dig up a freaking piece of paper?

"Sweetheart, are you okay?"

I look up to find Lexi, crouched on the floor in front of me. "Yes. No. I don't know."

"Glad that's all cleared up, then." She smiles and pats my knee, falling onto the floor by my feet. "Look, I know you're angry, but if you don't mind me saying so, you seemed a tiny bit unforgiving."

"That's because I am unforgiving. Jake lied to me, Lex, and not about something insignificant. He's my freaking stepbrother. How disgusting is that?"

"Well, this is Tennessee."

I cut her a not-funny look. "And because of his lie, our

entire relationship has been based on misinformation and me being misled."

"So let me ask you this, then. What would you have done if Jake had told you about Ella Mae that very first night? Forget all about the fact that nobody else in town knew, and you were a virtual stranger. Forget all about the fact that he didn't know if he could trust you with his secret, much less even liked you enough to want to share. Would you have ever spoken to him again?"

"I don't know," I say, even though I do know. "Maybe." *No way.*

But Lexi sees right through my lie. "Put yourself in his shoes, Gi. By the time he realized he liked you, it was too late. He was already vulnerable."

My sister is right, I know she is. My vision blurs, and my voice dies down to a whisper. "Whose side are you on?"

"Yours, silly rabbit." She reaches around my knee for my hand, pulling it into her lap and squeezing it between both of hers. "Always and forever, I'm on yours."

The bedroom door swings open, and a bleary-eyed Jake steps into the hall. His gaze searches out mine but I turn my head, pressing my lips together, biting down until I feel pain. I'm still processing Lexi's message, and my tears are dangerously close to the surface. I focus instead on the piece of paper clutched in Jake's hand.

Because I will not let Jake see me cry.

"Take it," he says, offering the sheet to me.

I pull the letter from his fingers. "I'll make a copy and get the original back to you."

"Don't bother. I don't want it back."

If his words didn't tell me his meaning, his crumpled brow does. First his mother, then Ella Mae, now me. So far this letter has brought him nothing but heartache and loss, and keeping it would only serve as a reminder.

I nod and push to a stand, gesturing to Lexi and the door. "Let's go."

Bo steps into the hall, his gaze bouncing from mine to the paper in my fist. "But what about the letter?"

"We'll read it at home." I reach for the knob and swing the door open.

But Bo doesn't move. He lifts his palms in the air and holds them there. "Then why did we come all the way over here? I want to read it now."

"Fine. We'll read it in the car."

Bo starts to object further, but Cal silences him with a hand on his biceps. "C'mon, son. Let's get back to your daddy."

With one last longing look at the letter, Bo files past Cal, out the door and down the stairs. My uncle follows him without another word.

I help Lexi up and pull her toward the stairs. At the door she pauses, then turns back and wiggles her fingers in a wave. "I'm so sorry, Jakey."

Jake waits until I peek at him through my lashes to give his reply. "No sorrier than I am."

33

Dear Brian,

As I sit here writing your name, I wonder if you still go by Brian. Your parents were of course free to choose their own name for you, but to me, you'll always be Brian.

You were born Brian Mitchell Cooper, a name you share with my father, your biological grandfather. You kind of looked like him, too. Long lashes dark as coal, face scrunched up like a bulldog chewing on a hornet, hollering your little lungs out. He died of a heart attack last July, but of course you wouldn't know that. I wonder if you've grown into his thick black hair, or if your feet are long and bony like his were.

I don't know anything about you. Are you handsome and smart and funny? Do you love thunderstorms, skinny-dipping and lemon pie? Do you believe in God? Have you ever loved someone so much it hurts? I wonder so many things, mostly if a tiny little part of me—I pray the best part—made it inside of you.

But the one thing I've never wondered is how your life would have been if I'd kept you. I have so many regrets, but giving you up for adoption that day in August is not one of them.

I know those words are not easy to hear, and probably aren't the ones you thought you'd find when you tore open this letter. They don't mean I didn't come this close to changing my mind when the nurse took you from me, didn't cry myself to sleep your whole first year with a piece of me missing, didn't think about your angel face every single day. For the past eighteen years I've searched my soul and can't find any hint of not wanting to keep you. It would be like not wanting air. And yet, I know handing you to that nurse was the best decision I ever made.

I loved you enough to give you a better life. Isn't that the most clichéd phrase on the planet? Still, it's true. I handed you over to parents who could give you everything this world has to offer, ones who could love you like you deserved to be loved.

Because Lord knows I couldn't. My life hasn't exactly been a shining example of how a person is supposed to live. Twice divorced and headed for a third, married to a man I no longer love and sleeping with a man whose idea of love terrifies me, sexually, emotionally, physically. Talk about a cliché. I'm the biggest one there is.

But the good news is, I finally get it. I finally understand why I've been running around town like a harlot, searching in another man's bed for something that wasn't there. It's because I've been trying to fill the hole that losing you left inside of me. I should have known better than to try to fill it with the next-door neighbor, a man who is as malicious on the inside as he is beautiful and charming on the outside.

Love should bring you joy and not drive you to despair. It should make you want to laugh and sing and skip, not weep. It should be measured in stomach butterflies and skipped heartbeats, not in bruises and broken spirits. If nothing else, Dean taught me these lessons, but he did so the hard way, with threats and fists and fury.

You're probably wondering why on earth I'm telling you all this. And why reach out to you now, after almost two decades?

You see, Brian, I'm pregnant. And this little baby growing inside me is dragging up so many memories of how I felt when I found out there was you. Shocked. Scared. Unsure which of two men got me in this way.

Except this time, I'm also determined. Determined to keep this baby, and raise him or her by myself. Determined to do better, be better, love better. And this time around, I am determined enough to be a real mother.

I'm so sorry I wasn't ready to be yours.

All my love,

Ella Mae

34

"Holy mother of Christ." Woefully inadequate words, I know, but they're the first ones I could think of to do the situation any sort of justice.

Next to me on the backseat of Bo's parked car, Lexi puffs out a breath, short and sharp as if she'd been holding it in the entire time it took her to read Ella Mae's letter. "No fucking shit."

The Andrews sisters are nothing if not eloquent.

"If Dean was abusive," Bo says, twisting in the driver's seat to face Lexi and me, his tone filled with excited anger, "then maybe he was capable of murder, too."

Lexi and I don't respond. As scientifically brilliant as our brother is, he is the last to grasp the letter's biggest implication: that our father and his attorney have had evidence that could have released our father from prison, or at least gotten him a new trial, and they did nothing. Nothing.

Cal makes a scoffing sound and shakes his head. "That there's a half-cocked conclusion if I ever did hear one. There's not one word on that paper to suggest Dean Sullivan was capable of anything more than cheating on his wife."

I cock my head and study my uncle, slumped in the passenger's seat. If Dad's known about the letter for a good five years, I have to assume Cal has, too. As his attorney, as his brother, why didn't Cal do anything? Why did he let my father waste the last years of his life away in prison?

"What are you talking about?" Bo stabs a finger at the letter, still lying on the middle console. "It says right here she was scared of him, that his idea of love was with insults and fists."

"Son, as a scientist, you should know better than anybody in this car the danger in making assumptions based on anything other than the straight-up facts. Maybe Ella Mae was exaggerating. Maybe she was using some fancy-ass metaphor, or said it out of spite for something Dean had done. The point is, we don't know and we never will, because Ella Mae's not here to ask."

Lexi looks over at me. "But Dean is."

Cal twists to face us so fast that both Lexi and I jump a good inch off the backseat. "No. You two will not go over there again. Not even to borrow a doggone cup of sugar. Do you understand me?"

And this is where I lose it—my patience, as well as my faith that Uncle Cal is working only in Dad's best interests. I push up to the edge of the backseat, leaning my entire upper body into the front seat.

"No, Cal, I don't understand why I shouldn't talk to Dean. There are, however, some things I do understand. Like that you lied to me about the affair, about Dad knowing about the affair, about Dad knowing it was with Dean, about the letter. Shall I go on? Because with a little effort, I could probably come up with a couple more."

"I suggest you don't be usin' that tone on me, baby girl. I'm still your elder, and you'll treat me with respect."

"What are you going to do? Ground me? Besides the fact that I'm thirty-four, you no longer have the authority, something you lost when you looked me straight in the face and lied the first time."

Cal jolts like someone stuck him in the backside with a pitchfork, but he doesn't raise his voice. "Out of protection for your father. I already told you that."

"Protection from what? He already knew everything! As a matter of fact, I'm starting to think the only person you're trying to protect here is yourself—" Cal's face turns an alarming shade of purple, but I raise my voice and crank up my pitch anyway "—for fucking up so spectacularly when you decided not to expose Dean Sullivan as Ella Mae's lover at the trial."

"You are on dangerously thin ice, young lady."

"Yeah? Well, so what, because you're fired."

Next to him, Bo's eyes go wide and he fidgets on the vinyl seat, but he doesn't challenge my decision. Neither, I notice, does Lexi.

Any leftover facade of composure Cal managed to hide behind collapses. He sputters around for a bit, then says, "I'm what?"

"Fired. Canned. Dismissed. Sent packing. Your services as our father's attorney are no longer desired."

He pushes off the dashboard until he's facing the backseat, his indignant air giving off fumes, choking the oxygen out of Bo's car. "You can't fire me. I have power of attorney, which pretty much makes me the ultimate authority as far as your father is concerned."

I snort. "That's pretty damn convenient, since you've always liked to think of yourself as the Lord God. Well, I hate to tell you, Jesus, but you're nobody's savior."

"Enough!" Lexi hooks a finger through a belt loop on

my jeans and tugs my bottom back onto the seat. "Hush up, both of you. Let's just all settle way the hell down, okay? Insults and blame aren't getting us anywhere but pissed."

Cal and I don't agree, but we both draw a deep, calming breath, and we hush up.

Lexi takes in our bunched shoulders and scowls. "You know things have gone to pot when I'm the voice of reason. All right, Cal. Gia makes a number of reasonable points. Perhaps you would care to refute them?"

My sister should have known better than to give the floor—especially such a poorly defined floor—to a seasoned attorney. With a nod to Lexi and another withering glare at me, Cal straightens in the passenger's seat, fills his lungs with air and proceeds to refute my points one by one. He talks, and he talks, and he talks, pausing only long enough to haul another giant breath and talk some more. The shadows grow stubby and the sun rises higher and higher in the sky, and Cal is talking still. After forever, we lose interest. Bo closes his eyes and leans his head back, Lexi stops bothering to stifle her yawns or cover her gaping mouth, and I find myself lamenting the state of my own cuticles. If Cal's intention is to bore us to death, he damn near succeeds.

But he doesn't succeed in convincing me. His verbiage is lengthier than it is persuasive, mostly because it is built on three questionable arguments: 1) that he didn't learn about Dean until after the first (and only) appeal, 2) that without Ella Mae or Dean or another eyewitness around to corroborate, any talk of an affair between Ella Mae and Dean is just that, talk, otherwise known in courtrooms and judges' chambers as hearsay, and thus inadmissible and 3) ditto for the letter.

Finally, Cal launches his closing argument. Tennessee

vs. Ray Andrews has been and gone. The case is closed. And now, with our father at home on his deathbed, we should be putting our energy into making his last days as comfortable and pleasurable for him as possible, rather than in arguing about what could have been.

In that respect, at least, I suppose Cal is right. We're too late to save Dad from either death or prison.

But judge and jury are not the only courts in Rogersville.

I slide Ella Mae's letter from the middle console, and Cal is still too busy expatiating to pay much notice when I fold the paper along its seams and tuck it in my coat pocket. Lexi watches me silently, her expression confirming she approves. Because if the affair between Dean and Ella Mae is the proverbial smoking gun, then I'm holding the silver bullet. And by now I think it's safe to assume that the Rogersville court of public opinion won't mind one little bit that it's hearsay.

A chirp from inside my pocket rips the needle off the Cal recording, especially when it's followed by a symphony of electronic beeps and dings from every seat in the car. We fumble frantically in our jeans and jackets for our phones.

When Cal finds his and breaks the silence first, we all know what's coming. He turns to Bo, his face grim. "Son, how fast can you get us home?"

Though we don't speak on the short ride home from town, I think all of us are assuming the worst. Even more so when Fannie throws open the door and motions for us to hurry as we're pulling into the driveway. We take off at a dead sprint for the house.

I rush inside, breathless and stiff with panic, and in the very back of my mind notice that Keith Urban is crooning from a radio somewhere, and the air is thick with the cloying aroma of freshly baked cookies. A tray of them—peanut butter sugar cookies, by the looks and smell of them—balances across Dad's lap. Dad picks up the plate and smiles. Smiles.

Cal blinks at Fannie. "I thought you said this was an emergency."

"It is. Ray is having a good morning, and I wanted y'all to be here for it. Coffee?"

"I'll take mine with a shot of bourbon." Lexi tugs on her scarf, loosening it around her neck, and collapses onto the couch. "You people are killin' me."

Fannie nods and shuffles off to the kitchen.

"Everybody sit down," Dad says. "I've made some important decisions I'd like to talk to y'all about."

After a few exchanged looks we sit, Cal at the wing chair by Dad's shoulder, the rest of us either on the couch or in chairs by the foot of his bed. Once Dad is satisfied he's got our complete attention, he begins.

"Call somebody over at Davis and Son. That old Clyde Davis was a mean son of a bitch, but his people always did plan the best funerals. They'll know how to spread the word about the service. Is Reverend Bulloch still alive?"

Lexi nods. "He's about a hundred and twelve, but yeah. He's alive."

"Good. Ask him to say a few words, and I mean a few. He likes to talk into next week, and by now he's probably too blind to notice if half the place falls asleep." Dad's gaze lands on me. "I'd like you to give the eulogy."

I sink farther into the couch. "Me? Why me?"

"Because you always were the best at seeing both sides of the coin. I think forgiveness would be a relevant topic all around, don't you? No wailing or gnashing of teeth, you hear? Just tell things like you see them. And anybody else who has something to say is welcome to also, good or bad. I'm sick of worrying myself to death about which one it's gonna be."

Dad chuckles, but no one else sees the humor in his statement.

"Bo, I want you to make sure the service feels like something I'd approve of. I don't know what all they do at funerals nowadays, but you and I always did have the same taste, so just choose whatever you think is best. I trust you."

Bo clears his throat. He's nervous, fiddling with the zipper on his puffy coat. "I'll do you proud."

"I know you will, son." Dad turns to my sister.

"Can you handle the money? It's not much, but you'll know how to pinch it enough so the insurance covers the cremation, cost of a simple service and a nice dinner for y'all afterward. And don't have other people spending theirs, especially on flowers I'll never see. If they want to give something, get 'em to donate to the hospice that sent us Frannie, okay?"

Fannie, I think.

Lexi's bottom lip quivers and her face is flushed, but she sits up straighter next to me and looks damn pleased. And then my father turns to Cal, hauling another breath as we hold ours, waiting.

"I hardly dare to ask any more of you, Cal, but I'm gonna need you to take care of my ashes."

Cal sucks in a sob, one he covers by scrounging around in the blanket for Dad's bony hand. "Of course."

"You know that spot up at the top of Roan Mountain, where Rosalie and I used to go camping back after we just got married?" He pauses to receive Cal's nod. "I want you to go up there this summer when the flowers are at their peak. You know where, on the Tennessee side at the high knob. Make sure you find a spot with the best view of the bluffs, then pick the prettiest rhododendron bush and put half of me there. At the very least I'll be good fertilizer."

Cal nods again, then clears his throat. "And the other half?"

"The other half of me goes in Ella Mae's garden."

At first I don't understand. An avid gardener, Ella Mae kept the yard full of blooms pretty much all year around, but she's been dead for almost two decades. What flowers didn't follow her to an early grave have been taken over by crabgrass and overgrown with weeds.

Cal must understand, though, because his face goes thunderous. "No. That garden is to remember her by, not you. I won't put you there."

Ah, Dad means the memorial garden in town. I can't say I blame him. I'd be hard-pressed to think of a more beautiful final resting spot.

But Cal shakes his head so hard his cheeks wobble.

"I'm a dyin' man. These are my last wishes."

My uncle pops off his chair, his body looming above Dad's. "These past sixteen years I've done everything you asked. Everything! Even when I didn't agree, even when it wasn't in your best interests. But this is something I will not do, do you hear me? You are not gonna spend eternity in that woman's garden."

"Technically, it would be only half of me."

"Not even one teeny tiny flake of you. It would be a goddamn travesty."

"That seems a bit harsh, don't you think?" Bo says, stepping to his feet to look our uncle in the eyes. "Besides, it's not our decision to make. It's Dad's, and I think we need to respect his wishes."

"I am respecting his wishes, dammit." Something about

the way he looks at Dad as he says it—and something about the way Dad looks away—makes me think he means other wishes, more secrets Lexi and Bo and I don't know about. "But this is where I draw the line. I'll respect every wish but this one."

Dad dribbles a hand at Cal and Bo. "Sit down, both of you, and listen up. I spent the first half of my life loving Rosalie, and the second half Ella Mae. I still love them both. It's only appropriate I share my everlastin' life with them equally, too."

"It's illegal," Cal says, something in his tone grasping at straws. "I can't just go spreading your ashes around wherever you see fit."

"Do it in the dark." Dad hisses out a breathy laugh. "I won't tattle, I promise."

Cal doesn't find him the least bit funny. "I'm not gonna do it, Ray. Forget it."

I think about all the possible reasons Cal might have to refuse. Because it's against the law, because he doesn't think it's proper, because he's worried what others might say. None of them seem strong enough for Cal to call it a "goddamn travesty."

But even if Dad somehow manages to convince his brother to agree to this last wish, I'm not entirely certain Cal would actually carry it out. He's already lied and threatened to pull the power-of-attorney card. What would keep him from doing either of those things after Dad is gone?

"I'll do it," I blurt without thinking. Only once my brain catches up with my mouth, I know I actually mean it. "I'll spread your ashes wherever you want me to."

My father's head swivels to me, another rare grin blooming on his face. "That's my girl."

Cal spears me with a look that before today would've had me quaking in my sneakers. "Oh, hell no, you won't."

"Yes she will, and I'll help." Lexi scoots to the edge of the couch and smiles around me at Dad. "The tulips will be up in a few weeks, and they get prettier every year. They're in the perfect spot, too, up by the thinkin' bench."

Bo shoots Cal an apologetic look. "I'm helping, too."

Cal's furious expression says it all, but for the first time I can remember, he's speechless.

Dad ignores his brother's fury, turning back to us with a fierce expression. "One last thing, and it's the most important. I want you kids to promise—no, swear to me that you'll figure out how to make peace with what happened. Find a place for it inside you somewhere and tuck it away tight, because that's the only way you'll ever be able to move on. Make sure your heads and your hearts are free for better things, for more important things. Things like falling in love and building a life with somebody. Okay?"

Regret sears the backs of my eyes, and I turn to look out the window. I don't tell him that's what I thought I was already doing—moving on, falling in love and building a life with Jake. Because what's left to tell him about now? Only a hollow ache in the center of my chest.

As if reading my thoughts, Lexi slides her perfect and tidy hand into mine and gives it a squeeze.

"Son?" Dad says, and Bo looks up, his eyes rimmed with red. "I'm sorry I wasn't there for your wedding. Cal showed me the pictures, and it was beautiful. Amy's beautiful. As soon as you're done here, I want you to get yourself back home to your wife and start making me some grandbabies. Promise?"

Bo's eyes widen and his mouth twists, just briefly, and I suspect he's thinking the same thing as I am: grandbabies you'll never see. His quick nod releases two fat tears that slide down his cheeks. "I promise," he whispers.

Dad turns to me and Lexi, still hand in hand on the couch, and his expression softens. "Just look at the two of you, connected at the hip again. I never understood y'all's connection, but I'm awful glad for it, especially now. Does a father good right here." He thumps a palm against his chest. "You're going to need each other in the coming months, so no more fighting, you hear?"

I nod and clutch at Lexi's hand, but no harder than she's clutching mine, a silent promise between sisters to never lose touch again. One I am certain, with every ounce of everything inside of me, both of us intend to fulfill.

Satisfied, Dad lifts the plate on his lap into the air. "Now that that's settled, who wants one of Frannie's cookies?"

35

Upstairs, I slide Ella Mae's letter from my pocket and spread it out on my bedroom floor. The pages are brittle with age, the edges decorated with a yellow tinge, but her script is smooth and easy to read, even on my tiny iPhone screen. I email the images to Jeffrey, along with a text message to look at them and call me asap, sit on my bed and wait.

Less than two minutes later, my phone rings.

"You've been a busy bee."

"You don't know the half of it." I kick off my shoes, peel off my socks, pop the button on my jeans. I just took my last sleeping pill, and I can't wait for it to hit so I can forget this horrendous day. "Both Cal and Dad knew about everything. The affair, Dean, even the letter. Ella Mae's son showed it to them over five years ago. Cal said by the time he learned about Dean, it was too late to save Dad."

"Cal's lying."

I snort, standing to peel off my pants. "Oh, you think? He gave me some bullshit about the letter being hearsay, but—"

"No, I mean he's lying about the timing. Allison Sullivan told me Cal came to her with knowledge of the affair before the trial even began."

My hands freeze and I straighten, my jeans bunched around my knees. "Then why wouldn't Cal have exposed Dean as Ella Mae's lover when he took the stand?"

"Because Allison informed him Dean had an alibi."

His words hit me like a blow to the head. My vision goes dark and blurry, then explodes in a burst of white. "What?"

"Dean was with Allison that night, from sometime right before ten until fourteen minutes past one, which I'm sure I don't have to remind you is a good hour past Ella Mae's time of death. The details are stamped in her memory forever, she said, because she spent those three and a half hours tied up, while Dean beat and raped her."

"Oh—" My voice falters, and I have to try again. "Oh, my God."

"I know. She says she's been waiting sixteen years for someone other than Cal to come and ask her side of the story. Until now, nobody ever did." And then Jeffrey says the words my brain is still struggling to comprehend, the words that smash the last shred of hope still hanging inside me. "Dean Sullivan is an evil, abusive shit, Gia, but he didn't kill Ella Mae."

I swallow the bile rushing up my throat and whisper, "Then who?"

"I don't know, but maybe…" He sighs, and I hear all sorts of things I don't want to hear behind it. Doubt. Regret. Suspicion. "Maybe I need to take another hard look at my research."

Thank God the bed is behind me, because at that moment my legs give out. I half moan, half grunt as my butt hits the mattress.

"Look, I'm not saying I think your father is guilty, but maybe neither is Cal. Sounds like he kept the affair with Dean under wraps because he knew Dean was innocent. At that point, the only thing introducing testimony around the affair would have done is give your father a motive."

"Which, clearly, he had."

"Let's not jump to any concl—"

A woman's singsong voice interrupts him, something about powering down his phone. Jeffrey responds with a humph.

"Are you on a plane?"

"Yeah, still on the ground in Chicago but headed your way. I want to take another hard look at my research, but after that you and I will sit down and—" His tone turns choppy and annoyed. "Look, lady, this conversation is important, okay? I'll be off in just a minute."

Her reply comes through loud and 4G clear. "Sir, now!"

Another sigh. "I'll call you when I know more."

The line goes dead and I curl into a ball on my bed, staring at the wallpaper for so long the tiny burst of pink and purple flowers blurs. Jeffrey's words echo in my mind. *I'm not saying I think your father is guilty.* But instinct tells me that by saying those words out loud, Jeffrey just said exactly that, that he thinks my father might be guilty.

Nausea swirls and rolls in my belly.

An alibi. Dean Sullivan had an alibi, which means the affair is not only hearsay, it's irrelevant hearsay. And the more I think about it, the more I realize his alibi wiped away any hope I had that my father was telling the truth. Because if Dean didn't kill Ella Mae, that leaves only one person who had both motive and opportunity.

And just like that, my father shifts back up to prime suspect in my mind.

* * *

The sleeping pill does its work, because someone shakes me awake later that same day. Is it the same day? Outside my window the sky is purple with either dawn or dusk, I have no idea which. I roll over and see Lexi looming above me in today's (yesterday's?) clothes, my cell phone in her hand.

"What's up?" I ask. "Is Dad okay?"

"The same." My sister hands me my phone. "These things work better if you actually answer them, you know. I've been listening to it beep for the past hour."

I bolt to sitting and snatch it out of her hand, checking my missed calls. Four from Jake, a couple from local numbers I don't recognize and exactly none from Jeffrey. I check the time and see it's almost six. Jeffrey should be back by now. Why hasn't he called? My stomach sinks at the thought of what his silence might mean.

Lexi sinks onto the bed next to me. "I made things awful hard on you this past month, didn't I?"

I pat her knee. "Like Dad said. You're here now. That's all that matters."

"No. No, it's not. I did it all on purpose, you know. Skipping out on you in Roadkill, running off at the bank, letting you take care of Dad all by yourself—"

"How about the vomiting? Was that on purpose, too?"

"Public vomiting is never on purpose. But getting drunk and causing a scene, that was on purpose. All my way of getting back at you for leaving." She glances at me through her lashes. "Juvenile, right?"

"A little." I butt her with a shoulder, load my words with a teasing tone. "But nobody's ever accused you of being mature."

She purses her lips into the teasing pout she perfected

back in high school. "Uh, hello? Ella Mae used to always say I was too big for my britches."

I giggle. "That's not what she meant and you know it."

Her smile fades just a tad, and she reaches for my hand. "I've missed you, sis."

"I've missed you, too. More than you could ever imagine."

"Then stay." She twists on the bed to look at me then, not letting go of my hand, her smile on the verge of crumbling into tears. "Just for a little while. I know you still have mountain water in your veins, I can smell it on you. And I don't think I can go through losing Dad and you again. It's too much."

My staying is, of course, inextricably tied to Jake. But the fury I felt at discovering his lie no longer pulses in my chest. The pain I felt at his betrayal no longer pinches my heart. The grudge I held up between us like armor has melted, soft and useless, at my feet. Because how can I resent him for anything when I'm back to suspecting—no, believing—my father was his mother's killer?

But I can't tell my sister any of this, because then I'd have to tell her about Dean's alibi. The only reason she's here is because of the affair, and the tiny cracks it made in her conviction that our father was absolutely, without doubt guilty of murder. If I remove the possibility of Dean's hand in Ella Mae's death, I remove Lexi, and likely Bo, as well, from this house and what's left of Dad's life. And as selfish as it sounds, I'm not ready to lose either of them yet.

I settle on ambiguity. "I can't stay, Lex. This town is too small for both me and Jake, and running into him every day would be too much. The pain would kill me."

My sister wraps an arm around my waist and presses her head to my shoulder, and her compassion burns at the backs of my eyes. "You really don't think you'll ever be able to move past his lie?"

I don't answer, mostly because I can't tell her my leaving is no longer about the lie. We fall silent for a long moment.

And then from somewhere outside, I hear voices. Men's and women's, low and high and everywhere in between. At first it's just a jumble of words, then slowly, melodically, they come together as one in song.

Lexi sits up straight, cocks her head. "Is that 'Kumbaya'?"

I crawl to the window and look out over the yard, where a good fifty people stand huddled, their candles flickering in the fading light. Behind them Maple Street is a parking lot, its edges lined with their cars and SUVs and vans and trucks. Jake's truck, parked by the mailbox. My gaze flits back to the crowd and there he is, front and center, with a Starbucks cup in one hand and a candle in the other, watching me in the window.

"It is," Lexi says, coming up beside me. "It's freaking 'Kumbaya.' Jeez, couldn't they have chosen a less cliché song? Next thing you know they'll break into 'Amazing Grace.'"

Her words may be snarky, but her tone is anything but. My sister grips the windowsill with both hands and looks out over the scene on the lawn—folks we've known all our lives, friends and former classmates and neighbors—and her pretty pink lips curl into a smile.

She nudges me with an elbow. "You seein' who I'm seein'?"

My voice is barely a whisper. "I'm seein'."

Jake catches us watching and lifts the candle in a wave.

"Maybe writing the eulogy will help."

"What do you mean?"

She looks over at me. "It's supposed to be about for-giveness, right? Maybe you'll figure out how to give him some of yours."

I turn back to the window, my gaze sliding automatically to Jake. "You're not going to give up, are you?"

Lexi wriggles her fingers in the window, and Jake smiles—a beautiful smile, a devastating smile—up at us in the window.

"If you forgiving him means I get to keep you here with me, never."

I look away from my sister, settling my focus anywhere but the familiar curve of Jake's mouth. Pain pierces my heart and shreds my stomach. The truth is, Jake is already forgiven. I no longer care that he lied.

What I'm more concerned with is how repulsed he would be at the thought of lying next to the daughter of the man who murdered his mother.

After a long moment, I push off the bed, pull on my jeans and leave the room.

That night, thanks to the afternoon's drug-induced coma, I can't sleep. Long after the sky turns black with night, long after Jake and the others on the front lawn climb into their cars and return to the warmth of their homes, long after the house is dark and quiet and still, my body hums with energy.

Jeffrey had called earlier, and the news hadn't been good. He's dropping the chapter about my father's case, removing his story from the book entirely. Jeffrey was more than a little surprised when I told him I'd honor my promise for an interview, but not until after my father's memorial, which, according to Fannie, will be any day now. Hopefully by then I'll know what I want to say.

For sixteen years, I've been trying to outrun my doubt, pretending that ignoring the feeling would make it grow tiny enough to shove in the back of a closet, or under the bed. When the possibility of Dean's hand in the murder presented itself, I latched on to it with both hands. I treated it like my salvation. But what was it Lexi told me? Reasonable doubt is still doubt. I should have listened better to mine.

I lie here in my old room, watching shadows dance on the ceiling, and realize I'm listening now.

36

There is an immeasurable gulf between what donors think humanitarian aid is capable of, and what it delivers. What our websites and brochures will never tell you is that your twenty-dollar donation won't fix poverty or end hunger, in fact won't even come close. We won't reveal that places that sucked before the disaster will still suck three years later. We'll neglect to mention that relief organizations screw up, frequently and spectacularly, because by definition disasters are chaotic and unpredictable and humans are…well, human.

We'll never say any of these things, because aid organizations do make a difference. By providing food and water and medicine, we are making things a little more bearable, a little less awful, for a short period of time. Even if we're doing it all wrong, we're at least doing something, and that's one step closer than doing nothing at all.

Which is what I tell myself as I sneak down the stairs in my sweats and bare feet. That by going to confront my father in the middle of the night with what I think I know, I'm at least doing something.

Like every night, Fannie's left the oven light burning in the kitchen before disappearing up to her room. Its golden glow works its way across the living room floor, falling into shadows halfway to Dad's bed, blanketing the rest of the room in splotches of black and gray. I stop in the doorway a moment in order to allow my eyes to adjust to the inky darkness.

A breathy but rhythmic rattle tells me my father is the lumpy form on the hospital bed, sound asleep. I go to him, tugging on the elastic holding my hair, letting my curls fall loose and free all around my shoulders. A niggle of guilt pushes at the lining of my belly but I ignore it, reaching for Dad's arm instead. It takes a few shakes, but then Dad opens his eyes with a snort.

"Huh?" He whips his head up and swivels it back and forth, searching for me in the dark. "Who's there?"

"It's just me." I wrap a palm around his forearm and grip until he stills. I want him to be paying close attention when I say my next words: "Ella Mae."

He jerks back as though I just poked him with a live wire, and then his dying muscles give out. His limbs, his head, his jaw all go slack. Only his eyes move, the lids blinking rapidly at me. "What?"

"It's me. Ella Mae."

Dad's mouth snaps shut and his nostrils flare. The sound of his heavy breathing fills the room. He shakes his head violently. "You can't be here. You're dead."

"No, Ray, it's real." I pick up his hand, hold it in mine. "I'm real."

He snatches his hand away, his lip curling in either horror or disgust. "Are you here for revenge? 'Cause I'm already dyin'."

My heart heaves and cracks at the mean edge to both

his mouth and his tone, aimed at the woman I loved like my mother. I choke back my tears, dipping my chin and cocking my head a tiny bit to the right the way she used to do, and I disguise my lie in a Tennessee drawl. "I know the truth, Ray."

His eyes go wide, and they stare dry and unblinking into mine. "You can't know. Nobody knows but me and Cal. I was so careful."

"Not careful enough. I saw you."

"Liar! You couldn't have seen me. I had on different clothes. I was wearing a ski mask. You never knew it was me!"

Just because I was expecting a confession doesn't make it any easier to hear. I sway, and sixteen years' worth of suspicion and sorrow slides down my cheeks. I open my mouth to tell him that I hate him for stealing Ella Mae from me. That he deserved every one of those sixteen years in prison, and I wish he would live to see at least sixteen more. That he is going to burn in hell for what he did.

And then his face curls inward and he reaches for me with both hands, his fists latching on to the hem of my sweatshirt, and the words die in my throat.

"I loved you, Ella Mae." Her name catches in his chest, emerges on the tail end of a sob. "I would've stayed with you forever if only you'd loved me back. Why couldn't you love me back?" He doesn't wait for me to answer, just hauls air into his lungs and wails loud enough to wake the whole house. "Why didn't you love me back?"

He breaks down then, his body racked with sobs his lungs are too weak to fuel with much more than wheezy rattles. My father asked me to talk about forgiveness, but the only thing I feel now is a bone-deep sorrow—for Ella Mae, for me and Bo and Lexi, for Cal and Jake. But mostly, for my father. For the daddy I once knew and the murderer he'd become. For the man who lost a woman's love, and the man I'm about to lose all over again.

"Tell me you forgive me." His grip on my shirt tightens, and his muscles give a weak squeeze to pull me closer. "I'm begging you. Let me die in peace."

I watch him for a long moment, thinking he doesn't deserve an ounce of peace. But I'm not going to be like Lexi. I won't let my bitterness and anger and hatred eat me alive. I won't let it pull me under.

Every single decision I've made in the past sixteen years has been motivated by an attempt to escape my past. I meant my words to Jake, though. I'm done running.

But in order to stay put anywhere—in order to still the gypsy in my soul—I have to scrounge up a teeny tiny scrap of forgiveness for my father, even if I will never be able to forgive his action.

And if I can't do either of those things just yet, the least I can do is give him peace.

"Go back to sleep." I untangle my shirt from his fists and place both his palms gently on his chest. "I forgive you."

"That was one hell of a performance."

Cal's voice doesn't startle me. Though I didn't notice him sitting in the corner of the living room when I confronted my father, I heard his movement, and shortly after, his footsteps, as I stumbled into the kitchen. So though I'm not particularly surprised he followed me, it's his tone—impressed, almost reverent—that shocks me. I mop up my face with the sleeve of my sweatshirt and turn to face my uncle.

"I figured it was worth a try." My voice comes out far calmer than I feel. I lift a shoulder and look straight into

Cal's eyes. "I was tired of waiting around for someone to volunteer the truth."

"Well, like I said, bravo." The dim light in the kitchen paints angry purple shadows under his eyes, across his forehead, around his mouth, where worry and grief have etched new lines in his face. He reaches past me, flicking on the water boiler with a knuckle. "I sure could use a whiskey toddy. How 'bout you?"

He takes my silence as a yes, because he pulls two mugs from the drainer by the sink, rummages around in a cabinet for honey, gives both mugs a generous squirt.

"I tell you what, though, baby girl. You certainly had the element of surprise on your side, 'cause your father and I never saw that one coming. Not in a million years. And I'm not being the least bit facetious when I say I don't think I could have done any better myself."

"How long have you known?"

What I don't say is that my question is a test. If Cal lies to me now, I will march out of this kitchen and this house, and I will never, ever speak to him again. Not even to give him my condolences at his brother's death. He must detect something in either my tone or my stance, because he adds an extra glug of Jack Daniel's to both mugs, tops them with boiling water and drops in two spoons.

And then he picks them up by the handles and gestures to the kitchen table. "Let's sit, shall we? My knees aren't what they used to be."

We settle in at the kitchen table, and Cal pushes a steaming mug across its surface to me. "You know I'm breaching attorney-client privilege if I tell you."

"You know I'm walking out of here and never speaking to you again if you don't."

Cal smiles. "Touché, baby girl." He gives the spoon a

spin, watching the milky mixture swirl around and around in his mug. "I was the first phone call your father made that night. He was barely making any sense he was so hysterical, going on and on about how Ella Mae was making a fool of him, that she was a cheatin' whore, that he had to do it. When I asked him what, what did he have to do? he said, calm as could be, 'I killed her, Cal.'"

Even though I knew it was coming, I suck in a breath.

"My reaction was a little more colorful. After I was through cussin' him out, I told him to call 9-1-1 and turn himself in. That's when he hung up on me."

Cal pauses to take a sip of his toddy. I grip the handle of mine hard enough to snap the ceramic in two.

"By the time I made it to Rogersville, the police were already here. Your father was being treated for shock and a head injury. He'd rammed himself into the doorpost hard enough to give himself a mild concussion, but of course the police didn't know that. By then he'd already fed them the story about intruders, and I have to give it to him, he did a damn good job. Breakin' into his own door, clearin' any evidence he was the one to drag Ella Mae down the stairs. If Dean Sullivan hadn't been looking out his living room window at two in the morning your father would've gotten away with it."

"And yet you still defended him." Though the words may be accusatory, my tone is not. I'm suddenly exhausted by all the bitterness and blame. I only want to understand.

Cal doesn't seem to take offense. "I didn't have a choice, baby girl. Your daddy taught me how to pitch a baseball and shoot a BB gun and skin a rabbit with a Swiss Army knife. He bought me my first beer, and when the time came, my first pack of Trojan condoms. Up until that very night,

I'd spent my entire life worshipping that man. What was I supposed to do?"

"You were supposed to let justice take care of him."

Only, as I say the words, I realize that is exactly what Cal's done. My father went to prison for murder despite having the Tennessee Tiger by his side. His appeals stalled after only one attempt. Cal's defense wasn't accidentally shoddy. He threw the most prominent, the most important case of his life on purpose.

"You should have told us. Bo and Lexi and me. We deserved to know the truth."

"You think I don't know that? But telling you kids was the one thing your father wouldn't budge on. He cried and carried on like a mule in heat. So your father and I made a deal. He agreed to spend the rest of his life in prison for what he'd done, and I agreed to not tell the police or you kids what I knew."

Whoever said the worst thing about the wait is not knowing was right. For sixteen years I'd waited for the truth. Now that I know, something inside of me breaks open, lets go. Of the anger, the fear, the bitterness. I let go of it all.

"What ever happened to the baby?"

Cal shrugs. "Your father never knew about a baby until the letter."

I don't believe him, not for a second.

Cal must read the doubt on my expression, because he says, "Now that you know the truth, I don't have any more reasons to lie. Your father didn't know, and it didn't come up in the autopsy, so I've always assumed nature cleaned up its own mess." He reaches across the table, drapes a palm over my hand. "I know I should've told you, baby girl, and I'm sorrier than you'll ever know. I just pray one day you kids'll be able to move past all this tragedy and be happy."

I think about my siblings sleeping upstairs, clueless to the drama unfolding beneath them, and my heart gives a painful squeeze. They've just gotten their father back, and now they're about to lose him all over again.

"Somebody has to tell Bo and Lexi."

"I know." Cal's words come out on a sigh. "But I can't tell them what I just told you. I've already said too much."

"Fine. Tell them Dad confessed to me. That's all they need to know."

He drops his head in a nod, studies the table. "I'll tell them in the morning."

"Tell them now."

Cal raises his head, and I hold his gaze, daring him to disagree. Finally, after a long moment, he winces, then nods.

And then I think of someone else who deserves to know, and my heart flops around like one of those bluegill Bo used to fish out of the Holston River when we were little. I push back my chair and stand, looking around for wherever I left my keys. I find them on top of the microwave.

"Where are you going?"

"To town." I stuff my feet into my boots, on the mat by the kitchen door. "Because there's only one person on the planet who can tell Jake who murdered his mother, and that's me."

37

When you're in a hurry, one point seven miles can feel like a million, and the time it takes to drive there an eternity. Tonight, the trip to Roadkill feels almost instant, like I blink my eyes and I'm there, parked in front of Jake's door two seconds later.

If I were thinking straight, I might be surprised to see the lights are still on behind the thick etched windows, even more surprised to see a solitary Jake, hunched over a glass of amber liquid at his bar. Instead, I pocket my keys and breeze through the door like it isn't rapidly approaching dawn.

Jake looks up and I try to ignore the shiver rippling up my arms. The late hour and bourbon have slowed his reactions, and it takes a few seconds for his eyes to focus on whoever just walked through his door, a few more to recognize that it's me. And then eyes so dark brown they're almost black bore into mine with not pleasure to see me, but resignation.

He thunks down his glass with a heavy arm. "If you're

coming to tell me we're through, you don't have to bother. I already got the message, at least three times now."

"That's not why I'm here." He blinks at me, and I catch a brief glimmer of hope before I shake my head. "That's not why, either."

Jake gives me a disappointed nod, then returns to his bourbon and takes a long, slow pull. There's only an inch or two left in the bottle on the bar next to him, and I wonder how much of that he's drunk tonight. Judging by his glassy, red eyes and sloppy movements, I suspect most of it.

"Are you drunk? Because I have something to say, and I need you to remember it in the morning."

He drains his glass with one hand, reaches for the bottle with the other. "Well, then, you better hang on, 'cause I'm not nearly drunk enough." He turns the bottle upside down over his glass until it's empty, then drops it behind the bar where it falls to the rubber mat with a dull thunk.

"Never mind." I turn for the door. "I'll come back tomorrow."

"No." For someone with a bottle of bourbon in his system, Jake is fast. He's off his stool and across the room faster than I can reach for the handle. "Don't leave. Please. I'm listening."

I drop the handle, suck in a breath, force myself to meet his gaze. "I figured it out, Jake."

He tries to pull up that smile I love so much, but it doesn't quite make it up his cheeks. "Seeing as my veins are currently filled with more booze than blood, you're going to have to be a little more specific. Figured what out?"

I look up at him and my heart whimpers. Why does he make me want to laugh instead of cry, why does he have to stand so close, and why do I want to jump in his arms and bury my face in his neck and forget the words I came here to say?

The weight of the past few days hits me, and a sob bursts up my throat. Jake doesn't hesitate. He pulls me into his arms and holds me upright while I fall apart, wiping my tears with his thumbs and murmuring comforting words into my curls. His gentleness breaks my heart even more, and it's a long time before I can do anything other than lean into him and cry.

"Is it your father? Did he...?"

I shake my head into his chest, and then I shrug. "I don't know. Maybe by now..." His arms tighten around me in response, and I know I have to tell him right this instant, before I lose whatever's left of my nerve. I breathe deep, taking in as much as I can of his scent and his strength, untangle myself from his arms, step back far enough to look into his eyes and force myself to say the words. "Dean Sullivan didn't kill Ella Mae."

"What? What are you talking about?"

"He has an alibi, Jake. He couldn't have murdered her."

Jake shakes his head, thrusts a hand through his hair. "Then what about all those things he told us? That he was sorry, that he didn't mean to do it. What was that all about?"

"Who knows? The man's been a raging alcoholic for almost two decades now. He's probably got all of twelve brain cells left in his pickled head." Fresh tears well in my eyes, and my voice drops to barely a whisper. "But he's not who killed Ella Mae."

Understanding flashes across his expression and then is wiped away, like he hears the message behind my words yet refuses to accept it as truth. I don't blame him. Like Jake, I can almost see our life. I would find a job at a nearby nonprofit and plan Sunday-afternoon dinners with Bo and

Lexi. At night, Jake and I would sneak upstairs with a pan of that night's special and a bottle of Bordeaux to share in his bed. Afterward, we'd make love to the thumps of music and laughter coming from the bar beneath us. His love could heal my grief at my father's betrayal, teach me to find peace in this place.

If only Jake wasn't Ella Mae's son. If only Dean was Ella Mae's killer. If only, if only, if only.

Jake leads me to a bar stool, the very same bar stool where we started. He picks me up—literally wraps his hands around my waist and lifts me off the ground—and settles me onto it. He points to his glass, still half full, on the bar between us. When I don't go to pick it up, he pushes it into my hand and waits until I down a good gulp.

Jake gives the liquid courage time to hit my stomach, warm my blood, loosen my tongue. And then he says, "Start at the beginning."

"Allison Sullivan told Jeffrey that Dean was with her." Bile swirls in my throat but I swallow it down, force myself to look him in the eyes. "From ten until after one the night Ella Mae was murdered. She remembers exactly, because that's how long Dean beat and raped her."

Jake sobers in an instant. His body, his expression, the flicker of hope in his eyes, all go dead. He shakes his head and leans back. "Don't say it."

"I have to. There have already been too many secrets."

"I mean it, Gia." His face is so ferocious, I have to remind myself his rage is not directed at me. Not really. "Do not tell me his name."

"But I don't have to say the name, do I?" I whisper, smiling sadly through my tears. "You've already figured it out." When he doesn't respond, I whisper, "He admit-

ted it to me tonight. Cal confirmed it. Ray Andrews murdered Ella Mae."

I watch as every emotion I feared most competes on
Jake's face. Grief, disgust, hatred, despair. He snatches the
glass from my hand and goes to lift it to his mouth, then
reconsiders halfway there. Rearing back with a roar, he
pitches the tumbler clear across the room, leaving a trail of
liquid down his jeans and across the floor. The glass hits
the far wall and explodes in a cloud of bourbon fumes and
crystal shards. And then he swipes a hand down his chin,
not quite looking at me.

"It doesn't matter." His voice is desperate in a way that
is more, I think, to convince himself than to sway me.
"What's done is done."

"Get real, Jake. I saw your face just now. I can't spend
the rest of my life wondering when you'll decide you hate
me more than you love me."

"I could never hate you."

"For a second or two, you just did," I whisper, and my
heart breaks in two when he doesn't deny it.

He shakes his head. "We can figure this out. We can
get past this."

I push to a stand. "You were right, you know. Those millions of decisions we make every day—coffee or tea, buy
or rent, love me or don't?—in the end they're all irrelevant.
You could have told me the truth about who you were that
very first second we met or the next day or the next, and
maybe I would've gotten over it, maybe I wouldn't have. It
doesn't matter, because all of our choices are irrelevant."

He grabs for me, but I step back and he swipes air. He
tries again and ends up clutching a handful of my sweatshirt in his fist, tugging me toward him.

"Don't you see, Jake? Our fates had already been decided

for us long before we met. Not by God or the universe or whatever higher power you choose to believe in, but by our parents. When your mother decided to sleep with the neighbor, and my father decided to kill her for it, you and I were destined to pay for something neither of us had a hand in."

"Gia…"

I wait for whatever he's about to say next, but it doesn't come. Maybe because of the alcohol, maybe because he's still trying to figure out what, exactly, there is left to say.

Gently, I peel his fingers away from the fabric of my shirt and he lets me. Jake doesn't reach for me again. His hands hang limp at his sides. When I turn and head for the door, when I step onto the sidewalk and into my car, no one stops me. When I gun the gas and head for home, no one chases me. Jake doesn't follow.

By the time I push through the door at home, two things have happened. First of all, Dad has died, judging by the look of compassion Fannie gives me and the unabashed tears on Cal's cheeks when I step into the living room.

Cal's also made good on his promise to tell the truth. I deduce this mainly from my siblings—Bo in a sobbing, crumpled heap at the foot of the couch and Lexi, who almost mows me down in her hurry to get out the door.

"Where are you going?"

She gives me a get-real look. "I told you so. All these years I knew with every ounce inside me he was guilty. I don't know why I let you talk me into coming."

Bo lifts his head, blinks at me through bloodshot eyes. "So it's true? He really did confess to killing Ella Mae?"

"Of course he did." Lexi puts everything she's got in her voice. Fury, indignation, conviction, contempt. Yet I still hear the tiniest thread of hope.

"Shut up!" Bo shrieks, surprising us with both his volume and his vehemence. "I want to hear it from Gia."

"I'm so sorry, BoBo." My voice drops to a whisper. "But it's true."

He makes a choking sound and buries his face in his hands.

I turn to Lexi, my voice hardening to match her tone. "Don't even think about leaving."

My sister shakes her perfect ponytail, shifts her designer bag onto a shoulder and stomps across the Rooms To Go carpet.

But I'm faster. I sprint around her, spread my arms wide, press my back against the door. A human wall between Lexi and outside.

Lexi dips her head, says from between clenched teeth, "Move."

I don't. "Listen to me first. I know—"

She hitches a thumb to the left. "Move, dammit." This time she loads her words with a silent *or else.*

I plant my feet firmer into the floor. "I let you ditch me once. I'm not going to let you do it again. We have about a million things to do, even more decisions to make."

"Decisions? What kind of decisions?"

"Well, for one, we promised Dad a memorial."

"A memorial." She grunts. "Lemme give you a little tip for future reference. When your father makes a deathbed confession that he really is guilty of the murder he claimed for sixteen years not to have committed, his last wishes can go to hell right along with him."

"But what about his remains?"

"Put 'em in a garbage bag and drop 'em in the Holston River for all I care. I will certainly not be touching them." She glares over her shoulder at Cal. "And if you put his ashes anywhere even two hundred miles upwind of Ella Mae's park, you can go to hell, too."

Cal pushes to a stand, looking every bit his sixty-three years. "I'll take care of his ashes, and don't worry. They won't be anywhere near here."

Lexi turns back to me. "Now that that's settled…" She raises an expectant brow.

When I don't move, she pushes me aside, yanks open the door without another word and marches across the porch toward the stairs. I follow her to the edge of the porch.

"Lexi, wait!"

She doesn't slow.

By the mailbox, a cluster of five or six gray-haired women look up from their candles with shocked expressions. Their presence here strikes me as downright absurd, considering Lexi's desertion and Dad's confession, and I am about to give a bitter laugh when suddenly, the weight of the situation hits me like an anvil to the temple. They don't know. Folks in Rogersville still think Dad is innocent. I had been so concerned with telling my siblings and Jake, I hadn't thought about the rest of the town.

My sister clearly hasn't given them a second thought, either, because she tears up the walkway to her car, not slowing, not looking back. A shot of fresh red-hot rage scorches a path up my spine.

"You selfish bitch!"

Lexi looks over her shoulder just long enough to roll her cornflower eyes. "You're gonna have to try a little harder than that, girlfriend. I've been called much worse."

Silly me. Lexi is right, she has been called a lot worse, and mostly by me. I ramp up my insult to a slight Lexi will comprehend.

"Selfish, ass-ugly, thunder-thighed, bad-root-jobbed bitch. And your jeans are too tight!"

"Uh-oh," Bo mutters from somewhere behind me.

A quick burst of snickers erupts from the spectators up by the mailbox, a group whose members seem to have multiplied. At least three new cars have tripled our audience.

But none of them could ever accuse me of not knowing my sister. She skids to a stop and wheels around, her expression so deathly calm that if I weren't so furious, I would find it hilarious. Or it would scare me shitless, either one.

"Did you just call me fat?"

Of course that's the one she picked up on. My gaze flits to the crowd up at the street. Their candles hang by their sides, their mouths half open in unabashed curiosity. Vigil-holders turned rubberneckers.

"Can we please discuss this inside?"

She takes three threatening steps back up the walkway. "I said, did you just call me *fat?*" Her last word echoes throughout the valley.

I come down the porch stairs, moving closer and dropping my voice so that hopefully, not all of Rogersville will hear what I say next. "The insult I was going for was selfish. Have you taken even one second to think about anyone other than yourself? Use that pretty little brain of yours to think about what Dad's confession might've meant for the rest of us. What it might have meant for me."

Understanding blooms across her brow. "You told Jake?"

I nod.

"And?"

Tears spring to my eyes, answer enough for Lexi. She drops her bag on the grass and closes the distance between us, pulling me into a hug.

"Aw, baby. I'm so sorry."

If nothing else, at least this past month has given me back my sister. I clutch her closer, inhale her sugar-sweet scent. No matter what happens next, I will not allow us to lose touch again.

There's movement to our left, movement I don't take much note of until the shape acquires a voice. "Well, isn't this sweet? Two bitches for the price of one."

Lexi and I freeze, and the blood drains from my face. Not from the source of the voice or even his words, but the unmistakable threat they both carry.

As one, every person in the yard turns to where Dean is standing, in his filthy pajamas and bare feet, his greasy hair sticking up on one side. How the man is still upright is beyond me. He is, for lack of better words, completely wasted. One hand flails through the air for balance. The other hand, his right, is steady as all the rocks holding up Rock City.

Which is unfortunate, because his right hand is the one holding the gun.

38

Ella Mae Andrews, March 1994

When the phone rang for the third time in a row, Ella Mae knew it was Dean. She knew without getting up from where she lay on the couch he was plastered against his living room window again, phone pressed to his ear and staring daggers across the yard. And by now she knew him well enough to be more than a tiny bit afraid. Afraid of how he made her feel. Afraid of how he hurt her. Avoiding him seemed like the safest option.

The sharp rings died abruptly, and Ella Mae puffed a sigh of relief as the house around her fell silent. She closed her eyes and nestled deeper into the couch. Was she this bone-tired last time she was pregnant? Like every step was uphill, every simple task a chore? She honestly couldn't remember that far back. It was as if her brain was clogged with cotton balls or something. She gave in to the confusion, letting her exhaustion pull her under.

And then a door slammed and a voice carried across the lawn. "Ella Mae!"

Shit. Dean, and loud enough for all of Appalachia to hear.

She jumped off the couch and scrambled down the hall-way to the front door. But she wasn't fast enough.

"Goddammit, Ella Mae, I know you're in there!" His voice echoed through the house, his fists pounded against the wood. "Open up, before I break the door down."

Ella Mae didn't have a lick of doubt he would do it, too. She flipped the lock and opened up just wide enough to stick her head through. "Jesus, Dean! Do you want the en-tire street to know our business? What if somebody heard you?"

"You didn't leave me with much choice. I've been call-ing you for days." His eyes narrowed to accusing slits. "Are you avoiding me?"

"No, I'm not avoiding you." She planted her bare feet in the door opening, not swinging the door any wider, not inviting him in. Even though Gia and Ray were off visit-ing colleges and she'd just seen Allison disappear down the driveway with the girls. Ella Mae didn't trust herself with Dean near. His pull on her was still too dangerous. "I've just been so tired."

Dean studied her with obvious disbelief, and Ella Mae tried not to fidget. That last time with Dean, in that hotel room off exit 23, he'd taken things too far, with his toys and with his fists. The blow he'd dealt her had worked like a cold shower, washing away Ella Mae's lust and showing her a side of Dean she didn't like, a kinky side, a painful side, one with handcuffs and paddles and clamps and angry hands. After that day, she began to see this affair with Dean for what it was. Sick. Perverse. Over.

"C'mon, baby, let me in." He smiled that smile of his, and his voice took on that low, crooning quality he knew from experience made her squirm with lust.

But the mother she wanted to become this time around wouldn't lose her mind over her married neighbor, no matter how charming, no matter how handsome. Ella Mae bit down on her bottom lip, and she didn't let him in.

He propped a palm high on the wall and leaned close enough for her to feel his warm breath on her cheek when he said his next words. "Please? I'll make it worth your while."

Oh, Ella Mae knew he would, and then some. At the thought of how he might make it worth her while, something down there stirred. Despite her best intentions to end this affair, despite her determination to no longer be affected by Dean Sullivan, she still wanted him, dammit. Her body was a traitor, a goddamn traitor. She had to grip the doorjamb to keep herself from pouncing.

Dean could tell he was wearing her down. He smiled, leaned even closer and dropped his voice until it was like warm caramel, smooth and creamy and so damn sweet. His hand curled around her wrist. "Baby, I've missed you so much these past few days, I can barely sleep. Let me in and I'll prove how much I missed you, I promise."

She pressed a hand to her fluttering belly, still flat despite her baby growing underneath. The reminder snapped her right out of Dean's spell, gave her the strength to take a single step back and break his grasp.

"Go home, Dean."

Ella Mae pushed on the wood, and the last thing she noticed were Dean's eyes, widening in astonishment, right before the door exploded. The hinges groaned, and the wood made a crunching sound when it crashed into the wall behind it, missing Ella Mae's shoulder by less than an inch.

Faster than she could blink, Dean was inside the house. He kicked the door shut, seized Ella Mae, whirled her around. One hand grabbed a fistful of hair and yanked, forcing a sharp whimper up her throat before she could stop herself. Ella Mae knew better than to scream.

Dean would like it if she screamed.

"You think that after everything that's happened between us—" his words squeezed, deep and deadly, through clenched teeth "—you can send me away? I own you, Ella Mae Andrews. I don't intend to go home until you've learned that little lesson."

Ella Mae couldn't have responded if she'd wanted to because he covered her mouth with his. When his tongue batted up against her front teeth, he jerked painfully on her hair, pulling Ella Mae's head back until her mouth fell open.

What Dean did then wasn't even remotely a kiss. It was rape by tongue, invading her mouth and consuming her soul and stealing her breath until Ella Mae's vision went dark around the corners. She flapped her arms by his shoulders until he lifted his head and she gulped air, but he didn't let her go.

He smacked her cheek, not too hard, but hard enough to sting. She made a sound of surprise, and he clapped a palm over her mouth.

"Are you going to be a good girl?"

Ella Mae nodded. By now she knew there was no refusing him. He was too strong, and far too determined. She figured her best tactic was to play along, pretend she was just as crazy for him as he was certifiably insane. And then, as soon as his pants hit the floor, she would run upstairs, lock herself in her bedroom and call the police.

She forced her body to relax in his arms. When his grip on her loosened, she pressed herself flush against him and made another sound, a throatier sound, and he smiled in approval. He dropped his hand from her mouth, and Ella Mae dropped to her knees. She reached for his belt buckle.

"That's a very good girl."

"No, Dean." She licked her lips and gave him a smoldering look through her lashes. "I'm a very bad girl, and as soon as I'm done here, I think I'm gonna want a spanking."

Ella Mae peeled his jeans and boxers down his legs in one smooth motion, leaving them both jumbled around his ankles. Dean was more than ready. He threw back his head in anticipation.

Now.

She braced her palms on Dean's bare thighs and shoved with all her strength, using his body as leverage to push up and out, to give her a head start up the stairs. For a split hair of a second, she thought she might make it.

"You're gonna be sorry you did that."

Ella Mae already was.

Because instead of hitting air when she'd pushed him, Dean's shoulders rebounded right off the front door. She wasn't even halfway up the staircase when he tugged his pants to his hips and caught up to her, all in five seconds flat.

She was even sorrier when Dean snatched one of her ankles out of the air, and Ella Mae dropped to the steps with a scream. Pain burst up a shoulder, across a hip bone, down a calf. With one flick of his arm, Dean flipped Ella Mae over like a sirloin steak. She felt a dull pop, somewhere way down deep inside, and warmth spread across her abdomen.

"You thought you could get away from me?" His lip curled in an ugly sneer. "Think again, bitch."

He raped her right there on the stairs. First on her back, and then he flipped her over and raped her again. And again and again and again, every which way. Ella Mae tried to keep still. She tried not to scream or cry or fight back, because she knew it only wound him up more, made his fists fly even faster.

But there were a handful of times she couldn't help herself. She squealed or whimpered or wailed. The pain was too much.

And once—just once—she'd cried out in pleasure. She hated herself for it, hated her body for still responding to Dean's touch, but she hated Dean more.

And then, as suddenly as he'd started, Dean's body went still.

"What the...?" He looked down, and his brow crumpled in surprise. "Jesus, Ella Mae, you're bleeding."

39

One of the hardest things in the world is to look some-one in the eye when they're aiming a gun at your heart, but that's just what I do. I untangle myself from my sister and turn to face Dean Sullivan, doing my best to stare at his face and not down the barrel of his gun. My heart rate rockets up to a billion times ten.

"Have you seen what those animals did to my house?"

His words are so slurred they're almost incoherent, but I know without asking he's talking about the bloodred *A* slashed across his front siding, and the newer, even bigger, *liar* in black block letters. I want to tell him I had noth-ing to do with the graffiti, but my tongue won't cooperate. Maybe it's because I feel at least partly responsible for the vandalism of his home, even though I wasn't technically the one wielding the can of spray paint.

"Folks are saying I committed perjury, maybe even mur-der."

I nod. "I know, and I'm really sorry, but—"

My apology seems to infuriate him. His brows dip and his lips curl in accusation. "You should be sorry, dammit.

I've turned into a freaking joke. Rogersville's own loony tune. All because of your family."

He punctuates the last word by stabbing the gun in our direction, and a gasp goes through the crowd. Even as drunk as he is, his right arm is steadier than it should be and the distance close enough to make it a fairly easy shot. I pinch my eyes shut and brace myself for a bullet that doesn't come.

My mind flies through my options. Surely by now someone had enough sense to call the police. Maybe I can keep Dean talking until they get here or he passes out, whichever comes first. Or Lexi and I could make a run for the house and pray the Jack Daniel's has derailed his aim, but what if Dean takes his vexation out on the crowd? I chance a glance at them, wide-eyed and frozen to the pavement at the end of the driveway, and I want to scream in frustration. This is Tennessee, for crap's sake, where guns are allowed in bars. Where are the vigilantes when you need them?

I turn back to Dean with the only ammunition I have that will take away his. "I know you didn't murder Ella Mae."

"Damn straight I didn't. I loved Ella Mae. I would've never hurt her."

I hear Lexi take in air for what I know will be a smart-ass comment, but I elbow her in the ribs before she can get it out. If she gets Dean even more riled up, he won't hear my next words.

"Dean, listen to me. You didn't murder Ella Mae. My father murdered Ella Mae."

A gasp rises from the crowd to my right, and someone mutters, "I knew it," but I don't turn. I watch for Dean's reaction, which is, quite frankly, anticlimactic.

He lifts a sloppy but apathetic shoulder. "I know. Because she was gonna leave him for me."

Now isn't the best time to tell him about the letter, or point out Ella Mae was planning to leave them both. But still. Dean is missing my point. I just told him, in front of a couple dozen loose-mouthed witnesses, that my father killed Ella Mae, so why is Dean still aiming a gun at my chest?

Lexi goes for her most appeasing tone. "How 'bout this, Mr. Sullivan? You take yourself and your weapon back inside to your whiskey, these fine folks will head into town and—"

"Shut up."

"—tell everybody that Ray's the killer, and Gia and Bo and I will forget this ever happened. That way everybody wins, right?"

"I said, shut up!" He swivels his gun between me and my sister. "You two are trying to trick me."

Lexi's hand throttles my fingers. "Nobody's trying to trick you, I swear."

I chance a glance up the porch. Bo is frozen in shock at the edge, strangling the railing with both hands, but I don't see either Cal or Fannie. Even more people have materialized up at the mailbox, sneaking out of their houses and through the woods to watch the show, but none of them seem to be reaching for either a cell phone or a concealed weapon. And where the *hell* is Jimmy?

Relief floods my senses and loosens my bones when I hear an engine roaring in the distance, then bubbles into intense, giddy joy when Jake's truck crests the hill. He stops with a screech of brakes at the mailbox.

Dean's reactions are delayed and unsteady, but after a few extra beats, he swivels his body to Jake's parked truck. A warning scream sticks in my throat.

Through the front windshield, Jake's eyes find mine

for a brief second, and he winks. There's nothing the least bit flirtatious about the gesture. It's meant to calm me, to reassure me.

It doesn't work.

Jake slides out of the cab, confidently, casually, like people point deadly weapons at his head every day. He doles out greetings to the crowd as if this is a typical Tuesday morning visit. When he strolls his way down the drive, straight at Dean and his pistol, he might as well be whistling Dixie.

"Somebody decide to have a party and forget to call me?" Jake's voice is measured and even, and I don't know how he does it, but he manages to pull up a sincere smile.

"You again." Dean's spiteful tone, combined with the look of pure hatred on his face, has me dropping my gaze to his trigger finger, watching for even the slightest twitch. "Hold it right there, boy."

Jake holds it there, a good ten-foot shot away, and he holds up both palms. "Why don't you put that gun down, Mr. Sullivan, and we'll talk this out."

"Talking's what got me into this mess in the first place. Talking about what I saw that night. Talking about the baby. If you don't mind, I think I'm all talked out."

"I don't mind at all." Jake glances over his shoulder at the people huddled together by the mailbox, then back to Dean. "In fact, why don't I talk instead? Because I came over here with something to say, and it's just as good I do so with an audience."

And then he does the unthinkable. He turns his back on the man holding the gun and faces me.

Behind him, Dean looks stumped, and his shooting arm drops a good half foot.

"You left before I could tell you you were wrong," Jake

says as if we're the only two people on the front lawn, as if a confused Dean wasn't swiveling his gun, back and forth, between me and Jake.

I shake my head, not understanding, not caring that I don't understand, not concerned about anything other than Dean's bullets.

"You said all of our choices were irrelevant," he says, inching to the right, "and maybe some of them are. But not the most important one, the one where I choose to love you, and you choose to love me back. I choose you, Gia. Choose to love me back."

Greg Lawson's mother presses a fleshy hand to her even fleshier chest. "Aw, ain't that just the sweetest thing I ever did hear?"

Jake gives her an appreciative nod. "I thank you for saying so, Mary."

"But you were right, too," he tells me, taking another step. "There have been too many secrets, and I'm gonna do something about that." He swivels his body to face the crowd. "Thirty-four years ago, Ella Mae Andrews had a baby boy. She was young and scared at the time, but mature enough to know she couldn't give her son the life he deserved so she found a loving couple who could. I thank God every day for her sacrifice, because I'm that boy. I'm Ella Mae's son."

There are a few gasps, the loudest of which comes from Dean, and a flurry of whispers makes its way through the crowd. Jake uses the distraction. He takes a few subtle steps to his right, sweeping his gaze over Lexi and me until it lands on Bo, stock-still on the edge of the porch. An entire conversation passes between the two men in an instant, communicated not in spoken words but in subtly raised brows and squinted eyes and pinched mouths. Bo dips his head in understanding. Lexi cringes closer to my side. My heart stops.

Jake looks over at me, and he doesn't say a word, but then again, he doesn't have to. His eyes say everything I could ever hope to hear.

And then he returns his attention to the crowd. "I know I should've told you the truth that very first night I rode into town, and I know I should be sorry, but I'm not. Because if I had told you folks—" he points a long arm at me, shifting more to his right and planting himself directly in the line between the barrel of Dean's gun and me "—then that gorgeous woman over there would've never loved me, and I would've never loved her back."

My breath catches in my throat, and a shudder pummels my torso. I will not have Jake taking my bullet. I shake my head, frantic.

Out of the corner of my eye, I see Bo duck around the corner of the porch and slip out of sight.

Jake holds my gaze, ignores my protests. "You and I are connected by our pasts, by people who made sometimes stupid decisions we had absolutely no control over. But here's something we can control. Let's forget about the people who came before us, and not allow their mistakes to influence you and me. Let's hold each other up despite the way our parents beat each other down. Let's write our own happy ending. Because whatever happened sixteen years ago has nothing to do with you and me, except that it brought us here to this place."

It's not his words, as beautiful as they are, but his willingness to step into a bullet's path for me that does it. I'm about to rush into his embrace when a shot pierces the air and sends the cluster of spectators into a frenzy. They scatter like a pack of hunted quail, flying apart and taking cover behind their cars. I barely notice, because I'm concentrating on Jake's body, which goes stiff with shock. I scream his name, but he stops me with a palm in the air.

"I'm okay. I'm not shot."

Jake holds up his other hand and slowly turns to face Dean, giving me a clear view of him, pointing the smoking barrel into the brand-new blue sky.

"Jesus Christ," Lexi says on a sigh.

A warning shot. My knees wobble with relief.

"You have no idea," Dean slurs, right as Jake steps between us again, "no goddamn idea, what my life has been like since that murdering sonovabitch took Ella Mae. I lost my job, my family, my life. All because of Ray Andrews. He was supposed to go away for life. He deserved the motherfucking needle."

In the corner of my vision, I catch a shape coming up the hill to my left.

"And then you people—" I wish I could see Dean, so I knew which people, and where he's pointing his gun "—start blabbering about me and Ella Mae all over town, and suddenly everybody's calling me a liar and wrecking my house. I'm not a liar, dammit! I saw Ray Andr—"

A blur I briefly recognize as Bo shoots from behind a bush and tackles Dean. Lexi is lightning fast, too, shoving me out of the way, and I slide across the lawn, a tangle of grass and leaves and limbs. I come to a sudden stop at a tree, slamming into the trunk with my shoulder hard enough that I wonder if I'm the one who was hit.

Because sometime in the space between Bo tackling Dean and Lexi pushing me halfway across the yard, Dean pinched off another shot.

And then I see Bo holding Dean at gunpoint and Lexi rushing forward to a body, lying motionless on the driveway. I crawl over and push her out of the way, barely noticing the sound of sirens growing closer through the valley, the crowd of concerned faces watching down all around us, the way my tears soak with blood into a growing puddle on Jake's flannel shirt.

How many times have I watched someone die in the field? Too many to count. Maybe I have been overexposed by all the disasters I've seen, made less sensitive to all the suffering around me, because that moment of last breath has never scared me. To be the last face someone sees in this lifetime is a beautiful thing. A precious, priceless gift.

Now, though, I'm afraid of death. Terrified. I know this when Jake won't open his eyes, not when I press a hand over his wound, dangerously close to where his heart is, spurting blood, too much blood into my palm, squeezing sticky and warm between my fingers. Not when I hold his limp hand in the ambulance, careening and wailing through the hills to Hawkins County Memorial, and beg him to hold on, just a little longer. Not when I cry into his chest and tell him I love him, right before they whisk him away from me and into the emergency room.

Now I see there is nothing beautiful about death. Death is not precious or priceless. For the person close to the dying soul—a parent, a lover, a child—death is not a gift but a thief.

40

I lean back on the bench, and late-afternoon sunlight filters through the pink clouds of cherry tree blossoms above my head. It's May, a full three months after I was called home to take care of Dad, and I'm still here, in Rogersville.

And surprisingly, not all of my time here has been bad. Lexi was right. My blood, like hers and Bo's, *is* mixed with mountain water, and this place—this town and the mountains and rivers and valleys that surround it—is as much a part of me as my skin and bones. It whispers for me to stay, even while another part, a larger part, tells me it's time to go.

Beyond my outstretched feet, Ella Mae's Memorial Garden blooms like a springtime carpet, a riot of hydrangeas and peonies and lilacs and even a few straggler tulips, swaying above fledgling grass shoots. Lexi was right about that, too. This is the perfect spot.

The wind kicks up, and the shirt I pilfered from Jake's drawer dances and bucks around me like a tethered kite. When I stand, it flaps around my shoulders, straining for the sky and beyond, and my gypsy soul stirs. Where will the kite take me this time? To Africa? Asia? The Arby's down the road? Wherever disaster strikes next, I suppose.

My name, called out by a familiar throaty voice, floats up the hill on a fresh breeze. I turn and there she is, Sexy Lexi Andrews, sashaying up the pea gravel walkway like it's a catwalk. "How did I know I'd find you up here?"

I grin. Lexi knows the thinking bench is where I've spent the better part of the past three months, watching plants nudge their way through the soil and, well, *thinking*. About Dad and Ella Mae. About Lexi and Bo and Cal and Dean. About Jake. Most of all, I think about Jake and how he was right, too. What happened here all those years ago has nothing to do with him and me, but wisdom like his is easy to miss when you're in the eye of the storm.

"Everybody's down at the truck, waiting." She jerks a manicured thumb down the path she came in on. "You coming?"

"Yeah, I was just…" I spread my arms wide and look around, like the answer is tucked behind the fronds and flowers. "I don't know. Letting go, I guess."

She gives me a dubious look. Letting go is a concept Lexi has never considered. "Just like that?"

"Just like that."

Other than to purse her pretty lips, Lexi doesn't respond, and I don't push it. I know she's not ready, may never be ready. She's already told me she was relieved to learn the truth about Dad. As much as she wanted to believe he was innocent, she said she should have known something was off when forgiveness never felt as comfortable as her blame, as if we were talking about a pair of worn-in jeans, or an old flannel shirt.

But she's finally managed to let go of some of her hatred, at least toward Dad. All that anger had to go somewhere, though, so she picked it up and transferred it over to Cal. When I remind her he spent the entire thirteen and a half minutes we were at gunpoint using his lawyer voice on the 9-1-1 operator, ordering the police to hurry the hell up before he sued the entire state of Tennessee for negligence, she tells me it doesn't matter. She says she will never forgive him for lying for Dad, and I have no reason not to believe her.

"It's not too late to change your mind, you know," she says softly, her voice pulsing with hope. "One of my clients runs the YMCA in Kingsport. He'll know where to start, who to talk to…" She pauses to take in my expression, and hers falls. "You're not going to change your mind, are you?"

I don't shake my head, but I don't nod, either. I just head down the hill, not stopping until I'm right in front of her.

"It's not for forever," I say as much to Lexi as to myself. "I'll be back soon, I promise."

"That's what you said last time." When I don't respond, she snorts. "Okay, fine. You *might* have said something like that last time, but it was hard to hear over your gunning engine and squealing tires. Those old track marks are still on the driveway, you know. They smoked for days."

I laugh at the same time a sob pushes up my throat. I'm ready to leave, but at the same time, it shatters my heart to go.

I don't have to tell any of this to Lexi. She always could read my mind. "Me, too," she whispers, and the fresh tears in her eyes mirror mine. She links her arm through mine, tugging me down the path. "But it's time."

We walk in silence for a bit, our shoes crunching in the gravel.

Jake said we can't change our pasts, and he was right about that, too. Trying to change what happened with my father and Ella Mae, with Dean and Cal, with me and Jake, would be like trying to stuff the flowers back down into the soil…impossible.

What's important is what comes next. Do we spend the rest of our days chasing someone else's disasters, filled with hate and resentment? Do we put what happened in a box and shove it to the back of our closets, refusing to forgive or at the very least, pretending to forget? Or do we somehow learn to adjust and make peace?

As for me, I choose the last. I plan to take Jake's advice and figure out how to not let my past influence my future. I plan to write my own happy ending.

Lexi and I emerge onto Main Street's empty sidewalk, a few blocks down from Roadkill, now owned by a nice couple from Mount Carmel. Jake's truck idles, packed and fueled at the curb. Bo and Amy push off the bumper when they see us coming.

"Make sure to check the tires and top off the oil on your way out," Bo says, gesturing to the truck. "Washer fluid might be a little low, too."

I could tell him I had the truck checked out, bumper to bumper, just yesterday, but I don't. If measuring sticks and air pumps are how Bo wants to express his love, who am I to complain? Instead, I pull him into a fierce hug and kiss him on the cheek.

"Thanks, bro. I'll see you soon."

He nods brusquely and hands me off to Amy, then blinks at the concrete while Lexi and I share our final, tearful goodbye.

"Call me when you get to wherever you're going, okay?" Lexi thinks better of it, shakes her head. "Or actually, no. Scratch that. Call me anytime, I don't care when. Just call me. Often."

"Every single day."

"Okay, well, not *that* often. I have a life, you know."

Sharp footfalls sound behind me, heavy boots on concrete. I turn, and my heart gives a happy flip at the sight of Jake. Hair a little longer, frame a little thinner, but my point is, he's still here.

I gesture to the battered duffel in his fist. "Do you have everything?"

He tosses the bag in the bed of his truck, then steps close, as close as you can get without touching, and tucks a curl behind my ear. "Everything I need."

"God, y'all are disgusting," Lexi says, but there's a smile in her voice. She shoos us into the truck. "Leave already."

Once we're settled, Jake behind the wheel and me pushed up against him until there is not a sliver of space between us, Lexi leans her arms over the open passenger window. "You take care of my baby sister, you hear me?"

"I hear you," Jake says. "I'll bring her back, too."

Lexi slaps the side of the truck and steps back, taking up next to Bo and Amy on the sidewalk, while Jake works the gearshift into Drive.

"Ready?"

I deposit a kiss on his pec, an inch or two to the right of his scar, and nod.

He reaches for the wheel, then pauses. "Uh, where are we going, exactly?"

Somewhere on this planet, seas are churning, locusts are swarming, plates are shifting under the earth's crust. Who knows where the next disaster will strike, or how long we have until it does. I want to make every second until then count.

I swing my feet up onto the dash, blow a kiss to my family and point straight down Main. "Just drive."

* * * * *

ACKNOWLEDGMENTS

Writing a book is a lonely venture, and I am blessed to be surrounded by people who don't put up with my attempts at seclusion for very long.

To my agent, Nikki Terpilowski, and my editor, Rachel Burkot. Thank you for loving this story as much as I do, for all the ways you helped me shape it into a book, for your enthusiasm in sending it out into the world. I feel as though I won the literary jackpot with you both.

To the sweetest sistahs a girl could ask for: Lara Chapman, Koreen Myers, Alex Ratcliff. Your support, critiques, shoulders, advice, cheerleading, laughs and friendship make my world a much brighter place. And to Margie Lawson, who gave me my sistahs and taught me more about the craft than I thought was possible. I'm not exaggerating when I say this book would not exist without you and your brilliant coaching. Thanks for sitting on my shoulder while I write.

To the lovely ladies of Altitude—Nancy Davis, Marquette Dreesch, Sima Lal Gupta, Angelique Kilkelly, Jen Robinson, Amanda Sapra and Tracy Willoughby. You gals have been there every step of the way, and you've made the long road bearable. Thanks for always having my back and cheering me on.

To Genevieve Bos, for your generosity, business sense and all-around fabulousness, and to my early readers and cheerleaders—Kimberly Barnett, Mellissa Steadman Barney, Elizabeth and Greg Baxendale, Christy Brown, Lisa Campagna, Jamie Gallo, Kathy Kay, Dorothy Peterson, Jennifer Richardson, Tanya Sam, Alan and Teresa Schaefer, and K. C. Young. Katennia Dula, I'm so glad we're on each other's team.

To my *literatuurgroep*—Jiska van Ede, Kiki Edelman, Carolien van der Lande, Alette Stache, Petra Strickland, Irene Tyler, Jacqueline Waning and Riëtte van Winden—for agreeing to read an English-language book at a Dutch book club, and for letting it be this one.

To my parents. Thanks for being proud of my writing before you read the very first word.

To Ewoud—my best friend, my biggest fan, my traveling partner and partner in crime. Life with you is an adventure.

And finally, to Evan and Isabella. No matter where in this world I end up, my favorite place will always be wherever you are.

QUESTIONS FOR DISCUSSION

1. In *The Last Breath*, the story begins with Gia returning home to care for her dying father, a man she hasn't seen or spoken to in sixteen years. She's not convinced he's guilty of murdering her stepmother, but she's not certain he's innocent, either. Would you have returned home in this case?

2. Why do you think Gia chose a career chasing disasters around the planet? Was it to feed her wanderlust, to get away from her past in Rogersville or something else entirely? Does it matter if her reasons were not purely altruistic, as long as she's helping others?

3. Alternatively, do you understand Lexi's reasons for remaining in Rogersville, and Jake's for settling there? Are their methods of coping with their traumas better or worse than Gia's?

4. Think about the bonds of family—the obligations that hold them together and the secrets that can tear them

apart. What do you think the author was trying to say with Gia's story?

5. Have you or someone you know ever been caught up in a destructive and abusive relationship? How did reading about Ella Mae and Dean make you feel about that relationship? Did it change any of your thoughts or beliefs about how that relationship played out?

6. Gia keeps finding herself in situations where she's either disappointed by her family members, or she feels she's disappointing them. Is there anything she should have handled differently?

7. At one point, Gia realizes that Cal's defense wasn't accidentally shoddy, that he threw the most prominent and important case of his life on purpose. Do you understand Cal's choice to defend his brother, while also ensuring Ray paid for what he did? What about Cal's promise to keep Ray's secret from his children?

8. Do you understand Jake's reasons for keeping his true identity secret from the people in Rogersville? What about from Gia? Was he right or wrong in not telling?

9. After her father's deathbed confession, Gia forgives her father, even if she will never be able to forgive his action. Further, according to Gia, "And if I can't do either of those things just yet, the least I can do is give him peace." Could you do the same in her position?

10. Where do you think Gia and Jake end up? What do their lives look like a year or two or ten down the line?

A CONVERSATION WITH KIMBERLY BELLE

What was your inspiration for this story? Where did the plot and characters come from, and what helped them to take shape in your mind and then come to life on paper?

Unfortunately, tragedies like Ella Mae's happen every day, so finding a story spark can sometimes be as easy as turning on the news. For me, though, what makes a story compelling is not the tragedy, but how it affects the people left in its aftermath. How do they cope; how do their relationships change? In the case of Gia, when her father swears he didn't do this awful thing everyone says he did, how does she decide who and what to believe? These are some of the questions I loved exploring in this story.

As for where I find my characters, Gia was a gift from the writing gods. She came to me almost fully formed, her name and physical attributes, her strengths and weaknesses already in place. Lexi and Jake, too, to a large extent. I had to work a little harder for the others, mining my memories for some of the more colorful folks, embellishing them to really make them pop. Folks like Fannie, for example. I'm not exaggerating, not even a little bit, when I say there are a million Fannies puttering up and down the hills of Appalachia.

What about the setting? Why Tennessee? What did you want to convey by giving the book a small-town feel, and with the homecoming element for Gia?

The easy answer is that I grew up in eastern Tennessee and wanted to showcase the natural beauty of the Appalachians, but there was more to my reasoning than that. I wanted a place that for Gia would look and sound and smell like home, one that would slam her with a strong sense of belonging while at the same time stifling her with its small-town, small-minded feel. A place where the mountains are big and wide, but the towns are tiny and insular. Where everybody knows your business, and they won't hesitate to act as if it's theirs. Eastern Tennessee's dichotomy served Gia's story perfectly.

How, if at all, do you relate to Gia? How are you different? Is there anything she does that you would never do yourself?

I imagine every writer puts at least a little bit of herself in her characters, and I'm no exception. Like Gia, I grew up in eastern Tennessee, in a small town about a half hour from Rogersville, and have more than a little gypsy in my soul. I worked in nonprofits for years (albeit a desk job), and many of Gia's frustrations about what organizations are and are not capable of accomplishing were mine, as well.

But that's kind of where our similarities end. Gia had this horrible, awful thing happen in her family when she was eighteen, something I can only imagine in fiction, but instead of succumbing to her tragedy, she channeled it into a career helping others. She's so broken, yet so brave and strong. Returning home was the hardest thing ever, yet she not only did it, she rediscovered her roots, reconnected with her siblings and fell in love. I would have been a puddle on the floor.

What proved most challenging in writing this story? What was the greatest pleasure that you took from it?

Writing Dean and Ella Mae's story was extremely difficult and took me to dark and scary places. I think a lot of people can relate to losing yourself in a relationship. To getting so caught up in another person that you push aside all the voices that say he's bad, he's wrong, he's going to hurt you in ways you never dreamed you could be hurt. Maybe not to the extent that Dean hurt Ella Mae, but still. I have a daughter, and all I could think about while writing their story was, how do I prevent my daughter from becoming an Ella Mae?

At the same time, I'm a romantic at heart, so the best part of writing this story was easily Gia and Jake. They had everything going against them, yet their love was so strong, so genuine and sweet. They had to work really hard for it, but they deserved their happy ending, and I was glad to give it to them.

Did you know every plot twist and decision your characters would make—and furthermore, the book's outcome—before you started writing? Or did the characters surprise you and lead you to stray from original plotting at all?

By the time I sit down to write, I always have the basics of the story in my head. I know where it begins, who the major players are, the themes and big-picture messages, and the plot points, including a general sense of the ending. But characters always surprise me. I had no idea, for example, that Gia would pretend to be Ella Mae when she went downstairs to coax a deathbed confession from her father. She did that all by herself. And I didn't decide on the true identity of Ella Mae's killer—Ray or Dean or someone else entirely—until about the halfway point. Writers talk a lot about writing the story that wants to be told. I try to do just that, to point my plot and characters in a general direction while also giving them room to take an unexpected turn.

Can you describe your writing process? Are you an outliner? Do you write scenes consecutively, or jump around? Do you keep a daily schedule?

I'm a planner, but I don't outline, and with the exception of one or two candy-bar scenes (Jake painting Gia's house was one of them, and my favorite scene in the book), I write the story in order. I do a lot of polishing as I go, as I find I can't move forward until the characters feel authentic and the plot points ring true. It takes me longer to get to the end, but it's typically a pretty clean first draft.

And yes, when I'm working on a story, I sit my butt in a chair for a big chunk of every day, slogging toward a daily word-count goal. Sometimes those words suck, sometimes they don't. But words make sentences, and sentences make paragraphs and chapters and eventually an entire story.

*Read on for a sneak peek at
Kimberly Belle's gripping
new psychological thriller,*
Stranger in the Lake.

I untie the dock cleats and shove the boat into water as gray as the sky. Sometime in the past few hours, gunmetal clouds have rolled over the mountaintops, shooting down icy gusts that froth the surface of Lake Crosby into a million white peaks. My stomach churns, and not from the water's chop.

Maybe morning sickness, maybe nerves at the words I need to say to my new husband out loud.

Surprise! I'm pregnant.

I sink onto the helm seat and shove my hands into the pockets of my new down jacket. A gift from Paul, who has impeccable taste—the kind that comes from good breeding and a big bank account. We've only ever spoken about children in the vaguest of terms. Things like "this room would make a good nursery" or "we would make pretty babies," the "one day" silent but implied. He and his first wife never tried for a baby before she died, a little over four years ago. I haven't known him a year. This wasn't exactly the plan.

But neither was falling for a man eleven years older than me, a man who always claimed he'd never marry again. The thirty-seven-year-old wealthy widower falls for a gas station clerk from the muddy side of the mountain, both of us touched by tragedy. A combination that everybody from our town said would never work.

"I don't give a damn what people think," Paul is constantly telling me. "I love you and you love me, and that's all that matters."

But now... My hand feels under the jacket to my still-flat stomach. What will he think about this little surprise blooming inside my belly? I have no idea.

His mother, the people in town, friends who've known him all his life. I know exactly what they'll say.

They'll say that this baby was no accident. That the littlest Keller will cement my place at the family dinner table in a way the three carats on my ring finger can't. That marriages are temporary, but children are until the end of time. That now he's *really* trapped.

Sugar daddy, sugar baby, baby daddy.

By now the wind has pushed me away from the dock, and I start the engine and swing the boat around. Paul and I live on a cove, but the currents here are swift, the water dangerously deep. The hill his house is perched on doesn't stop at the shoreline, but plunges to depths of up to three hundred feet. There's a whole town buried down there, tucked in the hills of what was once a thriving valley. Homes, roads, farms, schools. Graveyards. Whenever anything manages to wriggle loose—a battered shingle, an algae-covered shoe, a slimy dog collar—it ends up here, in Skeleton Cove.

Halfway to the town's center, I ease up on the throttle going around the point to Buck Knob Cove and look westward, over the water and mountains and endless smoky skies. I've never lived anywhere else but Lake Crosby, North Carolina—have never even considered it—and still the raw beauty of this place can take my breath away. These mountains are as much a part of me as my own skin and bones, the connection as real as the cells multiplying in my belly. If I close my eyes, I can feel the plates shifting under my feet. I am the mountains and the mountains are me. I couldn't live anyplace else if I tried.

It's the one thing I can't resent my mother for, I suppose, choosing this place to have a family—not that she was much of a parent. I mostly raised myself, and then I raised my brother, Chet, which is how I know love can only go so far. Love doesn't put food on the table. Love doesn't pay the rent or the creditors who come banging at the door. A baby needs so much more than love.

People say I married Paul for the money, but that's just not true. I married him because I love him, and I love him for all the things he provides. A mortgage-free roof over my head and a belly stuffed with nutritious, organic food. Health insurance and car insurance and cell phone and internet. The freedom of never having to choose between going cold or going hungry again. A life that is safe and stable and secure.

And really, when you think about it, isn't *security* just another word for *love*?

2

The town of Lake Crosby isn't much, just three square blocks and some change, but it's the only town in the southern Appalachians perched at the edge of the water, which makes it a popular tourist spot. Paul's office is at the far end of the first block, tucked between a fudge shop and Stuart's Craft Cocktails, which, as far as I can tell, is just another way to say "pretentious bar." Most of the businesses here are pretentious, farm-to-table restaurants and specialty boutiques selling all things overpriced and unnecessary.

For people like Paul, town is a place to socialize and make money—in his case, by selling custom house designs for the million-dollar lots that sit high on the hills or line the lakeshores. My old friends serve his drinks and wait his tables—but only the lucky ones. There are ten times more locals than there are jobs.

The covered terrace for the cocktail lounge is quiet, a result of the off-season and the incoming weather, the sign on the door still flipped to Closed. I'm passing the empty hostess stand when I notice movement at the very back, a tattered shadow peeling away from the wall. Jax—the town loon, the crazy old man who lives in the woods. Most people turn away from him, either out of pity or fear, but not me. For some reason I can't put into words, I've never been afraid to look him straight on.

He takes a couple of halting steps, like he doesn't want to be seen—and he probably doesn't. Jax is like a deer you come up on in a meadow, one blink and he's gone. But this time he doesn't run.

His gaze flicks around, searching the street behind me. "Where's Paul." A statement, not a question.

Slowly, so not to spook him, I point to the sleek double doors on the next building, golden light spilling out the windows of Keller Architecture. "Did you check inside?"

Jax shakes his head. "I need to talk to him. It's important."

Like every time he emerges from out of the woods, curiosity bubbles in my chest. Once upon a time, Jax had everything going for him. High school prom king and star quarterback, the golden boy with a golden future, and one of Paul's two best friends. Their picture still sits atop his desk in the study, Paul and Jax and Micah, all tanned chests and straightened smiles, three teenage boys with the world at their feet.

Now he's Batty Jax, the raggedy, bearded boogeyman parents use as a warning. Do your homework, stay out of trouble, and don't end up like Jax.

He clings to the murky back of the terrace, sticking to the shaded spots where it's too dark for me to make out much more than a halo of matted hair, the jutting edges of an oversized jacket, long, lean thighs. His face is dark, too, the combination of a life outdoors and dirt.

"Do you want me to give Paul a message? Or if you stay right there, I can send him out. I know he'll want to see you."

Actually, I don't know; I only assume. Jax is the source of a slew of rumors and petty gossip, but for Paul, he's a painful subject, one he doesn't like to talk about. As far as I know, the two haven't spoken since high school graduation—not an easy thing to do in a town where everybody knows everybody.

Jax glances up the street, in the direction of far-off voices floating on the icy wind. I don't follow his gaze, but I can tell from the way his body turns skittish that someone is coming this way, moving closer.

"Do you need anything? Some money, maybe?"

Good thing those people aren't within earshot, because they would laugh at the absurdity of the trailer-park girl turned married-up wifey offering the son of an insurance tycoon some cash. Not that Jax's father didn't disown him ages ago or that I have more than a couple of bucks in my pocket, but still.

Jax shakes his head again. "Tell Paul I need to talk to him. Tell him to hurry."

Before I can ask what for, he's off, planting a palm on the railing and springing over in one easy leap, his body light as a pole vaulter. He hits the cement and takes off up the alley. I dash forward until I'm flush with the railing, peering down the long passage between Paul's building and the cocktail lounge, but it's empty. Jax is already gone.

I push through the doors of Keller Architecture, an open space with cleared desks and darkened computer screens. The whiteboard on the back wall has already been wiped clean, too, one of the many tasks Paul requires his staff to do daily. It's nearing five, and other than his lead designer, Gwen, hunched over a drawing at her drafting table, the office is empty.

She nods at my desk. "Perfect timing. I just finished the Curtis Cottage drawings."

Calling a seven-thousand-square-foot house a "cottage" is ridiculous, as are whatever reasons Tom Curtis and his wife, a couple well into their seventies, gave Paul for wanting six bedrooms and two kitchens in what is essentially a weekend home. But the Curtises are typical Keller Architecture clients—privileged, demanding and more than a little entitled. They like Paul because he's one of them. Having a desk is probably ridiculous, too, since I only work twenty hours a week, and for most of them I'm anywhere but here. My role is client relations, which consists mainly of hauling my ass to wherever the clients are so I can put out fires and talk them off the latest ledge. The job and the desk are one of the many perks of being married to a Keller.

"Thanks." I tuck the Curtis designs under an arm and move toward the hallway to my left, a sleek tunnel of wood and steel that ends in Paul's glass-walled office. "I'm here to pick up Paul. There's something wrong with his car."

When he called earlier to tell me his car was dead in the lot, I thought he was joking. Engine trouble is what happens to my ancient Civic, not Paul's fancy Range Rover, a brand-new supercharged machine with a dashboard that belongs in a cockpit. *More money than sense*, my mother would say about Paul if she were here, and now, I guess, about me.

Gwen leans back in her chair, wagging a mechanical pencil between two slim fingers. "Yeah, the dealer is sending a tow truck and a replacement car, but they just called to say they're delayed. He said he had a couple of errands to run."

I frown. "Who, the tow truck driver?"

"No, Paul." She swivels in her chair, reaching across the desk behind her for a straightedge. "He should be back any sec."

I thank her and head for the door.

On the sidewalk, I fire off a quick text to Paul. I'm here, where are you?

I wait for a reply that doesn't come. The screen goes dark, then black. I slip the phone into my jacket pocket and start walking.

In a town like Lake Crosby, there are only so many places Paul could be. The market, the pharmacy, the shop where he buys his ties and socks. I pop into all of them, but no one's seen him since this morning. Back on the sidewalk, I pull out my phone and give him a call. It rings once, then shoots me to voice mail. I hit End and look up and down the mostly deserted street.

"Hey, Charlie," somebody calls from across the road, two single lanes separated by a parking strip, and I whirl around, spotting Wade's familiar face over the cars and SUVs. One of my brother's former classmates, a known troublemaker who dropped out sophomore year because he was too busy cooking meth and raising hell. He leans against the ivory siding of the bed-and-breakfast, holding what I sincerely hope is a hand-rolled cigarette.

"It's Charlotte," I say, but I don't know why I bother.

On my sixteenth birthday, I plunked down more than a hundred hard-earned dollars at the courthouse to change my name. But no matter how many times I correct the people who knew me back when—people who populate the trailer parks and shacks along the mountain range, people like Wade and me—no matter how many times I tell them I'm not that person anymore, to them I'll always be Charlie.

He flicks the cigarette butt into the gutter and tilts his head up the street. "I just saw your old man coming out of the coffee shop." Emphasis on the *old man*. "If you hurry, you can probably catch him."

STRANGER IN THE LAKE

I mumble a thanks, then head in that direction.

Just past the market, I spot Paul at the far end of a side street, a paper cup clutched in his hand. He's wearing the clothes I watched him pull on this morning—a North Face fleece, a navy cashmere sweater, dark jeans, leather lace-up boots, but no coat. No hat or scarf or gloves. Paul always dresses like this, without a second thought as to the elements. That fleece might be fine for the quick jogs from the house to his car to the office door, but with the wind skimming up the lake, he must be freezing.

The woman he's talking to is more properly dressed. Boots and a black wool coat, the big buttons fastened all the way to a neck cloaked in a double-wrapped scarf. A knitted hat is pulled low over her ears and hair, leaving only a slice of her face—from this angle, her profile—exposed.

"There you are," I say, and they both turn.

A short but awkward silence. If I didn't know better, I'd think he looks surprised to see me.

"Charlotte, hi. I was just…" He glances at the woman, then back to me. "What are you doing here?"

"You asked me to pick you up. Didn't you get my text?"

With his free hand, he wriggles his cell from his pocket and checks the screen. "Oh. Sorry, I must have had it on Silent. I was on my way back to the office, but then I got to talking and…well, you know how that goes." He gives me a sheepish smile. It's a known fact that Paul is a talker, and like in most small towns, there's always someone to talk to.

But I don't know this woman.

I take in her milky skin and sky blue eyes, the light smattering of freckles across her nose and high cheekbones, and I'm positive I've never seen her before. She's the kind of pretty a person would remember, almost beautiful even, though she's nothing like his type. Paul likes his women curvy and exotic, with dark hair and ambiguous coloring. This woman is bony, her skin so pale it's almost translucent.

I step closer, holding up my hand in a wave. "Hi, I'm Charlotte Keller. Paul's wife."

The woman gives me a polite smile, but her gaze flits to Paul. She murmurs something, and I'm pretty sure it's "Keller."

The hairs soldier on the back of my neck, even though I've never been the jealous type. It's always seemed like such a waste of energy to me, being possessive and suspicious of a man who claims to love you. Either you believe him or you don't—or so I've always thought. Paul tells me he loves me all the time, and I believe him.

But this woman wouldn't be the first around these parts to try to snag herself a Keller.

"Are you ready?" I say, looking at Paul. "Because I came in the boat, and we need to get home before this weather blows in."

The talk of rain does the trick, and Paul snaps out of whatever I walked into here. He gives me that smile he saves only for me, and a rush of something warm hits me hard, right behind the knees.

People who say Paul and I are wrong together don't get that we've been waiting for each other all our lives. His first wife's death, my convict father and meth-head mother, they broke us for a reason, so all these years later our jagged edges would fit together perfectly, like two pieces of the same fractured puzzle. The first time Paul took my hand, the world just…started making sense.

And now there's a baby, a perfect little piece of Paul and me, an accidental miracle that somehow busted through the birth control. Maybe it's not a fluke but a sign, the universe's way of telling me something good is coming. A new life. A new chance to get things right.

All of a sudden and out of nowhere I feel it, this burning in my chest, an overwhelming, desperate fire for this baby that's taken root in my belly. I want it to grow and kick and thrive. I want it with everything inside me.

"Let's go home." Without so much as a backward glance at the woman, Paul takes my hand and leads me to the boat.

We're smack in the middle of Lake Crosby when it starts to snow, lazy fat flakes dancing down from a canopy of white. Flurries, but there's more coming. Those are snow clouds spilling over the mountaintops.

Paul has the bow pointed to home and the throttle buried, and I don't blame him. His fleece was bad enough in town, where there were warm shops to duck in and brick buildings to huddle behind. Out here on the open water the wind is fierce, and he might as well be shirtless.

He's hunched low behind the windshield, steering the boat with his knees, his hands shoved deep in his pits for warmth. I take in his blue lips, his chattering teeth, and wince. I should have brought his coat.

Tell him. Just open your mouth and say I'm pregnant. *Do it now.*

"Hey, Paul?" The words get lost in the roar of the engine, but there's no stopping now. Not when I've finally summoned my courage. I tap him on the shoulder and try again. *"Paul."*

He pulls back on the throttle, slowing the boat to a crawl. "What's wrong? Did you forget something?"

I shake my head. An hour ago, I left the house with exactly two items, the boat keys and my cell phone, both of which are here with me now. The keys dangle from the ignition, and I tucked my cell in the cubby by my seat, along with the Curtis Cottage drawings.

"You know how I've been feeling kinda out of sorts?" I don't have to tick off my symptoms—the bouts of nausea, the bone-tiredness I can't seem to shake. Paul brought me chicken soup from the market in town, covered me with blankets whenever I'd nap on the couch.

"You had the flu."

"That's what I thought, too. But who has the flu for three whole weeks?"

I stare at him hard, waiting for the realization to hit, but Paul's face is a complete blank. I can't tell if it's because he doesn't understand where I'm going with this, or if he's trying to contain his panic—or worse, suspicion. Will he accuse me of flicking my pills into the toilet, of forgetting to take them on purpose? His mother certainly will.

I look away. "Anyway, it wasn't the flu."

He reaches up and kills the engine. All around us, the air goes quiet the way it can only here, in the middle of a lake cradled between mountains and trees. A strange kind of muffled silence punctuated by the far-off cry of a hawk.

Paul swivels on his seat to face me, his voice laced with worry. "What is it? Are you sick?"

"No." My answer is swift, and I make sure to look him in the eyes. Paul's already lost one wife. Of course his mind would go there. I probably should have led with my good health. "No, I'm fine. Better than fine. Healthy as can be."

My heart is pounding now, but that's to be expected. I think of the matching pink lines on the sticks, wrapped in toilet paper and buried at the bottom of the wastebasket. The instructions said one line may come out lighter than the other, but any hint of a second line meant I was pregnant. All three times I pulled a new one from the wrapper and peed on it just in case the ones before it were defective, the lines were so pink they were almost purple.

I see the second the quarter drops. Paul huffs out a breath, and the twin lines between his eyebrows smooth out. "Are you saying what I think you're saying?" He sounds stunned, not angry. In fact, he kind of sounds the opposite, happy and hopeful—but maybe that's just me.

Still. I bite down on a smile. "That depends. What do you think I'm saying?"

"Charlotte McCreedy Keller, don't play games with me. My brittle old heart can't take it." He stands, reaching for me with icy hands, pulling me out of my chair. "Are you going to make me the happiest man on the planet? Are you going to make me a father?" He wraps his hands around my biceps and gives them a little jiggle. His eyes are gleaming, his smile stretched clear to his sideburns. "Are you?"

After a second or two, I nod.

Paul whoops, and a flock of swallows bursts from a bush on the shore, birds and batting wings swirling in the air. Suddenly I'm in the air, too, my legs wrapped around Paul's waist, his hands firm on my backside. He twirls me around in the tiny space between the seats, and I laugh, from relief and at Paul's reaction—a stunned but unapologetic joy.

"You're pretty strong for an old man."

"I'm not an old man. I am *the* man. My swimmers are bad*ass*. They are *fierce*." I laugh, and he puts me down. "How do you feel? Any other symptoms?"

"A little tired still, and kinda pukey in the mornings. Once I eat something, I'm usually fine."

"This is…this is amazing. I can't wait to tell everybody. Let's go home and make some calls."

"Paul, can we just…I don't know…keep this quiet for a little while longer? At least until I see the doctor and she gives us the green light. I want to know everything's okay before we go telling the whole world."

Worry flits across his brow. "What, you think this baby might not stick?"

"No, but it's still so early. I want to see this baby with my own two eyes and be sure. Let's just wait until after the first ultrasound, okay?"

"Okay, but so you know, I have a good feeling about this little guy. He's going to be fine."

I lift a brow. "Little *guy*?"

"Well, yeah. An adorable baby Keller to carry on the name." He presses a hand over my lower stomach and smiles. "Paul Junior."

Now, *that* his mother would approve of, a carbon copy of her precious son. I think back to Diana's reaction when we told her we were getting married, the fake smile that tried to crack open her cheeks when Chet walked me down the aisle. I am not what she pictured for Paul—I'm too young, too unpolished, too poor and crass. She thinks that sometime very soon, her son will snap to his senses.

But a baby… A baby changes everything.

"What if it's a Paulette?"

Paul makes a face. "*God*, no. I can't saddle my daughter with a name like Paulette. She'll grow up and go on *Dr. Phil*, talking about how we ruined her life. She'll never speak to us again."

Neglect, alcoholism, a felon father and a mother who had no business ever pushing out kids—now, those are some things to bellyache about on national television. This baby will have everything Chet and I didn't: a real house with real walls to keep out of the cold, a fridge filled with food, clothes that don't come from a church basement bin. Two parents who stick around, who don't disappear for days at a time or get carted off to jail.

And, as corny as it sounds, love.

I smile over our hands at my husband. "I do have one more request."

"For the love of my life? The mother of my child?" He lifts my hand to his lips, presses a frosty kiss to my knuckle. "Absolutely anything."

"When it's time, you get to tell your mother."